THE

THE FIRM

John Grisham

ARROW BOOKS

Arrow Books Limited
20 Vauxhall Bridge Road, London SW1V 2SA

An imprint of the Random Century Group

London Melbourne Sydney Auckland Johannesburg
and agencies throughout the world

First published in Great Britain by Century in 1991
Arrow edition 1991

7 9 10 8 6

Printed and bound in Great Britain by
Cox & Wyman Ltd, Reading

ISBN 0 09 983000 0

To Renée

I

THE SENIOR PARTNER studied the résumé for the hundredth time and again found nothing he disliked about Mitchell Y. McDeere, at least not on paper. He had the brains, the ambition, the good looks. And he was hungry; with his background, he had to be. He was married, and that was mandatory. The firm had never hired an unmarried lawyer, and it frowned heavily on divorce, as well as womanizing and drinking. Drug testing was in the contract. He had a degree in accounting, passed the CPA exam the first time he took it and wanted to be a tax lawyer, which of course was a requirement with a tax firm. He was white, and the firm had never hired a black. They managed this by being secretive and clubbish and never soliciting job applications. Other firms solicited, and hired blacks. This firm recruited, and remained lily white. Plus, the firm was in Memphis, of all places, and the top blacks wanted New York or Washington or Chicago. McDeere was a male, and there were no women in the firm. That mistake had been made in the mid-seventies when they recruited the number one grad from Harvard, who happened to be a she and a wizard at taxation. She lasted four turbulent years and was killed in a car wreck.

1

He looked good, on paper. He was their top choice. In fac for this year there were no other prospects. The list was ve short. It was McDeere or no one.

The managing partner, Royce McKnight, studied a dossi labeled "Mitchell Y. McDeere—Harvard." An inch thick wi small print and a few photographs, it had been prepared I some ex-CIA agents in a private intelligence outfit in Bethesd They were clients of the firm and each year did the investig: ing for no fee. It was easy work, they said, checking out unsu pecting law students. They learned, for instance, that he pr ferred to leave the Northeast, that he was holding three j offers, two in New York and one in Chicago, and that t highest offer was $76,000 and the lowest was $68,000. He w in demand. He had been given the opportunity to cheat on securities exam during his second year. He declined, and ma the highest grade in the class. Two months ago he had be offered cocaine at a law school party. He said no and left whe everyone began snorting. He drank an occasional beer, b drinking was expensive and he had no money. He owed clo to $23,000 in student loans. He was hungry.

Royce McKnight flipped through the dossier and smile McDeere was their man.

Lamar Quin was thirty-two and not yet a partner. He ha been brought along to look young and act young and project youthful image for Bendini, Lambert & Locke, which in fa was a young firm, since most of the partners retired in the late forties or early fifties with money to burn. He would ma partner in this firm. With a six-figure income guaranteed f the rest of his life, Lamar could enjoy the twelve-hundre dollar tailored suits that hung so comfortably from his ta athletic frame. He strolled nonchalantly across the thousan dollar-a-day suite and poured another cup of decaf. I checked his watch. He glanced at the two partners sitting the small conference table near the windows.

Precisely at two-thirty someone knocked on the door. Lam looked at the partners, who slid the résumé and dossier into a open briefcase. All three reached for their jackets. Lamar bu toned his top button and opened the door.

"Mitchell McDeere?" he asked with a huge smile and a han thrust forward.

"Yes." They shook hands violently.

"Nice to meet you, Mitchell. I'm Lamar Quin."

"My pleasure. Please call me Mitch." He stepped inside and ickly surveyed the spacious room.

"Sure, Mitch." Lamar grabbed his shoulder and led him ross the suite, where the partners introduced themselves. ey were exceedingly warm and cordial. They offered him ffee, then water. They sat around a shiny mahogany confere table and exchanged pleasantries. McDeere unbuttoned s coat and crossed his legs. He was now a seasoned veteran in e search for employment, and he knew they wanted him. He axed. With three job offers from three of the most prestis firms in the country, he did not need this interview, this m. He could afford to be a little overconfident now. He was ere out of curiosity. And he longed for warmer weather.

Oliver Lambert, the senior partner, leaned forward on his bows and took control of the preliminary chitchat. He was b and engaging with a mellow, almost professional baritone. t sixty-one, he was the grandfather of the firm and spent ost of his time administering and balancing the enormous os of some of the richest lawyers in the country. He was the unselor, the one the younger associates went to with their ubles. Mr. Lambert also handled the recruiting, and it was s mission to sign Mitchell Y. McDeere.

"Are you tired of interviewing?" asked Oliver Lambert.

"Not really. It's part of it."

Yes, yes, they all agreed. Seemed like yesterday they were terviewing and submitting résumés and scared to death they ouldn't find a job and three years of sweat and torture would down the drain. They knew what he was going through, all ght.

"May I ask a question?" Mitch asked.

"Certainly."

"Sure."

"Anything."

"Why are we interviewing in this hotel room? The other ms interview on campus through the placement office."

"Good question." They all nodded and looked at each other d agreed it was a good question.

"Perhaps I can answer that, Mitch." said Royce McKnight,

3

the managing partner. "You must understand our firm. We a
different, and we take pride in that. We have forty-one la
yers, so we are small compared with other firms. We don't hi
too many people; about one every other year. We offer t
highest salary and fringes in the country, and I'm not exagg
ating. So we are very selective. We selected you. The letter y
received last month was sent after we screened over two tho
sand third year law students at the best schools. Only o
letter was sent. We don't advertise openings and we don't s
licit applications. We keep a low profile, and we do things d
ferently. That's our explanation."

"Fair enough. What kind of firm is it?"

"Tax. Some securities, real estate and banking, but eigh
percent is tax work. That's why we wanted to meet yo
Mitch. You have an incredibly strong tax background."

"Why'd you go to Western Kentucky?" asked Oliver La
bert.

"Simple. They offered me a full scholarship to play footba
Had it not been for that, college would've been impossible.

"Tell us about your family."

"Why is that important?"

"It's very important to us, Mitch," Royce McKnight sa
warmly.

They all say that, thought McDeere. "Okay, my father w
killed in the coal mines when I was seven years old. M
mother remarried and lives in Florida. I had two brothe
Rusty was killed in Vietnam. I have a brother named R
McDeere."

"Where is he?"

"I'm afraid that's none of your business." He stared at Roy
McKnight and exposed a mammoth chip on his shoulder. T
dossier, oddly, was silent on Ray.

"I'm sorry," the managing partner said softly.

"Mitch, our firm is in Memphis," Lamar said. "Does th
bother you?"

"Not at all. I'm not fond of cold weather."

"Have you ever been to Memphis?"

"No."

"We'll have you down soon. You'll love it."

Mitch smiled and nodded and played along. Were these gu

rious? How could he consider such a small firm in such a
small town when Wall Street was waiting?

"How are you ranked in your class?" Mr. Lambert asked.

"Top five." Not top five percent, but top five. That was
enough of an answer for all of them. Top five out of three
hundred. He could have said number three, a fraction away
from number two, and within striking distance of number
one. But he didn't. They came from inferior schools—Chicago,
Columbia and Vanderbilt, as he recalled from a cursory examination of Martindale-Hubbell's Legal Directory. He knew
they would not dwell on academics.

"Why did you select Harvard?"

"Actually, Harvard selected me. I applied at several schools
and was accepted everywhere. Harvard offered more financial
assistance. I thought it was the best school. Still do."

"You've done quite well here, Mitch," Mr. Lambert said,
admiring the résumé. The dossier was in the briefcase, under
the table.

"Thank you. I've worked hard."

"You made extremely high grades in your tax and securities
courses."

"That's where my interest lies."

"We've reviewed your writing sample, and it's quite impressive."

"Thank you. I enjoy research."

They nodded and acknowledged this obvious lie. It was part
of the ritual. No law student or lawyer in his right mind enjoyed research, yet, without fail, every prospective associate
professed a deep love for the library.

"Tell us about your wife," Royce McKnight said, almost
meekly. They braced for another reprimand. But it was a standard, nonsacred area explored by every firm.

"Her name is Abby. She has a degree in elementary education from Western Kentucky. We graduated one week and got
married the next. For the past three years she's taught at a
private kindergarten near Boston College."

"And is the marriage—"

"We're very happy. We've known each other since high
school."

5

"What position did you play?" asked Lamar, in the directi
of less sensitive matters.

"Quarterback. I was heavily recruited until I messed up
knee in my last high school game. Everyone disappeared e
cept Western Kentucky. I played off and on for four yea
even started some as a junior, but the knee would never he
up."

"How'd you make straight A's and play football?"

"I put the books first."

"I don't imagine Western Kentucky is much of an acaden
school," Lamar blurted with a stupid grin, and immediate
wished he could take it back. Lambert and McKnight frown
and acknowledged the mistake.

"Sort of like Kansas State," Mitch replied. They froze, all
them froze, and for a few seconds stared incredulously at ea
other. This guy McDeere knew Lamar Quin went to Kans
State. He had never met Lamar Quin and had no idea w
would appear on behalf of the firm and conduct the intervie
Yet, he knew. He had gone to Martindale-Hubbell's a
checked them out. He had read the biographical sketches of
of the forty-one lawyers in the firm, and in a split second
had recalled that Lamar Quin, just one of the forty-one, h
gone to Kansas State. Damn, they were impressed.

"I guess that came out wrong," Lamar apologized.

"No problem." Mitch smiled warmly. It was forgotten.

Oliver Lambert cleared his throat and decided to get pe
sonal again. "Mitch, our firm frowns on drinking and chasin
women. We're not a bunch of Holy Rollers, but we put bu
ness ahead of everything. We keep low profiles and we wo
very hard. And we make plenty of money."

"I can live with all that."

"We reserve the right to test any member of the firm f
drug use."

"I don't use drugs."

"Good. What's your religious affiliation?"

"Methodist."

"Good. You'll find a wide variety in our firm. Catholics, Ba
tists, Episcopalians. It's really none of our business, but v
like to know. We want stable families. Happy lawyers are pr
ductive lawyers. That's why we ask these questions."

Mitch smiled and nodded. He'd heard this before.

The three looked at each other, then at Mitch. This meant they had reached the point in the interview where the interviewee was supposed to ask one or two intelligent questions. Mitch recrossed his legs. Money, that was the big question, particularly how it compared to his other offers. If it isn't enough, thought Mitch, then it was nice to meet you fellas. If the pay is attractive, *then* we can discuss families and marriages and football and churches. But, he knew, like all the other firms they had to shadowbox around the issue until things got awkward and it was apparent they had discussed everything in the world but money. So, hit them with a soft question first.

"What type of work will I do initially?"

They nodded and approved of the question. Lambert and McKnight looked at Lamar. This answer was his.

"We have something similar to a two-year apprenticeship, though we don't call it that. We'll send you all over the country to tax seminars. Your education is far from over. You'll spend two weeks next winter in Washington at the American Tax Institute. We take great pride in our technical expertise, and the training is continual, for all of us. If you want to pursue a master's in taxation, we'll pay for it. As far as practicing law, it won't be very exciting for the first two years. You'll do a lot of research and generally boring stuff. But you'll be paid handsomely."

"How much?"

Lamar looked at Royce McKnight, who eyed Mitch and said, "We'll discuss the compensation and other benefits when you come to Memphis."

"I want a ballpark figure or I may not come to Memphis." He smiled, arrogant but cordial. He spoke like a man with three job offers.

The partners smiled at each other, and Mr. Lambert spoke first. "Okay. A base salary of eighty thousand the first year, plus bonuses. Eighty-five the second year, plus bonuses. A low-interest mortgage so you can buy a home. Two country club memberships. And a new BMW. You pick the color, of course."

They focused on his lips, and waited for the wrinkles to

7

form on his cheeks and the teeth to break through. He tried
conceal a smile, but it was impossible. He chuckled.

"That's incredible," he mumbled. Eighty thousand in Me
phis equaled a hundred and twenty thousand in New Yo
Did the man say BMW! His Mazda hatchback had a milli
miles on it and for the moment had to be jump-started wh
he saved for a rebuilt starter.

"Plus a few more fringes we'll be glad to discuss in Me
phis."

Suddenly he had a strong desire to visit Memphis. Wasn't
by the river?

The smile vanished and he regained his composure.
looked sternly, importantly at Oliver Lambert and said, as
he'd forgotten about the money and the home and the BM'
"Tell me about your firm."

"Forty-one lawyers. Last year we earned more per lawy
than any firm our size or larger. That includes every big fir
in the country. We take only rich clients—corporations, ban
and wealthy people who pay our healthy fees and never co
plain. We've developed a specialty in international taxatio
and it's both exciting and very profitable. We deal only wi
people who can pay."

"How long does it take to make partner?"

"On the average, ten years, and it's a hard ten years. It's n
unusual for our partners to earn half a million a year, and mo
retire before they're fifty. You've got to pay your dues, put
eighty-hour weeks, but it's worth it when you make partner

Lamar leaned forward. "You don't have to be a partner
earn six figures. I've been with the firm seven years, and we
over a hundred thousand four years ago."

Mitch thought about this for a second and figured by th
time he was thirty he could be well over a hundred thousan
maybe close to two hundred thousand. At the age of thirty!

They watched him carefully and knew exactly what he wa
calculating.

"What's an international tax firm doing in Memphis?"
asked.

That brought smiles. Mr. Lambert removed his readin
glasses and twirled them. "Now that's a good question. M
Bendini founded the firm in 1944. He had been a tax lawyer i

8

iladelphia and had picked up some wealthy clients in the uth. He got a wild hair and landed in Memphis. For twenty-e years he hired nothing but tax lawyers, and the firm pros-ed nicely down there. None of us are from Memphis, but have grown to love it. It's a very pleasant old Southern vn. By the way, Mr. Bendini died in 1970."

'How many partners in the firm?"

'Twenty, active. We try to keep a ratio of one partner for :h associate. That's high for the industry, but we like it. ;ain, we do things differently."

'All of our partners are multi-millionaires by the age of ·ty-five," Royce McKnight said.

'All of them?"

'Yes, sir. We don't guarantee it, but if you join our firm, put ten hard years, make partner and put in ten more years, and u're not a millionaire at the age of forty-five, you'll be the st in twenty years."

"That's an impressive statistic."

"It's an impressive firm, Mitch," Oliver Lambert said, "and :'re very proud of it. We're a close knit fraternity. We're all and we take care of each other. We don't have the cut-roat competition the big firms are famous for. We're very reful whom we hire, and our goal is for each new associate to come a partner as soon as possible. Toward that end we vest an enormous amount of time and money in ourselves, pecially our new people. It is a rare, extremely rare occasion hen a lawyer leaves our firm. It is simply unheard of. We go e extra mile to keep careers on track. We want our people ppy. We think it is the most profitable way to operate."

"I have another impressive statistic," Mr. McKnight added. .ast year, for firms our size or larger, the average turnover te among associates was twenty-eight percent. At Bendini, mbert & Locke, it was zero. Year before, zero. It's been a ng time since a lawyer left our firm."

They watched him carefully to make sure all of this sank in. .ch term and each condition of the employment was impor-nt, but the permanence, the finality of his acceptance over-adowed all other items on the checklist. They explained as st they could, for now. Further explanation would come .er.

9

Of course, they knew much more than they could talk abo
For instance, his mother lived in a cheap trailer park in Pa
ma City Beach, remarried to a retired truck driver with
violent drinking problem. They knew she had received $41,0
from the mine explosion, squandered most of it, then we
crazy after her oldest son was killed in Vietnam. They kn
he had been neglected, raised in poverty by his brother F
(whom they could not find) and some sympathetic relativ
The poverty hurt, and they assumed, correctly, it had bred
intense desire to succeed. He had worked thirty hours a we
at an all night convenience store while playing football a
making perfect grades. They knew he seldom slept. Th
knew he was hungry. He was their man.

"Would you like to come visit us?" asked Oliver Lamber

"When?" asked Mitch, dreaming of a black 318i with a s
roof.

The ancient Mazda hatchback with three hubcaps and a ba
cracked windshield hung in the gutter with its front whe
sideways, aiming at the curb, preventing a roll down the h
Abby grabbed the door handle on the inside, yanked twice a
opened the door. She inserted the key, pressed the clutch a
turned the wheel. The Mazda began a slow roll. As it gain
speed, she held her breath, released the clutch and bit her
until the unmuffled rotary engine began whining.

With three job offers on the table, a new car was fo
months away. She could last. For three years they had endur
poverty in a two room student apartment on a campus cover
with Porsches and little Mercedes convertibles. For the m
part they had ignored the snubs from the classmates and c
workers in this bastion of East Coast snobbery. They we
hillbillies from Kentucky, with few friends. But they had e
dured and succeeded quite nicely all to themselves.

She preferred Chicago to New York, even for a lower sala
largely because it was further from Boston and closer to Ke
tucky. But Mitch remained noncommittal, characteristica
weighing it all carefully and keeping most of it to himself. S
had not been invited to visit New York and Chicago with h
husband. And she was tired of guessing. She wanted an a
swer.

She parked illegally on the hill nearest the apartment and walked two blocks. Their unit was one of thirty in a two-story all-brick rectangle. Abby stood outside her door and fumbled through the purse looking for keys. Suddenly, the door jerked open. He grabbed her, yanked her inside the tiny apartment, threw her on the sofa and attacked her neck with his lips. She yelled and giggled as arms and legs thrashed about. They kissed, one of those long, wet, ten minute embraces with groping and fondling and moaning, the kind they had enjoyed as teenagers when kissing was fun and mysterious and the ultimate.

"My goodness," she said when they finished. "What's the occasion?"

"Do you smell anything?" Mitch asked.

She looked away and sniffed. "Well, yes. What is it?"

"Chicken chow mein and egg foo yung. From Wong Boys."

"Okay, what's the occasion?"

"Plus an expensive bottle of Chablis. It's even got a cork."

"What have you done, Mitch?"

"Follow me." On the small, painted kitchen table, among the legal pads and casebooks, sat a large bottle of wine and a sack of Chinese food. They shoved the law school paraphernalia aside and spread the food. Mitch opened the wine and filled two plastic wineglasses.

"I had a great interview today," he said.

"Who?"

"Remember that firm in Memphis I received a letter from last month?"

"Yes. You weren't too impressed."

"That's the one. I'm very impressed. It's all tax work and the money looks good."

"How good?"

He ceremoniously dipped chow mein from the container onto both plates, then ripped open the tiny packages of soy sauce. She waited for an answer. He opened another container and began dividing the egg foo yung. He sipped his wine and smacked his lips.

"How much?" she repeated.

"More than Chicago. More than Wall Street."

She took a long, deliberate drink of wine and eyed him sus-

11

piciously. Her brown eyes narrowed and glowed. The e
brows lowered and the forehead wrinkled. She waited.

"How much?"

"Eighty thousand, first year, plus bonuses. Eighty-five, s
ond year, plus bonuses." He said this nonchalantly wh
studying the celery bits in the chow mein.

"Eighty thousand," she repeated.

"Eighty thousand, babe. Eighty thousand bucks in Me
phis, Tennessee, is about the same as a hundred and twen
thousand bucks in New York."

"Who wants New York?" she asked.

"Plus a low-interest mortgage loan."

That word—mortgage—had not been uttered in the apa
ment in a long time. In fact, she could not, at the mome
recall the last discussion about a home or anything related
one. For months now it had been accepted that they would r
some place until some distant, unimaginable point in the
ture when they achieved affluence and would then qualify
a large mortgage.

She sat her glass of wine on the table and said matter-
factly, "I didn't hear that."

"A low-interest mortgage loan. The firm loans enou
money to buy a house. It's very important to these guys t
their associates look prosperous, so they give us the money a
much lower rate."

"You mean as in a *home*, with grass around it and shrubs

"Yep. Not some overpriced apartment in Manhattan, bu
three bedroom house in the suburbs with a driveway and
two car garage where we can park the BMW."

The reaction was delayed by a second or two, but she fina
said, "BMW? Whose BMW?"

"Ours, babe. Our BMW. The firm leases a new one a
gives us the keys. It's sort of like a signing bonus for a fir
round draft pick. It's worth another five thousand a year.
pick the color, of course. I think black would be nice. What
you think?"

"No more clunkers. No more leftovers. No more hand-n
downs," she said as she slowly shook her head.

He crunched on a mouthful of noodles and smiled at h
She was dreaming, he could tell, probably of furniture, a

paper, and perhaps a pool before too long. And babies, dark eyed children with light brown hair.

And there are some other benefits to be discussed later."

"I don't understand, Mitch. Why are they so generous?"

"I asked that question. They're very selective, and they take of pride in paying top dollar. They go for the best and 't mind shelling out the bucks. Their turnover rate is zero. , I think it costs more to entice the top people to Mem-."

"It would be closer to home," she said without looking at.

"I don't have a home. It would be closer to your parents, and worries me."

She deflected this, as she did most of his comments about her ily. "You'd be closer to Ray."

He nodded, bit into an egg roll and imagined her parents' visit, that sweet moment when they pulled into the drive-y in their well-used Cadillac and stared in shock at the new nch colonial with two new cars in the garage. They would n with envy and wonder how the poor kid with no family no status could afford all this at twenty-five and fresh out aw school. They would force painful smiles and comment how nice everything was, and before long Mr. Sutherland uld break down and ask how much the house cost and tch would tell him to mind his own business and it would ve the old man crazy. They'd leave after a short visit and urn to Kentucky, where all their friends would hear how at the daughter and the son-in-law were doing down in mphis. Abby would be sorry they couldn't get along but uldn't say much. From the start they had treated him like a er. He was so unworthy they had boycotted the small wed-g.

"Have you ever been to Memphis?" he asked.

"Once when I was a little girl. Some kind of convention for church. All I remember is the river."

"They want us to visit."

"Us! You mean I'm invited?"

"Yes. They insist on you coming."

13

"When?"

"Couple of weeks. They'll fly us down Thursday aftern͏ for the weekend."

"I like this firm already."

2

THE FIVE-STORY BUILDING had been built a hundred years earlier by a cotton merchant and his sons after the Reconstruction, during the revival of cotton ...ing in Memphis. It sat in the middle of Cotton Row on ...nt Street near the river. Through its halls and doors and ...ss its desks, millions of bales of cotton had been purchased ...m the Mississippi and Arkansas deltas and sold around the ...ld. Deserted, neglected, then renovated time and again ...e the first war, it had been purchased for good in 1951 by ...aggressive tax lawyer named Anthony Bendini. He reno-...ed it yet again and began filling it with lawyers. He re-...ned it the Bendini Building.

...e pampered the building, indulged it, coddled it, each year ...ing another layer of luxury to his landmark. He fortified it, ...ing doors and windows and hiring armed guards to protect ...nd its occupants. He added elevators, electronic surveil-...ce, security codes, closed-circuit television, a weight room, ...eam room, locker rooms and a partners' dining room on the ...h floor with a captivating view of the river.

...n twenty years he built the richest law firm in Memphis, ..., indisputably, the quietest. Secrecy was his passion. Every

associate hired by the firm was indoctrinated in the evils of
loose tongue. Everything was confidential. Salaries, perks,
vancement and, most especially, clients. Divulging firm b
ness, the young associates were warned, could delay
awarding of the holy grail—a partnership. Nothing left
fortress on Front Street. Wives were told not to ask, or w
lied to. The associates were expected to work hard, keep q
and spend their healthy paychecks. They did, without exc
tion.

With forty-one lawyers, the firm was the fourth larges
Memphis. Its members did not advertise or seek public
They were clannish and did not fraternize with other lawy
Their wives played tennis and bridge and shopped am
themselves. Bendini, Lambert & Locke was a big family,
sorts. A rather rich family.

At 10 A.M. on a Friday, the firm limo stopped on Front Str
and Mr. Mitchell Y. McDeere emerged. He politely than
the driver, and admired the vehicle as it drove away. His f
limo ride. He stood on the sidewalk next to a streetlight a
admired the quaint, picturesque, yet somehow imposing ho
of the quiet Bendini firm. It was a far cry from the gargant
steel-and-glass erections inhabited by New York's finest or
enormous cylinder he had visited in Chicago. But he instan
knew he would like it. It was less pretentious. It was more
himself.

Lamar Quin walked through the front door and down
steps. He yelled at Mitch and waved him over. He had
them at the airport the night before and checked them into
Peabody—"the South's Grand Hotel."

"Good morning, Mitch! How was your night?" They sh
hands like lost friends.

"Very nice. It's a great hotel."

"We knew you'd like it. Everybody likes the Peabody."

They stepped into the front foyer, where a small billbo
greeted Mr. Mitchell Y. McDeere, the guest of the day. A w
dressed, but unattractive receptionist smiled warmly and s
her name was Sylvia and if he needed anything while he
in Memphis just let her know. He thanked her. Lamar led
to a long hallway where he began the guided tour. He

16

ned the layout of the building and introduced Mitch to
ous secretaries and paralegals as they walked. In the main
ary on the second floor a crowd of lawyers circled the
nmoth conference table and consumed pastries and coffee.
y became silent when the guest entered.

liver Lambert greeted Mitch and introduced him to the
g. There were about twenty in all, most of the associates in
firm, and most barely older than the guest. The partners
e too busy, Lamar had explained, and would meet him
r at a private lunch. He stood at the end of the table as Mr.
nbert called for quiet.

Gentlemen, this is Mitchell McDeere. You've all heard
ut him, and here he is. He is our number one choice this
r, our number one draft pick, so to speak. He is being ro-
nced by the big boys in New York and Chicago and who
ws where else, so we have to sell him on our little firm here
Memphis." They smiled and nodded their approval. The
st was embarrassed.

He will finish at Harvard in two months and will graduate
h honors. He's an associate editor of the *Harvard Law Re-
v*." This made an impression, Mitch could tell. "He did his
lergraduate work at Western Kentucky, where he gradu-
d summa cum laude." This was not quite as impressive.
e also played football for four years, starting as quarterback
junior year." Now they were really impressed. A few ap-
red to be in awe, as if staring at Joe Namath.

he senior partner continued his monologue while Mitch
od awkwardly beside him. He droned on about how selec-
e they had always been and how well Mitch would fit in.
tch stuffed his hands in his pockets and quit listening. He
died the group. They were young, successful and affluent.
e dress code appeared to be strict, but no different than
w York or Chicago. Dark gray or navy wool suits, white or
e cotton button downs, medium starch, and silk ties. Noth-
bold or nonconforming. Maybe a couple of bow ties, but
hing more daring. Neatness was mandatory. No beards,
staches or hair over the ears. There were a couple of
mps, but good looks dominated.

Mr. Lambert was winding down. "Lamar will give Mitch a
r of our offices, so you'll have a chance to chat with him

17

later. Let's make him welcome. Tonight he and his lovely, I do mean lovely, wife, Abby, will eat ribs at the Rendezv and of course tomorrow night is the firm dinner at my pl I'll ask you to be on your best behavior." He smiled and loo at the guest. "Mitch, if you get tired of Lamar, let me kr and we'll get someone more qualified."

He shook hands with each one of them again as they and tried to remember as many names as possible.

"Let's start the tour," Lamar said when the room clea "This, of course, is a library, and we have identical ones each of the first four floors. We also use them for large m ings. The books vary from floor to floor, so you never kn where your research will lead you. We have two full-time brarians, and we use microfilm and microfiche extensively. a rule, we don't do any research outside the building. Th are over a hundred thousand volumes, including every c ceivable tax reporting service. That's more than some schools. If you need a book we don't have, just tell a librari

They walked past the lengthy conference table and betw dozens of rows of books. "A hundred thousand volum Mitch mumbled.

"Yeah, we spend almost half a million a year on upke supplements and new books. The partners are always grip about it, but they wouldn't think of cutting back. It's one the largest private law libraries in the country, and w proud of it."

"It's pretty impressive."

"We try to make research as painless as possible. You kn what a bore it is and how much time can be wasted looking the right materials. You'll spend a lot of time here the first t years, so we try to make it pleasant."

Behind a cluttered workbench in a rear corner, one of librarians introduced himself and gave a brief tour of the co puter room, where a dozen terminals stood ready to assist w the latest computerized research. He offered to demonstr the latest, truly incredible software, but Lamar said t might stop by later.

"He's a nice guy," Lamar said as they left the library. " pay him forty thousand a year just to keep up with the boo It's amazing."

ruly amazing, thought Mitch.

he second floor was virtually identical to the first, third
fourth. The center of each floor was filled with secretaries,
r desks, file cabinets, copiers and the other necessary ma-
es. On one side of the open area was the library, and on
other was a configuration of smaller conference rooms and
es.

You won't see any pretty secretaries," Lamar said softly as
y watched them work. "It seems to be an unwritten firm
. Oliver Lambert goes out of his way to hire the oldest and
eliest ones he can find. Of course, some have been here for
nty years and have forgotten more law than we learned in
school."

They seem kind of plump," Mitch observed, almost to him-
.

Yeah, it's part of the overall strategy to encourage us to
p our hands in our pockets. Philandering is strictly forbid-
, and to my knowledge has never happened."

And if it does?"

Who knows. The secretary would be fired, of course. And I
pose the lawyer would be severely punished. It might cost
artnership. No one wants to find out, especially with this
ch of cows."

They dress nice."

Don't get me wrong. We hire only the best legal secretaries
we pay more than any other firm in town. You're looking
he best, not necessarily the prettiest. We require experience
maturity. Lambert won't hire anyone under thirty."

One per lawyer?"

Yes, until you're a partner. Then you'll get another, and by
n you'll need one. Nathan Locke has three, all with twenty
rs' experience, and he keeps them jumping."

Where's his office?"

Fourth floor. It's off limits."

Mitch started to ask, but didn't.

The corner offices were 25 by 25, Lamar explained, and oc-
ied by the most senior partners. Power offices, he called
m, with great admiration. They were decorated to each in-
idual's taste with no expense spared and vacated only at
rement or death, then fought over by the younger partners.

Lamar flipped a switch in one and they stepped inside, c[losing] the door behind them. "Nice view, huh," he said as Mi[tch] walked to the windows and looked at the river moving eve[r] slowly beyond Riverside Drive.

"How do you get this office?" Mitch asked as he admire[d a] barge inching under the bridge leading to Arkansas.

"Takes time, and when you get here you'll be very weal[thy] and very busy, and you won't have time to enjoy the view[."]

"Whose is it?"

"Victor Milligan. He's head of tax, and a very nice m[an.] Originally from New England, he's been here for twenty-[five] years and calls Memphis home." Lamar stuck his hands in [his] pockets and walked around the room. "The hardwood flo[ors] and ceilings came with the building, over a hundred years a[go.] Most of the building is carpeted, but in a few spots the w[ood] was not damaged. You'll have the option of rugs and car[pet] when you get here."

"I like the wood. What about the rug?"

"Some kind of antique Persian. I don't know its history. [The] desk was used by his great-grandfather, who was a judge [of] some sort in Rhode Island, or so he says. He's full of crap, [so] you never know when he's blowing smoke."

"Where is he?"

"Vacation, I think. Did they tell you about vacations?"

"No."

"You get two weeks a year for the first five years. Paid [of] course. Then three weeks until you become a partner, t[hen] you take whatever you want. The firm has a chalet in Va[il, a] cabin on a lake in Manitoba and two condos on Seven M[ile] Beach on Grand Cayman Island. They're free, but you nee[d to] book early. Partners get priority. After that it's first come. [The] Caymans are extremely popular in the firm. It's an inter[na]tional tax haven and a lot of our trips are written off. I th[ink] Milligan's there now, probably scuba diving and calling [it] business."

Through one of his tax courses, Mitch had heard of the C[ay]man Islands and knew they were somewhere in the Caribbe[an.] He started to ask exactly where, but decided to check it h[im]self.

"Only two weeks?" he asked.

20

Uh, yeah. Is that a problem?"

No, not really. The firms in New York are offering at least
e." He spoke like a discriminating critic of expensive vaca-
s. He wasn't. Except for the three day weekend they re-
ed to as a honeymoon, and an occasional drive through
w England, he had never participated in a vacation and had
er left the country.

You can get an additional week, unpaid."

Mitch nodded as though this was acceptable. They left Milli-
s office and continued the tour. The hallway ran in a long
angle with the attorneys' offices to the outside, all with
dows, sunlight, views. Those with views of the river were
e prestigious, Lamar explained, and usually occupied by
ners. There were waiting lists.

he conference rooms, libraries and secretarial desks were
he inside of the hallway, away from the windows and dis-
tions.

he associates' offices were smaller—15 by 15—but richly
orated and much more imposing than any associates' offices
ad seen in New York or Chicago. The firm spent a small
une on design consultants, Lamar said. Money, it seemed,
v on trees. The younger lawyers were friendly and talka-
and seemed to welcome the interruption. Most gave brief
imonials to the greatness of the firm and of Memphis. The
town kind of grows on you, they kept telling him, but it
s time. They, too, had been recruited by the big boys in
hington and on Wall Street, and they had no regrets.

he partners were busier, but just as nice. He had been
fully selected, he was told again and again, and he would
n. It was his kind of firm. They promised to talk more
ing lunch.

hour earlier, Kay Quin had left the kids with the baby
se and the maid and met Abby for brunch at the Peabody.
was a smalltown girl, much like Abby. She had married
aar after college and lived in Nashville for three years
le he studied law at Vanderbilt. Lamar made so much
ey she quit work and had two babies in fourteen months.
v that she had retired and finished her childbearing, she
it most of her time with the garden club and the heart fund

21

and the country club and the PTA and the church. Despite
money and the affluence, she was modest and unpretenti
and apparently determined to stay that way regardless of
husband's success. Abby found a friend.

After croissants and eggs Benedict, they sat in the lobb
the hotel, drinking coffee and watching the ducks swin
circles around the fountain. Kay had suggested a quick tou
Memphis with a late lunch near her home. Maybe some sh
ping.

"Have they mentioned the low-interest loan?" she asked.

"Yes, at the first interview."

"They'll want you to buy a house when you move h
Most people can't afford a house when they leave law sch
so the firm loans you the money at a lower rate and holds
mortgage."

"How low?"

"I don't know. It's been seven years since we moved h
and we've bought another house since then. It'll be a barg
believe me. The firm will see to it that you own a home.
sort of an unwritten rule."

"Why is it so important?"

"Several reasons. First of all, they want you down here. T
firm is very selective, and they usually get who they want.
Memphis is not exactly in the spotlight, so they have to o
more. Also, the firm is very demanding, especially on the a
ciates. There's pressure, overwork, eighty-hour weeks
time away from home. It won't be easy on either of you,
the firm knows it. The theory is that a strong marriage me
a happy lawyer, and a happy lawyer is a productive lawyer
the bottom line is profits. Always profits.

"And there's another reason. These guys—all guys,
women—take a lot of pride in their wealth, and everyon
expected to look and act affluent. It would be an insult to
firm if an associate was forced to live in an apartment. T
want you in a house, and after five years in a bigger house
we have some time this afternoon, I'll show you some of
partners' homes. When you see them, you won't mind
eighty-hour weeks."

"I'm used to them now."

"That's good, but law school doesn't compare with t

...metimes they'll work a hundred hours a week during tax
...on."

...bby smiled and shook her head as if this impressed her a
...t deal. "Do you work?"

...No. Most of us don't work. The money is there, so we're
...forced to, and we get little help with the kids from our
...bands. Of course, working is not forbidden."

...forbidden by whom?"

...The firm."

...would hope not." Abby repeated the word "forbidden" to
...self, but let it pass.

...ay sipped her coffee and watched the ducks. A small boy
...dered away from his mother and stood near the fountain.
... you plan to start a family?" Kay asked.

...Maybe in a couple of years."

...Babies are encouraged."

...By whom?"

...The firm."

...Why should the firm care if we have children?"

...Again, stable families. A new baby is a big deal around the
...e. They send flowers and gifts to the hospital. You're
...ted like a queen. Your husband gets a week off, but he'll be
...busy to take it. They put a thousand dollars in a trust fund
...college. It's a lot of fun."

...Sounds like a big fraternity."

...It's more like a big family. Our social life revolves around
...firm, and that's important because none of us are from
...mphis. We're all transplants."

...That's nice, but I don't want anyone telling me when to
...k and when to quit and when to have children."

...Don't worry. They're very protective of each other, but the
...a does not meddle."

...I'm beginning to wonder."

...Relax, Abby. The firm is like a family. They're great peo-
...and Memphis is a wonderful old town to live in and raise
.... The cost of living is much lower and life moves at a
...ver pace. You're probably considering the bigger towns. So
...we, but I'll take Memphis any day over the big cities."

...Do I get the grand tour?"

...That's why I'm here. I thought we'd start downtown, then

head out east and look at the nicer neighborhoods, maybe ║
at some houses and eat lunch at my favorite restaurant."

"Sounds like fun."

Kay paid for the coffee, as she had the brunch, and they ║
the Peabody in the Quin family's new Mercedes.

The dining room, as it was simply called, covered the west ║
of the fifth floor above Riverside Drive and high above ║
river in the distance. A row of eight-foot windows lined ║
wall and provided a fascinating view of the tugboats, pad║
wheelers, barges, docks and bridges.

The room was protected turf, a sanctuary for those law║
talented and ambitious enough to be called partners in ║
quiet Bendini firm. They gathered each day for lunches ║
pared by Jessie Frances, a huge, temperamental old b║
woman, and served by her husband, Roosevelt, who w║
white gloves and an odd-fitting, faded, wrinkled hand║
down tux given to him by Mr. Bendini himself shortly be║
his death. They also gathered for coffee and doughnuts s║
mornings to discuss firm business and, occasionally, for a g║
of wine in the late afternoon to celebrate a good month o║
exceptionally large fee. It was for partners only, and mayb║
occasional guest such as a blue chip client or prospective ║
cruit. The associates could dine there twice a year, only t║
—and records were kept—and then only at the invitation ║
partner.

Adjacent to the dining room was a small kitchen where ║
sie Frances performed, and where she had cooked the ║
meal for Mr. Bendini and a few others twenty-six years ear║
For twenty-six years she had cooked Southern food and║
nored requests to experiment and try dishes she had tro║
pronouncing. "Don't eat it if you don't like it," was her s║
dard reply. Judging from the scraps Roosevelt collected fr║
the tables, the food was eaten and enjoyed immensely. ║
posted the week's menu on Monday, asked that reservation║
made by ten each day and held grudges for years if some║
canceled or didn't show. She and Roosevelt worked four h║
each day and were paid a thousand each month.

Mitch sat at a table with Lamar Quin, Oliver Lambert ║

rce McKnight. The entrée was prime ribs, served with
d okra and boiled squash.

She laid off the grease today," Mr. Lambert observed.

It's delicious," Mitch said.

Is your system accustomed to grease?"

Yes. They cook this way in Kentucky."

I joined this firm in 1955," Mr. McKnight said, "and I come
n New Jersey, right? Out of suspicion, I avoided most
thern dishes as much as possible. Everything is battered
fried in animal fat, right? Then Mr. Bendini decides to
n up this little café. He hires Jessie Frances, and I've had
rtburn for the past twenty years. Fried ripe tomatoes, fried
en tomatoes, fried eggplant, fried okra, fried squash, fried
thing and everything. One day Victor Milligan said too
ch. He's from Connecticut, right? And Jessie Frances had
pped up a batch of fried dill pickles. Can you imagine?
d dill pickles! Milligan said something ugly to Roosevelt
he reported it to Jessie Frances. She walked out the back
r and quit. Stayed gone for a week. Roosevelt wanted to
rk, but she kept him at home. Finally, Mr. Bendini
othed things over and she agreed to return if there were no
plaints. But she also cut back on the grease. I think we'll
ive ten years longer."

It's delicious," said Lamar as he buttered another roll.

It's always delicious," added Mr. Lambert as Roosevelt
ked by. "Her food is rich and fattening, but we seldom
s lunch."

Mitch ate cautiously, engaged in nervous chitchat and tried
ppear completely at ease. It was difficult. Surrounded by
nently successful lawyers, all millionaires, in their exclu-
, lavishly ornamented dining suite, he felt as if he was on
owed ground. Lamar's presence was comforting, as was
osevelt's.

When it was apparent Mitch had finished eating, Oliver
mbert wiped his mouth, rose slowly and tapped his tea glass
h his spoon. "Gentlemen, could I have your attention."

he room became silent as the twenty or so partners turned
he head table. They laid their napkins down and stared at
guest. Somewhere on each of their desks was a copy of the
sier. Two months earlier they had voted unanimously to

make him their number one pick. They knew he ran f
miles a day, did not smoke, was allergic to sulfites, had
tonsils, had a blue Mazda, had a crazy mother and once th
three interceptions in one quarter. They knew he took noth
stronger than aspirin even when he was sick, and that he
hungry enough to work a hundred hours a week if they as
They liked him. He was good-looking, athletic-looking
man's man with a brilliant mind and a lean body.

"As you know, we have a very special guest today, M
McDeere. He will soon graduate with honors from F
vard—"

"Hear! Hear!" said a couple of Harvard alumni.

"Yes, thank you. He and his wife, Abby, are staying at
Peabody this weekend as our guests. Mitch will finish in
top five out of three hundred and has been heavily recrui
We want him here, and I know you will speak to him before
leaves. Tonight he will have dinner with Lamar and I
Quin, and then tomorrow night is the dinner at my place.
are all expected to attend." Mitch smiled awkwardly at
partners as Mr. Lambert rambled on about the greatness of
firm. When he finished, they continued eating as Roose
served bread pudding and coffee.

Kay's favorite restaurant was a chic East Memphis hangout
the young affluent. A thousand ferns hung from everywh
and the jukebox played nothing but early sixties. The daiqu
were served in tall souvenir glasses.

"One is enough," Kay warned.

"I'm not much of a drinker."

They ordered the quiche of the day and sipped daiquiri

"Does Mitch drink?"

"Very little. He's an athlete and very particular about
body. An occasional beer or glass of wine, nothing stron
How about Lamar?"

"About the same. He really discovered beer in law sch
but he has trouble with his weight. The firm frowns on dri
ing."

"That's admirable, but why is it their business?"

"Because alcohol and lawyers go together like blood
vampires. Most lawyers drink like fish, and the professio

26

;ued with alcoholism. I think it starts in law school. At
derbilt, someone was always tapping a keg of beer. Prob-
the same at Harvard. The job has a lot of pressure, and that
lly means a lot of booze. These guys aren't a bunch of
otalers, mind you, but they keep it under control. A
thy lawyer is a productive lawyer."

guess that makes sense. Mitch says there's no turnover."
t's rather permanent. I can't recall anyone leaving in the
n years we've been here. The money's great and they're
ful about whom they hire. They don't want anyone with
ily money."

'm not sure I follow."

They won't hire a lawyer with other sources of income.
y want them young and hungry. It's a question of loyalty.
l your money comes from one source, then you tend to be
 loyal to that source. The firm demands extreme loyalty.
ar says there's never talk of leaving. They're all happy,
 either rich or getting that way. And if one wanted to
e, he couldn't find as much money with another firm.
y'll offer Mitch whatever it takes to get you down here.
y take great pride in paying more."

Why no female lawyers?"

They tried it once. She was a real bitch and kept the place
n uproar. Most women lawyers walk around with chips on
r shoulders looking for fights. They're hard to deal with.
ar says they're afraid to hire one because they couldn't fire
if she didn't work out, with affirmative action and all."

he quiche arrived and they declined another round of dai-
is. Hundreds of young professionals crowded under the
ds of ferns, and the restaurant grew festive. Smokey
inson sang softly from the jukebox.

've got a great idea," Kay said. "I know a realtor. Let's call
and go look at some houses."

What kind of houses?"

'or you and Mitch. For the newest associate at Bendini,
bert & Locke. She can show you several in your price
ge."

don't know our price range."

'd say a hundred to a hundred and fifty thousand. The last

associate bought in Oakgrove, and I'm sure he paid somet[hing] like that."

Abby leaned forward and almost whispered, "How m[uch] would the notes be?"

"I don't know. But you'll be able to afford it. Around a t[hou]sand a month, maybe a little more."

Abby stared at her and swallowed hard. The small ap[art]ments in Manhattan were renting for twice that. "Let's [give] her a call."

As expected, Royce McKnight's office was a power one w[ith a] great view. It was in one of the prized corners on the fo[urth] floor, down the hall from Nathan Locke. Lamar excused [him]self, and the managing partner asked Mitch to have a seat [at a] small conference table next to the sofa. A secretary was [sent] for coffee.

McKnight asked him about his visit so far, and Mitch sai[d he] was quite impressed.

"Mitch, I want to nail down the specifics of our offer."

"Certainly."

"The base salary is eighty thousand for the first year. W[hen] you pass the bar exam you receive a five thousand dollar r[aise.] Not a bonus, but a raise. The exam is given sometime in [Au]gust and you'll spend most of your summer reviewing fo[r it.] We have our own bar study courses and you'll receive ex[ten]sive tutoring from some of the partners. This is done prima[rily] on firm time. As you know, most firms put you to work [and] expect you to study on your own time. Not us. No associat[e in] this firm has ever flunked the bar exam, and we're not wor[ried] about you breaking with tradition. Eighty thousand initi[ally,] up to eighty-five in six months. Once you've been here a y[ear] you'll be raised to ninety thousand, plus you'll get a bo[nus] each December based on the profits and performance du[ring] the prior twelve months. Last year the average bonus for a[sso]ciates was nine thousand. As you know, profit sharing [for] associates is extremely rare for law firms. Any questions a[bout] the salary?"

"What happens after the second year?"

"Your base salary is raised about ten percent a year until [you]

me a partner. Neither the raises nor the bonuses are guar-
ed. They are based on performance."

air enough."

As you know, it is very important to us that you buy a
e. It adds stability and prestige and we're very concerned
t these things, especially with our associates. The firm
ides a low-interest mortgage loan, thirty years, fixed rate,
assumable should you decide to sell in a few years. It's a
shot deal, available only for your first home. After that
re on your own."

What kind of rate?"

As low as possible without running afoul with the IRS.
rent market rate is around ten, ten and a half. We should
ble to get you a rate of seven to eight percent. We represent
e banks, and they assist us. With this salary, you'll have no
ble qualifying. In fact, the firm will sign on as a guarantor
cessary."

That's very generous, Mr. McKnight."

t's important to us. And we don't lose any money on the
. Once you find a house, our real estate section handles
ything. All you have to do is move in."

What about the BMW?"

r. McKnight chuckled. "We started that about ten years
and it's proved to be quite an inducement. It's very simple.
pick out a BMW, one of the smaller ones, we lease it for
e years and give you the keys. We pay for tags, insurance,
ntenance. At the end of three years you can buy it from the
ng company for the fair market value. It's also a one shot
"

That's very tempting."

We know."

r. McKnight looked at his legal pad. "We provide com-
e medical and dental coverage for the entire family. Preg-
ies, checkups, braces, everything. Paid entirely by the
"

itch nodded, but was not impressed. This was standard.

We have a retirement plan second to none. For every dollar
invest, the firm matches it with two, provided, however,
invest at least ten percent of your base pay. Let's say you
at eighty, and the first year you set aside eight thousand.

The firm kicks in sixteen, so you've got twenty-four after first year. A money pro in New York handles it and last our retirement earned nineteen percent. Not bad. Invest twenty years and you're a millionaire at forty-five, just of tirement. One stipulation: If you bail out before twenty y you lose everything but the money you put in, with no inc earned on that money."

"Sounds rather harsh."

"No, actually it's rather generous. Find me another fir company matching two to one. There are none, to my kn edge. It's our way of taking care of ourselves. Many of partners retire at fifty, some at forty-five. We have no ma tory retirement, and some work into their sixties and se ties. To each his own. Our goal is simply to ensure a gene pension and make early retirement an option."

"How many retired partners do you have?"

"Twenty or so. You'll see them around here from tim time. They like to come in and have lunch and a few office space. Did Lamar cover vacations?"

"Yes."

"Good. Book early, especially for Vail and the Caymans. buy the air fare, but the condos are free. We do a lot of busi in the Caymans and from time to time we'll send you dow two or three days and write the whole thing off. Those are not counted as vacation, and you'll get one every yea so. We work hard, Mitch, and we recognize the value o sure."

Mitch nodded his approval and dreamed of lying on a drenched beach in the Caribbean, sipping on a pina colada watching string bikinis.

"Did Lamar mention the signing bonus?"

"No, but it sounds interesting."

"If you join our firm we hand you a check for five thous We prefer that you spend the bulk of it on a new wardr After seven years of jeans and flannel shirts, your invento suits is probably low, and we realize it. Appearance is important to us. We expect our attorneys to dress sharp conservative. There's no dress code, but you'll get the ture."

Did he say five thousand dollars? For clothes? Mitch

ly owned two suits, and he was wearing one of them. He
t a straight face and did not smile.

"Any questions?"

"Yes. The large firms are infamous for being sweatshops
re the associates are flooded with tedious research and
ed away in some library for the first three years. I want no
t of that. I don't mind doing my share of research and I
ize I will be the low man on the pole. But I don't want to
arch and write briefs for the entire firm. I'd like to work
a real clients and their real problems."

Mr. McKnight listened intently and waited with his re-
rsed answer. "I understand, Mitch. You're right, it is a real
plem in the big firms. But not here. For the first six
ks you'll do little but study for the bar exam. When that's
r, you begin practicing law. You'll be assigned to a partner,
his clients will become your clients. You'll do most of his
arch and, of course, your own, and occasionally you'll be
ed to assist someone else with the preparation of a brief or
e research. We want you happy. We take pride in our zero
nover rate, and we go the extra mile to keep careers on
k. If you can't get along with your partner, we'll find an-
er one. If you discover you don't like tax, we'll let you try
ırities or banking. It's your decision. The firm will soon
est a lot of money in Mitch McDeere, and we want him to
productive."

Mitch sipped his coffee and searched for another question.
McKnight glanced at his checklist.

"We pay all moving expenses to Memphis."

"That won't be much. Just a small rental truck."

"Anything else, Mitch?"

"No, sir. I can't think of anything."

The checklist was folded and placed in the file. The partner
ed both elbows on the table and leaned forward. "Mitch,
re not pushing, but we need an answer as soon as possible.
ou go elsewhere, we must then continue to interview. It's a
gthy process, and we'd like our new man to start by July 1."

"Ten days soon enough?"

"That's fine. Say by March 30?"

"Sure, but I'll contact you before then." Mitch excused him-
, and found Lamar waiting in the hall outside McKnight's
ce. They agreed on seven for dinner.

3

THERE WERE no law offices on the fifth floor of
Bendini Building. The partners' dining room
kitchen occupied the west end, some unused and
painted storage rooms sat locked and empty in the center, t
a thick concrete wall sealed off the remaining third of the fl
A small metal door with a button beside it and a camera ov
hung in the center of the wall and opened into a small r
where an armed guard watched the door and monitored a v
of closed circuit screens. A hallway zigzagged through a n
of cramped offices and workrooms where an assortmen
characters went secretly about their business of watching
gathering information. The windows to the outside w
sealed with paint and covered with blinds. The sunlight st
no chance of penetrating the fortress.

DeVasher, head of security, occupied the largest of
small, plain offices. The lone certificate on his bare walls re
nized him for thirty years of dedicated service as a detec
with the New Orleans Police Department. He was of med
build with a slight belly, thick shoulders and chest and a h
perfectly round head that smiled with great reluctance.
wrinkled shirt was mercifully unbuttoned at the collar,

ing his bulging neck to sag unrestricted. A thick polyester
hung on the coatrack with a badly worn blazer.

Monday morning after the McDeere visit, Oliver Lambert
od before the small metal door and stared at the camera
r it. He pushed the button twice, waited and was finally
red through security. He walked quickly through the
mped hallway and entered the cluttered office. DeVasher
w smoke from a Dutch Masters into a smokeless ashtray
l shoved papers in all directions until wood was visible on
desk.

Mornin', Ollie. I guess you want to talk about McDeere."
DeVasher was the only person in the Bendini Building who
ed him Ollie to his face.

Yes, among other things."

Well, he had a good time, was impressed with the firm,
d Memphis okay and will probably sign on."

Where were your people?"

We had the rooms on both sides at the hotel. His room was
ed, of course, as was the limo and the phone and everything
. The usual, Ollie."

Let's get specific."

Okay. Thursday night they checked in late and went to
d. Little discussion. Friday night he told her all about the
n, the offices, the people, said you were a real nice man. I
ught you'd like that."

Get on with it."

Told her about the fancy dining room and his little lunch
h the partners. Gave her the specifics on the offer and they
re ecstatic. Much better than his other offers. She wants a
ne with a driveway and a sidewalk and trees and a back-
d. He said she could have one."

Any problems with the firm?"

Not really. He commented on the absence of blacks and
men, but it didn't seem to bother him."

What about his wife?"

She had a ball. She likes the town, and she and Quin's wife
it off. They looked at houses Friday afternoon, and she saw
ouple she liked."

You get any addresses?"

Of course, Ollie. Saturday morning they called the limo

and rode all over town. Very impressed with the limo. [...]
driver stayed away from the bad sections, and they looke[...]
more houses. I think they decided on one, 1231 East Mea[...]
brook. It's empty. Realtor by the name of Betsy Bell wa[...]
them through it. Asking one-forty, but will take less. Nee[...]
move it."

"That's a nice part of town. How old is the house?"

"Ten, fifteen years. Three thousand square feet. Sort [...]
colonial-looking job. It's nice enough for one of your b[...]
Ollie."

"Are you sure that's the one they want?"

"For now anyway. They discussed maybe coming back [...]
month or so to look at some more. You might want to fly t[...]
back as soon as they accept. That's normal procedure, ain'[...]

"Yes. We'll handle that. What about the salary?"

"Most impressed. Highest one so far. They talked and ta[...]
about the money. Salary, retirement, mortgage, BMW, bo[...]
everything. They couldn't believe it. Kids must really[...]
broke."

"They are. You think we got him, huh?"

"I'd bet on it. He said once that the firm may not b[...]
prestigious as the ones on Wall Street, but the lawyers [...]
just as qualified and a lot nicer. I think he'll sign on, yea[...]

"Any suspicions?"

"Not really. Quin evidently told him to stay away f[...]
Locke's office. He told his wife that no one ever went in t[...]
but some secretaries and a handful of partners. But he [...]
Quin said Locke was eccentric and not that friendly. I d[...]
think he's suspicious, though. She said the firm seemed [...]
cerned about some things that were none of its business.[...]

"Such as?"

"Personal matters. Children, working wives, etc. [...]
seemed a bit irritated, but I think it was more of an obse[...]
tion. She told Mitch Saturday morning that she woul[...]
damned if any bunch of lawyers would tell her when to v[...]
and when to have babies. But I don't think it's a problem[...]

"Does he realize how permanent this place is?"

"I think so. There was no mention of putting in a few y[...]
and moving on. I think he got the message. He wants to [...]
partner, like all of them. He's broke and wants the mone[...]

What about the dinner at my place?"

They were nervous, but had a good time. Very impressed your place. Really liked your wife."

ex?"

very night. Sounded like a honeymoon in there."

What'd they do?"

We couldn't see, remember. Sounded normal. Nothing y. I thought of you and how much you like pictures, and I telling myself we should've rigged up some cameras for Ollie."

hut up, DeVasher."

Maybe next time."

ey were silent as DeVasher looked at a notepad. He bed his cigar in the ashtray and smiled to himself.

ll in all," he said, "it's a strong marriage. They seemed to ery intimate. Your driver said they held hands all week- Not a cross word for three days. That's pretty good, ain't ut who am I? I've been married three times myself."

hat's understandable. What about children?"

ouple of years. She wants to work some, then get preg- ."

What's your opinion of this guy?"

ery good, very decent young man. Also very ambitious. I k he's driven and he won't quit until he's at the top. He'll some chances, bend some rules if necessary."

lie smiled. "That's what I wanted to hear."

wo phone calls. Both to her mother in Kentucky. Noth- remarkable."

What about his family?"

Never mentioned."

No word on Ray?"

We're still looking, Ollie. Give us some time."

eVasher closed the McDeere file and opened another, h thicker one. Lambert rubbed his temples and stared at floor. "What's the latest?" he asked softly.

t's not good, Ollie. I'm convinced Hodge and Kozinski are king together now. Last week the FBI got a warrant and ked Kozinski's house. Found our wiretaps. They told him ouse was bugged, but of course they don't know who did ozinski tells Hodge last Friday while they're hiding in the third-floor library. We got a bug nearby, and we pick up and pieces. Not much, but we know they talked about wiretaps. They're convinced everything is bugged, and suspect us. They're very careful where they talk."

"Why would the FBI bother with a search warrant?"

"Good question. Probably for our benefit. To make t look real legal and proper. They respect us."

"Which agent?"

"Tarrance. He's in charge, evidently."

"Is he good?"

"He's okay. Young, green, overzealous, but competent. no match for our men."

"How often has he talked to Kozinski?"

"There's no way to know. They figure we're listenin everybody's real careful. We know of four meetings in th month, but I suspect more."

"How much has he spilled?"

"Not much, I hope. They're still shadowboxing. The conversation we got was a week ago and he didn't say n He's bad scared. They're coaxing a lot, but not getting n He hasn't yet made the decision to cooperate. They proached him, remember. At least we think they approa him. They shook him up pretty bad and he was ready to deal. Now he's having second thoughts. But he's still in tact with them, and that's what worries me."

"Does his wife know?"

"I don't think so. She knows he's acting strange, and he her it's office pressure."

"What about Hodge?"

"Still ain't talked to the Fibbies, as far as we know. He Kozinski talk a lot, or whisper I should say. Hodge keeps ing he's scared to death of the FBI, that they don't play and they cheat and play dirty. He won't move without K ski."

"What if Kozinski is eliminated?"

"Hodge will be a new man. But I don't think we've rea that point. Dammit, Ollie, he ain't some hotshot thug who in the way. He's a very nice young man, with kids an that."

36

"Your compassion is overwhelming. I guess you think I en-
this. Hell, I practically raised these boys."

"We'll get them back in line, then, before this thing goes too
, New York's getting suspicious, Ollie. They're asking a lot
questions."

"Who?"

"Lazarov."

"What have you told them, DeVasher?"

"Everything. That's my job. They want you in New York
after tomorrow, for a full briefing."

"What do they want?"

"Answers. And plans."

"Plans for what?"

"Preliminary plans to eliminate Kozinski, Hodge and Tar-
ce, should it become necessary."

"Tarrance! Are you crazy, DeVasher? We can't eliminate a
. They'll send in the troops."

"Lazarov is stupid, Ollie. You know that. He's an idiot, but I
't think we should tell him."

"I think I will. I think I'll go to New York and tell Lazarov
s a complete fool."

"You do that, Ollie. You do that."

Oliver Lambert jumped from his seat and headed for the
or. "Watch McDeere for another month."

"Sure, Ollie. You betcha. He'll sign. Don't worry."

4

T HE MAZDA was sold for two hundred dollars, a most of the money was immediately invested in twelve foot U-Haul rental truck. He would be re bursed in Memphis. Half of the odd assortment of furnit was given or thrown away, and when loaded the truck hel refrigerator, a bed, a dresser and chest of drawers, a sm color television, boxes of dishes, clothes and junk and an sofa which was taken out of sentiment and would not last l in the new location.

Abby held Hearsay, the mutt, as Mitch worked his v through Boston and headed south, far south toward the pr ise of better things. For three days they drove the back roa enjoyed the countryside, sang along with the radio, slept cheap motels and talked of the house, the BMW, new fur ture, children, affluence. They rolled down the windows a let the wind blow as the truck approached top speeds of alm forty-five miles per hour. At one point, somewhere in Penns vania, Abby mentioned that perhaps they could stop in K tucky for a brief visit. Mitch said nothing, but chose a ro through the Carolinas and Georgia, never venturing wit

hundred miles of any point on the Kentucky border.
by let it pass.

hey arrived in Memphis on a Thursday morning, and, as
mised, the black 318i sat under the carport as though it
onged there. He stared at the car. She stared at the house.
e lawn was thick, green and neatly trimmed. The hedges
been manicured. The marigolds were in bloom.

he keys were found under a bucket in the utility room, as
mised.

After the first test drive, they quickly unloaded the truck
ore the neighbors could inspect the sparse belongings. The
Haul was returned to the nearest dealer. Another test drive.
An interior designer, the same one who would do his office,
ved after noon and brought with her samples of carpet,
nt, floor coverings, curtains, drapes, wallpaper. Abby found
idea of a designer a bit hilarious after their apartment in
nbridge, but played along. Mitch was immediately bored,
excused himself for another test drive. He toured the tree
d, quiet, shady streets of this handsome neighborhood of
ich he was now a member. He smiled as boys on bicycles
pped and whistled at his new car. He waved at the postman
lking down the sidewalk sweating profusely. Here he was,
tchell Y. McDeere, twenty-five years old and one week out
aw school, and he had arrived.

At three, they followed the designer to an upscale furniture
re where the manager politely informed them that Mr. Oli-
Lambert had already made arrangements for their credit,
hey so chose, and there was in fact no limit on what they
ld buy and finance. They bought a houseful. Mitch
wned from time to time, and twice vetoed items as too ex-
sive, but Abby ruled the day. The designer complimented
time and again on her marvelous taste, and said she would
Mitch on Monday, to do his office. Marvelous, he said.

th a map of the city, they set out for the Quin residence.
by had seen the house during the first visit, but did not
member how to find it. It was in a section of town called
ickasaw Gardens, and she remembered the wooded lots,
ge houses and professionally landscaped front yards. They

parked in the driveway behind the new Mercedes and the Mercedes.

The maid nodded politely, but did not smile. She led th to the living room, and left them. The house was dark quiet—no children, no voices, no one. They admired the fu ture and waited. They mumbled quietly, then grew impati Yes, they agreed, they had in fact been invited to dinner this night, Thursday, June 25, at 6 P.M. Mitch checked watch again and said something about it being rude. T waited.

From the hallway, Kay emerged and attempted to sm Her eyes were puffy and glazed, with mascara leaking fr the corners. Tears flowed freely down her cheeks, and she h a handkerchief over her mouth. She hugged Abby and sat n to her on the sofa. She bit the handkerchief and cried lou

Mitch knelt before her. "Kay, what's happened?"

She bit harder and shook her head. Abby squeezed her kr and Mitch patted the other one. They watched her fearfu expecting the worst. Was it Lamar or one of the kids?

"There's been a tragedy," she said through the quiet s bing.

"Who is it?" Mitch asked.

She wiped her eyes and breathed deeply. "Two member the firm, Marty Kozinski and Joe Hodge, were killed today. were very close to them."

Mitch sat on the coffee table. He remembered Marty Koz ski from the second visit in April. He had joined Lamar Mitch for lunch at a deli on Front Street. He was next in l for a partnership, but had seemed less than enthused. Mi could not place Joe Hodge.

"What happened?" he asked.

She had stopped crying, but the tears continued. She wi her face again and looked at him. "We're not sure. They w on Grand Cayman, scuba diving. There was some kind of explosion on a boat, and we think they drowned. Lamar s details were sketchy. There was a firm meeting a few ho ago, and they were all told about it. Lamar barely made home."

"Where is he?"

"By the pool. He's waiting for you."

40

e sat in a white metal lawn chair next to a small table with
all umbrella, a few feet from the edge of the pool. Near a
er bed, a circular lawn sprinkler rattled and hissed and
wed forth water in a perfect arc which included the table,
rella, chair and Lamar Quin. He was soaked. Water
ped from his nose, ears and hair. The blue cotton shirt and
l pants were saturated. He wore no socks or shoes.

e sat motionless, never flinching with each additional
sing. He had lost touch. Some distant object on the side
e attracted and held his attention. An unopened bottle of
neken sat in a puddle on the concrete beside his chair.

itch surveyed the back lawn, in part to make sure the
hbors could not see. They could not. An eight-foot cypress
e ensured complete privacy. He walked around the pool
stopped at the edge of the dry area. Lamar noticed him,
ded, attempted a weak smile and motioned to a wet chair.
ch pulled it a few feet away and sat down, just as the next
age of water landed.

is stare returned to the fence, or whatever it was in the
ance. For an eternity they sat and listened to the thrashing
d of the sprinkler. Lamar would sometimes shake his head
attempt to mumble. Mitch smiled awkwardly, unsure of
t, if anything, needed to be said.

Lamar, I'm very sorry," he finally offered.

e acknowledged this and looked at Mitch. "Me too."

I wish I could say something."

is eyes left the fence, and he cocked his head sideways in
ch's direction. His dark hair was soaked and hung in his
. The eyes were red and pained. He stared, and waited
l the next round of water passed over.

I know. But there's nothing to say. I'm sorry it had to hap-
now, today. We didn't feel like cooking."

That should be the least of your concern. I lost my appetite
oment ago."

Do you remember them?" he asked, blowing water from
lips.

I remember Kozinski, but not Hodge."

Marty Kozinski was one of my best friends. From Chicago.
joined the firm three years ahead of me and was next in
for a partnership. A great lawyer, one we all admired and

41

turned to. Probably the best negotiator in the firm. Very ○ and dry under pressure."

He wiped his eyebrows and stared at the ground. Wher talked the water dripped from his nose and interfered with enunciation. "Three kids. His twin girls are a month o than our son, and they've always played together." He cl his eyes, bit his lip and started crying.

Mitch wanted to leave. He tried not to look at his frie "I'm very sorry, Lamar. Very sorry."

After a few minutes, the crying stopped, but the water tinued. Mitch surveyed the spacious lawn in search of the ○ side faucet. Twice he summoned the courage to ask if he cc turn off the sprinkler, and twice he decided he could la: Lamar could. Maybe it helped. He checked his watch. D ness was an hour and a half away.

"What about the accident?" Mitch finally asked.

"We weren't told much. They were scuba diving and th was an explosion on the boat. The dive captain was also ki A native of the islands. They're trying to get the bodies h now."

"Where were their wives?"

"At home, thankfully. It was a business trip."

"I can't picture Hodge."

"Joe was a tall blond-headed guy who didn't say much. kind you meet but don't remember. He was a Harvard r like yourself."

"How old was he?"

"He and Marty were both thirty-four. He would've m partner after Marty. They were very close. I guess we're close, especially now."

With all ten fingernails he combed his hair straight back. stood and walked to dry ground. Water poured from his sl tail and the cuffs of his pants. He stopped near Mitch looked blankly at the treetops next door. "How's the BMV

"It's great. A fine car. Thanks for delivering it."

"When did you arrive?"

"This morning. I've already put a thousand miles on it.

"Did the interior woman show up?"

"Yeah. She and Abby spent next year's salary."

"That's nice. Nice house. We're glad you're here, Mitch. I'm
st sorry about the circumstances. You'll like it here."

"You don't have to apologize."

"I still don't believe it. I'm numb, paralyzed. I shudder at
e thought of seeing Marty's wife and the kids. I'd rather be
shed with a bullwhip than go over there."

The women appeared, walked across the wooden patio deck
d down the steps to the pool. Kay found the faucet and the
rinkler was silenced.

hey left Chickasaw Gardens and drove west with the traffic
ward downtown, into the fading sun. They held hands, but
id little. Mitch opened the sunroof and rolled down the win-
ws. Abby picked through a box of old cassettes and found
ringsteen. The stereo worked fine. "Hungry Heart" blew
om the windows as the little shiny roadster made its way
ward the river. The warm, sticky, humid Memphis summer
r settled in with the dark. Softball fields came to life as teams
fat men with tight polyester pants and lime-green and fluo-
scent-yellow shirts laid chalk lines and prepared to do battle.
rs full of teenagers crowded into fast-food joints to drink
er and gossip and check out the opposite sex. Mitch began to
ile. He tried to forget about Lamar, and Kozinski and
odge. Why should he be sad? They were not his friends. He
as sorry for their families, but he did not really know these
ople. And he, Mitchell Y. McDeere, a poor kid with no fami-
, had much to be happy about. Beautiful wife, new house,
w car, new job, new Harvard degree. A brilliant mind and a
lid body that did not gain weight and needed little sleep.
ghty thousand a year, for now. In two years he could be in
x figures, and all he had to do was work ninety hours a week.
ece of cake.

He pulled into a self-serve and pumped fifteen gallons. He
id inside and bought a six-pack of Michelob. Abby opened
vo, and they darted back into the traffic. He was smiling now.

"Let's eat," he said.

"We're not exactly dressed," she said.

He stared at her long, brown legs. She wore a white cotton
irt, above the knees, with a white cotton button-down. He

had shorts, deck shoes and a faded black polo. "With legs li[ke] that, you could get us into any restaurant in New York."

"How about the Rendezvous? The dress seemed casual."

"Great idea."

They paid to park in a lot downtown and walked two bloc[ks] to a narrow alley. The smell of barbecue mixed with the sum[mer] air and hung like a fog close to the pavement. The arom[a] filtered gently through the nose, mouth and eyes and caused [a] rippling sensation deep in the stomach. Smoke poured into t[he] alley from vents running underground into the massive ove[n] where the best pork ribs were barbecued in the best barbec[ue] restaurant in a city known for world-class barbecue. The Re[n]dezvous was downstairs, beneath the alley, beneath an ancie[nt] red-brick building that would have been demolished decad[es] earlier had it not been for the famous tenant in the baseme[nt.]

There was always a crowd and a waiting list, but Thursda[ys] were slow, it seemed. They were led through the cavernou[s,] sprawling, noisy restaurant and shown a small table with a re[d-] checked tablecloth. There were stares along the way. Alwa[ys] stares. Men stopped eating, froze with ribs hanging from the[ir] teeth, as Abby McDeere glided by like a model on a runwa[y.] She had stopped traffic from a sidewalk in Boston. Whistl[es] and catcalls were a way of life. And her husband was used [to] it. He took great pride in his beautiful wife.

An angry black man with a red apron stood before the[m.] "Okay, sir," he demanded.

The menus were mats on the tables, and completely unne[c]essary. Ribs, ribs and ribs.

"Two whole orders, cheese plate, pitcher of beer," Mit[ch] shot back at him. The waiter wrote nothing, but turned an[d] screamed in the direction of the entrance: "Gimme two who[le,] cheese, pitcher!"

When he left, Mitch grabbed her leg under the table. S[he] slapped his hand.

"You're beautiful," he said. "When was the last time I to[ld] you that you are beautiful?"

"About two hours ago."

"Two hours! How thoughtless of me!"

"Don't let it happen again."

He grabbed her leg again and rubbed the knee. She allowe[d]

She smiled seductively at him, dimples forming perfectly, eth shining in the dim light, soft pale brown eyes glowing. er dark brunet hair was straight and fell perfectly a few ches below her shoulders.

The beer arrived and the waiter filled two mugs without ying a word. Abby took a small drink and stopped smiling.

"Do you think Lamar's okay?" she asked.

"I don't know. I thought at first he was drunk. I felt like an iot sitting there watching him get soaked."

"Poor guy. Kay said the funerals will probably be Monday, they can get the bodies back in time."

"Let's talk about something else. I don't like funerals, any neral, even when I'm there out of respect and don't know e deceased. I've had some bad experiences with funerals."

The ribs arrived. They were served on paper plates with uminum foil to catch the grease. A small dish of slaw and one baked beans sat around a foot long slab of dry ribs sprinkled avily with the secret sauce. They dug in with fingers.

"What would you like to talk about?" she asked.

"Getting pregnant."

"I thought we were going to wait a few years."

"We are. But I think we should practice diligently until en."

"We've practiced in every roadside motel between here and oston."

"I know, but not in our new home." Mitch ripped two ribs art, slinging sauce into his eyebrows.

"We just moved in this morning."

"I know. What're we waiting for?"

"Mitch, you act as though you've been neglected."

"I have, since this morning. I suggest we do it tonight, as on as we get home, to sort of christen our new house."

"We'll see."

"Is it a date? Look, did you see that guy over there? He's out to break his neck trying to see some leg. I oughta go over d whip his ass."

"Yes. It's a date. Don't worry about those guys. They're star- g at you. They think you're cute."

"Very funny."

Mitch stripped his ribs clean and ate half of hers. When the

45

beer was gone, he paid the check and they climbed into t▯ alley. He drove carefully across town and found the name of street he recognized from one of his many road trips of t▯ day. After two wrong turns, he found Meadowbrook, and th▯ the home of Mr. and Mrs. Mitchell Y. McDeere.

The mattress and box springs were stacked on the floor ▯ the master bedroom, surrounded by boxes. Hearsay hid und▯ a lamp on the floor and watched as they practiced.

Four days later, on what should have been his first day behi▯ his new desk, Mitch and his lovely wife joined the remaini▯ thirty-nine members of the firm, and their lovely wives, they paid their last respects to Martin S. Kozinski. The cath dral was full. Oliver Lambert offered a eulogy so eloquent a▯ touching not even Mitchell McDeere, who had buried a fath▯ and a brother, could resist chill bumps. Abby's eyes watered the sight of the widow and the children.

That afternoon, they met again in the Presbyterian chur▯ in East Memphis to say farewell to Joseph M. Hodge.

5

THE SMALL LOBBY outside Royce McKnight's office was empty when Mitch arrived precisely at eight-thirty, on schedule. He hummed and coughed and began to wait anxiously. From behind two file cabinets an ancient blue-haired secretary appeared and scowled in his general direction. When it was apparent he was not welcome, he introduced himself and explained he was to meet Mr. McKnight at this appointed hour. She smiled and introduced herself as Louise, Mr. McKnight's personal secretary, for thirty-one years now. Coffee? Yes, he said, black. She disappeared and returned with a cup and saucer. She notified her boss through the intercom and instructed Mitch to have a seat. She recognized him now. One of the other secretaries had pointed him out during the funerals yesterday.

She apologized for the somber atmosphere around the place. No one felt like working, she explained, and it would be days before things were normal. They were such nice young men. The phone rang and she explained that Mr. McKnight was in an important meeting and could not be disturbed. It rang again, she listened, and escorted him into the managing partner's office.

Oliver Lambert and Royce McKnight greeted Mitch and introduced him to two other partners, Victor Milligan and Avery Tolleson. They sat around a small conference table. Louise was sent for more coffee. Milligan was head of tax, and Tolleson, at forty-one, was one of the younger partners.

"Mitch, we apologize for such a depressing beginning," McKnight said. "We appreciate your presence at the funerals yesterday, and we're sorry your first day as a member of our firm was one of such sadness."

"I felt I belonged at the funerals," Mitch said.

"We're very proud of you, and we have great plans for you. We've just lost two of our finest lawyers, both of whom did nothing but tax, so we'll be asking more of you. All of us will have to work a little harder."

Louise arrived with a tray of coffee. Silver coffee server, fine china.

"We are quite saddened," said Oliver Lambert. "So please bear with us."

They all nodded and frowned at the table. Royce McKnight looked at some notes on a legal pad.

"Mitch, I think we've covered this before. At this firm, we assign each associate to a partner, who acts as a supervisor and mentor. These relationships are very important. We try to match you with a partner with whom you will be compatible and able to work closely, and we're usually right. We have made mistakes. Wrong chemistry, or whatever, but when that happens we simply reassign the associate. Avery Tolleson will be your partner."

Mitch smiled awkwardly at his new partner.

"You will be under his direction, and the cases and files you work on will be his. Virtually all of it will be tax work."

"That's fine."

"Before I forget it, I'd like to have lunch today," Tolleson said.

"Certainly," Mitch said.

"Take my limo," Mr. Lambert said.

"I had planned to," said Tolleson.

"When do I get a limo?" Mitch asked.

They smiled, and seemed to appreciate the relief. "In about twenty years," said Mr. Lambert.

"I can wait."

"How's the BMW?" asked Victor Milligan.

"Great. It's ready for the five-thousand-mile service."

"Did you get moved in okay?"

"Yes, everything's fine. I appreciate the firm's assistance in everything. You've made us feel very welcome, and Abby and I are extremely grateful."

McKnight quit smiling and returned to the legal pad. "As we told you, Mitch, the bar exam has priority. You've got six weeks to study for it and we assist in every way possible. We have our own review courses directed by our members. All areas of the exam will be covered and your progress will be closely watched by all of us, especially Avery. At least half of each day will be spent on bar review, and most of your spare time as well. No associate in this firm has ever failed the exam."

"I won't be the first."

"If you flunk it, we take away the BMW," Tolleson said with a slight grin.

"Your secretary will be a lady named Nina Huff. She's been with the firm more than eight years. Sort of temperamental, not much to look at, but very capable. She knows a lot of law and has a tendency to give advice, especially to the newer attorneys. It'll be up to you to keep her in place. If you can't get along with her, we'll move her."

"Where's my office?"

"Second floor, down the hall from Avery. The interior woman will be here this afternoon to pick out the desk and furnishings. As much as possible, follow her advice."

Lamar was also on the second floor, and at the moment that thought was comforting. He thought of him sitting by the pool, soaking wet, crying and mumbling incoherently.

McKnight spoke. "Mitch, I'm afraid I neglected to cover something that should've been discussed during the first visit here."

He waited, and finally said, "Okay, what is it?"

The partners watched McKnight intently. "We've never allowed an associate to begin his career burdened with student loans. We prefer that you find other things to worry about, and other ways to spend your money. How much do you owe?"

Mitch sipped his coffee and thought rapidly. "Almo twenty-three thousand."

"Have the documents on Louise's desk first thing in th morning."

"You, uh, mean the firm satisfies the loans?"

"That's our policy. Unless you object."

"No objection. I don't quite know what to say."

"You don't have to say anything. We've done it for ever associate for the past fifteen years. Just get the paperwork Louise."

"That's very generous, Mr. McKnight."

"Yes, it is."

Avery Tolleson talked incessantly as the limo moved slow through the noontime traffic. Mitch reminded him of himsel he said. A poor kid from a broken home, raised by foster fam lies throughout southwest Texas, then put on the streets aft high school. He worked the night shift in a shoe factory finance junior college. An academic scholarship to UTE opened the door. He graduated with honors, applied to eleve law schools and chose Stanford. He finished number two in h class and turned down offers from every big firm on the We Coast. He wanted to do tax work, nothing but tax work. Ol ver Lambert had recruited him sixteen years ago, back whe the firm had fewer than thirty lawyers.

He had a wife and two kids, but said little about the famil He talked about money. His passion, he called it. The fir million was in the bank. The second was two years away. A four hundred thousand a year gross, it wouldn't take long. H specialty was forming partnerships to purchase supertanker He was the premier specialist in his field and worked at thre hundred an hour, sixty, sometimes seventy hours a week.

Mitch would start at a hundred bucks an hour, at least fiv hours a day until he passed the bar and got his license. The eight hours a day would be expected, at one-fifty an hour. Bil ing was the lifeblood of the firm. Everything revolved aroun it. Promotions, raises, bonuses, survival, success, everythin revolved around how well one was billing. Especially the ne guys. The quickest route to a reprimand was to neglect th daily billing records. Avery could not remember such a repr

and. It was simply unheard of for a member of the firm to
nore his billing.

The average for associates was one-seventy-five per hour.
or partners, three hundred. Milligan got four hundred an
our from a couple of his clients, and Nathan Locke once got
ve hundred an hour for some tax work that involved swap-
ng assets in several foreign countries. Five hundred bucks an
our! Avery relished the thought, and computed five hundred
er hour by fifty hours per week at fifty weeks per year. One
illion two hundred fifty thousand a year! That's how you
ake money in this business. You get a bunch of lawyers
orking by the hour and you build a dynasty. The more law-
ers you get, the more money the partners make.

Don't ignore the billing, he warned. That's the first rule of
rvival. If there were no files to bill on, immediately report to
s office. He had plenty. On the tenth day of each month the
artners review the prior month's billing during one of their
clusive luncheons. It's a big ceremony. Royce McKnight
ads out each lawyer's name, then the total of his monthly
lling. The competition among the partners is intense, but
od-spirited. They're all getting rich, right? It's very motiva-
onal. As for the associates, nothing is said to the low man
less it's his second straight month. Oliver Lambert will say
mething in passing. No one has ever finished low for three
raight months. Bonuses can be earned by associates for exor-
tant billing. Partnerships are based on one's track record for
nerating fees. So don't ignore it, he warned again. It must
ways have priority—after the bar exam, of course.

The bar exam was a nuisance, an ordeal that must be en-
ured, a rite of passage, and nothing any Harvard man should
ar. Just concentrate on the review courses, he said, and try to
member everything he had just learned in law school.

The limo wheeled into a side street between two tall build-
gs and stopped in front of a small canopy that extended from
e curb to a black metal door. Avery looked at his watch and
id to the driver, "Be back at two."

Two hours for lunch, thought Mitch. That's over six hun-
red dollars in billable time. What a waste.

The Manhattan Club occupied the top floor of a ten story
ffice building which had last been fully occupied in the early

fifties. Avery referred to the structure as a dump, but w
quick to point out that the club was the most exclusive lun
and dinner refuge in the city. It offered excellent food in a
all-white rich-male, plush environment. Powerful lunches f
powerful people. Bankers, lawyers, executives, entrepreneu
a few politicians and a few aristocrats. A gold-plated elevat
ran nonstop past the deserted offices and stopped on the e
gant tenth floor. The maître d' called Mr. Tolleson by nan
and asked about his good friends Oliver Lambert and Natha
Locke. He expressed sympathies for the loss of Mr. Kozins
and Mr. Hodge. Avery thanked him and introduced the nev
est member of the firm. The favorite table was waiting in th
corner. A courtly black man named Ellis delivered the menu

"The firm does not allow drinking at lunch," Avery said
he opened his menu.

"I don't drink during lunch."

"That's good. What'll you have?"

"Tea, with ice."

"Iced tea, for him," Avery said to the waiter. "Bring me
Bombay martini on the rocks with three olives."

Mitch bit his tongue and grinned behind the menu.

"We have too many rules," Avery mumbled.

The first martini led to a second, but he quit after two. H
ordered for both of them. Broiled fish of some sort. The speci
of the day. He watched his weight carefully, he said. He al
worked out daily at a health club, his own health club. H
invited Mitch to come sweat with him. Maybe after the b
exam. There were the usual questions about football in colleg
and the standard denials of any greatness.

Mitch asked about the children. He said they lived wit
their mother.

The fish was raw and the baked potato was hard. Mitc
picked at his plate, ate his salad slowly and listened as h
partner talked about most of the other people present fe
lunch. The mayor was seated at a large table with some Jap
nese. One of the firm's bankers was at the next table. Ther
were some other big-shot lawyers and corporate types, all ea
ing furiously and importantly, powerfully. The atmosphe
was stuffy. According to Avery, every member of the club w

52

compelling figure, a potent force both in his field and in the
ty. Avery was at home.

They both declined dessert and ordered coffee. He would be
pected to be in the office by nine each morning, Avery ex-
ained as he lit a Montesino. The secretaries would be there
eight-thirty. Nine to five, but no one worked eight hours a
y. Personally, he was in the office by eight, and seldom left
fore six. He could bill twelve hours each day, every day,
gardless of how many hours he actually worked. Twelve a
y, five days a week, at three hundred an hour, for fifty
eeks. Nine hundred thousand dollars! In billable time! That
as his goal. Last year he had billed seven hundred thousand,
t there had been some personal problems. The firm didn't
re if Mitch came in at 6 A.M. or 9 A.M., as long as the work
as done.

"What time are the doors unlocked?" Mitch asked.

Everyone has a key, he explained, so he could come and go
he pleased. Security was tight, but the guards were accus-
med to workaholics. Some of the work habits were legend-
y. Victor Milligan, in his younger days, worked sixteen
urs a day, seven days a week, until he made partner. Then
e quit working on Sundays. He had a heart attack and gave
p Saturdays. His doctor put him on ten hour days, five days a
eek, and he hasn't been happy since. Marty Kozinski knew
l the janitors by first name. He was a 9 A.M. man who wanted
have breakfast with the kids. He would come in at nine and
ave at midnight. Nathan Locke claims he can't work well
ter the secretaries arrive, so he comes in at six. It would be a
sgrace to start later. Here's a man sixty-one years old, worth
n million, and works from six in the morning until eight at
ght five days a week and then a half day on Saturday. If he
tired, he'd die.

Nobody punched a clock, the partner explained. Come and
as you please. Just get the work done.

Mitch said he got the message. Sixteen hours a day would be
othing new.

Avery complimented him on the new suit. There was an
nwritten dress code, and it was apparent Mitch had caught
. Avery had a tailor, an old Korean in South Memphis, he

would recommend when Mitch could afford it. Fifteen hundred a suit. Mitch said he would wait a year or two.

An attorney from one of the bigger firms interrupted and
spoke to Avery. He offered his sympathies and asked about th
families. He and Joe Hodge had worked together on a case la
year, and he couldn't believe it. Avery introduced him
Mitch. He was at the funeral, he said. They waited for him
leave, but he rambled on and on about how sorry he was.
was obvious he wanted details. Avery offered none, and l
finally left.

By two, the power lunches were losing steam, and th
crowd thinned. Avery signed the check, and the maître d' le
them to the door. The chauffeur stood patiently by the rear
the limo. Mitch crawled into the back and sank into the heav
leather seat. He watched the buildings and the traffic. I
looked at the pedestrians scurrying along the hot sidewall
and wondered how many of them had seen the inside of a lim
or the inside of the Manhattan Club. How many of the
would be rich in ten years? He smiled, and felt good. Harva
was a million miles away. Harvard with no student loans. Ke
tucky was in another world. His past was forgotten. He ha
arrived.

The decorator was waiting in his office. Avery excused himse
and asked Mitch to be in his office in an hour to begin wor
She had books full of office furniture and samples of ever
thing. He asked for suggestions, listened with as much intere
as he could muster, then told her he trusted her judgment an
she could pick out whatever she felt was appropriate. She like
the solid cherry work desk, no drawers, burgundy leathe
wing chairs and a very expensive oriental rug. Mitch said
was marvelous.

She left and he sat behind the old desk, one that looked fir
and would have suited him except that it was considered use
and therefore not good enough for a new lawyer at Bendin
Lambert & Locke. The office was fifteen by fifteen, with tw
six-foot windows facing north and staring directly into th
second floor of the old building next door. Not much of a viev
With a strain, he could see a glimpse of the river to the nortl
west. The walls were sheet-rock and bare. She had picked ou

ne artwork. He determined that the Ego Wall would face
: desk, behind the wing chairs. The diplomas, etc., would
ve to be mounted and framed. The office was big, for an
ociate. Much larger than the cubbyholes where the rookies
re placed in New York and Chicago. It would do for a cou-
: of years. Then on to one with a better view. Then a corner
ice, one of those power ones.

Miss Nina Huff knocked on the door and introduced herself
the secretary. She was a heavyset woman of forty-five, and
th one glance it was not difficult to understand why she was
ll single. With no family to support, it was evident she spent
r money on clothes and makeup—all to no avail. Mitch won-
red why she did not invest in a fitness counselor. She in-
med him forthrightly that she had been with the firm eight
d a half years now and knew all there was to know about
ice procedure. If he had a question, just ask her. He thanked
r for that. She had been in the typing pool and was grateful
the return to general secretarial duties. He nodded as
ugh he understood completely. She asked if he knew how
operate the dictating equipment. Yes, he said. In fact, the
ar before he had worked for a three-hundred-man firm on
ll Street and that firm owned the very latest in office tech-
logy. But if he had a problem he would ask her, he prom-
d.

"What's your wife's name?" she asked.

"Why is that important?" he asked.

"Because when she calls, I would like to know her name so
at I can be real sweet and friendly to her on the phone."

"Abby."

"How do you like your coffee?"

"Black, but I'll fix it myself."

"I don't mind fixing your coffee for you. It's part of the job."

"I'll fix it myself."

"All the secretaries do it."

"If you ever touch my coffee, I'll see to it that you're sent to
: mail room to lick stamps."

"We have an automated licker. Do they lick stamps on Wall
reet?"

"It was a figure of speech."

55

"Well, I've memorized your wife's name and we've settl
the issue of coffee, so I guess I'm ready to start."

"In the morning. Be here at eight-thirty."

"Yes, boss." She left and Mitch smiled to himself. She wa
real smart-ass, but she would be fun.

Lamar was next. He was late for a meeting with Nath
Locke, but he wanted to stop by and check on his friend. I
was pleased their offices were close. He apologized again
last Thursday's dinner. Yes, he and Kay and the kids would
there at seven to inspect the new house and the furniture.

Hunter Quin was five. His sister Holly was seven. They bo
ate the spaghetti with perfect manners from the brand-n
dining table and dutifully ignored the grown-up talk circul
ing around them. Abby watched the two and dreamed of I
bies. Mitch thought they were cute, but was not inspired. I
was busy recalling the events of the day.

The women ate quickly, then left to look at the furnit
and talk about the remodeling. The children took Hearsay
the backyard.

"I'm a little surprised they put you with Tolleson," Lam
said, wiping his mouth.

"Why is that?"

"I don't think he's ever supervised an associate."

"Any particular reason?"

"Not really. He's a great guy, but not much of a tea
player. Sort of a loner. Prefers to work by himself. He and I
wife are having some problems, and there's talk that they'
separated. But he keeps it to himself."

Mitch pushed his plate away and sipped the iced tea. "Is h
good lawyer?"

"Yes, very good. They're all good if they make partner. A I
of his clients are rich people with millions to put in tax sh
ters. He sets up limited partnerships. Many of his shelters a
risky, and he's known for his willingness to take chances a
fight with the IRS later. Most of his clients are big-time ri
takers. You'll do a lot of research looking for ways to bend t
tax laws. It'll be fun."

"He spent half of lunch lecturing on billing."

"It's vital. There's always the pressure to bill more a

ore. All we have to sell is our time. Once you pass the bar ur billing will be monitored weekly by Tolleson and Royce cKnight. It's all computerized and they can tell down to the ne how productive you are. You'll be expected to bill thirty forty hours a week for the first six months. Then fifty for a uple of years. Before they'll consider you for partner, you've t to hit sixty hours a week consistently over a period of ars. No active partner bills less than sixty a week—most of it the maximum rate."

"That's a lot of hours."

"Sounds that way, but it's deceptive. Most good lawyers can ork eight or nine hours a day and bill twelve. It's called dding. It's not exactly fair to the client, but it's something erybody does. The great firms have been built by padding es. It's the name of the game."

"Sounds unethical."

"So is ambulance chasing by plaintiff's lawyers. It's unethi- l for a dope lawyer to take his fee in cash if he has a reason to lieve the money is dirty. A lot of things are unethical. What out the doctor who sees a hundred Medicare patients a day? the one who performs unnecessary surgery? Some of the st unethical people I've met have been my own clients. It's sy to pad a file when your client is a multimillionaire who nts to screw the government and wants you to do it legally. e all do it."

"Do they teach it?"

"No. You just sort of learn it. You'll start off working long, azy hours, but you can't do it forever. So you start taking ortcuts. Believe me, Mitch, after you've been with us a year u'll know how to work ten hours and bill twice that much. s sort of a sixth sense lawyers acquire."

"What else will I acquire?"

Lamar rattled his ice cubes and thought for a moment. "A rtain amount of cynicism. This business works on you. hen you were in law school you had some noble idea of what lawyer should be. A champion of individual rights; a de- der of the Constitution; a guardian of the oppressed; an vocate for your client's principles. Then after you practice r six months you realize we're nothing but hired guns. outhpieces for sale to the highest bidder, available to any-

57

body, any crook, any sleazebag with enough money to pay o
outrageous fees. Nothing shocks you. It's supposed to be
honorable profession, but you'll meet so many crooked la
yers you'll want to quit and find an honest job. Yeah, Mit
you'll get cynical. And it's sad, really."

"You shouldn't be telling me this at this stage of my caree

"The money makes up for it. It's amazing how much drud
ery you can endure at two hundred thousand a year."

"Drudgery? You make it sound terrible."

"I'm sorry. It's not that bad. My perspective on life chang
radically last Thursday."

"You want to look at the house? It's marvelous."

"Maybe some other time. Let's just talk."

6

A T FIVE A.M. the alarm clock exploded on the new bed
table under the new lamp, and was immediately silenced. Mitch staggered through the dark house and
ind Hearsay waiting at the back door. He released him into
e backyard and headed for the shower. Twenty minutes
er he found his wife under the covers and kissed her good-
e. She did not respond.

With no traffic to fight, the office was ten minutes away. He
d decided his day would start at five-thirty, unless someone
uld top that, then he would be there at five, or four-thirty, or
enever it took to be first. Sleep was a nuisance. He would be
e first lawyer to arrive at the Bendini Building on this day,
d every day until he became a partner. If it took the others
ycars, he could do it in seven. He would become the young-
partner in the history of the firm, he had decided.

The vacant lot next to the Bendini Building had a ten-foot
ain link fence around it and a guard by the gate. There was a
rking place inside with his name spraypainted between the
llow lines. He stopped by the gate and waited. The uni-
med guard emerged from the darkness and approached the

driver's door. Mitch pushed a button, lowered the window a produced a plastic card with his picture on it.

"You must be the new man," the guard said as he held t card.

"Yes. Mitch McDeere."

"I can read. I should've known by the car."

"What's your name?" Mitch asked.

"Dutch Hendrix. Worked for the Memphis Police Depa ment for thirty-three years."

"Nice to meet you, Dutch."

"Yeah. Same to you. You start early, don't you?"

Mitch smiled and took the ID card. "No, I thought everyo would be here."

Dutch managed a smile. "You're the first. Mr. Locke will along shortly."

The gate opened and Dutch ordered him through. He fou his name in white on the asphalt and parked the spotless BM all by itself on the third row from the building. He grabbed empty burgundy eel-skin attaché case from the rear seat a gently closed the door. Another guard waited by the rear e trance. Mitch introduced himself and watched as the door w unlocked. He checked his watch. Exactly five-thirty. He w relieved that this hour was early enough. The rest of the fi was still asleep.

He flipped on the light switch in his office, and laid t attaché case on the temporary desk. He headed for the coff room down the hall, turning on lights as he went. The coff pot was one of those industrial sizes with multi-levels, mul burners, multi-pots and no apparent instructions on how operate any of it. He studied this machine for a moment as emptied a pack of coffee into the filter. He poured wat through one of the holes in the top and smiled when it beg dripping in the right place.

In one corner of his office were three cardboard boxes full books, files, legal pads and class notes he had accumulated the previous three years. He sat the first one on his desk a began removing its contents. The materials were categoriz and placed in neat little piles around the desk.

After two cups of coffee, he found the bar review materi in box number three. He walked to the window and open

blinds. It was still dark. He did not notice the figure sud-
ly appear in the doorway.

Good morning!"

Mitch spun from the window and gawked at the man. "You
ed me," he said, and breathed deeply.

I'm sorry. I'm Nathan Locke. I don't believe we've met."

I'm Mitch McDeere. The new man." They shook hands.

Yes, I know. I apologize for not meeting you earlier. I was
y during your earlier visits. I think I saw you at the funer-
Monday."

Mitch nodded and knew for certain he had never been
hin a hundred yards of Nathan Locke. He would have re-
mbered. It was the eyes, the cold black eyes with layers of
:k wrinkles around them. Great eyes. Unforgettable eyes.
. hair was white and thin on top with thickets around the
s, and the whiteness contrasted sharply with the rest of his
:. When he spoke, the eyes narrowed and the black pupils
wed fiercely. Sinister eyes. Knowing eyes.

Maybe so," Mitch said, captivated by the most evil face he
ever encountered. "Maybe so."

I see you're an early riser."

Yes, sir."

Well, good to have you."

Nathan Locke withdrew from the doorway and disap-
red. Mitch checked the hall, then closed the door. No won-
they keep him on the fourth floor away from everyone, he
ught. Now he understood why he didn't meet Nathan
:ke before he signed on. He might have had second
ughts. Probably hid him from all the prospective recruits.
. had, without a doubt, the most ominous, evil presence
:ch had ever felt. It was the eyes, he said to himself again, as
propped his feet on the desk and sipped coffee. The eyes.

Mitch expected, Nina brought food when she reported at
ht-thirty. She offered Mitch a doughnut, and he took two.
: inquired as to whether she should bring enough food
ry morning, and Mitch said he thought it would be nice of

What's that?" she asked, pointing at the stacks of files and
es on the desk.

61

"That's our project for the day. We need to get this s[...]
organized."

"No dictating?"

"Not yet. I meet with Avery in a few minutes. I need [...]
mess filed away in some order."

"How exciting," she said as she headed for the coffee ro[...]

Avery Tolleson was waiting with a thick, expandable [...]
which he handed to Mitch. "This is the Capps file. Part o[...]
Our client's name is Sonny Capps. He lives in Houston n[...]
but grew up in Arkansas. Worth about thirty million [...]
keeps his thumb on every penny of it. His father gave him [...]
old barge line just before he died, and he turned it into [...]
largest towing service on the Mississippi River. Now he [...]
ships, or boats, as he calls them, all over the world. We [...]
eighty percent of his legal work, everything but the litigati[...]
He wants to set up another limited partnership to purch[...]
another fleet of tankers, this one from the family of some d[...]
Chink in Hong Kong. Capps is usually the general partr[...]
and he'll bring in as many as twenty-five limited partners [...]
spread the risk and pool their resources. This deal is wo[...]
about sixty-five million. I've done several limited partnersh[...]
for him and they're all different, all complicated. And he [...]
extremely difficult to deal with. He's a perfectionist and thi[...]
he knows more than I do. You will not be talking to him. [...]
fact, no one here talks to him but me. That file is a portior[...]
the last partnership I did for him. It contains, among ot[...]
things, a prospectus, an agreement to form a partnership, [...]
ters of intent, disclosure statements and the limited partr[...]
ship agreement itself. Read every word of it. Then I want y[...]
to prepare a rough draft of the partnership agreement for t[...]
venture."

The file suddenly grew heavier. Perhaps five-thirty was [...]
early enough.

The partner continued. "We have about forty days, acco[...]
ing to Capps, so we're already behind. Marty Kozinski [...]
helping with this one, and as soon as I review his file I'll giv[...]
to you. Any questions?"

"What about the research?"

"Most of it is current, but you'll need to update it. Ca[...]
earned over nine million last year and paid a pittance in ta[...]

doesn't believe in paying taxes, and holds me personally
~~onsible~~ for every dime that's sent in. It's all legal, of
~~rse~~, but my point is that this is high-pressure work. Mil-
~~s~~ of dollars in investment and tax savings are at stake. The
~~ture~~ will be scrutinized by the governments of at least
~~ee~~ countries. So be careful."

~~M~~itch flipped through the documents. "How many hours a
do I work on this?"

As many as possible. I know the bar exam is important, but
~~s~~ Sonny Capps. He paid us almost a half a million last year
~~egal~~ fees."

I'll get it done."

I know you will. As I told you, your rate is one hundred an
~~ur~~. Nina will go over the time records with you today. Re-
~~mber~~, don't ignore the billing."

How could I forget?"

~~ver~~ Lambert and Nathan Locke stood before the metal door
the fifth floor and stared at the camera above. Something
~~ked~~ loudly and the door opened. A guard nodded. DeVa-
~~r~~ waited in his office.

Good morning, Ollie," he said quietly while ignoring the
~~er~~ partner.

What's the latest?" Locke snapped in DeVasher's direction
~~hout~~ looking at him.

From where?" DeVasher asked calmly.

Chicago."

They're very anxious up there, Nat. Regardless of what
~~u~~ believe, they don't like to get their hands dirty. And,
~~nkly~~, they just don't understand why they have to."

What do you mean?"

They're asking some tough questions, like why can't we
~~p~~ our people in line?"

And what're you telling them?"

That everything's okay. Wonderful. The great Bendini firm
~~solid~~. The leaks have been plugged. Business as usual. No
~~oblems~~."

How much damage did they do?" asked Oliver Lambert.

We're not sure. We'll never be sure, but I don't think they
~~r~~ talked. They had decided to, no doubt about that, but I

don't think they did. We've got it from a pretty good sou
there were FBI agents en route to the island the day of
accident, so we think they planned to rendezvous to spill th
guts."

"How do you know this?" asked Locke.

"Come on, Nat. We've got our sources. Plus, we had ped
all over the island. We do good work, you know."

"Evidently."

"Was it messy?"

"No, no. Very professional."

"How'd the native get in the way?"

"We had to make it look good, Ollie."

"What about the authorities down there?"

"What authorities? It's a tiny, peaceful island, Ollie. I
year they had one murder and four diving accidents. As fa
they're concerned, it's just another accident. Three accider
drownings."

"What about the FBI?" asked Locke.

"Don't know."

"I thought you had a source."

"We do. But we can't find him. We've heard nothing as
yesterday. Our people are still on the island and they've
ticed nothing unusual."

"How long will you stay there?"

"Couple of weeks."

"What happens if the FBI shows up?" asked Locke.

"We watch them real close. We'll see them when they get
the plane. We'll follow them to their hotel rooms. We may e
bug their phones. We'll know what they eat for breakfast a
what they talk about. We'll assign three of our guys for ev
one of theirs, and when they go to the toilet we'll know
There ain't nothing for them to find, Nat. I told you it wa
clean job, very professional. No evidence. Relax."

"This makes me sick, DeVasher," Lambert said.

"You think I like it, Ollie? What do you want us to do?
back and let them talk? Come on, Ollie, we're all humar
didn't want to do it, but Lazarov said do it. You wanna ar
with Lazarov, go ahead. They'll find you floating somewh
Those boys were up to no good. They should've kept qu

ven their little fancy cars and played big-shot lawyers. No,
y gotta get sanctimonious."

Nathan Locke lit a cigarette and blew a heavy cloud of
oke in the general direction of DeVasher. The three sat in
nce for a moment as the smoke settled across his desk. He
red at Black Eyes but said nothing.

Oliver Lambert stood and stared at the blank wall next to
door. "Why did you want to see us?" he asked.

DeVasher took a deep breath. "Chicago wants to bug the
ne phones of all nonpartners."

"I told you," Lambert said to Locke.

"It wasn't my idea, but they insist on it. They're very ner-
us up there, and they wanna take some extra precautions.
u can't blame them."

"Don't you think it's going a bit too far?" asked Lambert.

"Yeah, it's totally unnecessary. But Chicago doesn't think
"

"When?" asked Locke.

"Next week or so. It'll take a few days."

"All of them?"

"Yes. That's what they said."

"Even McDeere?"

"Yes. Even McDeere. I think Tarrance will try again, and he
ght start at the bottom this time."

"I met McDeere this morning," said Locke. "He was here before
."

"Five thirty-two," answered DeVasher.

e law school memorabilia were removed to the floor and the
pps file spread across the desk. Nina brought a chicken salad
dwich back from lunch, and he ate it as he read and as she
d away the junk on the floor. Shortly after one, Wally Hud-
, or J. Walter Hudson as the firm letterhead declared him,
ived to begin the study for the bar exam. Contracts were his
cialty. He was a five-year member of the firm and the only
rginia man, which he found odd because Virginia had the
st law school in the country, in his opinion. He had spent
 last two years developing a new review course for the con-
cts section of the exam. He was quite anxious to try it on
neone, and McDeere happened to be the man. He handed

Mitch a heavy three-ring notebook that was at least four inch thick and weighed as much as the Capps file.

The exam would last for four days and consist of three par Wally explained. The first day would be a four-hour multip choice exam on ethics. Gill Vaughn, one of the partners, w the resident expert on ethics and would supervise that porti of the review. The second day would be an eight-hour exa known simply as multi-state. It covered most areas of the l common to all states. It, too, was multiple choice and the qu tions were very deceptive. Then the heavy action. Days th and four would be eight hours each and cover fifteen areas substantive law. Contracts, Uniform Commercial Code, r estate, torts, domestic relations, wills, estates, taxation, wo men's compensation, constitutional law, federal trial pro dure, criminal procedure, corporations, partnerships, ins ance and debtor-creditor relations. All answers would be essay form, and the questions would emphasize Tennessee la The firm had a review plan for each of the fifteen sections

"You mean fifteen of these?" Mitch asked as he lifted t notebook.

Wally smiled. "Yes. We're very thorough. No one in this fi has ever flunked—"

"I know. I know. I won't be the first."

"You and I will meet at least once a week for the next weeks to go through the materials. Each session will last ab two hours, so you can plan accordingly. I would suggest ea Wednesday at three."

"Morning or afternoon?"

"Afternoon."

"That's fine."

"As you know, contracts and the Uniform Commerc Code go hand in hand, so I've incorporated the UCC into th materials. We'll cover both, but it'll take more time. A typi bar exam is loaded with commercial transactions. Those pr lems make great essay questions, so that notebook will be v important. I've included actual questions from old exan along with the model answers. It's fascinating reading."

"I can't wait."

"Take the first eighty pages for next week. You'll find so essay questions you'll need to answer."

You mean homework?"

Absolutely. I'll grade it next week. It's very important to ctice these questions each week."

This could be worse than law school."

It's much more important than law school. We take it very iously. We have a committee to monitor your progress from w until you sit for the exam. We'll be watching very sely."

Who's on the committee?"

Myself, Avery Tolleson, Royce McKnight, Randall Dunbar Kendall Mahan. We'll meet each Friday to assess your gress."

Vally produced a smaller, letter-sized notebook and laid it the desk. "This is your daily log. You are to record the urs spent studying for the exam and the subjects studied. I'll k it up every Friday morning before the committee meets. y questions?"

I can't think of any," Mitch said as he laid the notebook on of the Capps file.

Good. See you next Wednesday at three."

ess than ten seconds after he left, Randall Dunbar walked with a thick notebook remarkably similar to the one left ind by Wally. In fact, it was identical, but not quite as k. Dunbar was head of real estate and had handled the chase and sale of the McDeere home in May. He handed ch the notebook, labeled *Real Estate Law*, and explained his specialty was the most critical part of the exam. rything goes back to property, he said. He had carefully pre- ed the materials himself over the past ten years and con- ed that he had often thought of publishing them as an horitative work on property rights and land financing. He ld need at least one hour a week, preferably on Tuesday rnoon. He talked for an hour about how different the exam thirty years ago when he took it.

endall Mahan added a new twist. He wanted to meet on urday mornings. Early, say seven-thirty.

No problem," Mitch said as he took the notebook and ed it next to the others. This one was for constitutional , a favorite of Kendall's, although he seldom got to use it, said. It was the most important section of the exam, or at

least it had been when he took it five years ago. He had p
lished an article on First Amendment rights in the *Colum*
Law Review in his senior year there. A copy of it was in
notebook, in case Mitch wanted to read it. He promised to
so almost immediately.

The procession continued throughout the afternoon u
half of the firm had stopped by with notebooks, assignment
homework and requests for weekly meetings. No fewer t
six reminded him that no member of the firm had ever fa
the bar exam.

When his secretary said goodbye at five, the small desk
covered with enough bar review materials to choke a ten m
firm. Unable to speak, he simply smiled at her and returne
Wally's version of contract law. Food crossed his mind an h
later. Then, for the first time in twelve hours, he though
Abby. He called her.

"I won't be home for a while," he said.

"But I'm cooking dinner."

"Leave it on the stove," he said, somewhat shortly.

There was a pause. "When will you be home?" she as
with slow, precise words.

"In a few hours."

"A few hours. You've already been there half the day."

"That's right, and I've got much more to do."

"But it's your first day."

"You wouldn't believe it if I told you."

"Are you all right?"

"I'm fine. I'll be home later."

The starting engine awakened Dutch Hendrix, and he jum
to his feet. The gate opened and he waited by it as the last
left the lot. It stopped next to him.

"Evenin', Dutch," Mitch said.

"You just now leaving?"

"Yeah, busy day."

Dutch flashed his light at his wrist and checked the ti
Eleven-thirty.

"Well, be careful," Dutch said.

"Yeah. See you in a few hours."

The BMW turned onto Front Street and raced away into

ht. A few hours, thought Dutch. The rookies were indeed
azing. Eighteen, twenty hours a day, six days a week. Some-
es seven. They all planned to be the world's greatest lawyer
l make a million dollars overnight. Sometimes they worked
und the clock, slept at their desks. He had seen it all. But
y couldn't last. The human body was not meant for such
se. After about six months they lost steam. They would cut
k to fifteen hours a day, six days a week. Then five and a
f. Then twelve hours a day.

No one could work a hundred hours a week for more than
months.

7

O NE SECRETARY dug through a file cabinet in sea
of something Avery needed immediately. The ot
secretary stood in front of his desk with a steno p
occasionally writing down the instructions he gave when
stopped yelling into the receiver of his phone and listened
whoever was on the other end. Three red lights were blink
on the phone. When he spoke into the receiver the secreta
spoke sharply to each other. Mitch walked slowly into the
fice and stood by the door.

"Quiet!" Avery yelled to the secretaries.

The one in the file cabinet slammed the drawer and wen
the next file cabinet, where she bent over and pulled the l
tom drawer. Avery snapped his fingers at the other one a
pointed at his desk calendar. He hung up without saying go
bye.

"What's my schedule for today?" he asked while pullin
file from his credenza.

"Ten A.M. meeting with the IRS downtown. One P.M. m
ing with Nathan Locke on the Spinosa file. Three-thirty, p
ners' meeting. Tomorrow you're in tax court all day, a
you're supposed to prepare all day today."

Great. Cancel everything. Check the flights to Houston urday afternoon and the return flights Monday, early Mon-."

Yes, sir."

Mitch! Where's the Capps file?"

On my desk."

How much have you done?"

I've read through most of it."

We need to get in high gear. That was Sonny Capps on the ne. He wants to meet Saturday morning in Houston, and wants a rough draft of the limited partnership agreement."

Mitch felt a nervous pain in his empty stomach. If he re-ed correctly, the agreement was a hundred and forty some es long.

Just a rough draft," Avery said as he pointed to a secretary.

No problem," Mitch said with as much confidence as he ld muster. "It may not be perfect, but I'll have a rough ft."

I need it by noon Saturday, as perfect as possible. I'll get of my secretaries to show Nina where the form agree-nts are in the memory bank. That will save some dictation typing. I know this is unfair, but there's nothing fair ut Sonny Capps. He's very demanding. He told me the deal st close in twenty days or it's dead. Everything is waiting us."

I'll get it done."

Good. Let's meet at eight in the morning to see where we "

Avery punched one of the blinking lights and began arguing the receiver. Mitch walked to his office and looked for the pps file under the fifteen notebooks. Nina stuck her head in door.

Oliver Lambert wants to see you."

When?" Mitch asked.

As soon as you can get there."

Mitch looked at his watch. Three hours at the office and he s ready to call it a day. "Can it wait?"

I don't think so. Mr. Lambert doesn't usually wait for any-ly."

I see."

"You'd better go."

"What does he want?"

"His secretary didn't say."

He put on his coat, straightened his tie and raced upstairs to the fourth floor, where Mr. Lambert's secretary was waiting. She introduced herself and informed him she had been with the firm for thirty-one years. In fact, she was the second secretary hired by Mr. Anthony Bendini after he moved to Memphis. Ida Renfroe was her name, but everyone called her Mrs. Ida. She showed him into the big office and closed the door.

Oliver Lambert stood behind his desk and removed his reading glasses. He smiled warmly and laid his pipe in the brass holder. "Good morning, Mitch," he said softly, as if time meant nothing. "Let's sit over there." He waved to the sofa.

"Would you like coffee?" Mr. Lambert asked.

"No, thanks."

Mitch sank into the couch and the partner sat in a stiff wing chair, two feet away and three feet higher. Mitch unbuttoned his coat and tried to relax. He crossed his legs and glanced at his new pair of Cole-Haans. Two hundred bucks. That was an hour's work for an associate at this money-printing factory. He tried to relax. But he could feel the panic in Avery's voice and see the desperation in his eyes when he held the phone and listened to this Capps fellow on the other end. This, his second full day on the job, and his head was pounding and his stomach hurting.

Mr. Lambert smiled downward with his best sincere grandfatherly smile. It was time for a lecture of some sort. He wore a brilliant white shirt, button-down, all-cotton, pinpoint, with a small, dark silk bow tie which bestowed upon him a look of extreme intelligence and wisdom. As always, he was tanned beyond the usual midsummer Memphis scorched bronzeness. His teeth sparkled like diamonds. A sixty-year-old model.

"Just a couple of things, Mitch," he said. "I understand you've become quite busy."

"Yes, sir, quite."

"Panic is a way of life in a major law firm, and clients like Sonny Capps can cause ulcers. Our clients are our only assets, so we kill ourselves for them."

Mitch smiled and frowned at the same time.

"Two things, Mitch. First, my wife and I want you and by to have dinner with us Saturday. We dine out quite en, and we enjoy having our friends with us. I am some-at of a chef myself, and I appreciate fine food and drink. We ally reserve a large table at one of our favorite restaurants own, invite our friends and spend the evening with a nine-rse meal and the rarest of wines. Will you and Abby be free Saturday?"

"Of course."

"Kendall Mahan, Wally Hudson, Lamar Quin and their es will also be there."

"We'd be delighted."

"Good. My favorite place in Memphis is Justine's. It's an old nch restaurant with exquisite cuisine and an impressive e list. Say seven Saturday?"

"We'll be there."

"Second, there's something we need to discuss. I'm sure 're aware of it, but it's worth mentioning. It's very impor-t to us. I know they taught you at Harvard that there exists onfidential relationship between yourself, as a lawyer, and r client. It's a privileged relationship and you can never be ced to divulge anything a client tells you. It's strictly confi-tial. It's a violation of our ethics if we discuss our client's iness. Now, this applies to every lawyer, but at this firm we e this professional relationship very seriously. We don't dis-s a client's business with anyone. Not other lawyers. Not uses. Sometimes, not even each other. As a rule, we don't at home, and our wives have learned not to ask. The less say, the better off you are. Mr. Bendini was a great be-er in secrecy, and he taught us well. You will never hear a mber of this firm mention even so much as a client's name side this building. That's how serious we are."

Where's he going with this? Mitch asked himself. Any sec-l year law student could give this speech. "I understand , Mr. Lambert, and you don't have to worry about me."

'Loose tongues lose lawsuits.' That was Mr. Bendini's tto, and he applied it to everything. We simply do not dis-s our clients' business with anyone, and that includes our es. We're very quiet, very secretive, and we like it that way. 'll meet other lawyers around town and sooner or later they'll ask something about our firm, or about a client. don't talk, understand?"

"Of course, Mr. Lambert."

"Good. We're very proud of you, Mitch. You'll make a gr lawyer. And a very rich lawyer. See you Saturday."

Mrs. Ida had a message for Mitch. Mr. Tolleson needed h at once. He thanked her and raced down the stairs, down hallway, past his office, to the big one in the corner. Th were now three secretaries digging and whispering to e other while the boss yelled into the telephone. Mitch foun safe spot in a chair by the door and watched the circus. T women pulled files and notebooks and mumbled in stra tongues among themselves. Occasionally Avery would s his fingers and point here and there and they would jump scared rabbits.

After a few minutes he slammed the phone down, ag without saying goodbye. He glared at Mitch.

"Sonny Capps again. The Chinese want seventy-five mil and he's agreed to pay it. There will be forty-one limited p ners instead of twenty-five. We have twenty days, or the de off."

Two of the secretaries walked over to Mitch and han him thick expandable files.

"Can you handle it?" Avery asked, almost with a sneer. secretaries looked at him.

Mitch grabbed the files and headed for the door. "Of cou I can handle it. Is that all?"

"It's enough. I don't want you to work on anything but t file between now and Saturday, understand?"

"Yes, boss."

In his office he removed the bar review materials, all fifte notebooks, and piled them in a corner. The Capps file arranged neatly across the desk. He breathed deeply and be reading. There was a knock at the door.

"Who is it?"

Nina stuck her head through. "I hate to tell you this, your new furniture is here."

He rubbed his temples and mumbled incoherently.

"Perhaps you could work in the library for a couple hours."

Perhaps."

hey repacked the Capps file and moved the fifteen note-
ks into the hall, where two large black men waited with a
of bulky cardboard boxes and an oriental rug.

Jina followed him to the second floor library.

I'm supposed to meet with Lamar Quin at two to study for
bar exam. Call him and cancel. Tell him I'll explain later."

You have a two o'clock meeting with Gill Vaughn," she
.

Cancel that one too."

He's a partner."

Cancel it. I'll make it up later."

It's not wise."

Just do as I say."

You're the boss."

Thank you."

e paperhanger was a short muscle-bound woman advanced
ears but conditioned to hard work and superbly trained.
almost forty years now, she explained to Abby, she had
g expensive paper in the finest homes in Memphis. She
ed constantly, but wasted no motion. She cut precisely,
a surgeon, then applied glue like an artist. While it dried,
removed her tape measure from her leather work belt and
lyzed the remaining corner of the dining room. She mum-
d numbers which Abby could not decipher. She gauged the
gth and height in four different places, then committed it
to memory. She ascended the stepladder and instructed
by to hand her a roll of paper. It fit perfectly. She pressed it
ly to the wall and commented for the hundredth time on
 nice the paper was, how expensive, how long it would
 good and last. She liked the color too. It blended wonder-
y with the curtains and the rug. Abby had long since
wn tired of saying thanks. She nodded and looked at her
ch. It was time to start dinner.

Vhen the wall was finished, Abby announced it was quit-
 time and asked her to return at nine the next morning.
 lady said certainly, and began cleaning up her mess. She
 being paid twelve dollars an hour, cash, and was agreeable
lmost anything. Abby admired the room. They would fin-

75

ish it tomorrow, and the wallpapering would be complete
cept for two bathrooms and the den. The painting was sch
uled to begin next week. The glue from the paper and the
lacquer from the mantel and the newness of the furniture co
bined for a wonderful fresh aroma. Just like a new house.

Abby said goodbye to the paperhanger and went to the b
room where she undressed and lay across her bed. She cal
her husband, spoke briefly to Nina and was told he was i
meeting and would be a while. Nina said he would call. A
stretched her long, sore legs and rubbed her shoulders.
ceiling fan spun slowly above her. Mitch would be ho
eventually. He would work a hundred hours a week fo
while, then cut back to eighty. She could wait.

She awoke an hour later and jumped from the bed. It
almost six. Veal piccata. Veal piccata. She stepped into a pai
khaki walking shorts and slipped on a white polo. She ra
the kitchen, which was finished except for some paint and a
of curtains due in next week. She found the recipe in a p
cookbook and arranged the ingredients neatly on the coun
top. There had been little red meat in law school, maybe
occasional hamburger steak. When she cooked, it had b
chicken this or chicken that. There had been a lot of sa
wiches and hot dogs.

But now, with all this sudden affluence, it was time to le
to cook. In the first week she prepared something new ev
night, and they ate whenever he got home. She planned
meals, studied the cookbooks, experimented with the sau
For no apparent reason, Mitch liked Italian food, and w
spaghetti and pork capellini tried and perfected, it was t
for veal piccata. She pounded the veal scallops with a ma
until they were thin enough, then laid them in flour seaso
with salt and pepper. She put a pan of water on the burner
the linguine. She poured a glass of Chablis and turned on
radio. She had called the office twice since lunch, and he
not found time to return the calls. She thought of cal
again, but said no. It was his turn. Dinner would be fixed,
they would eat whenever he got home.

The scallops were sautéed in hot oil for three minutes u
the veal was tender; then removed. She poured the oil from
pan and added wine and lemon juice until it was boiling.

aped and stirred the pan to thicken the sauce. She returned veal to the pan, and added mushrooms and artichokes and ter. She covered the pan and let it simmer.

he fried bacon, sliced tomatoes, cooked linguine and red another glass of wine. By seven, dinner was ready; on and tomato salad with tubettini, veal piccate, and garlic ad in the oven. He had not called. She took her wine to the io and looked around the backyard. Hearsay ran from un- the shrubs. Together they walked the length of the yard, veying the Bermuda and stopping under the two large oaks. e remains of a long-abandoned tree house were scattered ong the middle branches of the largest oak. Initials were ved on its trunk. A piece of rope hung from the other. She nd a rubber ball, threw it and watched as the dog chased it. listened for the phone through the kitchen window. It did ring.

earsay froze, then growled at something next door. Mr. e emerged from a row of perfectly trimmed box hedges und his patio. Sweat dripped from his nose and his cotton ershirt was soaked. He removed his green gloves, and no- d Abby across the chain-link fence, under her tree. He led. He looked at her brown legs and smiled. He wiped his ehead with a sweaty forearm and headed for the fence.

"How are you?" he asked, breathing heavy. His thick gray r dripped and clung to his scalp.

"Just fine, Mr. Rice. How are you?"

"Hot. Must be a hundred degrees."

Abby slowly walked to the fence to chat. She had caught his res for a week now, but did not mind. He was at least sev- y and probably harmless. Let him look. Plus, he was a liv- , breathing, sweating human who could talk and maintain a versation to some degree. The paperhanger had been her y source of dialogue since Mitch left before dawn.

"Your lawn looks great," she said.

He wiped again and spat on the ground. "Great? You call s great? This belongs in a magazine. I've never seen a put- green look this good. I deserve garden of the month, but y won't give it to me. Where's your husband?"

"At the office. He's working late."

"It's almost eight. He must've left before sunup this morn-

ing. I take my walk at six-thirty, and he's already gone. Wh
with him?"

"He likes to work."

"If I had a wife like you, I'd stay at home. Couldn't make
leave."

Abby smiled at the compliment. "How is Mrs. Rice?"

He frowned, then yanked a weed out of the fence. "Not
good, I'm afraid. Not too good." He looked away and bit
lip. Mrs. Rice was almost dead with cancer. There were
children. She had a year, the doctors said. A year at the m
They had removed most of her stomach, and the tumors w
now in the lungs. She weighed ninety pounds and seldom
the bed. During their first visit across the fence his e
watered when he talked of her and of how he would be al
after fifty-one years.

"Naw, they won't give me garden of the month. Wrong p
of town. It always goes to those rich folks who hire yard b
to do all the work while they sit by the pool and sip daiqu
It does look good, doesn't it?"

"It's incredible. How many times a week do you mow?"

"Three or four. Depends on the rain. You want me to m
yours?"

"No. I want Mitch to mow it."

"He ain't got time, seems like. I'll watch it, and if it nee
little trim, I'll come over."

Abby turned and looked at the kitchen window. "Do
hear the phone?" she asked, walking away. Mr. Rice pointe
his hearing aid.

She said goodbye and ran to the house. The phone stop
when she lifted the receiver. It was eight-thirty, almost d
She called the office, but no one answered. Maybe he was d
ing home.

An hour before midnight, the phone rang. Except for it
the light snoring, the second floor office was without a sou
His feet were on the new desk, crossed at the ankles and nu
from lack of circulation. The rest of the body slouched c
fortably in the thick leather executive chair. He slumpe
one side and intermittently exhaled the sounds of a deep sl
The Capps file was strewn over the desk and one formid

78

king document was held firmly against his stomach. His
es were on the floor, next to the desk, next to a pile of
uments from the Capps file. An empty potato chip bag was
ween the shoes.

fter a dozen rings he moved, then jumped at the phone. It
 his wife.

Why haven't you called?" she asked, coolly, yet with a
ht touch of concern.

I'm sorry. I fell asleep. What time is it?" He rubbed his eyes
 focused on his watch.

Eleven. I wish you would call."

I did call. No one answered."

When?"

Between eight and nine. Where were you?"

he did not answer. She waited. "Are you coming home?"

No. I need to work all night."

All night? You can't work all night, Mitch."

Of course I can work all night. Happens all the time
und here. It's expected."

I expected you home, Mitch. And the least you could've
 e was call. Dinner is still on the stove."

I'm sorry. I'm up to my ears in deadlines and I lost track of
 e. I apologize."

here was silence for a moment as she considered the apol-
 . "Will this become a habit, Mitch?"

It might."

I see. When do you think you might be home?"

Are you scared?"

No, I'm not scared. I'm going to bed."

I'll come in around seven for a shower."

That's nice. If I'm asleep, don't wake me."

he hung up. He looked at the receiver, then put it in place.
 the fifth floor a security agent chuckled to himself. " 'Don't
 ke me.' That's good," he said as he pushed a button on the
 nputerized recorder. He punched three buttons and spoke
 a small mike. "Hey, Dutch, wake up down there."

Dutch woke up and leaned to the intercom. "Yeah, what is

This is Marcus upstairs, I think our boy plans to stay all
 ht."

"What's his problem?"

"Right now it's his wife. He forgot to call her and she fix[e] real nice supper."

"Aw, that's too bad. We've heard that before, ain't we?"

"Yeah, every rookie does it the first week. Anyway, he [t] her he ain't coming home till in the morning. So go bac[k] sleep."

Marcus pushed some more buttons and returned to his m[a]zine.

Abby was waiting when the sun peeked between the oak tr[ees]. She sipped coffee and held the dog and listened to the q[uiet] sounds of her neighborhood stirring to life. Sleep had b[een] fitful. A hot shower had not eased the fatigue. She wo[re] white terry-cloth bathrobe, one of his, and nothing else. [Her] hair was wet and pulled straight back.

A car door slammed and the dog pointed inside the ho[use]. She heard him unlock the kitchen door, and moments later [the] sliding door to the patio opened. He laid his coat on a be[nch] near the door and walked over to her.

"Good morning," he said, then sat down across the wi[de] table.

She gave him a fake smile. "Good morning to you."

"You're up early," he said in an effort at friendliness. It [did] not work. She smiled again and sipped her coffee.

He breathed deeply and gazed across the yard. "Still m[ad] about last night, I see."

"Not really. I don't carry a grudge."

"I said I was sorry, and I meant it. I tried to call once."

"You could've called again."

"Please don't divorce me, Abby. I swear it will never h[ap]pen again. Just don't leave me."

She managed a genuine grin. "You look terrible," she sa[id].

"What's under the robe?"

"Nothing."

"Let's see."

"Why don't you take a nap? You look haggard."

"Thanks. But I've got a nine o'clock meeting with Av[ery.] And a ten o'clock meeting with Avery."

"Are they trying to kill you the first week?"

Yes, but they can't do it. I'm too much of a man. Let's go
a shower."

"I've taken one."

"Naked?"

"Yes."

"Tell me about it. Tell me every detail."

"If you'd come home at a decent hour you wouldn't feel
craved."

"I'm sure it'll happen again, dear. There will be plenty of
nighters. You didn't complain in law school when I studied
and the clock."

"It was different. I endured law school because I knew it
uld soon end. But now you're a lawyer and you will be for a
g time. Is this part of it? Will you always work a thousand
rs a week?"

"Abby, this is my first week."

"That's what worries me. It will only get worse."

"Sure it will. That's part of it, Abby. It's a cutthroat busi-
s where the weak are eaten and the strong get rich. It's a
athon. He who endures wins the gold."

"And dies at the finish line."

"I don't believe this. We moved here a week ago, and you're
ady worried about my health."

he sipped the coffee and rubbed the dog. She was beautiful.
h tired eyes, no makeup, and wet hair, she was beautiful.
stood, walked behind her and kissed her on the cheek. "I
you," he whispered.

he clutched his hand on her shoulder. "Go take a shower.
fix breakfast."

he table was arranged to perfection. Her grandmother's
a was taken from the cabinet and used for the first time in
new home. Candles were lit in silver candlesticks. Grape-
t juice was poured in the crystal tea glasses. Linen napkins
matched the tablecloth were folded on the plates. When
inished his shower and changed into a new Burberry glen
d, he walked to the dining room and whistled.

"What's the occasion?"

"It's a special breakfast, for a special husband."

He sat and admired the china. The food was warming in a

covered silver dish. "What'd you cook?" he asked, smacking
lips. She pointed and he removed the lid. He stared at it.

"What's this?" he asked without looking at her.

"Veal piccata."

"Veal what?"

"Veal piccata."

He glanced at his watch. "I thought it was breakfast tir

"I cooked it for dinner last night, and I suggest you eat

"Veal piccata for breakfast?"

She grinned firmly and shook her head slightly. He loo
again at the dish, and for a second or two analyzed the si
tion.

Finally, he said, "Smells good."

ATURDAY MORNING. He slept in and didn't get to
the office until seven. He didn't shave, wore jeans, an old
button down, no socks and Bass loafers. Law school attire.
he Capps agreement had been printed and reprinted late
ay. He made some further revisions, and Nina ran it again
ght Friday night. He assumed she had little or no social
so he didn't hesitate to ask her to work late. She said she
't mind overtime, so he asked her to work Saturday morn-

e arrived at nine, wearing a pair of jeans that would fit a
guard. He handed her the agreement, all two hundred
six pages, with his latest changes, and asked her to run it
he fourth time. He was to meet with Avery at ten.

e office changed on Saturday. All of the associates were
, as well as most of the partners and a few of the secretar-
There were no clients, thus no dress code. There was
gh denim to launch a cattle drive. No ties. Some of the
pier ones wore their finest starched Duckheads with heavi-
arched button-downs and seemed to crackle when they
ed.

t the pressure was there, at least for Mitchell Y. McDeere,

the newest associate. He had canceled his bar review meet
on Thursday, Friday and Saturday, and the fifteen noteb
sat on the shelf, gathering dust and reminding him tha
would indeed become the first member to flunk the bar e:

At ten the fourth revision was complete, and Nina cer
niously laid it on Mitch's desk and left for the coffee roor
had grown to two hundred and nineteen pages. He had
every word four times and researched the tax code provis
until they were memorized. He marched down the hall to
partner's office and laid it on the desk. A secretary was pac
a mammoth briefcase while the boss talked on the phone.

"How many pages?" Avery asked when he hung up.

"Over two hundred."

"This is quite impressive. How rough is it?"

"Not very. That's the fourth revision since yesterday m
ing. It's almost perfect."

"We'll see. I'll read it on the plane, then Capps will re:
with a magnifying glass. If he finds one mistake he'll raise
for an hour and threaten not to pay. How many hours ai
this?"

"Fifty-four and a half, since Wednesday."

"I know I've pushed, and I apologize. You've had a t
first week. But our clients sometimes push hard, and
won't be the last time we break our necks for someone
pays us two hundred dollars an hour. It's part of the busin

"I don't mind it. I'm behind on the bar review, but I
catch up."

"Is that little Hudson twerp giving you a hard time?"

"No."

"If he does, let me know. He's only a five year man, an
enjoys playing professor. Thinks he's a real academic. I d
particularly like him."

"He's no problem."

Avery placed the agreement in the briefcase. "Where are
prospectus and other documents?"

"I've done a very rough draft of each. You said we
twenty days."

"We do, but let's get it done. Capps starts demanding th
long before their deadlines. Are you working tomorrow?"

'I hadn't planned on it. In fact, my wife has sort of insisted
: go to church."

Avery shook his head. "Wives can really get in the way,
n't they?" He said this without expecting a reply.

Mitch did not respond.

'Let's have Capps finished by next Saturday."

'Fine. No problem," Mitch said.

'Have we discussed Koker-Hanks?" Avery asked while rum-
aging through a file.

'No."

'Here it is. Koker-Hanks is a big general contractor out of
nsas City. Keeps about a hundred million under contract,
over the country. An outfit out of Denver called Holloway
others has offered to buy Koker-Hanks. They want to swap
me stock, some assets, some contracts, and throw in some
sh. Pretty complicated deal. Familiarize yourself with the
:, and we'll discuss it Tuesday morning when I get back."

'How much time do we have?"

'Thirty days."

It was not quite as thick as the Capps file, but just as impos-
g. "Thirty days," Mitch mumbled.

'The deal is worth eighty million, and we'll rake off two
ndred grand in fees. Not a bad deal. Every time you look at
it file, charge it for an hour. Work on it whenever you can.
fact, if the name Koker-Hanks crosses your mind while
u're driving to work, stick it for an hour. The sky's the limit
this one."

Avery relished the thought of a client who would pay re-
rdless of the charges. Mitch said goodbye and returned to his
ice.

out the time the cocktails were finished, while they studied
: wine list and listened to Oliver Lambert's comparison of
: nuances, the subtleties, the distinctions of each of the
ench wines, about the time Mitch and Abby realized they
uld much rather be home eating a pizza and watching TV,
o men with the correct key entered the shiny black BMW in
: parking lot of Justine's. They wore coats and ties and
ked inconspicuous. They sped away innocently and drove
oss midtown to the new home of Mr. and Mrs. McDeere.

They parked the BMW where it belonged, in the carport. T
driver produced another key, and the two entered the hou
Hearsay was locked in a closet in the washroom.

In the dark, a small leather attaché case was placed on
dining table. Thin disposable rubber gloves were pulled a
stretched over the hands, and each took a small flashlight.

"Do the phones first," one said.

They worked quickly, in the dark. The receiver from
kitchen phone was unplugged and laid on the table. The
crophone was unscrewed and examined. A tiny drop-in tra
mitter, the size of a raisin, was glued in the cavity of the
ceiver and held firmly in place for ten seconds. When the g
became firm, the microphone was replaced and the recei
was plugged into the phone and hung on the kitchen wall. T
voices, or signals, would be transmitted to a small receiver
be installed in the attic. A larger transmitter next to the
ceiver would send the signals across town to an antenna on
of the Bendini Building. Using the AC lines as a power sour
the small bugs in the phones would transmit indefinitely.

"Get the one in the den."

The attaché case was moved to a sofa. Above the reclin
they drove a small nail into a ridge in the paneling, then
moved it. A thin black cylinder, one twentieth of an inch
one inch, was carefully placed in the hole. It was cemented
place with a dab of black epoxy. The microphone was inv
ble. A wire, the thickness of a human hair, was gently fitt
into the seam of the paneling and run to the ceiling. It wou
be connected to a receiver in the attic.

Identical mikes were hidden in the walls of each bedroo
The men found the retractable stairs in the main hallway a
climbed into the attic. One removed the receiver and transm
ter from the case while the other painstakingly pulled the ti
wires from the walls. When he gathered them, he wrapp
them together and laid them under the insulation and r
them to a corner where his partner was placing the transm
ter in an old cardboard box. An AC line was spliced and wir
to the unit to provide power and transmission. A small a
tenna was raised to within an inch of the roof decking.

Their breathing became heavier in the sweltering heat
the dark attic. The small plastic casing of an old radio w

ed around the transmitter, and they scattered insulation
l old clothing around it. It was in a remote corner and not
ly to be noticed for months, maybe years. And if it was
ticed, it would appear to be only worthless junk. It could be
ked up and thrown away without suspicion. They admired
ir handiwork for a second, then descended the stairs.
They meticulously covered their tracks and were finished in
minutes.

Hearsay was released from the closet, and the men crept
o the carport. They backed quickly out the driveway and
d into the night.

As the baked pompano was served, the BMW parked quietly
t to the restaurant. The driver fished through his pockets
l found the key to a maroon Jaguar, property of Mr.
ndall Mahan, attorney-at-law. The two technicians locked
BMW and slid into the Jag. The Mahans lived much closer
n the McDeeres, and judging from the floor plans, the job
uld be quicker.

the fifth floor of the Bendini Building, Marcus stared at a
el of blinking lights and waited for some signal from 1231
t Meadowbrook. The dinner party had broken up thirty
nutes earlier, and it was time to listen. A tiny yellow light
hed weakly, and he draped a headset over his ears. He
hed a button to record. He waited. A green light beside the
le McD6 began flashing. It was the bedroom wall. The sig-
s grew clearer, voices, at first faint, then very clear. He
reased the volume. And listened.

"Jill Mahan is a bitch," the female, Mrs. McDeere, was say-
. "The more she drank, the bitchier she got."

"I think she's a blue blood of some sort," Mr. McDeere re-
ed.

"Her husband is okay, but she's a real snot," Mrs. McDeere
d.

"Are you drunk?" asked Mr. McDeere.

"Almost. I'm ready for passionate sex."

Marcus increased the volume and leaned toward the blink-
lights.

"Take your clothes off," demanded Mrs. McDeere.

"We haven't done this in a while," said Mr. McDeere.

87

Marcus stood and hovered above the switches and lights
"And whose fault is that?" she asked.
"I haven't forgotten how. You're beautiful."
"Get in the bed," she said.
Marcus turned the dial marked VOLUME until it would go
further. He smiled at the lights and breathed heavily. He lov
these associates, fresh from law school and full of energy. A
smiled at the sounds of their lovemaking. He closed his ey
and watched them.

9

THE CAPPS CRISIS passed in two weeks without disaster, thanks largely to a string of eighteen hour days by the newest member of the firm, a member who had not passed the bar exam and who was too busy practicing law worry about it. In July he billed an average of fifty-nine rs a week, a firm record for a nonlawyer. Avery proudly rmed the partners at the monthly meeting that McDeere's rk was remarkable for a rookie. The Capps deal was closed ee days ahead of schedule, thanks to McDeere. The docu-nts totaled four hundred pages, all perfect, all meticulously arched, drafted and redrafted by McDeere. Koker-Hanks uld close within a month, thanks to McDeere, and the firm uld earn close to a quarter of a mill. He was a machine.

liver Lambert expressed concern over his study habits. e bar exam was less than three weeks away, and it was ious to all that McDeere was not ready. He had canceled f his review sessions in July and had logged less than nty hours. Avery said not to worry, his boy would be dy.

ifteen days before the exam, Mitch finally complained. He about to flunk it, he explained to Avery over lunch at the

Club, and he needed time to study. Lots of tir
d cram it in for the next two weeks and pass by
of his ass. But he had to be left alone. No deadlines.
emergencies. No all-nighters. He pleaded. Avery listened ca
fully, and apologized. He promised to ignore him for the n
two weeks. Mitch said thanks.

On the first Monday in August, a firm meeting was called
the main library on the first floor. It was the meeting room,
largest of the four libraries, the showplace. Half the lawy
sat around the antique cherry conference table with twe
chairs under it. The rest stood next to the shelves of th
leather law books which had not been opened in decades.
ery member was present, even Nathan Locke. He arrived l
and stood next to the door by himself. He spoke to no one, a
no one looked at him. Mitch stole a glance at Black Eyes wh
possible.

The mood was somber. No smiles. Beth Kozinski and La
Hodge were escorted through the door by Oliver Lamb
They were seated at the front of the room facing a wall wh
two veiled portraits hung. They held hands and tried to sm
Mr. Lambert stood with his back to the wall and faced
small audience.

He spoke softly, his rich baritone exuding sympathy a
compassion. He almost whispered at first, but the power of
voice made every sound and every syllable clear through
the room. He looked at the two widows and told of the d
sadness the firm felt, how they would always be taken care
as long as there was a firm. He talked of Marty and Joe,
their first few years with the firm, of their importance to
firm, of the vast voids their deaths created. He spoke of th
love for their families, their dedication to their homes.

The man was eloquent. He spoke in prose, with no fo
thought as to what the next sentence would be. The wido
cried softly and wiped their eyes. And then some of the clo
ones, Lamar Quin and Doug Turney, began to sniffle.

When he had said enough, he unveiled the portrait of M
tin Kozinski. It was an emotional moment. There were me
tears. There would be a scholarship established at the Chica
Law School in his name. The firm would set up trusts for
children's education. The family would be taken care of. B

t her lip, but cried louder. The seasoned, hardened, tough-as-
ails negotiators of the great Bendini firm swallowed rapidly
d avoided looking at each other. Only Nathan Locke was
moved. He glared at the wall with his penetrating lasers and
nored the ceremony.

Then the portrait of Joe Hodge, and a similar biography,
milar scholarship and trust funds. Mitch had heard a rumor
at Hodge purchased a two-million-dollar life insurance poli-
four months before his death

When the eulogies were complete, Nathan Locke disap-
ared through the door. The lawyers surrounded the widows
d offered quiet words and embraces. Mitch did not know
em and had nothing to say. He walked to the front wall and
amined the paintings. Next to those of Kozinski and Hodge
ere three slightly smaller, but equally dignified portraits.
he one of the woman caught his attention. The brass plate
ad: "Alice Knauss 1948–1977."

"She was a mistake," Avery said under his breath as he
epped next to his associate.

"What do you mean?" Mitch asked.

"Typical female lawyer. Came here from Harvard, number
ne in her class and carrying a chip because she was a female.
hought every man alive was a sexist and it was her mission in
e to eliminate discrimination. Super-bitch. After six months
e all hated her but couldn't get rid of her. She forced two
rtners into early retirement. Milligan still blames her for his
art attack. He was her partner."

"Was she a good lawyer?"

"Very good, but it was impossible to appreciate her talents.
e was so contentious about everything."

"What happened to her?"

"Car wreck. Killed by a drunk driver. It was really tragic."

"Was she the first woman?"

"Yes, and the last, unless we get sued."

Mitch nodded to the next portrait. "Who was he?"

"Robert Lamm. He was a good friend of mine. Emory Law
hool in Atlanta. He was about three years ahead of me."

"What happened?"

"No one knows. He was an avid hunter. We hunted moose
Wyoming one winter. In 1970 he was deer hunting in Ar-

91

kansas and turned up missing. They found him a month late
in a ravine with a hole through his head. Autopsy said th
bullet entered through the rear of his skull and blew awa
most of his face. They speculate the shot was fired from a hig
powered rifle at long range. It was probably an accident, b
we'll never know. I could never imagine anyone wanting t
kill Bobby Lamm."

The last portrait was of John Mickel, 1940–1984. "What ha
pened to him?" Mitch whispered.

"Probably the most tragic of all. He was not a strong ma
and the pressure got to him. He drank a lot, and started drug
Then his wife left him and they had a bitter divorce. The fir
was embarrassed. After he had been here ten years, he bega
to fear he would not become a partner. The drinking g
worse. We spent a small fortune on treatment, shrinks, ever
thing. But nothing worked. He became depressed, then su
cidal. He wrote a seven-page suicide note and blew his brair
out."

"That's terrible."

"Sure was."

"Where'd they find him?"

Avery cleared his throat and glanced around the room. "I
your office."

"What!"

"Yeah, but they cleaned it up."

"You're kidding!"

"No, I'm serious. It was years ago, and the office has bee
used since then. It's okay."

Mitch was speechless.

"You're not superstitious, are you?" Avery asked with
nasty grin.

"Of course not."

"I guess I should've told you, but it's not something we ta
about."

"Can I change offices?"

"Sure. Just flunk the bar exam and we'll give you one o
those paralegal offices in the basement."

"If I flunk it, it'll be because of you."

"Yes, but you won't flunk it, will you?"

"If you can pass it, so can I."

om 5 A.M. to 7 A.M. the Bendini building was empty and
iet. Nathan Locke arrived around six, but went straight to
s office and locked the door. At seven, the associates began
pearing and voices could be heard. By seven-thirty the firm
d a quorum, and a handful of secretaries punched in. By
ght the halls were full and it was chaos as usual. Concentra-
on became difficult. Interruptions were routine. Phones
eped incessantly. By nine, all lawyers, paralegals, clerks and
cretaries were either present or accounted for.

Mitch treasured the solitude of the early hours. He moved
s clock up thirty minutes and began waking Dutch at five,
stead of five-thirty. After making two pots of coffee, he
amed the dark halls flipping light switches and inspecting
e building. Occasionally, on a clear morning, he would stand
fore the window in Lamar's office and watch the dawn break
ver the mighty Mississippi below. He would count the barges
ned neatly before their tugboats plowing slowly upriver. He
atched the trucks inch across the bridge in the distance. But
wasted little time. He dictated letters, briefs, summaries,
emorandums and a hundred other documents for Nina to
pe and Avery to review. He crammed for the bar exam.

The morning after the ceremony for the dead lawyers, he
und himself in the library on the first floor looking for a
eatise when he again noticed the five portraits. He walked to
e wall and stared at them, remembering the brief obituaries
ven by Avery. Five dead lawyers in fifteen years. It was a
angerous place to work. On a legal pad he scribbled their
ames and the years they died. It was five-thirty.

Something moved in the hallway, and he jerked to his right.
the darkness he saw Black Eyes watching. He stepped for-
ard to the door and glared at Mitch. "What are you doing?"
e demanded.

Mitch faced him and attempted a smile. "Good morning to
ou. It happens I am studying for the bar exam."

Locke glanced at the portraits and then stared at Mitch. "I
e. Why are you so interested in them?"

"Just curious. This firm has had its share of tragedy."

"They're all dead. A real tragedy will occur if you don't pass
e bar exam."

"I intend to pass it."

"I've heard otherwise. Your study habits are causing concern among the partners."

"Are the partners concerned about my excessive billing?"

"Don't get smart. You were told the bar exam has priorit over everything. An employee with no license is of no use this firm."

Mitch thought of a dozen smart retorts, but let it pass. Loc stepped backward and disappeared. In his office with the doc closed, Mitch hid the names and dates in a drawer and opene a review book on constitutional law.

IO

THE SATURDAY after the bar exam Mitch avoided his office and his house and spent the morning digging in the flower beds and waiting. With the remodeling complete, the house was now presentable, and of course the first guests had to be her parents. Abby had cleaned and polished for a week, and it was now time. She promised they wouldn't stay long, no more than a few hours. He promised to be as nice as possible.

Mitch had washed and waxed both new cars and they looked as if they had just left the showroom. The lawn had been manicured by a kid down the street. Mr. Rice had applied fertilizer for a month and it looked like a puttin' green, as he liked to say.

At noon they arrived, and he reluctantly left the flower beds. He smiled and greeted them and excused himself to go clean up. He could tell they were uncomfortable, and he wanted it that way. He took a long shower as Abby showed them every piece of furniture and every inch of wallpaper. These things impressed the Sutherlands. Small things always did. They dwelt on the things others did or did not have. He was the president of a small county bank that had been on the

95

verge of collapse for ten years. She was too good to work an had spent all of her adult life seeking social advancement in town where there was none to be had. She had traced h ancestry to royalty in one of the old countries, and this ha always impressed the coal miners in Danesboro, Kentuck With so much blue blood in her veins, it had fallen her duty do nothing but drink hot tea, play bridge, talk of her husband money, condemn the less fortunate and work tirelessly in th Garden Club. He was a stuffed shirt who jumped when sh barked and lived in eternal fear of making her mad. As a tea they had relentlessly pushed their daughter from birth to the best, achieve the best, but most importantly, marry th best. Their daughter had rebelled and married a poor kid wit no family except a crazy mother and a criminal brother.

"Nice place you've got here, Mitch," Mr. Sutherland said an effort to break the ice. They sat for lunch and began passin dishes.

"Thanks." Nothing else, just thanks. He concentrated the food. There would be no smiles from him at lunch. Th less he said, the more uncomfortable they would be. H wanted them to feel awkward, guilty, wrong. He wanted the to sweat, to bleed. It had been their decision to boycott th wedding. It had been their stones cast, not his.

"Everything is so lovely," her mother gushed in his dire tion.

"Thanks."

"We're so proud of it, Mother," Abby said.

The conversation immediately went to the remodeling. Th men ate in silence as the women chattered on and on abou what the decorator did to this room and that one. At time Abby was almost desperate to fill in the gaps with words abou whatever came to mind. Mitch almost felt sorry for her, but kept his eyes on the table. The butter knife could have cut th tension.

"So you've found a job?" Mrs. Sutherland asked.

"Yes. I start a week from Monday. I'll be teaching thir graders at St. Andrew's Episcopal School."

"Teaching doesn't pay much," her father blurted.

He's relentless, thought Mitch.

"I'm not concerned with money, Dad. I'm a teacher. To m

t's the most important profession in the world. If I wanted money, I would've gone to medical school."

"Third-graders," her mother said. "That's such a cute age. 'ou'll be wanting children before long."

Mitch had already decided that if anything would attract hese people to Memphis on a regular basis, it was grandchil-dren. And he had decided he could wait a long time. He had never been around children. There were no nieces or neph-ws, except for maybe a few unknown ones Ray had scattered round the country. And he had developed no affinity for chil-dren.

"Maybe in a few years, Mother."

Maybe after they're both dead, thought Mitch.

"You want children, don't you, Mitch?" asked the mother-in-law.

"Maybe in a few years."

Mr. Sutherland pushed his plate away and lit a cigarette. The issue of smoking had been repeatedly discussed in the days before the visit. Mitch wanted it banned completely from his house, especially by these people. They had argued vehe-mently, and Abby won.

"How was the bar exam?" the father-in-law asked.

This could be interesting, Mitch thought. "Grueling." Abby chewed her food nervously.

"Do you think you passed?"

"I hope so."

"When will you know?"

"Four to six weeks."

"How long did it last?"

"Four days."

"He's done nothing but study and work since we moved here. I haven't seen much of him this summer," Abby said.

Mitch smiled at his wife. The time away from home was lready a sore subject, and it was amusing to hear her condone t.

"What happens if you don't pass it?" her father asked.

"I don't know. I haven't thought about it."

"Do they give you a raise when you pass?"

Mitch decided to be nice, as he had promised. But it was lifficult. "Yes, a nice raise and a nice bonus."

"How many lawyers are in the firm?"

"Forty."

"My goodness," said Mrs. Sutherland. She lit up one of hers. "There's not that many in Dane County."

"Where's your office?" he asked.

"Downtown."

"Can we see it?" she asked.

"Maybe some other time. It's closed to visitors on Satur days." Mitch amused himself with his answer. Closed to vis tors, as if it was a museum.

Abby sensed disaster and began talking about the churc they had joined. It had four thousand members, a gymnasiur and bowling alley. She sang in the choir and taught eight-year olds in Sunday school. Mitch went when he was not working but he'd been working most Sundays.

"I'm happy to see you've found a church home, Abby," he father said piously. For years he had led the prayer each Sur day at the First Methodist Church in Danesboro, and the othe six days he had tirelessly practiced greed and manipulatior According to Ray, he had also steadily but discreetly pursue whiskey and women.

An awkward silence followed as the conversation came to halt. He lit another one. Keep smoking, old boy, Mitc thought. Keep smoking.

"Let's have dessert on the patio," Abby said. She bega clearing the table.

They bragged about his gardening skills, and he accepte the credit. The same kid down the street had pruned the tree pulled the weeds, trimmed the hedges and edged the patic Mitch was proficient only in pulling weeds and scooping do crap. He could also operate the lawn sprinkler, but usually le Mr. Rice do it.

Abby served strawberry shortcake and coffee. She looke helplessly at her husband, but he was noncommittal.

"This is a real nice place you've got here," her father said fo the third time as he surveyed the backyard. Mitch could see hi mind working. He had taken the measure of the house an neighborhood, and the curiosity was becoming unbearable How much did the place cost, dammit? That's what he wante to know. How much down? How much a month? Everything

He would keep pecking away until he could work in the questions somewhere.

"This is a lovely place," her mother said for the tenth time.

"When was it built?" her father asked.

Mitch laid his plate on the table and cleared his throat. He could sense it coming. "It's about fifteen years old," he answered.

"How many square feet?"

"About twenty-two hundred," Abby answered nervously. Mitch glared at her. His composure was vanishing.

"It's a lovely neighborhood," her mother added helpfully.

"New loan, or did you assume one?" her father asked, as if he were interviewing a loan applicant with weak collateral.

"It's a new loan," Mitch said, then waited. Abby waited and prayed.

He didn't wait, couldn't wait. "What'd you pay for it?"

Mitch breathed deeply and was about to say, "Too much." Abby was quicker. "We didn't pay too much, Daddy," she said firmly with a frown. "We're quite capable of managing our money."

Mitch managed a smile while biting his tongue.

Mrs. Sutherland was on her feet. "Let's go for a drive, shall we? I want to see the river and that new pyramid they've built beside it. Shall we? Come on, Harold."

Harold wanted more information about the house, but his wife was now tugging on his arm.

"Great idea," Abby said.

They loaded into the shiny new BMW and went to see the river. Abby asked them not to smoke in the new car. Mitch drove in silence and tried to be nice.

II

NINA ENTERED THE OFFICE in a rush with a stack of paperwork and laid it before her boss. "I need signatures," she demanded, and handed him his pen.

"What is all this?" Mitch asked as he dutifully scribbled his name.

"Don't ask. Just trust me."

"I found a misspelled word in the Landmark Partners agreement."

"It's the computer."

"Okay. Get the computer fixed."

"How late are you working tonight?"

Mitch scanned the documents and signed off on each. "I don't know. Why?"

"You look tired. Why don't you go home early, say around ten or ten-thirty, and get some rest. Your eyes are beginning to look like Nathan Locke's."

"Very funny."

"Your wife called."

"I'll call her in a minute."

When he finished she restacked the letters and documents

It's five o'clock. I'm leaving. Oliver Lambert is waiting on you in the first-floor library."

"Oliver Lambert! Waiting on me?"

"That's what I said. He called not more than five minutes go. Said it was very important."

Mitch straightened his tie and ran down the hall, down the airs, and walked casually into the library. Lambert, Avery nd what appeared to be most of the partners sat around the onference table. All of the associates were present, standing ehind the partners. The seat at the head of the table was mpty, and waiting. The room was quiet, almost solemn. here were no smiles. Lamar was close by and refused to look t him. Avery was sheepish, sort of embarrassed. Wally Hud- on twirled the end of his bow tie and slowly shook his head.

"Sit down, Mitch," Mr. Lambert said gravely. "We have omething to discuss with you." Doug Turney closed the door.

He sat and searched for any small sign of reassurance. None. he partners rolled their chairs in his direction, squeezing to- ether in the process. The associates surrounded him and lared downward.

"What is it?" he asked meekly, looking helplessly at Avery. mall beads of sweat surfaced above his eyebrows. His heart ounded like a jackhammer. His breathing was labored.

Oliver Lambert leaned across the edge of the table and re- oved his reading glasses. He frowned sincerely, as if this ould be painful. "We've just received a call from Nashville, ffitch, and we wanted to talk with you about it."

The bar exam. The bar exam. The bar exam. History had een made. An associate of the great Bendini firm had finally unked the bar exam. He glared at Avery, and wanted to cream, "It's all your fault!" Avery pinched his eyebrows as if migraine had hit and avoided eye contact. Lambert eyed the ther partners suspiciously and returned to McDeere.

"We were afraid this would happen, Mitch."

He wanted to speak, to explain that he deserved just one ore chance, that the exam would be given again in six onths and he would ace it, that he would not embarrass them gain. A thick pain hit below the belt.

"Yes, sir," he said humbly, in defeat.

Lambert moved in for the kill. "The folks in Nashville told

us that you made the highest score on the bar exam. Congratu lations, Counselor."

The room exploded with laughter and cheers. They gath ered around and shook his hand, patted his back and laughe at him. Avery rushed forward with a handkerchief and wipe his forehead. Kendall Mahan slammed three bottles of cham pagne on the table and began popping corks. A round wa poured into plastic wineglasses. He finally breathed and brok into a smile. He slugged the champagne, and they poured hi another glass.

Oliver Lambert placed his arm gently around Mitch's nec and spoke. "Mitch, we are very proud of you. You're the thir member of our firm to win the gold medal, and we think tha calls for a little bonus. I have here a firm check in the amoun of two thousand dollars, which I am presenting to you as small reward for this achievement."

There were whistles and catcalls.

"This is, of course, in addition to the substantial raise yo have just earned."

More whistles and catcalls. Mitch took the check but did n look at it.

Mr. Lambert raised his hand and asked for quiet. "On beha of the firm, I would like to present you with this." Lama handed him a package wrapped in brown paper. Mr. Lambe peeled it off and threw it on the table.

"It's a plaque which we prepared in anticipation of this day As you can also see, it is a bronzed replica of a piece of fir stationery, complete with every name. As you can see, th name of Mitchell Y. McDeere has been added to the lette head."

Mitch stood and awkwardly received the award. The colo had returned to his face, and the champagne was beginning t feel good. "Thank you," he said softly.

Three days later the Memphis paper published the names c the attorneys who passed the bar exam. Abby clipped the art cle for the scrapbook and sent copies to her parents and Ra

Mitch had discovered a deli three blocks from the Bendi Building between Front Street and Riverside Drive, near th river. It was a dark hole in the wall with few customers an easy chili dogs. He liked it because he could sneak away and proofread a document while he ate. Now that he was a full-grown associate, he could eat a hot dog for lunch and bill a hundred and fifty an hour.

A week after his name was in the paper, he sat by himself at a table in the rear of the deli and ate a chili dog with a fork. The place was empty. He read a prospectus an inch thick. The Greek who ran the place was asleep behind the cash register. A stranger approached his table and stopped a few feet away. He unraveled a piece of Juicy Fruit, making as much noise as possible. When it was apparent he was not being seen, he walked to the table and sat down. Mitch looked across the red-checkered tablecloth and laid the document next to the iced tea.

"Can I help you?" he asked.

The stranger glanced at the counter, glanced at the empty tables and glanced behind him. "You're McDeere, aren't you?" It was a rich brogue, undoubtedly Brooklyn. Mitch studied him carefully. He was about forty, with a short military hair-cut on the sides and a wisp of gray hair hanging almost to his eyebrows. The suit was a three-piece, navy in color, made of at least ninety percent polyester. The tie was cheap imitation silk. He wasn't much of a dresser, but there was a certain neatness about him. And an air of cockiness.

"Yeah. Who are you?" Mitch asked.

He grabbed his pocket and whipped out a badge. "Tarrance, Wayne Tarrance, special agent, FBI." He raised his eyebrows and waited for a response.

"Have a seat," Mitch said.

"Don't mind if I do."

"Do you want to frisk me?"

"Not till later. I just wanted to meet you. Saw your name in the paper and heard you were the new man at Bendini, Lambert & Locke."

"Why should that interest the FBI?"

"We watch that firm pretty close."

Mitch lost interest in the chili dog and slid the plate to the center of the table. He added more sweetener to his tea in a large styrofoam cup.

"Would you like something to drink?" Mitch asked.

"No, thanks."

"Why do you watch the Bendini firm?"

Tarrance smiled and looked toward the Greek. "I can't ally say at this point. We got our reasons, but I didn't co here to talk about that. I came here to meet you, and to wa you."

"To warn me?"

"Yes, to warn you about the firm."

"I'm listening."

"Three things. Number one, don't trust anyone. There's n a single person in that firm you can confide in. Rememb that. It will become important later on. Number two, eve word you utter, whether at home, at the office or anywhere the building, is likely to be recorded. They might even list to you in your car."

Mitch watched and listened intently. Tarrance was enjoyi this.

"And number three?" Mitch asked.

"Number three, money don't grow on trees."

"Would you care to elaborate?"

"I can't right now. I think you and I will become very clo I want you to trust me, and I know I'll have to earn your tru So I don't want to move too fast. We can't meet at your offi or my office, and we can't talk on the phone. So from time time I'll come find you. In the meantime, just remember th three things, and be careful."

Tarrance stood and reached for his wallet. "Here's my ca My home number is on the back. Use it only from a p phone."

Mitch studied the card. "Why should I be calling you?"

"You won't need to for a while. But keep the card."

Mitch placed it in his shirt pocket.

"There's one other thing," Tarrance said. "We saw you the funerals of Hodge and Kozinski. Sad, really sad. Th deaths were not accidental."

He looked down at Mitch with both hands in his pock and smiled.

"I don't understand."

Tarrance started for the door. "Gimme a call sometime, b be careful. Remember, they're listening."

. . . .

few minutes after four a horn honked and Dutch bolted to feet. He cursed and walked in front of the headlights.

"Dammit, Mitch. It's four o'clock. What're you doing here?"

"Sorry, Dutch. Couldn't sleep. Rough night." The gate ened.

By seven-thirty he had dictated enough work to keep Nina sy for two days. She bitched less when her nose was glued to monitor. His immediate goal was to become the first asso- te to justify a second secretary.

At eight o'clock he parked himself in Lamar's office and ited. He proofed a contract and drank coffee, and told mar's secretary to mind her own business. He arrived at ht-fifteen.

"We need to talk," Mitch said as he closed the door. If he ieved Tarrance, the office was bugged and the conversation uld be recorded. He was not sure whom to believe.

"You sound serious," Lamar said.

"Ever hear of a guy named Tarrance, Wayne Tarrance?"

"No."

"FBI."

Lamar closed his eyes. "FBI," he mumbled.

"That's right. He had a badge and everything."

"Where did you meet him?"

"He found me at Lansky's Deli on Union. He knew who I s, knew I'd just been admitted. Says he knows all about the m. They watch us real close."

"Have you told Avery?"

"No. No one but you. I'm not sure what to do."

Lamar picked up the phone. "We need to tell Avery. I think s has happened before."

"What's going on, Lamar?"

Lamar talked to Avery's secretary and said it was an emer- ncy. In a few seconds he was on the other end. "We've got a all problem, Avery. An FBI agent contacted Mitch yester- y. He's in my office."

Lamar listened, then said to Mitch, "He's got me on hold. d he was calling Lambert."

"I take it this is pretty serious," Mitch said.

105

"Yes, but don't worry. There's an explanation. It's happen before."

Lamar held the receiver closer and listened to the instructions. He hung up. "They want us in Lambert's office in minutes."

Avery, Royce McKnight, Oliver Lambert, Harold O'Ka and Nathan Locke were waiting. They stood nervous around the small conference table and tried to appear ca when Mitch entered the office.

"Have a seat," Nathan Locke said with a short, plastic smi "We want you to tell us everything."

"What's that?" Mitch pointed to a tape recorder in the ce ter of the table.

"We don't want to miss anything," Locke said, and point to an empty chair. Mitch sat and stared across the table Black Eyes. Avery sat between them. No one made a soun

"Okay. I was eating lunch yesterday at Lansky's Deli Union. This guy walks up and sits across my table. He kno my name. Shows me a badge and says his name is Wayne T rance, special agent, FBI. I look at the badge, and it's real. tells me he wants to meet because we'll get to know each oth They watch this firm real close and he warns me not to tru anyone. I ask him why, and he said he doesn't have time explain, but he will later. I don't know what to say, so I ju listen. He says he will contact me later. He gets up to leave a tells me they saw me at the funerals. Then he says the deat of Kozinski and Hodge were not accidents. And he leaves. T entire conversation lasted less than five minutes."

Black Eyes glared at Mitch and absorbed every word. "Ha you ever seen this man before?"

"Never."

"Whom did you tell?"

"Only Lamar. I told him first thing this morning."

"Your wife?"

"No."

"Did he leave you a phone number to call?"

"No."

"I want to know every word that was said," Locke manded.

'I've told you what I remember. I can't recall it verbatim."

'Are you certain?"

'Let me think a minute." A few things he would keep to nself. He stared at Black Eyes, and knew that Locke suscted more.

'Let's see. He said he saw my name in the paper and knew I s the new man here. That's it. I've covered everything. It s a very brief conversation."

'Try to remember everything," Locke persisted.

'I asked him if he wanted some of my tea. He declined."

The tape recorder was turned off, and the partners seemed relax a little. Locke walked to the window. "Mitch, we've d trouble with the FBI, as well as the IRS. It's been going on a number of years. Some of our clients are high rollers— ealthy individuals who make millions, spend millions and pect to pay little or no taxes. They pay us thousands of dol- s to legally avoid taxes. We have a reputation for being very gressive, and we don't mind taking chances if our clients struct us to. We're talking about very sophisticated business- n who understand risks. They pay dearly for our creative- ss. Some of the shelters and write-offs we set up have been allenged by the IRS. We've slugged it out with them in tax igation for the past twenty years. They don't like us, we n't like them. Some of our clients have not always possessed e highest degree of ethics, and they have been investigated d harassed by the FBI. For the past three years, we, too, have en harassed.

"Tarrance is a rookie looking for a big name. He's been here s than a year and has become a thorn. You are not to speak him again. Your brief conversation yesterday was probably corded. He is dangerous, extremely dangerous. He does not ay fair, and you'll learn soon enough that most of the feds n't play fair."

"How many of these clients have been convicted?"

"Not a single one. And we've won our share of litigation th the IRS."

"What about Kozinski and Hodge?"

"Good question," answered Oliver Lambert. "We don't ow what happened. It first appeared to be an accident, but

now we're not sure. There was a native of the islands on boa[r]
with Marty and Joe. He was the captain and divemaster. T[he]
authorities down there now tell us they suspect he was a k[ey]
link in a drug ring based in Jamaica and perhaps the explosi[on]
was aimed at him. He died, of course."

"I don't think we'll ever know," Royce McKnight adde[d]
"The police down there are not that sophisticated. We've ch[o]
sen to protect the families, and as far as we're concerned, [it]
was an accident. Frankly, we're not sure how to handle it."

"Don't breathe a word of this to anyone," Locke instruct[ed]
"Stay away from Tarrance, and if he contacts you again, let [us]
know immediately. Understand?"

"Yes, sir."

"Don't even tell your wife," Avery said.

Mitch nodded.

The grandfather's warmth returned to Oliver Lamber[t's]
face. He smiled and twirled his reading glasses. "Mitch, [we]
know this is frightening, but we've grown accustomed to [it.]
Let us handle it, and trust us. We are not afraid of Mr. T[ar]
rance, the FBI, the IRS or anybody else because we've do[ne]
nothing wrong. Anthony Bendini built this firm by ha[rd]
work, talent and uncompromising ethics. It has been drill[ed]
into all of us. Some of our clients have not been saints, but [no]
lawyer can dictate morals to his client. We don't want y[ou]
worrying about this. Stay away from this guy—he is ve[ry]
very dangerous. If you feed him, he'll get bolder and becom[e a]
nuisance."

Locke pointed a crooked finger at Mitch. "Further cont[act]
with Tarrance will jeopardize your future with this firm."

"I understand," Mitch said.

"He understands," Avery said defensively. Locke glared [at]
Tolleson.

"That's all we have, Mitch," Mr. Lambert said. "Be ca[u]
tious."

Mitch and Lamar hit the door and found the nearest sta[ir]
way.

"Get DeVasher," Locke said to Lambert, who was on t[he]
phone. Within two minutes the two senior partners had be[en]
cleared and were sitting before DeVasher's cluttered desk.

"Did you listen?" Locke asked.

Of course I listened to it, Nat. We heard every word the
said. You handled it real well. I think he's scared and will
from Tarrance."

What about Lazarov?"

I gotta tell him. He's the boss. We can't pretend it didn't
pen."

What will they do?"

Nothing serious. We'll watch the boy around the clock and
ck all his phone calls. And wait. He's not gonna move. It's
to Tarrance. He'll find him again, and the next time we'll
here. Try to keep him in the building as much as possible.
en he leaves, let us know, if you can. I don't think it's that
, really."

Why would they pick McDeere?" asked Locke.

New strategy, I guess. Kozinski and Hodge went to them,
member. Maybe they talked more than we thought. I don't
w. Maybe they figure McDeere is the most vulnerable be-
se he's fresh out of school and full of rookie idealism. And
ics—like our ethical friend Ollie here. That was good, Ollie,
good."

Shut up, DeVasher."

DeVasher quit smiling and bit his bottom lip. He let it pass.
looked at Locke. "You know what the next step is, don't
? If Tarrance keeps pushing, that idiot Lazarov will call me
day and tell me to remove him. Silence him. Put him in a
rel and drop him in the Gulf. And when that happens, all
ou honorable esquires will take your early retirement and
ve the country."

Lazarov wouldn't order a hit on an agent."

Oh, it would be a foolish move, but then Lazarov is a fool.
's very anxious about the situation down here. He calls a lot
asks all sorts of questions. I give him all sorts of answers.
netimes he listens, sometimes he cusses. Sometimes he says
gotta talk to the board. But if he tells me to take out
rance, then we'll take out Tarrance."

This makes me sick at my stomach," Lambert said.

You wanna get sick, Ollie. You let one of your little Gucci-
fered counselors get chummy with Tarrance and start talk-
, you'll get a helluva lot worse than sick. Now, I suggest

you boys keep McDeere so busy he won't have time to th
about Tarrance."

"My God, DeVasher, he works twenty hours a day.
started like fire and he hasn't slowed down."

"Just watch him close. Tell Lamar Quin to get real ti
with him so if he's got something on his mind, maybe h
unload."

"Good idea," said Locke. He looked at Ollie. "Let's hav
long talk with Quin. He's closest to McDeere, and maybe
can get closer."

"Look, boys," DeVasher said, "McDeere is scared right n
He won't make a move. If Tarrance contacts him again, h
do what he did today. He'll run straight to Lamar Quin.
showed us who he confides in."

"Did he tell his wife last night?" asked Locke.

"We're checking the tapes now. It'll take about an ho
We've got so damned many bugs in this city it takes six c
puters to find anything."

Mitch stared through the window in Lamar's office and
lected his words carefully. He said little. Suppose Tarra
was correct. Suppose everything was being recorded.

"Do you feel better?" Lamar asked.

"Yeah, I guess. It makes sense."

"It's happened before, just like Locke said."

"Who? Who was approached before?"

"I don't remember. Seems like it was three or four ye
ago."

"But you don't remember who it was?"

"No. Why is that important?"

"I'd just like to know. I don't understand why they wo
pick me, the new man, the one lawyer out of forty who kno
the least about this firm and its clients. Why would they p
me?"

"I don't know, Mitch. Look, why don't you do as Loc
suggested? Try to forget about it and run from this guy T
rance. You don't have to talk to him unless he's got a warra
Tell him to get lost if he shows up again. He's dangerous."

"Yeah, I guess you're right." Mitch forced a smile a

ded for the door. "We're still on for dinner tomorrow
ht?"

Sure. Kay wants to grill steaks and eat by the pool. Make it
, say around seven-thirty."

See you then."

12

THE GUARD called his name, frisked him and led ₠
to a large room where a row of small booths was oc
pied with visitors talking and whispering through th
metal screens.

"Number fourteen," the guard said, and pointed. Mi
walked to his booth and sat down. A minute later Ray
peared and sat between his dividers on the other side of
screen. Were it not for a scar on Ray's forehead and a ₠
wrinkles around the eyes, they could pass for twins. Both w
six-two, weighed about one-eighty, with light brown h
small blue eyes, high cheekbones and large chins. They ₠
always been told there was Indian blood in the family, but
dark skin had been lost through years in the coal mines.

Mitch had not been to Brushy Mountain in three ye
Three years and three months. They'd exchanged letters tw
a month, every month, for eight years now.

"How's your French?" Mitch finally asked. Ray's Army ₠
scores had revealed an amazing aptitude for languages. He ₠
served two years as a Vietnamese interpreter. He had m
tered German in six months while stationed there. Span

taken four years, but he was forced to learn it from a
tionary in the prison library. French was his latest project.

I'm fluent, I guess," Ray answered. "It's kinda hard to tell
here. I don't get much practice. Evidently they don't teach
nch in the projects, so most of these brothers here are uni-
gual. It's undoubtedly the most beautiful language."

Is it easy?"

Not as easy as German. Of course, it was easier to learn
rman since I was living there and everybody spoke it. Did
u know that fifty percent of our language comes from Ger-
n through Old English?"

No, I didn't know that."

It's true. English and German are first cousins."

What's next?"

Probably Italian. It's a Romance language like French and
anish and Portuguese. Maybe Russian. Maybe Greek. I've
n reading about the Greek isles. I plan to go there soon."

Mitch smiled. Ray was at least seven years away from pa-
e.

You think I'm kidding, don't you?" Ray asked. "I'm checkout of here, Mitchell, and it won't be long."

What are your plans?"

I can't talk. But I'm working on it."

Don't do it, Ray."

I'll need some help on the outside, and enough money to
me out of the country. A thousand should do it. You can
dle that, can't you? You won't be implicated."

Aren't they listening to us?"

Sometimes."

Let's talk about something else."

Sure. How's Abby?"

She's fine."

Where is she?"

Right now she's in church. She wanted to come, but I told
r she wouldn't get to see you."

I'd like to see her. Your letters sound like y'all are doing
l well. New house, cars, country club. I'm very proud of
u. You're the first McDeere in two generations to amount to
lamned thing."

"Our parents were good people, Ray. They had no opportunities and a lot of bad luck. They did the best they could."

Ray smiled and looked away. "Yeah, I guess so. Have y
talked to Mom?"

"It's been a while."

"Is she still in Florida?"

"I think so."

They paused and studied their fingers. They thought
their mother. Painful thoughts for the most part. There h
been happier times, when they were small and their father v
alive. She never recovered from his death, and after Rusty v
killed the aunts and uncles put her in an institution.

Ray took his finger and followed the small metal rods in
screen. He watched his finger. "Let's talk about somethi
else."

Mitch nodded in agreement. There was so much to t
about, but it was all in the past. They had nothing in comm
but the past, and it was best to leave it alone.

"You mentioned in a letter that one of your ex-cellmates i
private investigator in Memphis."

"Eddie Lomax. He was a Memphis cop for nine years, u
he got sent up for rape."

"Rape?"

"Yeah. He had a tough time here. Rapists are not well
garded around this place. Cops are hated. They almost kil
him until I stepped in. He's been out about three years nc
He writes me all the time. Does mainly divorce investi
tions."

"Is he in the phone book?"

"969-3838. Why do you need him?"

"I've got a lawyer buddy whose wife is fooling around, l
he can't catch her. Is this guy good?"

"Very good, so he says. He's made some money."

"Can I trust him?"

"Are you kidding? Tell him you're my brother and he'll
for you. He's gonna help me get out of here, he just does
know it. You might mention it to him."

"I wish you'd stop that."

A guard walked behind Mitch. "Three minutes," he said

"What can I send you?" Mitch asked.

"I'd like a real favor, if you don't mind."

"Anything."

"Go to a bookstore and look for one of those cassette courses how to speak Greek in twenty-four hours. That plus a eek-to-English dictionary would be nice."

"I'll send it next week."

"How about Italian too?"

"No problem."

"I'm undecided about whether to go to Sicily or the Greek s. It's really got me tore up. I asked the prison minister ut it, and he was of no help. I've thought of going to the rden. What do you think?"

Mitch chuckled and shook his head. "Why don't you go to stralia?"

"Great idea. Send me some tapes in Australian and a diction-
."

They both smiled, then stopped. They watched each other efully and waited for the guard to call time. Mitch looked at scar on Ray's forehead and thought of the countless bars and ntless fights that led to the inevitable killing. Self-defense, called it. For years he had wanted to cuss Ray for being so pid, but the anger had passed. Now he wanted to embrace and take him home and help him find a job.

"Don't feel sorry for me," Ray said.

"Abby wants to write you."

"I'd like that. I barely remember her as a small girl in nesboro, hanging around her daddy's bank on Main Street. l her to send me a picture. And I'd like a picture of your se. You're the first McDeere in a hundred years to own real te."

"I gotta go."

"Do me a favor. I think you need to find Mom, just to make e she's alive. Now that you're out of school, it would be e to reach out to her."

"I've thought about that."

"Think about it some more, okay?"

"Sure. I'll see you in a month or so."

· · · · ·

DeVasher sucked on a Roi-Tan and blew a lungful of smo[ke] into his air purifier. "We found Ray McDeere," he announc[ed] proudly.

"Where?" asked Ollie.

"Brushy Mountain State Prison. Convicted of second-deg[ree] murder in Nashville eight years ago and sentenced to fifte[en] years with no parole. Real name is Raymond McDee[re.] Thirty-one years old. No family. Served three years in [the] Army. Dishonorable discharge. A real loser."

"How'd you find him?"

"He was visited yesterday by his kid brother. We happen[ed] to be following. Twenty-four-hour surveillance, remember[?"]

"His conviction is public record. You should've found t[his] earlier."

"We would have, Ollie, if it was important. But it's not i[m]portant. We do our job."

"Fifteen years, huh? Who'd he kill?"

"The usual. A buncha drunks in a bar fighting over [a] woman. No weapon, though. Police and autopsy reports [say] he hit the victim twice with his fists and cracked his skull."

"Why the dishonorable discharge?"

"Gross insubordination. Plus, he assaulted an officer. I do[n't] know how he avoided a court-martial. Looks like a nasty ch[ar]acter."

"You're right, it's not important. What else do you kno[w?"]

"Not much. We've got the house wired, right? He has [not] mentioned Tarrance to his wife. In fact, we listen to this around the clock, and he ain't mentioned Tarrance to anyon[e."]

Ollie smiled and nodded his approval. He was proud [of] McDeere. What a lawyer.

"What about sex?"

"All we can do is listen, Ollie. But we listen real close, an[d I] don't think they've had any in two weeks. Of course, he's h[ere] sixteen hours a day going through the workaholic rookie co[un]selor routine that you guys instill. It sounds like she's gett[ing] tired of it. Could be the usual rookie's wife syndrome. She c[alls] her mother a lot—collect, so he won't know. She told her m[other] that he's changing and all that crap. She thinks he'll kill h[im]self working so hard. That's what we're hearing. So I do[n't] have any pictures, Ollie, and I'm sorry because I know h[ow]

116

ch you enjoy them. First chance we get, we'll have you
ne pictures."

Ollie glared at the wall but said nothing.

Listen, Ollie, I think we need to send the kid with Avery to
and Cayman on business. See if you can arrange it."

That's no problem. May I ask why?"

Not right now. You'll know later."

e building was in the low-rent section of downtown, a cou-
of blocks from the shadows of the modern steel-and-glass
vers which were packed together as if land was scarce in
mphis. A sign on a door directed one's attention upstairs,
ere Eddie Lomax, private investigator, maintained an office.
urs by appointment only. The door upstairs advertised in-
tigations of all types—divorces, accidents, missing relatives,
veillance. The ad in the phone book mentioned the police
ertise, but not the ending of that career. It listed eavesdrop-
g, countermeasures, child custody, photographs, courtroom
dence, voice-stress analysis, location of assets, insurance
ms and premarital background review. Bonded, insured,
nsed and available twenty-four hours a day. Ethical, reli-
e, confidential, peace of mind.

Mitch was impressed with the abundance of confidence. The
ointment was for 5 P.M., and he arrived a few minutes
ly. A shapely platinum blond with a constricting leather
rt and matching black boots asked for his name and pointed
n orange vinyl chair next to a window. Eddie would be a
nute. He inspected the chair, and noticing a fine layer of
t and several spots of what appeared to be grease, he de-
ned and said his back was sore. Tammy shrugged and re-
ned to her gum chewing and typing of some document;
tch speculated whether it was a premarital report, or maybe
rveillance summary, or perhaps a countermeasure attack
n. The ashtray on her desk was filled with butts smeared
h pink lipstick. While typing with her left hand, the right
instantly and precisely picked another cigarette from the
k and thrust it between her sticky lips. With remarkable
rdination, she flicked something with her left hand and a
ne shot to the tip of a very skinny and incredibly long liber-
d cigarette. When the flame disappeared, the lips instinc-

tively compacted and hardened around the tiny protrusi
and the entire body began to inhale. Letters became wor
words became sentences, sentences became paragraphs as s
tried desperately to fill her lungs. Finally, with an inch of
cigarette hanging as ashes, she swallowed, picked it from l
lips with two brilliant red fingernails and exhaled mighti
The smoke billowed toward the stained plaster ceiling, whe
it upset an existing cloud and swirled around a hanging fl
rescent light. She coughed, a hacking, irritating cough wh
reddened her face and gyrated her huge breasts until th
bounced dangerously close to the typewriter keys. S
grabbed a nearby cup and lapped up something, then re
serted the filter-tip 1000 and pecked away.

After two minutes, Mitch began to fear carbon monoxi
He spotted a small hole in the window, in a pane that for so
reason the spiders had not draped with cobwebs. He walked
within inches of the shredded, dust-laden curtains and tried
inhale in the direction of the opening. He felt sick. There w
more hacking and wheezing behind him. He tried to open t
window, but layers of cracked paint had long since welded
shut.

Just when he began to feel dizzy the typing and smoki
stopped.

"You a lawyer?"

Mitch turned from the window and looked at the secreta
She was now sitting on the edge of her desk, legs crossed, w
the black leather skirt well above her knees. She sipped a D
Pepsi.

"Yes."

"In a big firm?"

"Yes."

"I thought so. I could tell by your suit and your cute lit
preppie button-down with the silk paisley tie. I can alwa
spot the big-firm lawyers, as opposed to the ham-and-egg
who hang around City Court."

The smoke was clearing and Mitch was breathing easier. I
admired her legs, which for the moment were positioned j
so and demanded to be admired. She was now looking at l
shoes.

"You like the suit, huh?" he said.

It's expensive, I can tell. So's the tie. I'm not so sure about shirt and shoes."

Mitch studied the leather boots, the legs, the skirt and the ht sweater around the large breasts and tried to think of nething cute to say. She enjoyed this gazing back and forth, again sipped on her Diet Pepsi.

When she'd had enough, she nodded at Eddie's door and l, "You can go in now. Eddie's waiting."

The detective was on the phone, trying to convince some or old man that his son was in fact a homosexual. A very ive homosexual. He pointed to a wooden chair, and Mitch down. He saw two windows, both wide open, and breathed ier.

Eddie looked disgusted and covered the receiver. "He's cry-," he whispered to Mitch, who smiled obligingly, as if he s amused.

He wore blue lizard-skin boots with pointed toes, Levi's, a l-starched peach button-down, which was unbuttoned well the dark chest hair and exposed two heavy gold chains one which appeared to be turquoise. He favored Tom es or Humperdinck or one of those bushy-headed, dark-d singers with thick sideburns and solid chins.

I've got photographs," he said, and yanked the receiver m his ear when the old man screamed. He pulled five glossy ht-by-tens from a file and slid them across the desk into ch's lap. Yes, indeed, they were homosexuals, whoever they re. Eddie smiled at him proudly. The bodies were some- ere on a stage in what appeared to be a queer club. He laid m on the desk and looked at the window. They were of h quality, in color. Whoever took them had to have been in club. Mitch thought of the rape conviction. A cop sent up rape.

He slammed the phone down. "So you're Mitchell Deere! Nice to meet."

They shook hands across the desk. "My pleasure," Mitch l. "I saw Ray Sunday."

I feel like I've known you for years. You look just like Ray. told me you did. Told me all about you. I guess he told you ut me. The police background. The conviction. The rape. he explain to you it was statutory rape, and that the girl

was seventeen years old, looked twenty-five, and that I
framed?"

"He mentioned it. Ray doesn't say much. You know tha

"He's a helluva guy. I owe him my life, literally. They
most killed me in prison when they found out I was a cop.
stepped in and even the blacks backed down. He can hurt p
ple when he wants to."

"He's all the family I have."

"Yeah, I know. You bunk with a guy for years in an eight-
twelve cell and you learn all about him. He's talked about
for hours. When I was paroled you were thinking about
school."

"I finished in June of this year and went to work
Bendini, Lambert & Locke."

"Never heard of them."

"It's a tax and corporate firm on Front Street."

"I do a lot of sleazy divorce work for lawyers. Surveillan
taking pictures, like those, and gathering filth for court."
spoke quickly, with short, clipped words and sentences.
cowboy boots were placed gingerly on the desk for displ
"Plus, I've got some lawyers I run cases for. If I dig up a g
car wreck or personal-injury suit, I'll shop around to
who'll give me the best cut. That's how I bought this buildi
That's where the money is—personal injury. These lawy
take forty percent of the recovery. Forty percent!" He sh
his head in disgust as if he couldn't believe greedy lawy
actually lived and breathed in this city.

"You work by the hour?" Mitch asked.

"Thirty bucks, plus expenses. Last night I spent six hour
my van outside a Holiday Inn waiting for my client's husba
to leave his room with his whore so I could take more pictu
Six hours. That's a hundred eighty bucks for sitting on my
looking at dirty magazines and waiting. I also charged her
dinner."

Mitch listened intently, as if he wished he could do it.

Tammy stuck her head in the door and said she was leavi
A stale cloud followed her and Mitch looked at the windo
She slammed the door.

"She's a great gal," Eddie said. "She's got trouble with
husband. He's a truck driver who thinks he's Elvis. Got the

120

ck hair, ducktail, lamb-chop sideburns. Wears those thick
d sunglasses Elvis wore. When he's not on the road he sits
und the trailer listening to Elvis albums and watching
se terrible movies. They moved here from Ohio just so this
wn can be near the King's grave. Guess what his name is."

I have no idea."

Elvis. Elvis Aaron Hemphill. Had his name legally
nged after the King died. He does an impersonation rou-
e in dark nightclubs around the city. I saw him one night.
wore a white skintight jumpsuit unbuttoned to his navel,
ich would've been okay except he's got this gut that hangs
and looks like a bleached watermelon. It was pretty sad.
s voice is hilarious, sounds like one of those old Indian
efs chanting around the campfire."

So what's the problem?"

Women. You would not believe the Elvis nuts who visit this
. They flock to watch this buffoon act like the King. They
ow panties at him, big panties, panties made for heavy,
le lardasses, and he wipes his forehead and throws them
k. They give him their room numbers, and we suspect he
aks around and tries to play the big stud, just like Elvis. I
en't caught him yet."

Mitch could not think of any response to all this. He
nned like an idiot, like this was truly an incredible story.
max read him well.

You got trouble with your wife?"

No. Nothing like that. I need some information about four
ple. Three are dead, one is alive."

Sounds interesting. I'm listening."

Mitch pulled the notes from a pocket. "I assume this is
ctly confidential."

Of course it is. As confidential as you are with your client."

Mitch nodded in agreement, but thought of Tammy and
is and wondered why Lomax told him that story.

It must be confidential."

I said it would be. You can trust me."

Thirty bucks an hour?"

Twenty for you. Ray sent you, remember?"

I appreciate that."

Who are these people?"

"The three dead ones were once lawyers in our firm. Rob
Lamm was killed in 1970 in a hunting accident somewhere
Arkansas. Somewhere in the mountains. He was missing
about two weeks and they found him with a bullet in the he
There was an autopsy. That's all I know. Alice Knauss died
1977 in a car wreck here in Memphis. Supposedly a dru
driver hit her. John Mickel committed suicide in 1984. I
body was found in his office. There was a gun and a note."

"That's all you know?"

"That's it."

"What're you looking for?"

"I want to know as much as I can about how these peo
died. What were the circumstances surrounding each dea
Who investigated each death? Any unanswered questions
suspicions."

"What do you suspect?"

"At this point, nothing. I'm just curious."

"You're more than curious."

"Okay, I'm more than curious. But for now, let's leave i
that."

"Fair enough. Who's the fourth guy?"

"A man named Wayne Tarrance. He's an FBI agent here
Memphis."

"FBI!"

"Does that bother you?"

"Yes, it bothers me. I get forty an hour for cops."

"No problem."

"What do you want to know?"

"Check him out. How long has he been here? How long l
he been an agent? What's his reputation?"

"That's easy enough."

Mitch folded the paper and stuck it in his pocket. "H
long will this take?"

"About a month."

"That's fine."

"Say, what was the name of your firm?"

"Bendini, Lambert & Locke."

"Those two guys who got killed last summer—"

"They were members."

"Any suspicions?"

No."

Just thought I'd ask."

Listen, Eddie. You must be very careful with this. Don't
me at home or the office. I'll call you in about a month. I
pect I'm being watched very closely."

By whom?"

I wish I knew."

13

A VERY SMILED at the computer printout. "For month of October you billed an average of sixty- hours per week."

"I thought it was sixty-four," Mitch said.

"Sixty-one is good enough. In fact, we've never had a f year man average so high in one month. Is it legitimate?"

"No padding. In fact, I could've pushed it higher."

"How many hours are you working a week?"

"Between eighty-five and ninety. I could bill seventy-five wanted to."

"I wouldn't suggest it, at least not now. It could cause a li jealousy around here. The younger associates are watch you very closely."

"You want me to slow down?"

"Of course not. You and I are a month behind right n I'm just worried about the long hours. A little worried, th all. Most associates start like wildfire—eighty- and ninety-h weeks—but they burn out after a couple of months. Sixty- to seventy is about average. But you seem to have unu stamina."

"I don't require much sleep."

What does your wife think about it?"

Why is that important?"

Does she mind the long hours?"

Mitch glared at Avery, and for a second thought of the argu-
nt the previous night when he arrived home for dinner at
ee minutes before midnight. It was a controlled fight, but
worst one yet, and it promised to be followed by others.
ground was surrendered. Abby said she felt closer to Mr.
e next door than to her husband.

She understands. I told her I would make partner in two
rs and retire before I was thirty."

Looks like you're trying."

You're not complaining, are you? Every hour I billed last
nth was on one of your files, and you didn't seem too con-
ned about overworking me."

Avery laid the printout on his credenza and frowned at
ch. "I just don't want you to burn out or neglect things at
ne."

t seemed odd receiving marital advice from a man who had
his wife. He looked at Avery with as much contempt as he
ld generate. "You don't need to worry about what happens
ny house. As long as I produce around here you should be
py."

Avery leaned across the desk. "Look, Mitch, I'm not very
d at this sort of thing. This is coming from higher up.
nbert and McKnight are worried that maybe you're push-
a bit too hard. I mean, five o'clock in the morning, every
rning, even some Sundays. That's pretty intense, Mitch."

What did they say?"

Nothing much. Believe it or not, Mitch, those guys really
e about you and your family. They want happy lawyers
h happy wives. If everything is lovely, then the lawyers are
ductive. Lambert is especially paternalistic. He's planning
etire in a couple of years, and he's trying to relive his glory
rs through you and the other young guys. If he asks too
ny questions or gives a few lectures, take it in stride. He's
ned the right to be the grandfather around here."

Tell them I'm fine, Abby's fine, we're all happy and I'm
y productive."

Fine, now that that's out of the way, you and I leave for

Grand Cayman a week from tomorrow. I've got to meet w
some Caymanian bankers on behalf of Sonny Capps and th
other clients. Mainly business, but we always manage to w
in a little scuba diving and snorkeling. I told Royce McKni
you were needed, and he approved the trip. He said you pr
ably needed the R and R. Do you want to go?"

"Of course. I'm just a little surprised."

"It's business, so our wives won't be going. Lambert wa
little concerned that it may cause a problem at home."

"I think Mr. Lambert worries too much about what happ
at my home. Tell him I'm in control. No problems."

"So you're going?"

"Sure, I'm going. How long will we be there?"

"Couple of days. We'll stay in one of the firm's cond
Sonny Capps may stay in the other one. I'm trying to get
firm plane, but we may have to fly commercial."

"No problem with me."

Only two of the passengers on board the Cayman Airways
in Miami wore ties, and after the first round of compliment
rum punch Avery removed his and stuffed it in his coat poc
The punch was served by beautiful brown Caymanian st
ardesses with blue eyes and comely smiles. The women w
great down there, Avery said more than once.

Mitch sat by the window and tried to conceal the excitem
of his first trip out of the country. He had found a book on
Cayman Islands in a library. There were three islands, Gr
Cayman, Little Cayman and Cayman Brac. The two sma
ones were sparsely populated and seldom visited. Grand C
man had eighteen thousand people, twelve thousand registe
corporations and three hundred banks. The population
twenty percent white, twenty percent black, and the ot
sixty percent wasn't sure and didn't care. Georgetown,
capital, in recent years had become an international tax ha
with bankers as secretive as the Swiss. There were no inc
taxes, corporate taxes, capital-gains taxes, estate or gift ta
Certain companies and investments were given guaran
against taxation for fifty years. The islands were a depend
British territory with an unusually stable government. R

from import duties and tourism funded whatever govern-
t was necessary. There was no crime or unemployment.

rand Cayman was twenty-three miles long and eight miles
e in places, but from the air it looked much smaller. It was
all rock surrounded by clear, sapphire water.

he landing almost occurred in a lagoon, but at the last
nd a small asphalt strip came forth and caught the plane.
y disembarked and sang their way through customs. A
k boy grabbed Mitch's bags and threw them with Avery's
the trunk of a 1972 Ford LTD. Mitch tipped him gener-
y.

Seven Mile Beach!" Avery commanded as he turned up the
nants of his last rum punch.

Okay, mon," the driver drawled. He gunned the taxi and
rubber in the direction of Georgetown. The radio blared
ae. The driver shook and gyrated and kept a steady beat
his fingers on the steering wheel. He was on the wrong
of the road, but so was everybody else. Mitch sank into the
n seat and crossed his legs. The car had no air conditioning
pt for the open windows. The muggy tropical air rushed
ss his face and blew his hair. This was nice.

he island was flat, and the road into Georgetown was busy
small, dusty European cars, scooters and bicycles. The
es were small one-stories with tin roofs and neat, colorful
t jobs. The lawns were tiny with little grass, but the dirt
neatly swept. As they neared the town the houses became
s, two- and three-story white frame buildings where tour-
stood under the canopies and took refuge from the sun.

driver made a sharp turn and suddenly they were in the
st of a downtown crowded with modern bank buildings.
very assumed the role of tour guide. "There are banks here
everywhere. Germany, France, Great Britain, Canada,
n, Japan, Denmark. Even Saudi Arabia and Israel. Over
e hundred, at last count. It's become quite a tax haven.
bankers here are extremely quiet. They make the Swiss
like blabbermouths."

he taxi slowed in heavy traffic, and the breeze stopped. "I
a lot of Canadian banks," Mitch said.

That building right there is the Royal Bank of Montreal.

127

We'll be there at ten in the morning. Most of our business [will] be with Canadian banks."

"Any particular reason?"

"They're very safe, and very quiet."

The crowded street turned and dead-ended into ano[ther] one. Beyond the intersection the glittering blue of the Ca[rib]bean rose to the horizon. A cruise ship was anchored in [the] bay.

"That's Hogsty Bay," Avery said. "That's where the pir[ates] docked their ships three hundred years ago. Blackbeard h[im]self roamed these islands and buried his loot. They found s[ome] of it a few years ago in a cave east of here near Bodden Tow[n.]"

Mitch nodded as if he believed this tale. The driver smile[d in] the rearview mirror.

Avery wiped the sweat from his forehead. "This place [has] always attracted pirates. Once it was Blackbeard, now [it's] modern-day pirates who form corporations and hide t[heir] money here. Right, mon?"

"Right, mon," the driver replied.

"That's Seven Mile Beach," Avery said. "One of the m[ost] beautiful and most famous in the world. Right, mon?"

"Right, mon."

"Sand as white as sugar. Warm, clear water. Warm, beaut[iful] women. Right, mon?"

"Right, mon."

"Will they have the cookout tonight at the Palms?"

"Yes, mon. Six o'clock."

"That's next door to our condo. The Palms is a pop[ular] hotel with the hottest action on the beach."

Mitch smiled and watched the hotels pass. He recalled [the] interview at Harvard when Oliver Lambert preached ab[out] how the firm frowned on divorce and chasing women. A[nd] drinking. Perhaps Avery had missed those sermons. Per[haps] he hadn't.

The condos were in the center of Seven Mile Beach, [next] door to another complex and the Palms. As expected, the u[nits] owned by the firm were spacious and richly decorated. Av[ery] said they would sell for at least half a million each, but t[hey] weren't for sale. They were not for rent. They were sanct[uaries.]

or the weary lawyers of Bendini, Lambert & Locke. And a
very favored clients.

om the balcony off the second-floor bedroom, Mitch
:hed the small boats drift aimlessly over the sparkling sea.
 sun was beginning its descent and the small waves re-
ed its rays in a million directions. The cruise ship moved
ly away from the island. Dozens of people walked the
h, kicking sand, splashing in the water, chasing sand crabs
 drinking rum punch and Jamaican Red Stripe beer. The
hmic beat of Caribbean music drifted from the Palms,
re a large open-air thatched-roof bar attracted the
hcombers like a magnet. From a grass hut nearby they
ed snorkeling gear, catamarans and volleyballs.

very walked to the balcony in a pair of brilliant orange-
yellow flowered shorts. His body was lean and hard, with
lab. He owned part interest in a health club in Memphis
worked out every day. Evidently there were some tanning
; in the club. Mitch was impressed.

Iow do you like my outfit?" Avery asked.

Very nice. You'll fit right in."

've got another pair if you'd like."

No, thanks. I'll stick to my Western Kentucky gym shorts."

very sipped on a drink and took in the scenery. "I've been
 a dozen times, and I still get excited. I've thought about
ing down here."

That would be nice. You could walk the beach and chase
 crabs."

And play dominoes and drink Red Stripe. Have you ever
 a Red Stripe?"

Not that I recall."

Let's go get one."

he open-air bar was called Rumheads. It was packed with
sty tourists and a few locals who sat together around a
den table and played dominoes. Avery fought through the
vd and returned with two bottles. They found a seat next
ie domino game.

 think this is what I'll do when I retire. I'll come down
 and play dominoes for a living. And drink Red Stripe."

t's good beer."

And when I get tired of dominoes, I'll throw some darts."

He nodded to a corner where a group of drunk English●
were tossing darts at a board and cursing each other. "●
when I get tired of darts, well, who knows what I'll do. Ex●
me." He headed for a table on the patio where two s●
bikinis had just sat down. He introduced himself, and ●
asked him to have a seat. Mitch ordered another Red St●
and went to the beach. In the distance he could see the ●
buildings of Georgetown. He walked in that direction.

The food was placed on folding tables around the pool. Gr●
grouper, barbecued shark, pompano, fried shrimp, turtle
oysters, lobster and red snapper. It was all from the sea, an●
fresh. The guests crowded around the tables and served th●
selves while waiters scurried back and forth with gallon●
rum punch. They ate on small tables in the courtyard o●
looking Rumheads and the sea. A reggae band tuned up. ●
sun dipped behind a cloud, then over the horizon.

Mitch followed Avery through the buffet and, as expe●
to a table where the two women were waiting. They ●
sisters, both in their late twenties, both divorced, both ●
drunk. The one named Carrie had fallen in heat with Av●
and the other one, Julia, immediately began making eye●
Mitch. He wondered what Avery had told them.

"I see you're married," Julia whispered as she moved ne●
him.

"Yes, happily."

She smiled as if to accept the challenge. Avery and ●
woman winked at each other. Mitch grabbed a glass of pu●
and gulped it down.

He picked at his food and could think of nothing but A●
This would be hard to explain, if an explanation became ne●
sary. Having dinner with two attractive women who ●
barely dressed. It would be impossible to explain. The con●
sation became awkward at the table, and Mitch added noth●
A waiter set a large pitcher on the table, and it quickly ●
emptied. Avery became obnoxious. He told the women M●
had played for the New York Giants, had two Super B●
rings. Made a million bucks a year before a knee injury ru●
his career. Mitch shook his head and drank some more. J●
drooled at him and moved closer.

e band turned up the volume, and it was time to dance.
 the crowd moved to a wooden dance floor under two
, between the pool and the beach. "Let's dance!" Avery
d, and grabbed his woman. They ran through the tables
were soon lost in the crowd of jerking and lunging tour-

e felt her move closer, then her hand was on his leg. "Do
 wanna dance?" she asked.

No."

Good. Neither do I. What would you like to do?" She
ed her breasts on his biceps and gave her best seductive
e, only inches away.

 don't plan to do anything." He removed her hand.

w, come on. Let's have some fun. Your wife will never
v."

ook, you're a very lovely lady, but you're wasting your
 with me. It's still early. You've got plenty of time to pick
 real stud."

ou're cute."

e hand was back, and Mitch breathed deeply. "Why don't
 get lost."

 beg your pardon." The hand was gone.

 said, 'Get lost.' "

e backed away. "What's wrong with you?"

 have an aversion to communicable diseases. Get lost."

Why don't you get lost."

hat's a wonderful idea. I think I will get lost. Enjoyed
er."

itch grabbed a glass of rum punch and made his way
ugh the dancers to the bar. He ordered a Red Stripe and
 himself in a dark corner of the patio. The beach in front
m was deserted. The lights of a dozen boats moved slowly
s the water. Behind him were the sounds of the Barefoot
 and the laughter of the Caribbean night. Nice, he
ght, but it would be nicer with Abby. Maybe they would
ion here next summer. They needed time together, away
 home and the office. There was a distance between them
tance he could not define. Distance they could not discuss
oth felt. Distance he was afraid of.

What are you watching?" The voice startled him. She

walked to the table and sat next to him. She was a native, skin with blue or hazel eyes. It was impossible to tell in dark. But they were beautiful eyes, warm and uninhib Her dark curly hair was pulled back and hung almost to waist. She was an exotic mixture of black, white and prob Latin. And probably more. She wore a white bikini top very low and barely covering her large breasts and a brightly colored skirt with a slit to the waist that expose most everything when she sat and crossed her legs. No s

"Nothing, really," Mitch said.

She was young, with a childish smile that revealed pe teeth. "Where are you from?" she asked.

"The States."

She smiled and chuckled. "Of course you are. Where in States?" It was the soft, gentle, precise, confident Englis the Caribbean.

"Memphis."

"A lot of people come here from Memphis. A lot of div

"Do you live here?" he asked.

"Yes. All my life. My mother is a native. My father is England. He's gone now, back to where he came from."

"Would you like a drink?" he asked.

"Yes. Rum and soda."

He stood at the bar and waited for the drinks. A dull, vous something throbbed in his stomach. He could slide the darkness, disappear into the crowd and find his way t safety of the condo. He could lock the door and read a boo international tax havens. Pretty boring. Plus, Avery was by now with his hot little number. The girl was harmless rum and Red Stripe told him. They would have a coup drinks and say good night.

He returned with the drinks and sat across from the gi far away as possible. They were alone on the patio.

"Are you a diver?" she asked.

"No. Believe it or not, I'm here on business. I'm a law and I have meetings with some bankers in the morning."

"How long will you be here?"

"Couple of days." He was polite, but short. The less he the safer he would be. She recrossed her legs and smiled i cently. He felt weak.

"How old are you?" he asked.

"I'm twenty, and my name is Eilene. I'm old enough."

"I'm Mitch." His stomach flipped and he felt light-headed. He sipped rapidly on his beer. He glanced at his watch.

She watched with that same seductive smile. "You're very handsome."

This was unraveling in a hurry. Keep cool, he told himself, just keep cool.

"Thank you."

"Are you an athlete?"

"Sort of. Why do you ask?"

"You look like an athlete. You're very muscular and firm." It was the way she emphasized "firm" that made his stomach flip again. He admired her body and tried to think of some compliment that would not be suggestive. Forget it.

"Where do you work?" he asked, aiming for less sensual areas.

"I'm a clerk in a jewelry store in town."

"Where do you live?"

"In Georgetown. Where are you staying?"

"A condo next door." He nodded in the direction, and she looked to her left. She wanted to see the condo, he could tell. She sipped on her drink.

"Why aren't you at the party?" she asked.

"I'm not much on parties."

"Do you like the beach?"

"It's beautiful."

"It's prettier in the moonlight." That smile, again.

He could say nothing to this.

"There's a better bar about a mile down the beach," she said. "Let's go for a walk."

"I don't know, I should get back. I've got some work to do before morning."

She laughed and stood. "No one goes in this early in the Caymans. Come on. I owe you a drink."

"No. I'd better not."

She grabbed his hand, and he followed her off the patio onto the beach. They walked in silence until the Palms was out of sight and the music was growing dimmer. The moon was overhead and brighter now, and the beach was deserted. She

unsnapped something and removed her skirt, leaving nothi
but a string around her waist and a string running betwe
her legs. She rolled up the skirt and placed it around his ne
She took his hand.

Something said run. Throw the beer bottle in the oce
Throw the skirt in the sand. And run like hell. Run to
condo. Lock the door. Lock the windows. Run. Run. Run.

And something said to relax. It's harmless fun. Have a f
more drinks. If something happens, enjoy it. No one will e
know. Memphis is a thousand miles away. Avery won't kno
And what about Avery? What could he say? Everybody does
It had happened once before when he was in college, before
was married but after he was engaged. He had blamed it
too much beer, and had survived with no major scars. Ti
took care of it. Abby would never know.

Run. Run. Run.

They walked for a mile and there was no bar in sight. T
beach was darker. A cloud conveniently hid the moon. Th
had seen no one since Rumheads. She pulled his hand towa
two plastic beach chairs next to the water. "Let's rest,"
said. He finished his beer.

"You're not saying much," she said.

"What would you like for me to say?"

"Do you think I'm beautiful?"

"You are very beautiful. And you have a beautiful body."

She sat on the edge of her chair and splashed her feet in
water. "Let's go for a swim."

"I, uh, I'm not really in the mood."

"Come on, Mitch. I love the water."

"Go ahead. I'll watch."

She knelt beside him in the sand and faced him, incl
away. In slow motion, she reached behind her neck. She
hooked her bikini top, and it fell off, very slowly. Her brea
much larger now, lay on his left forearm. She handed the top to hi
"Hold this for me." It was soft and white and weighed less tha
millionth of an ounce. He was paralyzed and his breathing, heavy a
labored only seconds ago, had now ceased altogether.

She walked slowly into the water. The white string cove
nothing from the rear. Her long, dark, beautiful hair hung

waist. She waded knee deep, then turned to the beach.

"Come on, Mitch. The water feels great."

She flashed a brilliant smile and he could see it. He rubbed
bikini top and knew this would be his last chance to run.
t he was dizzy and weak. Running would require more
ength than he could possibly muster. He wanted to just sit
d maybe she would go away. Maybe she would drown.
aybe the tide would suddenly materialize and sweep her out
sea.

"Come on, Mitch."

He removed his shirt and waded into the water. She
tched him with a smile, and when he reached her, she took
hand and led him to deeper water. She locked her hands
und his neck, and they kissed. He found the strings. They
sed again.

She stopped abruptly and, without speaking, started for the
ach. He watched her. She sat on the sand, between the two
airs, and removed the rest of her bikini. He ducked under
water and held his breath for an eternity. When he sur-
ed, she was reclining, resting on her elbows in the sand. He
veyed the beach and, of course, saw no one. At that precise
tant, the moon ducked behind another cloud. There was not
oat or a catamaran or a dinghy or a swimmer or a snorkeler
anything or anybody moving on the water.

"I can't do this," he muttered through clenched teeth.

"What did you say, Mitch?"

"I can't do this!" he yelled.

"But I want you."

"I can't do it."

"Come on, Mitch. No one will ever know."

No one will ever know. No one will ever know. He walked
wly toward her. No one will ever know.

ere was complete silence in the rear of the taxi as the law-
s rode into Georgetown. They were late. They had over-
pt and missed breakfast. Neither felt particularly well.
ery looked especially haggard. His eyes were bloodshot and
face was pale. He had not shaved.

The driver stopped in heavy traffic in front of the Royal

Bank of Montreal. The heat and humidity were already 〈s〉
fling.

Randolph Osgood was the banker, a stuffy British type w〈ith〉
a navy double-breasted suit, horn-rimmed glasses, a large shi〈ny〉
forehead and a pointed nose. He greeted Avery like an 〈old〉
friend and introduced himself to Mitch. They were led t〈o a〉
large office on the second floor with a view of Hogsty B〈ay.〉
Two clerks were waiting.

"Exactly what do you need, Avery?" Osgood asked throu〈gh〉
his nose.

"Let's start off with some coffee. I need summaries of all 〈the〉
accounts of Sonny Capps, Al Coscia, Dolph Hemmba, Ratzl〈aff〉
Partners and Greene Group."

"Yes, and how far back would you like to go?"

"Six months. Every account."

Osgood snapped his fingers at one of the clerks. She left a〈nd〉
returned with a tray of coffee and pastries. The other cl〈erk〉
took notes.

"Of course, Avery, we'll need authorization and powers 〈of〉
attorney for each of these clients," Osgood said.

"They're on file," Avery said as he unpacked his briefca〈se.〉

"Yes, but they've expired. We'll need current ones. Eve〈ry〉
account."

"Very well." Avery slid a file across the table. "They're 〈all〉
there. Everything's current." He winked at Mitch.

A clerk took the file and spread the documents over the 〈ta〉
ble. Each instrument was scrutinized by both clerks, then 〈by〉
Osgood himself. The lawyers drank coffee and waited.

Osgood smiled and said, "It all appears to be in order. W〈e'll〉
get the records. What else do you need?"

"I need to establish three corporations. Two for Son〈ny〉
Capps and one for Greene Group. We'll follow the usual p〈ro〉
cedure. The bank will serve as registered agent, etc."

"I'll procure the necessary documents," Osgood said, a〈nd〉
looked at a clerk. "What else?"

"That's all for now."

"Very well. We should have these records within thirty m〈in〉
utes. Will you be joining me for lunch?"

"I'm sorry, Randolph. I must decline. Mitch and I hav〈e a〉
prior commitment. Maybe tomorrow."

Mitch knew nothing of a prior commitment, at least none he involved in.

"Perhaps," replied Osgood. He left the room with the clerks. ...very closed the door and removed his jacket. He walked to window and sipped coffee. "Look, Mitch. I'm sorry about night. Very sorry. I got drunk and quit thinking. I was ...ng to push that woman on you."

"Apology accepted. Don't let it happen again."

"It won't. I promise."

"Was she good?"

"I think so. I don't remember too much. What did you do ...h her sister?"

"She told me to get lost. I hit the beach and took a walk."

...very bit into a pastry and wiped his mouth. "You know I'm ...arated. We'll probably get a divorce in a year or so. I'm very ...reet because the divorce could get nasty. There's an un-...tten rule in the firm—what we do away from Memphis ...s away from Memphis. Understand?"

"Come on, Avery. You know I wouldn't tell."

"I know. I know."

Mitch was glad to hear of the unwritten rule, although he ...kened with the security that he had committed the perfect ...ne. He had thought of her in bed, the shower, the taxi, and ... he had trouble concentrating on anything. He had caught ...self looking at jewelry stores when they reached George-...n.

"I've got a question," Mitch said.

...very nodded and ate the pastry.

"When I was recruited a few months ago by Oliver Lambert McKnight and the gang, it was impressed upon me repeat-... that the firm frowned on divorce, women, booze, drugs, ...ything but hard work and money. That's why I took the ... I've seen the hard work and money, but now I'm seeing ...r things. Where did you go wrong? Or do all the guys do ...

"I don't like your question."

"I knew you wouldn't. But I'd like an answer. I deserve an ...wer. I feel like I was misled."

"So what are you going to do? Leave because I got drunk ... laid up with a whore?"

"I haven't thought about leaving."

"Good. Don't."

"But I'm entitled to an answer."

"Okay. Fair enough. I'm the biggest rogue in the firm, a they'll come down hard when I mention the divorce. I ch women now and then, but no one knows it. Or at least t can't catch me. I'm sure it's done by other partners, but yo never catch them. Not all of them, but a few. Most have v stable marriages and are forever faithful to their wives. I always been the bad boy, but they've tolerated me because so talented. They know I drink during lunch and sometime the office, and they know I violate some more of their sac rules, but they made me a partner because they need me. A now that I'm a partner, they can't do much about it. I'm that bad of a guy, Mitch."

"I didn't say you were."

"I'm not perfect. Some of them are, believe me. The machines, robots. They live, eat and sleep for Bendini, L bert & Locke. I like to have a little fun."

"So you're the exception—"

"Rather than the rule, yes. And I don't apologize for it.

"I didn't ask you for an apology. Just a clarification."

"Clear enough?"

"Yes. I've always admired your bluntness."

"And I admire your discipline. It's a strong man who remain faithful to his wife with the temptations you had night. I'm not that strong. Don't want to be."

Temptations. He had thought of inspecting the downto jewelry shops during lunch.

"Look, Avery, I'm not a Holy Roller, and I'm not shock I'm not one to judge—I've been judged all my life. I was confused about the rules, that's all."

"The rules never change. They're cast in concrete. Car in granite. Etched in stone. Violate too many and you're Or violate as many as you want, but just don't get caught.

"Fair enough."

Osgood and a group of clerks entered the room with co puter printouts and stacks of documents. They made neat p on the table and alphabetized it all.

"This should keep you busy for a day or so," Osgood s

th a forced smile. He snapped his fingers and the clerks appeared. "I'll be in my office if you need something."

"Yes, thanks," Avery said as he hovered over the first set of cuments. Mitch removed his coat and loosened his tie.

"Exactly what are we doing here?" he asked.

"Two things. First, we'll review the entries into all of these counts. We're looking primarily for interest earned, what e, how much, etc. We'll do a rough audit of each account to ke sure the interest is going where it is supposed to go. For ample, Dolph Hemmba sends his interest to nine different nks in the Bahamas. It's stupid, but it makes him happy. It's o impossible for anyone to follow, except me. He has about elve million in this bank, so it's worth keeping up with. He uld do this himself, but he feels better if I do it. At two-fifty hour, I don't mind. We'll check the interest this bank is ying on each account. The rate varies depending on a num-r of factors. It's discretionary with the bank, and this is a od way to keep them honest."

'I thought they were honest."

'They are, but they're bankers, remember."

'You're looking at close to thirty accounts here, and when : leave we'll know the exact balance, the interest earned and ere the interest is going. Second, we have to incorporate ee companies under Caymanian jurisdiction. It's fairly easy al work and could be done in Memphis. But the clients nk we must come here to do it. Remember, we're dealing th people who invest millions. A few thousand in legal fees esn't bother them."

Mitch flipped through a printout in the Hemmba stack. Who's this guy Hemmba? I haven't heard of him."

'I've got a lot of clients you haven't heard of. Hemmba is a farmer in Arkansas, one of the state's largest landowners."

'Twelve million dollars?"

'That's just in this bank."

'That's a lot of cotton and soybeans."

'Let's just say he has other ventures."

'Such as?"

'I really can't say."

'Legal or illegal?"

139

"Let's just say he's hiding twenty million plus interest various Caribbean banks from the IRS."

"Are we helping him?"

Avery spread the documents on one end of the table an began checking entries. Mitch watched and waited for an a swer. The silence grew heavier and it was obvious there wou not be one. He could press, but he had asked enough question for one day. He rolled up his sleeves and went to work.

At noon he learned about Avery's prior commitment. H woman was waiting at the condo for a little rendezvous. H suggested they break for a couple of hours and mentioned café downtown Mitch could try.

Instead of a café, Mitch found the Georgetown Library fo blocks from the bank. On the second floor he was directed the periodicals, where he found a shelf full of old editions *The Daily Caymanian*. He dug back six months and pulled t one dated June 27. He laid it on a small table by a windo overlooking the street. He glanced out the window, the looked closer. There was a man he had seen only momen earlier on the street by the bank. He was behind the wheel of battered yellow Chevette parked in a narrow drive across fro the library. He was a stocky, dark-haired, foreign-looking ty with a gaudy green-and-orange shirt and cheap touristy su glasses.

The same Chevette with the same driver had been parked front of the gift shop next to the bank, and now, momen later, it was parked four blocks away. A native on a bicyc stopped next to him and took a cigarette. The man in the c pointed at the library. The native left his bicycle and walke quickly across the street.

Mitch folded the newspaper and stuck it in his coat. H walked past the rows of shelves, found a *National Geograph* and sat down at a table. He studied the magazine and listen carefully as the native climbed the stairs, noticed him, walke behind him, seemed to pause as if to catch a glimpse of what was reading, then disappeared down the stairs. Mitch wait for a moment, then returned to the window. The native w taking another cigarette and talking to the man in t Chevette. He lit the cigarette and rode away.

Mitch spread the newspaper on the table and scanned the headline story of the two American lawyers and their dive guide who had been killed in a mysterious accident the day before. He made mental notes and returned the paper.

The Chevette was still watching. He walked in front of it, made the block and headed in the direction of the bank. The shopping district was squeezed tightly between the bank buildings and Hogsty Bay. The streets were narrow and crowded with tourists on foot, tourists on scooters, tourists in rented compacts. He removed his coat and ducked into a T-shirt shop with a pub upstairs. He climbed the stairs, ordered a Coke, and sat on the balcony.

Within minutes the native with the bicycle was at the bar, drinking a Red Stripe and watching from behind a hand printed menu.

Mitch sipped on the Coke and scanned the congestion below. No sign of the Chevette, but he knew it was close by. He saw another man stare at him from the street, then disappear. Then a woman. Was he paranoid? Then the Chevette turned the corner two blocks away and moved slowly beneath him.

He went to the T-shirt store and bought a pair of sunglasses. He walked for a block, then darted into an alley. He ran through the dark shade to the next street, then into a gift shop. He left through the back door, into an alley. He saw a large clothing store for tourists and entered through a side door. He watched the street closely and saw nothing. The racks were full of shorts and shirts of all colors—clothes the natives would not buy but the Americans loved. He stayed conservative— white shorts with a red knit pullover. He found a pair of straw sandals that sort of matched the hat he liked. The clerk giggled and showed him to a dressing room. He checked the street again. Nothing. The clothes fit, and he asked her if he could leave his suit and shoes in the back for a couple of hours. "No problem, mon," she said. He paid in cash, slipped her a ten and asked her to call a cab. She said he was very handsome.

He watched the street nervously until the cab arrived. He darted across the sidewalk, into the back seat. "Abanks Dive Lodge," he said.

"That's a long way, mon."

Mitch threw a twenty over the seat. "Get moving. Watc[h] your mirror. If someone is following, let me know."

He grabbed the money. "Okay, mon."

Mitch sat low under his new hat in the back seat as h[e] driver worked his way down Shedden Road, out of the sho[p]ping district, around Hogsty Bay, and headed east, past R[e] Bay, out of the city of Georgetown and onto the road to Bo[d]den Town.

"Who are you running from, mon?"

Mitch smiled and rolled down his window. "The Intern[al] Revenue Service." He thought that was cute, but the driv[er] seemed confused. There were no taxes and no tax collectors [in] the islands, he remembered. The driver continued in silenc[e].

According to the paper, the dive guide was Philip Abank[s,] son of Barry Abanks, the owner of the dive lodge. He w[as] nineteen when he was killed. The three had drowned when a[n] explosion of some sort hit their boat. A very mysterious expl[o]sion. The bodies had been found in eighty feet of water in fu[ll] scuba gear. There were no witnesses to the explosion and [no] explanations as to why it occurred two miles offshore in a[n] area not known for diving. The article said there were ma[ny] unanswered questions.

Bodden Town was a small village twenty minutes fro[m] Georgetown. The dive lodge was south of town on an isolat[ed] stretch of beach.

"Did anyone follow us?" Mitch asked.

The driver shook his head.

"Good job. Here's forty bucks." Mitch looked at his watc[h.] "It's almost one. Can you be here at exactly two-thirty?"

"No problem, mon."

The road ended at the edge of the beach and became a whi[te] rock parking area shaded by dozens of royal palms. The fro[nt] building of the lodge was a large, two-story home with a t[in] roof and an outer stairway leading to the center of the seco[nd] floor. The Grand House, it was called. It was painted a lig[ht] blue with neat white trim, and it was partially hidden by b[a?] vines and spider lilies. The handwrought fretwork w[as] painted pink. The solid wooden shutters were olive. It was t[he] office and eating room of Abanks Dive Lodge. To its right t[he] palm trees thinned and a small driveway curved around t[he] rand House and sloped downward to a large open area of hite rock. On each side was a group of a dozen or so atched-roof huts where divers roomed. A maze of wooden dewalks ran from the huts to the central point of the lodge, e open-air bar next to the water.

Mitch headed for the bar to the familiar sounds of reggae d laughter. It was similar to Rumheads, but without the owd. After a few minutes, the bartender, Henry, delivered a ed Stripe to Mitch.

"Where's Barry Abanks?" Mitch asked.

He nodded to the ocean and returned to the bar. Half a mile at, a boat cut slowly through the still water and made its way ward the lodge. Mitch ate the cheeseburger and watched the ominoes.

The boat docked at a pier between the bar and a larger hut ith the words DIVE SHOP hand painted over a window. The vers jumped from the boat with their equipment bags and, ithout exception, headed for the bar. A short, wiry man ood next to the boat and barked orders at the deckhands, who ere unloading empty scuba tanks onto the pier. He wore a hite baseball cap and not much else. A tiny black pouch cov- ed his crotch and most of his rear end. From the looks of his own leathery skin he hadn't worn much in the past fifty ars. He checked in at the dive shop, yelled at the dive cap- ins and deckhands and made his way to the bar. He ignored e crowd and went to the freezer, where he picked up a eineken, removed the top and took a long drink.

The bartender said something to Abanks and nodded to- ard Mitch. He opened another Heineken and walked to itch's table.

He did not smile. "Are you looking for me?" It was almost a eer.

"Are you Mr. Abanks?"

"That's me. What do you want?"

"I'd like to talk to you for a few minutes."

He gulped his beer and gazed at the ocean. "I'm too busy. I ve a dive boat leaving in forty minutes."

"My name is Mitch McDeere. I'm a lawyer from Memphis." Abanks glared at him with tiny brown eyes. Mitch had his tention. "So?"

143

"So, the two men who died with your son were friends mine. It won't take but a few minutes."

Abanks sat on a stool and rested on his elbows. "That's n one of my favorite subjects."

"I know. I'm sorry."

"The police instructed me not to talk to anyone."

"It's confidential. I swear."

Abanks squinted and stared at the brilliant blue water. H face and arms bore the scars of a life at sea, a life spent six feet down guiding novices through and around coral reefs a wrecked ships.

"What do you want to know?" he asked softly.

"Can we talk somewhere else?"

"Sure. Let's take a walk." He yelled at Henry and spoke to table of divers as he left. They walked on the beach.

"I'd like to talk about the accident," Mitch said.

"You can ask. I may not answer."

"What caused the explosion?"

"I don't know. Perhaps an air compressor. Perhaps so fuel. We are not certain. The boat was badly damaged a most of the clues went up in flames."

"Was it your boat?"

"Yes. One of my small ones. A thirty-footer. Your frien had chartered it for the morning."

"Where were the bodies found?"

"In eighty feet of water. There was nothing suspicio about the bodies, except that there were no burns or oth injuries that would indicate they had been in the explosion. I guess that makes the bodies very suspicious."

"The autopsies said they drowned."

"Yes, they drowned. But your friends were in full scu gear, which was later examined by one of my divemasters. worked perfectly. They were good divers."

"What about your son?"

"He was not in full gear. But he could swim like a fish."

"Where was the explosion?"

"They had been scheduled to dive along a series of reef fo mations at Roger's Wreck Point. Are you familiar with t island?"

"No."

"It's around the East Bay on Northeastern Point. Your
iends had never dived there, and my son suggested they try
. We knew your friends well. They were experienced divers
nd took it seriously. They always wanted a boat by them-
lves and didn't mind paying for it. And they always wanted
hilip as their dive captain. We don't know if they made any
ves on the Point. The boat was found burning two miles at
a, far from any of our dive sites."

"Could the boat have drifted?"

"Impossible. If there had been engine trouble, Philip would
ave used the radio. We have modern equipment, and our
vemasters are always in touch with the dive shop. There's no
ay the explosion could have occurred at the Point. No one
w it or heard it, and there's always someone around. Sec-
dly, a disabled boat could not drift two miles in that water.
nd, most importantly, the bodies were not on the boat, re-
ember. Suppose the boat did drift, how do you explain the
rifting of the bodies eighty feet below. They were found
ithin twenty meters of the boat."

"Who found them?"

"My men. We caught the bulletin over the radio, and I sent a
ew. We knew it was our boat, and my men started diving.
hey found the bodies within minutes."

"I know this is difficult to talk about."

Abanks finished his beer and threw the bottle in a wooden
arbage box. "Yes, it is. But time takes away the pain. Why are
ou so interested?"

"The families have a lot of questions."

"I am sorry for them. I met their wives last year. They spent
week with us. Such nice people."

"Is it possible they were simply exploring new territory
hen it happened?"

"Possible, yes. But not likely. Our boats report their move-
ents from one dive site to the next. That's standard proce-
ure. No exceptions. I have fired a dive captain for not clear-
g a site before going to the next. My son was the best captain
n the island. He grew up in these waters. He would never fail
 report his movements at sea. It's that simple. The police
lieve that is what happened, but they have to believe some-
ing. It's the only explanation they have."

"But how do they explain the condition of the bodies?"

"They can't. It's simply another diving accident as far as they're concerned."

"Was it an accident?"

"I think not."

The sandals had rubbed blisters by now, and Mitch removed them. They turned and started back to the lodge.

"If it wasn't an accident, what was it?"

Abanks walked and watched the ocean crawl along the beach. He smiled for the first time. "What are the other possibilities?"

"There's a rumor in Memphis that drugs could have been involved."

"Tell me about this rumor."

"We've heard that your son was active in a drug ring, that possibly he was using the boat that day to meet a supplier at sea, that there was a dispute and my friends got in the way."

Abanks smiled again and shook his head. "Not Philip. To my knowledge he never used drugs, and I know he didn't trade in them. He wasn't interested in money. Just women and diving."

"Not a chance?"

"No, not a chance. I've never heard this rumor, and I doubt if they know more in Memphis. This is a small island, and I would have heard it by now. It's completely false."

The conversation was over and they stopped near the bar. "I'll ask you a favor," Abanks said. "Do not mention any of this to the families. I cannot prove what I know to be true, so it's best if no one knows. Especially the families."

"I won't tell anyone. And I will ask you not to mention our conversation. Someone might follow me here and ask questions about my visit. Just say we talked about diving."

"As you wish."

"My wife and I will be here next spring for our vacation. I'll be sure to look you up."

14

ST. ANDREW'S EPISCOPAL SCHOOL was located behind the church of the same name on a densely wooded and perfectly manicured five-acre estate in the middle of midtown Memphis. The white and yellow brick was occasionally visible where the ivy had for some reason turned and pursued another course. Symmetrical rows of clipped boxwoods lined the sidewalks and the small playground. It was a one-story L-shaped building sitting quietly in the shadows of a dozen ancient oaks. Cherished for its exclusivity, St. Andrew's was the most expensive private school in Memphis for grades kindergarten through six. Affluent parents signed the waiting list shortly after birth.

Mitch stopped the BMW in the parking lot between the church and the school. Abby's burgundy Peugeot was three spaces down, sitting innocently. He was unexpected. The plane had landed an hour earlier, and he had stopped by the house to change into something lawyerly. He would see her, then back to his desk for a few hours at one hundred and fifty per.

He wanted to see her here, at the school, unannounced. A surprise attack. A countermove. He would say hello. He

147

missed her. He couldn't wait to see her, so he stopped by th
school. He would be brief, the first touch and feel and word
after that incident on the beach. Could she tell just by lookin
at him? Maybe she could read his eyes. Would she notice
slight strain in his voice? Not if she was surprised. Not if sh
was flattered by this visit.

He squeezed the steering wheel and stared at her car. Wha
an idiot! A stupid fool! Why didn't he run? Just throw her ski
in the sand and run like hell. But, of course, he didn't. He sai
what the hell, no one will ever know. So now he was suppose
to shrug it off and say what the hell, everybody does it.

On the plane he laid his plans. First, he would wait until la
this night and tell her the truth. He would not lie, had n
desire to live a lie. He would admit it and tell her exactly wha
happened. Maybe she would understand. Why, almost an
man—hell, virtually every man would have taken the dive. H
next move would depend on her reaction. If she was cool an
showed a trace of compassion, he would tell her he was sorr
so very sorry, and that it would never happen again. If she fe
all to pieces, he would beg, literally beg for forgiveness an
swear on the Bible that it was a mistake and would never ha
pen again. He would tell her how much he loved her an
worshipped her, and please just give him one more chanc
And if she started packing her bags, he would probably at th
point realize he should not have told her.

Deny. Deny. Deny. His criminal-law professor at Harvar
had been a radical named Moskowitz, who had made a nam
for himself defending terrorists and assassins and child fonc
lers. His theory of defense was simply: Deny! Deny! Deny
Never admit one fact or one piece of evidence that would ind
cate guilt.

He remembered Moskowitz as they landed in Miami, an
began working on Plan B, which called for this surprise vis
at the school and a late-night romantic dinner at her favorit
place. And no mention of anything but hard work in the Cay
mans. He opened the car door, thought of her beautiful smi
ing, trusting face and felt nauseous. A thick, dull pain han
mered deep in his stomach. He walked slowly in the lat
autumn breeze to the front door.

The hallway was empty and quiet. To his right was the o

ce of the headmaster. He waited for a moment in the hall, aited to be seen, but no one was there. He walked quietly aead until, at the third classroom, he heard the wonderful ice of his wife. She was plowing through multiplication ta- es when he stuck his head in the door and smiled. She froze, aen giggled. She excused herself, told them to stay in their ats and read the next page. She closed the door.

"What're you doing here?" she asked as he grabbed her and nned her to the wall. She glanced nervously up and down ae hall.

"I missed you," he said with conviction. He bear-hugged her r a good minute. He kissed her neck and tasted the sweetness her perfume. And then the girl returned. You piece of scum, hy didn't you run?

"When did you get in?" she asked, straightening her hair ad glancing down the hall.

"About an hour ago. You look wonderful."

Her eyes were wet. Those wonderfully honest eyes. "How as your trip?"

"Okay. I missed you. It's no fun when you're not around." Her smile widened and she looked away. "I missed you too." They held hands and walked toward the front door. "I'd like date tonight," he said.

"You're not working?"

"No. I'm not working. I'm going out with my wife to her vorite restaurant. We'll eat and drink expensive wine and ay out late, and then get naked when we get home."

"You did miss me." She kissed him again, on the lips, then oked down the hall. "But you better get out of here before meone sees you."

They walked quickly to the front door without being seen. He breathed deeply in the cool air and walked quickly to his r. He did it. He looked into those eyes, held her and kissed r like always. She suspected nothing. She was touched and en moved.

Vasher paced anxiously behind his desk and sucked ner- usly on a Roi-Tan. He sat in his worn swivel chair and tried concentrate on a memo, then he jumped to his feet and paced again. He checked his watch. He called his secretary. H called Oliver Lambert's secretary. He paced some more.

Finally, seventeen minutes after he was supposed to arriv Ollie was cleared through security and walked into DeVasher office.

DeVasher stood behind his desk and glared at Ollie. "You' late!"

"I'm very busy," Ollie answered as he sat in a worn Naug hyde chair. "What's so important?"

DeVasher's face instantly changed into a sly, evil smile. I dramatically opened a desk drawer and proudly threw a larg manila envelope across the desk into Ollie's lap. "Some of t best work we've ever done."

Lambert opened the envelope and gaped at the eight by te black-and-white photographs. He stared at each one, holdir them inches from his nose, memorizing each detail. DeVashe watched proudly.

Lambert reviewed them again and began breathing heavil "These are incredible."

"Yep. We thought so."

"Who's the girl?" Ollie asked, still staring.

"A local prostitute. Looks pretty good, doesn't she? We' never used her before, but you can bet we'll use her again."

"I want to meet her, and soon."

"No problem. I kinda figured you would."

"This is incredible. How'd she do it?"

"It looked difficult at first. He told the first girl to get los Avery had the other one, but your man wanted no part of h friend. He left and went to that little bar on the beach. That when our girl there showed up. She's a pro."

"Where were your people?"

"All over the place. Those were shot from behind a pal tree, about eighty feet away. Pretty good, aren't they?"

"Very good. Give the photographer a bonus. How long d they roll in the sand?"

"Long enough. They were very compatible."

"I think he really enjoyed himself."

"We were lucky. The beach was deserted and the timing w perfect."

Lambert raised a photograph toward the ceiling, in front of eyes. "Did you make me a set?" he asked from behind it.
"Of course, Ollie. I know how much you enjoy these ngs."

"I thought McDeere would be tougher than that."

"He's tough, but he's human. He's no dummy either. We're t sure, but we think he knew we were watching him the xt day during lunch. He seemed suspicious and began dart-g around the shopping district. Then he disappeared. He s an hour late for his meeting with Avery at the bank."

"Where'd he go?"

"We don't know. We were just watching out of curiosity, thing serious. Hell, he might've been in a bar downtown for we know. But he just disappeared."

"Watch him carefully. He worries me."

DeVasher waved another manila envelope. "Quit worrying, lie. We own him now! He would kill for us if he knew about se."

"What about Tarrance?"

"Not a sign. McDeere ain't mentioned it to anybody, at least t to anybody we're listening to. Tarrance is hard to trail netimes, but I think he's staying away."

"Keep your eyes open."

"Don't worry about my end, Ollie. You're the lawyer, the unselor, the esquire, and you get your eight-by-tens. You run e firm. I run the surveillance."

"How are things at the McDeere house?"

"Not too good. She was very cool to the trip."

"What'd she do when he was gone?"

"Well, she ain't one to sit around the house. Two nights she d Quin's wife went out to eat at a couple of those yuppie nts. Then to the movies. She was out one night with a oolteacher friend. She shopped a little.

She also called her mother a lot, collect. Evidently there's no e lost between our boy and her parents, and she wants to tch things up. She and her mom are tight and it really thers her because they can't be a big happy family. She nts to go home to Kentucky for Christmas, and she's afraid won't go for it. There's a lot of friction. A lot of undercur-ts. She tells her mom he works too much, and her mom

says it's because he wants to show them up. I don't like t
sound of it, Ollie. Bad vibes."

"Just keep listening. We've tried to slow him down, but h
a machine."

"Yeah, at a hundred and fifty an hour I know you want hi
to slack off. Why don't you cut all your associates back to for
hours a week so they can spend more time with their famili
You could cut your salary, sell a Jag or two, hock your o
lady's diamonds, maybe sell your mansion and buy a smal
house by the country club."

"Shut up, DeVasher."

Oliver Lambert stormed out of the office. DeVasher turn
red with his high-pitched laughter, then, when his office w
empty, he locked the photos in a file cabinet. "Mitch
McDeere," he said to himself with an immense smile, "no
you are ours."

15

ON A FRIDAY, at noon, two weeks before Christmas, Abby said goodbye to her students and left St. Andrew's for the holidays. At one, she parked in a lot full
Volvos and BMWs and Saabs and more Peugeots and
lked hurriedly through the cold rain into the crowded ter-
rium where the young affluent gathered to eat quiche and
itas and black bean soup among the plants. This was Kay
uin's current hot spot of the year, and this was the second
nch they'd had in a month. Kay was late, as usual.

It was a friendship still in the initial stages of development.
utious by nature, Abby had never been one to rush into
umminess with a stranger. The three years at Harvard had
en friendless, and she had learned a great deal of indepen-
nce. In six months in Memphis she had met a handful of
ospects at church and one at school, but she moved cau-
usly.

At first Kay Quin had pushed hard. She was at once a tour
ide, shopping consultant and even a decorator. But Abby
d moved slowly, learning a little with each visit and watch-
g her new friend carefully. They had eaten several times in
e Quin home. They had seen each other at firm dinners and

153

functions, but always in a crowd. And they had enjoyed ea
other's company over four long lunches at whatever happen
to be the hottest gathering place at that moment for the you
and beautiful Gold MasterCard holders in Memphis. Kay
ticed cars and homes and clothes, but pretended to ignore
all. Kay wanted to be a friend, a close friend, a confidante,
intimate. Abby kept the distance, slowly allowing her in.

The reproduction of a 1950s jukebox sat below Abby's tal
on the first level near the bar, where a standing-room cro
sipped and waited for tables. After ten minutes and two R
Orbisons, Kay emerged from the crowd at the front door a
looked upward to the third level. Abby smiled and waved.

They hugged and pecked each other properly on the chee
without transferring lipstick.

"Sorry I'm late," Kay said.

"That's okay. I'm used to it."

"This place is packed," Kay said, looking around in ama
ment. It was always packed. "So you're out of school?"

"Yes. As of an hour ago. I'm free until January 6."

They admired each other's outfits and commented on h
slim and in general how beautiful and young they were.

Christmas shopping at once became the topic, and th
talked of stores and sales and children until the wine arriv
Abby ordered scampi in a skillet, but Kay stuck with the
fern bar standby of broccoli quiche.

"What're your plans for Christmas?" Kay asked.

"None yet. I'd like to go to Kentucky to see my folks, h
I'm afraid Mitch won't go. I've dropped a couple of hints, bo
of which were ignored."

"He still doesn't like your parents?"

"There's been no change. In fact, we don't discuss them
don't know how to handle it."

"With great caution, I would imagine."

"Yeah, and great patience. My parents were wrong, bu
still need them. It's painful when the only man I've ever lov
can't tolerate my parents. I pray every day for a small mi
cle."

"Sounds like you need a rather large miracle. Is he worki
as hard as Lamar says?"

"I don't know how a person could work any harder. I

154

ghteen hours a day Monday through Friday, eight hours on
turday, and since Sunday is a day of rest, he puts in only five
six hours. He reserves a little time for me on Sunday."

"Do I hear a touch of frustration?"

"A lot of frustration, Kay. I've been patient, but it's getting
orse. I'm beginning to feel like a widow. I'm tired of sleeping
the couch waiting for him to get home."

"You're there for food and sex, huh?"

"I wish. He's too tired for sex. It's not a priority anymore.
nd this is a man who could never get enough. I mean, we
most killed each other in law school. Now, once a week if
n lucky. He comes home, eats if he has the energy and goes
bed. If I'm really lucky, he might talk to me for a few mines before he passes out. I'm starved for adult conversation,
ay. I spend seven hours a day with eight-year-olds, and I
ave words with more than three syllables. I try to explain
is to him, and he's snoring. Did you go through this with
amar?"

"Sort of. He worked seventy hours a week for the first year.
think they all do. It's kind of like initiation into the frater-
ty. A male ritual in which you have to prove your manliness.
ut most of them run out of gas after a year, and cut back to
xty or sixty-five hours. They still work hard, but not the
mikaze routine of the rookie year."

"Does Lamar work every Saturday?"

"Most Saturdays, for a few hours. Never on Sunday. I've
t my foot down. Of course, if there's a big deadline or it's
x season, then they all work around the clock. I think Mitch
s them puzzled."

"He's not slowing down any. In fact, he's possessed. Occa-
onally he won't come home until dawn. Then it's just a quick
ower, and back to the office."

"Lamar says he's already a legend around the office."

Abby sipped her wine and looked over the rail at the bar.
That's great. I'm married to a legend."

"Have you thought about children?"

"It requires sex, remember?"

"Come on, Abby, it can't be that bad."

"I'm not ready for children. I can't handle being a single
rent. I love my husband, but at this point in his life, he

155

would probably have a terribly important meeting and lea
me alone in the labor room. Eight centimeters dilated. I
thinks of nothing but that damned law firm."

Kay reached across the table and gently took Abby's han
"It'll be okay," she said with a firm smile and a wise look. "Tl
first year is the hardest. It gets better, I promise."

Abby smiled. "I'm sorry."

The waiter arrived with their food, and they ordered mo
wine. The scampi simmered in the butter-and-garlic sauce ar
produced a delicious aroma. The cold quiche was all alone or
bed of lettuce with a sickly tomato wedge.

Kay picked a glob of broccoli and chewed on it. "You kno
Abby, the firm encourages children."

"I don't care. Right now I don't like the firm. I'm competi
with the firm, and I'm losing badly. So I couldn't care less wh
they want. They will not plan my family for me. I don't u
derstand why they are so interested in things which are no
of their business. That place is eerie, Kay. I can't put my fing
on it, but those people make my skin crawl."

"They want happy lawyers with stable families."

"And I want my husband back. They're in the process
taking him away, so the family is not so stable. If they'd get
his back, perhaps we could be normal like everyone else ar
have a yard full of children. But not now."

The wine arrived, and the scampi cooled. She ate it slow
and drank her wine. Kay searched for less sensitive areas.

"Lamar said Mitch went to the Caymans last month."

"Yes. He and Avery were there for three days. Strictly bu
ness, or so he says. Have you been there?"

"Every year. It's a beautiful place with gorgeous beach
and warm water. We go in June of each year, when school
out. The firm owns two huge condos right on the beach."

"Mitch wants to vacation there in March, during my spri
break."

"You need to. Before we had kids, we did nothing but lie
the beach, drink rum and have sex. That's one reason the fir
furnishes the condos and, if you're lucky, the airplane. The
work hard, but they appreciate the need for leisure."

"Don't mention the firm to me, Kay. I don't want to he

ut what they like or dislike, or what they do or don't do, or at they encourage or discourage."

It'll get better, Abby. I promise. You must understand that ir husband and my husband are both very good lawyers, they could not earn this kind of money anywhere else. d you and I would be driving new Buicks instead of new geots and Mercedes-Benzes."

bby cut a shrimp in half and rolled it through the butter and lic. She stabbed a portion with a fork, then pushed her plate ay. The wineglass was empty. "I know, Kay, I know. But re is a hell of a lot more to life than a big yard and a Peut. No one around here seems to be aware of that. I swear, I nk we were happier living in a two-room student apartment Cambridge."

You've only been here a few months. Mitch will slow down ntually, and you'll get into your routine. Before long there l be little McDeeres running around the backyard, and bee you know it, Mitch will be a partner. Believe me, Abby, ngs will get much better. You're going through a period 've all been through, and we made it."

Thanks, Kay, I certainly hope you're right."

e park was a small one, two or three acres on a bluff above river. A row of cannons and two bronze statues memorial- d those brave Confederates who had fought to save the river the city. Under the monument to a general and his horse a o tucked himself away. His cardboard box and ragged quilt vided little shelter from the bitter cold and the tiny pellets frozen rain. Fifty yards below, the evening traffic rushed ng Riverside Drive. It was dark.

Mitch walked to the row of cannons and stood gazing at the er and the bridges leading to Arkansas. He zipped his rain- t and flipped the collar around his ears. He looked at his tch. He waited.

The Bendini Building was almost visible six blocks away. had parked in a garage in midtown and taken a taxi back to river. He was sure he had not been followed. He waited.

The icy wind blowing up from the river reddened his face reminded him of the winters in Kentucky after his parents re gone. Cold, bitter winters. Lonely, desolate winters. He

had worn someone else's coats, passed down from a cousin &
friend, and they had never been heavy enough. Secondh.
clothes. He dismissed those thoughts.

The frozen rain turned to sleet and the tiny pieces of
stuck in his hair and bounced on the sidewalk around him.
looked at his watch.

There were footsteps and a figure in a hurry walking tow
the cannons. Whoever it was stopped, then approached slow

"Mitch?" It was Eddie Lomax, dressed in jeans and a f
length rabbit coat. With his thick mustache and white cowl
hat he looked like an ad for a cigarette. The Marlboro Ma

"Yeah, it's me."

Lomax walked closer, to the other side of the cannon. T
stood like Confederate sentries watching the river.

"Have you been followed?" Mitch asked.

"No, I don't think so. You?"

"No."

Mitch stared at the traffic on Riverside Drive, and beyo
to the river. Lomax thrust his hands deep into his pock
"You talked to Ray, lately?" Lomax asked.

"No." The answer was short, as if to say, "I'm not stand
here in the sleet to chitchat."

"What'd you find?" Mitch asked, without looking.

Lomax lit a cigarette, and now he *was* the Marlboro M
"On the three lawyers, I found a little info. Alice Knauss w
killed in a car wreck in 1977. Police report said she was hit b
drunk driver, but oddly enough, no such driver was e
found. The wreck happened around midnight on a Wedr
day. She had worked late down at the office and was driv
home. She lived out east, in Sycamore View, and about a m
from her condo she gets hit head-on by a one-ton pickup. H
pened on New London Road. She was driving a fancy li
Fiat and it was blown to pieces. No witnesses. When the c
got there, the truck was empty. No sign of a driver. They
the plates and found that the truck had been stolen in St. Lo
three days earlier. No fingerprints or nothing."

"They dusted for prints?"

"Yeah. I know the investigator who handled it. They w
suspicious but had zero to go on. There was a broken bottle

158

iskey on the floorboard, so they blamed it on a drunk driver
d closed the file."

"Autopsy?"

"No. It was pretty obvious how she died."

"Sounds suspicious."

"Very much so. All three of them are suspicious. Robert
mm was the deer hunter in Arkansas. He and some friends
d a deer camp in Izard County in the Ozarks. They went
er two or three times a year during the season. After a
rning in the woods, everyone returned to the cabin but
mm. They searched for two weeks and found him in a ra-
.e, partially covered with leaves. He had been shot once
ough the head, and that's about all they know. They ruled
: suicide, but there was simply no evidence to begin an in-
tigation."

"So he was murdered?"

"Apparently so. Autopsy showed an entry at the base of the
all and an exit wound that removed most of his face. Suicide
uld have been impossible."

"It could have been an accident."

"Possibly. He could have caught a bullet intended for a deer,
: it's unlikely. He was found a good distance from the camp,
an area seldom used by hunters. His friends said they nei-
r heard nor saw other hunters the morning he disappeared.
alked to the sheriff, who is now the ex-sheriff, and he's con-
ced it was murder. He claims there was evidence that the
ly had been covered intentionally."

"Is that all?"

"Yeah, on Lamm."

"What about Mickel?"

"Pretty sad. He committed suicide in 1984 at the age of
rty-four. Shot himself in the right temple with a Smith &
sson .357. He left a lengthy farewell letter in which he told
ex-wife he hoped she would forgive him and all that crap.
d goodbye to the kids and his mother. Real touching."

"Was it in his handwriting?"

"Not exactly. It was typed, which was not unusual, because
typed a good bit. He had an IBM Selectric in his office, and
letter came from it. He had a terrible handwriting."

"So what's suspicious?"

"The gun. He never bought a gun in his life. No one kno
where it came from. No registration, no serial number, no
ing. One of his friends in the firm allegedly said something
the effect that Mickel had told him he had bought a gun
protection. Evidently he was having some emotional pr
lems."

"What do you think?"

Lomax threw his cigarette butt in the frozen rain on
sidewalk. He cupped his hands over his mouth and blew
them. "I don't know. I can't believe a tax lawyer with
knowledge of guns could obtain one without registration
serial number. If a guy like that wanted a gun, he would s
ply go to a gun shop, fill out the papers and buy a nice, sh
new piece. This gun was at least ten years old and had b
sanitized by professionals."

"Did the cops investigate?"

"Not really. It was open and shut."

"Did he sign the letter?"

"Yeah, but I don't know who verified the signature. He a
his wife had been divorced for a year, and she had moved b
to Baltimore."

Mitch buttoned the top button of his overcoat and shook
ice from his collar. The sleet was heavier, and the sidewalk v
covered. Tiny icicles were beginning to form under the bar
of the cannon. The traffic slowed on Riverside as wheels beg
to slide and spin.

"So what do you think of our little firm?" Mitch asked as
stared at the river in the distance.

"It's a dangerous place to work. They've lost five lawyers
the past fifteen years. That's not a very good safety record

"Five?"

"If you include Hodge and Kozinski. I've got a source tell
me there are some unanswered questions."

"I didn't hire you to investigate those two."

"And I'm not charging you for it. I got curious, that's a

"How much do I owe you?"

"Six-twenty."

"I'll pay cash. No records, okay?"

"Suits me. I prefer cash."

Mitch turned from the river and gazed at the tall buildi

160

ree blocks from the park. He was cold now, but in no hurry
leave. Lomax watched him from the corner of his eye.

"You've got problems, don't you, pal?"

"Wouldn't you say so?" Mitch answered.

"I wouldn't work there. I mean, I don't know all that you
, and I suspect you know a lot you're not telling. But we're
nding here in the sleet because we don't want to be seen. We
n't talk on the phone. We can't meet in your office. Now you
n't want to meet in my office. You think you're being fol-
wed all the time. You tell me to be careful and watch my rear
cause they, whoever they are, may be following me. You've
t five lawyers in that firm who've died under very suspicious
cumstances, and you act like you may be next. Yeah, I'd say
u got problems. Big problems."

"What about Tarrance?"

"One of their best agents; transferred in here about two
ars ago."

"From where?"

"New York."

The wino rolled from under the bronze horse and fell to the
ewalk. He grunted, staggered to his feet, retrieved his card-
ard box and quilt and left in the direction of downtown.
max jerked around and watched anxiously. "It's just a
mp," Mitch said. They both relaxed.

"Who are we hiding from?" Lomax asked.

"I wish I knew."

Lomax studied his face carefully. "I think you know."

Mitch said nothing.

"Look, Mitch, you're not paying me to get involved. I realize
at. But my instincts tell me you're in trouble, and I think
u need a friend, someone to trust. I can help, if you need me.
on't know who the bad guys are, but I'm convinced they're
ry dangerous."

"Thanks," Mitch said softly without looking, as if it was
ne for Lomax to leave and let him stand there in the sleet for
while.

"I would jump in that river for Ray McDeere, and I can
rtainly help his little brother."

161

Mitch nodded slightly, but said nothing. Lomax lit anoth
cigarette and kicked the ice from his lizard-skins. "Just call
anytime. And be careful. They're out there, and they play f
keeps."

16

A T THE INTERSECTION of Madison and Cooper in midtown, the old two-story buildings had been renovated into singles bars and watering holes and gift ~~ps~~ and a handful of good restaurants. The intersection was ~~wn~~ as Overton Square, and it provided Memphis with its ~~~~ nightlife. A playhouse and a bookstore added a touch of ~~ure~~. Trees lined the narrow median on Madison. The ~~kends~~ were rowdy with college students and sailors from ~~Navy~~ base, but on weeknights the restaurants were full but ~~et~~ and uncrowded. Paulette's, a quaint French place in a ~~te~~ stucco building, was noted for its wine list and desserts ~~the~~ gentle voice of the man at the Steinway. With sudden ~~~ence~~ came a collection of credit cards, and the McDeeres ~~used~~ theirs in a quest for the best restaurants in town. ~~lette's~~ was the favorite, so far.

~~itch~~ sat in the corner of the bar, drinking coffee and ~~ching~~ the front door. He was early, and had planned it that ~~.~~ He had called her three hours earlier and asked if he ~~d~~ have a date for seven. She asked why, and he said he ~~ld~~ explain later. Since the Caymans he had known some- ~~was~~ following, watching, listening. For the past month he had spoken carefully on the phone, had caught himself wa[tch]ing the rearview mirror, had even chosen his words aro[und] the house. Someone was watching and listening, he was s[ure].

Abby rushed in from the cold and glanced around the pa[rty] for her husband. He met her in the front of the bar and pec[ked] her on the cheek. She removed her coat, and they followed [the] maitre d' to a small table in a row of small tables which w[ere] all full with people within earshot. Mitch glanced around [for] another table, but there were none. He thanked him and [sat] across from his wife.

"What's the occasion?" she asked suspiciously.

"Do I need a reason to have dinner with my wife?"

"Yes. It's seven o'clock on Monday night, and you're n[ot at] the office. This is indeed a special occasion."

A waiter squeezed between their table and the next, [and] asked if they wanted a drink. Two white wines, please. M[itch] glanced around the dining room again and caught a glimps[e of] a gentleman sitting alone five tables away. The face loo[ked] familiar. When Mitch looked again, the face slid behin[d a] menu.

"What's the matter, Mitch?"

He laid his hand on hers and frowned. "Abby, we g[otta] talk."

Her hand flinched slightly and she stopped smiling. "A[bout] what?"

He lowered his voice. "About something very serious."

She exhaled deeply and said, "Can we wait for the win[e? I] might need it."

Mitch looked again at the face behind the menu. "We c[an't] talk here."

"Then why are we here?"

"Look, Abby, you know where the rest rooms are? D[own] the hall over there, to your right?"

"Yes, I know."

"There's a rear entrance at the end of the hall. It goes o[ut to] the side street behind the restaurant. I want you to go to [the] rest room, then out the door. I'll be waiting next to the stre[et.]"

She said nothing. Her eyebrows lowered and the eyes [nar]rowed. Her head leaned slightly to the right.

Trust me, Abby. I can explain later. I'll meet you outside
we'll find another place to eat. I can't talk in here."

You're scaring me."

Please," he said firmly, squeezing her hand. "Everything is
. I'll bring your coat."

he stood with her purse and left the room. Mitch looked
r his shoulder at the man with the familiar face, who sud-
ly stood and welcomed an elderly lady to his table. He did
notice Abby's exit.

n the street behind Paulette's, Mitch draped the coat over
by's shoulders and pointed eastward. "I can explain," he
more than once. A hundred feet down the street, they
ked between two buildings and came to the front entrance
he Bombay Bicycle Club, a singles bar with good food and
blues. Mitch looked at the headwaiter, then surveyed the
dining rooms, then pointed to a table in the rear corner.
at one," he said.

itch sat with his back to the wall and his face toward the
ing room and the front door. The corner was dark. Candles
he table. They ordered more wine.

bby sat motionless, staring at him, watching every move
waiting.

Do you remember a guy named Rick Acklin from Western
tucky?"

No," she said without moving her lips.

He played baseball, lived in the dorm. I think you may
e met him once. A very nice guy, real clean-cut, good stu-
t. I think he was from Bowling Green. We weren't good
nds, but we knew each other."

he shook her head and waited.

Well, he finished a year before we did and went to law
ool at Wake Forest. Now he's with the FBI. And he's work-
here in Memphis." He watched her closely to see if "FBI"
ld have an impact. It did not. "And today I'm eating lunch
Obloe's hot-dog place on Main Street, when Rick walks
out of nowhere and says hello. Just like it was a real
cidence. We chat for a few minutes, and another agent,
by the name of Tarrance, walks up and has a seat. It's the
nd time Tarrance has chased me down since I passed the
"

"The second . . . ?"

"Yes. Since August."

"And these are . . . FBI agents?"

"Yes, with badges and everything. Tarrance is a vete
agent from New York. Been here about two years. Acklin
rookie they brought in three months ago."

"What do they want?"

The wine arrived and Mitch looked around the club. A b
was tuning up on a small stage in a far corner. The bar
crowded with well-dressed professional types chitting
chatting relentlessly. The waiter pointed to the unopened mer
"Later," Mitch said rudely.

"Abby, I don't know what they want. The first visit wa
August, right after my name was printed in the paper for p
ing the bar." He sipped his wine and detailed play by play
first Tarrance visit at Lansky's Deli on Union, the warni
about whom not to trust and where not to talk, the meet
with Locke and Lambert and the other partners. He explai
their version of why the FBI was so interested in the firm
said that he discussed it with Lamar and believed every w
Locke and Lambert had said.

Abby hung on every word, but waited to start asking.

"And now, today, while I'm minding my own business,
ing a foot-long with onions, this guy I went to college w
walks up and tells me that they, the FBI, know for a fact t
my phones are bugged, my home is wired and somebody do
at Bendini, Lambert & Locke knows when I sneeze and tal
crap. Think of it, Abby, Rick Acklin was transferred here af
I passed the bar exam. Nice coincidence, huh?"

"But what do they want?"

"They won't say. They can't tell me, yet. They want me
trust them, and all that routine. I don't know, Abby. I have
idea what they're after. But they've chosen me for some r
son."

"Did you tell Lamar about this visit?"

"No. I haven't told anyone. Except you. And I don't plan
tell anyone."

She gulped the wine. "Our phones are tapped?"

"According to the FBI. But how do they know?"

'They're not stupid, Mitch. If the FBI told me my phones
re tapped, I'd believe them. You don't?"

'I don't know whom to believe. Locke and Lambert were so
ooth and believable when they explained how the firm
its with the IRS and the FBI. I want to believe them, but so
ch of it doesn't add up. Look at it this way—if the firm had
ich client who was shady and worthy of FBI scrutiny, why
uld the FBI pick me, the rookie, the one who knows the
st, and begin following me? What do I know? I work on files
neone else hands me. I have no clients of my own. I do as
told. Why not go after one of the partners?"

'Maybe they want you to squeal on the clients."

'No way. I'm a lawyer and sworn to secrecy about the af-
-s of clients. Everything I know about a client is strictly
fidential. The feds know that. No one expects a lawyer to
k about his clients."

'Have you seen any illegal deals?"

He cracked his knuckles and gazed around the dining room.
smiled at her. The wine had settled and was taking effect.
n not supposed to answer that question, even from you,
by. But the answer is no. I've worked on files for twenty of
ery's clients and a few other ones here and there, and I've
n nothing suspicious. Maybe a couple of risky tax shelters,
nothing illegal. I've got a few questions about the bank
ounts I saw in the Caymans, but nothing serious." Cay-
ns! His stomach dropped as he thought of the girl on the
ch. He felt sick.

The waiter loitered nearby and stared at the menus. "More
e," Mitch said, pointing at the glasses.

Abby leaned forward, near the candles, and looked bewil-
ed. "Okay, who tapped our phones?"

Assuming they're tapped, I have no idea. At the first meet-
in August, Tarrance implied it was someone from the firm.
ean, that's the way I took it. He said not to trust anyone at
firm, and that everything I said was subject to being heard
recorded. I assumed he meant they were doing it."

And what did Mr. Locke say about that?"

Nothing. I didn't tell him. I kept a few things to myself."

Someone has tapped our phones and wired our house?"

And maybe our cars. Rick Acklin made a big deal of it

today. He kept telling me not to say anything I didn't w
recorded."

"Mitch, this is incredible. Why would a law firm do tha

He shook his head slowly and looked into the empty wi
glass. "I have no idea, babe. No idea."

The waiter set two new wineglasses on the table and st
with his hands behind him. "Will you be ordering?" he asl

"In a few minutes," Abby said.

"We'll call you when we're ready," Mitch added.

"Do you believe it, Mitch?"

"I think something's up. There's more to the story."

She slowly folded her hands on the table and stared at l
with a look of utter fear. He told the story of Hodge
Kozinski, starting with Tarrance at the deli, then to the C
mans and being followed and the meeting with Abanks.
told her everything Abanks had said. Then Eddie Lomax
the deaths of Alice Knauss, Robert Lamm and John Micko

"I've lost my appetite," she said when he finished.

"So have I. But I feel better now that you know."

"Why didn't you tell me sooner?"

"I hoped it would go away. I hoped Tarrance would le
me alone and find someone else to torment. But he's here
stay. That's why Rick Acklin was transferred to Memphis.
work on me. I have been selected by the FBI for a missic
know nothing about."

"I feel weak."

"We have to be careful, Abby. We must continue to live a
we suspect nothing."

"I don't believe this. I'm sitting here listening to you, b
don't believe what you're telling me. This is not real, Mi
You expect me to live in a house that's wired and the pho
are tapped and someone, somewhere is listening to everyth
we say."

"Do you have a better idea?"

"Yeah. Let's hire this Lomax guy to inspect our house."

"I've thought of that. But what if he finds something? Th
about it. What if we know for sure that the house is win
What then? What if he breaks a device that's been plan
They, whoever in hell they are, will know that we know.
too dangerous, for now anyway. Maybe later."

This is crazy, Mitch. I guess we're supposed to run out in backyard to have a conversation."

Of course not. We could use the front yard."

At this moment, I don't appreciate your sense of humor."

Sorry. Look, Abby, let's be normal and patient for a while. rance has convinced me he's serious and he's not going to get about me. I can't stop him. He finds me, remember. I k they follow me and wait in ambush. For the time being, important that we carry on as usual."

Usual? Come to think of it, there's not much conversation und our house these days. I sort of feel sorry for them if y're waiting to hear meaningful dialogue. I talk to Hearsay t."

17

THE SNOW CLEARED long before Christmas, leav[ing] the ground wet and making way for the traditi[onal] Southern holiday weather of gray skies and cold r[ain]. Memphis had seen two white Christmases in the past ni[ne] years, and the experts predicted no more in the century.

There was snow in Kentucky, but the roads were c[lear]. Abby called her parents early Christmas morning after [she] packed. She was coming, she said, but she would be al[one]. They were disappointed, they said, and suggested that per[haps] she should stay if it was causing trouble. She insisted. It w[as a] ten-hour drive. Traffic would be light, and she would be th[ere] by dark.

Mitch said very little. He spread the morning paper on [the] floor next to the tree and pretended to concentrate as [she] loaded her car. The dog hid nearby under a chair, as if wai[ting] for an explosion. Their gifts had been opened and arran[ged] neatly on the couch. Clothes and perfume and albums, and [for] her, a full-length fox coat. For the first time in the young m[ar]riage, there was money to spend at Christmas.

She draped the coat over her arm and walked to the pa[tio]. "I'm leaving now," she said softly, but firmly.

He stood slowly and looked at her.

"I wish you would come with me," she said.

"Maybe next year." It was a lie, and they knew it. But it sounded good. It was promising.

"Please be careful."

"Take care of my dog."

"We'll be fine."

He took her shoulders and kissed her on the cheek. He looked at her and smiled. She was beautiful, much more so than when they married. At twenty-four, she looked her age, but the years were becoming very generous.

They walked to the carport, and he helped her into the car. They kissed again, and she backed down the driveway.

Merry Christmas, he said to himself. Merry Christmas, he said to the dog.

After an hour of watching the walls, he threw two changes of clothes in the BMW, placed Hearsay in the front seat and left town. He drove south on Interstate 55, out of Memphis, into Mississippi. The road was deserted, but he kept an eye on the rearview mirror. The dog whimpered precisely every sixty minutes, and Mitch would stop on the shoulder—if possible, just over a hill. He would find a cluster of trees where he could hide and watch the traffic while Hearsay did his business. He noticed nothing. After five stops, he was sure he was not being followed. They evidently took off Christmas Day.

In six hours he was in Mobile, and two hours later he crossed the bay at Pensacola and headed for the Emerald Coast of Florida. Highway 98 ran through the coastal towns of Navarre, Fort Walton Beach, Destin and Sandestin. It encountered clusters of condominiums and motels, miles of shopping centers, then strings of run-down amusement parks and low rent T-shirt shops, most of which had been locked and netted since Labor Day. Then it went for miles with no construction, no sprawl, just an awesome view of the snowy-white beaches and brilliant emerald waters of the Gulf. East of Destin, the highway narrowed and left the coast, and for an hour he drove alone on the two-lane with nothing to look at but the woods and an occasional self-serve gas station or quick-stop convenience store.

At dusk, he passed a high rise, and a sign said Panama C
Beach was eight miles ahead. The highway found the co
again at a point where it forked and offered a choice betw
the bypass to the north and the scenic route straight ahead
what was called the Miracle Strip. He chose the scenic ro
next to the beach—the strip that ran for fifteen miles by
water and was lined on both sides with condos, cheap mo
trailer parks, vacation cottages, fast-food joints and T-s
shops. This was Panama City Beach.

Most of the ten zillion condos were empty, but there we
few cars parked about and he assumed that some families va
tioned on the beach for Christmas. A hot-weather Christm
At least they're together, he said to himself. The dog bar
and they stopped by a pier where men from Pennsylvania
Ohio and Canada fished and watched the dark waters.

They cruised the Miracle Strip by themselves. Hea
stood on the door and took in the sights, barking at the o
sional flashing neon of a cinder-block motel advertising
openness and cheap rates. Christmas on the Miracle S
closed everything but a handful of diehard coffee shops
motels.

He stopped for gas at an all-night Texaco with a clerk v
seemed uncommonly friendly.

"San Luis Street?" Mitch asked.

"Yes, yes," the clerk said with an accent and pointed to
west. "Second traffic light to the right. First left. That's
Luis."

The neighborhood was a disorganized suburb of anti
mobile homes. Mobile, yes, but it was apparent they had
moved in decades. The trailers were packed tightly toge
like rows of dominoes. The short, narrow driveways see
inches apart and were filled with old pickups and rusted l
furniture. The streets were crowded with parked cars, j
cars, abandoned cars. Motorcycles and bicycles leaned on
trailer hitches and lawn-mower handles protruded from
neath each home. A sign called the place a retirement villa
"San Pedro Estates—A Half Mile from the Emerald Coast
was more like a slum on wheels, or a project with a tr
hitch.

He found San Luis Street and suddenly felt nervous. It

172

ding and narrow with smaller trailers in worse shape than other "retirement homes." He drove slowly, anxiously ching street numbers and observing the multitude of out-tate license plates. The street was empty except for the ked and abandoned cars.

he home at 486 San Luis was one of the oldest and smallest. vas scarcely bigger than a camper. The original paint job ed to be silver, but the paint was cracked and peeling, and irk green layer of mold covered the top and inched down-d to a point just above the windows. The screens were sing. One window above the trailer hitch was badly ked and held together with gray electrical tape. A small ered porch surrounded the only entrance. The storm door open, and through the screen Mitch could see a small r television and the silhouette of a man walking by.

his was not what he wanted. By choice, he had never met mother's second husband, and now was not the time. He ve on, wishing he had not come.

le found on the Strip the familiar marquee of a Holiday . It was empty, but open. He hid the BMW away from the way, and registered under the name of Eddie Lomax of esboro, Kentucky. He paid cash for a single room with an n view.

Panama City Beach phone book listed three Waffle Huts he Strip. He lay across the motel bed and dialed the first ber. No luck. He dialed the second number, and again d for Ida Ainsworth. Just a minute, he was told. He hung It was 11 P.M. He had slept for two hours.

he taxi took twenty minutes to arrive at the Holiday Inn, the driver began by explaining that he had been home ying leftover turkey with his wife and kids and kinfolks n the dispatcher called, and how it was Christmas and he ed to be with his family all day and not worry about work one day of the year. Mitch threw a twenty over the seat asked him to be quiet.

Vhat's at the Waffle Hut, man?" the driver asked.

ust drive."

Vaffles, right?" He laughed and mumbled to himself. He sted the radio volume and found his favorite soul station.

173

He glanced in the mirror, looked out the windows, whistle
bit, then said, "What brings you down here on Christmas?

"Looking for someone."

"Who?"

"A woman."

"Ain't we all. Anyone in particular?"

"An old friend."

"She at the Waffle Hut?"

"I think so."

"You some kinda private eye or something?"

"No."

"Seems mighty suspicious to me."

"Why don't you just drive."

The Waffle Hut was a small, rectangular, boxlike build
with a dozen tables and a long counter facing the grill, wh
everything was cooked in the open. Large plate-glass wind
lined one side next to the tables so the customers could tak
the Strip and the condos in the distance while they enjo
their pecan waffles and bacon. The small parking lot was
most full, and Mitch directed the driver to an empty slot n
the building.

"Ain't you getting out?" the driver asked.

"No. Keep the meter running."

"Man, this is strange."

"You'll get paid."

"You got that right."

Mitch leaned forward and rested his arms on the front s
The meter clicked softly as he studied the customers ins
The driver shook his head, slumped in the seat, but watc
out of curiosity.

In the corner next to the cigarette machine a table of
tourists with long shirts, white legs and black socks drank
fee, and all talked at the same time while glancing at
menus. The leader, the one with an unbuttoned shirt, a he
gold chain draped upon his chest hair, thick gray sideb
and a Phillies baseball cap, looked repeatedly toward the g
in search of a waitress.

"You see her?" asked the driver.

Mitch said nothing, then leaned forward and frowned.
appeared from nowhere and stood at the table with her

174

order book. The leader said something funny, and the fat
ple laughed. She never smiled, just kept writing. She was
l and much thinner. Almost too thin. The black-and-white
form fit snugly and squeezed her tiny waist. Her gray hair
 pulled tightly and hidden under the Waffle Hut bonnet.
 was fifty-one, and from the distance she looked her age.
thing worse. She seemed sharp. When she finished scrib-
g she snatched the menus from their hands, said something
ite, almost smiled, then disappeared. She moved quickly
ong the tables, pouring coffee, handing ketchup bottles and
ing orders to the cook.

Mitch relaxed. The meter ticked slowly.

Is that her?" asked the driver.

Yes."

What now?"

I don't know."

Well, we found her, didn't we?"

Mitch followed her movements and said nothing. She
red coffee for a man sitting alone. He said something, and
 smiled. A wonderful, gracious smile. A smile he had seen a
usand times in the darkness staring at the ceiling. His
ther's smile.

 light mist began to fall and the intermittent wipers
ned the windshield every ten seconds. It was almost mid-
ht, Christmas Day.

he driver tapped the wheel nervously and fidgeted. He
k lower in the seat, then changed stations. "How long we
na sit here?"

Not long."

Man, this is weird."

You'll be paid."

Man, money ain't everything. It's Christmas. I got kids at
ne, kinfolks visiting, turkey and wine to finish off, and here
n sitting at the Waffle Hut so you can look at some old
nan through the window."

It's my mother."

Your what!"

You heard me."

Man, oh man. I get all kinds."

Just shut up, okay?"

175

"Okay. Ain't you gonna talk to her? I mean it's Christm and you found your momma. You gotta go see her, don't yo

"No. Not now."

Mitch sat back in the seat and looked at the dark be across the highway. "Let's go."

At daybreak, he dressed in jeans and a sweatshirt, no socks shoes, and took Hearsay for a walk on the beach. They wal east, toward the first glow of orange peeking above the h zon. The waves broke gently thirty yards out and rolled etly onto shore. The sand was cool and wet. The sky was c and full of sea gulls talking incessantly among themsel Hearsay ran boldly into the sea, then retreated furiously wl the next wave of white foam approached. For a house dog, endless stretch of sand and water demanded exploration. ran a hundred yards ahead of Mitch.

After two miles they approached a pier, a large conc structure running two hundred feet from the beach into ocean. Hearsay, fearless now, darted onto it and ran t bucket of bait next to two men standing motionless and s ing down at the water. Mitch walked behind them, to the of the pier, where a dozen fishermen talked occasionally each other and waited for their lines to jump. The dog rub himself on Mitch's leg and grew still. A brilliant return of sun was in progress, and for miles the water glistened turned from black to green.

Mitch leaned on the railing and shivered in the cool w His bare feet were frozen and gritty. For miles along the be in both directions, the hotels and condos sat quietly and wa for the day. There was no one on the beach. Another jutted into the water miles away.

The fishermen spoke with the sharp, precise words of t from the North. Mitch listened long enough to learn the were not biting. He studied the sea. Looking southeast, thought of the Caymans, and Abanks. And the girl for a ment, then she was gone. He would return to the island March, for a vacation with his wife. Damn the girl. Surel would not see her. He would dive with Abanks and cultiva friendship. They would drink Heineken and Red Stripe at bar and talk of Hodge and Kozinski. He would follow who

176

following him. Now that Abby was an accomplice, she
uld assist him.

e man waited in the dark beside the Lincoln Town Car. He
vously checked his watch and glanced at the dimly lit side-
k that disappeared in front of the building. On the second
r a light was turned off. A minute later, the private eye
ked from the building toward the car. The man walked up
im.

Are you Eddie Lomax?" he asked anxiously.

omax slowed, then stopped. They were face to face. "Yeah.
o are you?"

he man kept his hands in his pockets. It was cold and
up, and he was shaking. "Al Kilbury. I need some help, Mr.
nax. Real bad. I'll pay you right now in cash, whatever you
at. Just help me."

It's late, pal."

Please. I've got the money. Name the price. You gotta help,
 Lomax." He pulled a roll of cash from his left pants
ket and stood ready to count.

omax looked at the money, then glanced over his shoulder.
hat's the problem?"

My wife. In an hour she's supposed to meet a man at a
el in South Memphis. I've got the room number and all. I
need you to go with me and take pictures of them coming
going."

How do you know this?"

Phone taps. She works with the man, and I've been suspi-
s. I'm a wealthy man, Mr. Lomax, and it's imperative I
 the divorce. I'll pay you a thousand in cash now." He
kly peeled off ten bills and offered them.

omax took the money. "Okay. Let me get my camera."

Please hurry. Everything's in cash, okay? No records."

Suits me," said Lomax as he walked toward the building.

wenty minutes later, the Lincoln rolled slowly through
 crowded parking lot of a Days Inn. Kilbury pointed to a
nd-floor room on the back side of the motel, then to a
king space next to a brown Chevy van. Lomax backed care-
y alongside the van and parked his Town Car. Kilbury
in pointed to the room, again checked his watch and again

told Lomax how much he appreciated his services. Lo[max]
thought of the money. A thousand bucks for two hours' w[ork].
Not bad. He unpacked a camera, loaded the film and gau[ged]
the light. Kilbury watched nervously, his eyes darting f[rom]
the camera to the room across the parking lot. He looked h[urt].
He talked of his wife and their wonderful years together,
why, oh why was she doing this?

Lomax listened and watched the rows of parked car[s in]
front of him. He held his camera.

He did not notice the door of the brown van. It quietly
slowly slid open, just three feet behind him. A man in a b[lack]
turtleneck wearing black gloves crouched low in the van [and]
waited. When the parking lot was still, he jumped from [the]
van, yanked open the left rear door of the Lincoln and f[ired]
three times into the back of Eddie's head. The shots, mu[ffled]
with a silencer, could not be heard outside the car.

Eddie slumped against the wheel, already dead. Kilb[ury]
bolted from the Lincoln, ran to the van and sped away w[ith]
the assassin.

18

AFTER THREE DAYS of unbillable time, of no production, of exile from their sanctuaries, of turkey and ham and cranberry sauce and new toys that came unasbled, the rested and rejuvenated lawyers of Bendini, Lam- & Locke returned to the fortress on Front Street with a geance. The parking lot was full by seven-thirty. They sat d and comfortable behind their heavy desks, drank coffee he gallons, meditated over mail and correspondence and uments and mumbled incoherently and furiously into their taphones. They barked orders at secretaries and clerks and legals, and at each other. There were a few "How was r Christmas?" greetings in the halls and around the coffee-, but small talk was cheap and unbillable. The sounds of writers, intercoms and secretaries all harmonized into one ious hum as the mint recovered from the nuisance of istmas. Oliver Lambert walked the halls, smiling with sat-tion and listening, just listening to the sounds of wealth g made by the hour.

t noon, Lamar walked into the office and leaned across the . Mitch was deep into an oil and gas deal in Indonesia. unch?" Lamar asked.

"No, thanks. I'm behind."

"Aren't we all. I thought we could run down to the F Street Deli for a bowl of chili."

"I'll pass. Thanks."

Lamar glanced over his shoulder at the door and le closer as if he had extraordinary news to share. "You k what today is, don't you?"

Mitch glanced at his watch. "The twenty-eighth."

"Right. And do you know what happens on the twe eighth of December of every year?"

"You have a bowel movement."

"Yes. And what else?"

"Okay. I give up. What happens?"

"At this very moment, in the dining room on the fifth fl all the partners are gathered for a lunch of roast duck French wine."

"Wine, for lunch?"

"Yes. It's a very special occasion."

"Okay?"

"After they eat for an hour, Roosevelt and Jessie Fra will leave and Lambert will lock the door. Then it's all partners, you see. Only the partners. And Lambert will l out a financial summary for the year. It's got all the part listed, and beside each name is a number that represents t total billing for the year. Then on the next page is a summ of the net profits after expenses. Then, based on product they divide the pie!"

Mitch hung on every word. "And?"

"And, last year the average piece of pie was three hun and thirty thousand. And, of course, it's expected to be higher this year. Goes up every year."

"Three hundred and thirty thousand," Mitch repe slowly.

"Yep. And that's just the average. Locke will get close million. Victor Milligan will run a close second."

"And what about us?"

"We get a piece too. A very small piece. Last year it around nine thousand, on the average. Depends on how you've been here and production."

"Can we go watch?"

"They wouldn't sell a ticket to the President. It's supposed
be a secret meeting, but we all know about it. Word will
gin drifting down late this afternoon."

"When do they vote on who to make the next partner?"

"Normally, it would be done today. But, according to ru-
or, there may not be a new partner this year because of
arty and Joe. I think Marty was next in line, then Joe. Now,
ey might wait a year or two."

"So who's next in line?"

Lamar stood straight and smiled proudly. "One year from
day, my friend, I will become a partner in Bendini, Lambert
Locke. I'm next in line, so don't get in my way this year."

"I heard it was Massengill—a Harvard man, I might add."

"Massengill doesn't have a prayer. I intend to bill a hundred
d forty hours a week for the next fifty-two weeks, and those
rds will beg me to become a partner. I'll go to the fourth
or, and Massengill will go to the basement with the parale-
ls."

"I'm putting my money on Massengill."

"He's a wimp. I'll run him into the ground. Let's go eat a
wl of chili, and I'll reveal my strategy."

"Thanks, but I need to work."

Lamar strutted from the office and passed Nina, who was
rrying a stack of papers. She laid them on a cluttered corner
the desk. "I'm going to lunch. Need anything?"

"No. Thanks. Yes, a Diet Coke."

The halls quietened during lunch as the secretaries escaped
e building and walked toward downtown to a dozen small
fés and delicatessens nearby. With half the lawyers on the
th floor counting their money, the gentle roar of commerce
ok an intermission.

Mitch found an apple on Nina's desk and rubbed it clean.
e opened a manual on IRS regulations, laid it on the copier
hind her desk and touched the green PRINT button. A red
rning lit up and flashed the message: INSERT FILE NUMBER.
e backed away and looked at the copier. Yes, it was a new
e. Next to the PRINT button was another that read BYPASS. He
ick his thumb on it. A shrill siren erupted from within the
chine, and the entire panel of buttons turned bright red. He

looked around helplessly, saw no one and frantically grabb
the instruction manual.

"What's going on here?" someone demanded over the wa
ing of the copier.

"I don't know!" Mitch yelled, waving the manual.

Lela Pointer, a secretary too old to walk from the buildi
for lunch, reached behind the machine and flipped a swit
The siren died.

"What the hell?" Mitch said, panting.

"Didn't they tell you?" she demanded, grabbing the manu
and placing it back in its place. She drilled a hole in him wi
her tiny fierce eyes, as if she had caught him in her purse.

"Obviously not. What's the deal?"

"We have a new copying system," she lectured downwa
through her nose. "It was installed the day after Christm
You must code in the file number before the machine w
copy. Your secretary was supposed to tell you."

"You mean this thing will not copy unless I punch in a t
digit number?"

"That's correct."

"What about copies in general, with no particular file?"

"Can't be done. Mr. Lambert says we lose too much mon
on unbilled copies. So, from now on, every copy is automa
cally billed to a file. You punch in the number first. The m
chine records the number of copies and sends it to the ma
terminal, where it goes on the client's billing account."

"What about personal copies?"

Lela shook her head in total frustration. "I can't believe yo
secretary didn't tell you all this."

"Well, she didn't, so why don't you help me out."

"You have a four-digit access number for yourself. At t
end of each month you'll be billed for your personal copies

Mitch stared at the machine and shook his head. "Why t
damned alarm system?"

"Mr. Lambert says that after thirty days they will cut off t
alarms. Right now, they're needed for people like you. H
very serious about this. Says we've been losing thousands
unbilled copies."

"Right. And I suppose every copier in the building has be
replaced."

She smiled with satisfaction. "Yes, all seventeen."

"Thanks." Mitch returned to his office in search of a file
mber.

three that afternoon, the celebration on the fifth floor came
a joyous conclusion, and the partners, now much wealthier
d slightly drunker, filed out of the dining room and de-
nded to their offices below. Avery, Oliver Lambert and Na-
n Locke walked the short hallway to the security wall and
shed the button. DeVasher was waiting.

He waved at the chairs in his office and told them to sit
wn: Lambert passed around hand wrapped Hondurans, and
eryone lit up.

"Well, I see we're all in a festive mood," DeVasher said with
neer. "How much was it? Three hundred and ninety thou-
d, average?"

"That's correct, DeVasher," Lambert said. "It was a very
od year." He puffed slowly and blew smoke rings at the
ling.

"Did we all have a wonderful Christmas?" DeVasher asked.

"What's on your mind?" Locke demanded.

"Merry Christmas to you too, Nat. Just a few things. I met
th Lazarov two days ago in New Orleans. He does not cele-
ate the birth of Christ, you know. I brought him up to date
the situation down here, with emphasis on McDeere and
e FBI. I assured him there had been no further contact since
initial meeting. He did not quite believe this and said we
uld check with their sources within the Bureau. I don't
ow what that means, but who am I to ask questions? He
tructed me to trail McDeere twenty-four hours a day for
next six months. I told him we were already doing so, sort
He does not want another Hodge-Kozinski situation. He's
y distressed about that. McDeere is not to leave the city on
n business unless at least two of us go with him."

"He's going to Washington in two weeks," Avery said.

"What for?"

"American Tax Institute. It's a four-day seminar that we
quire of all new associates. It's been promised to him, and
ll be very suspicious if it's canceled."

"We made his reservations in September," Ollie added.

"I'll see if I can clear it with Lazarov," DeVasher said. "G
me the dates, flights and hotel reservations. He won't l
this."

"What happened Christmas?" Locke asked.

"Not much. His wife went to her home in Kentucky. Sh
still there. McDeere took the dog and drove to Panama C
Beach, Florida. We think he went to see his mom, but we
not sure. Spent one night at a Holiday Inn on the beach. J
he and the dog. Pretty boring. Then he drove to Birmingha
stayed in another Holiday Inn, then early yesterday morni
he drove to Brushy Mountain to visit his brother. Harml
trip."

"What's he said to his wife?" asked Avery.

"Nothing, as far as we can tell. It's hard to hear everythin

"Who else are you watching?" asked Avery.

"We're listening to all of them, sort of sporadically. We h
no real suspects, other than McDeere, and that's just beca
of Tarrance. Right now all's quiet."

"He's got to go to Washington, DeVasher," Avery insist

"Okay, okay. I'll get it cleared with Lazarov. He'll make
send five men for surveillance. What an idiot."

Ernie's Airport Lounge was indeed near the airport. Mi
found it after three attempts and parked between two fo
wheel-drive swampmobiles with real mud caked on the ti
and headlights. The parking lot was full of such vehicles.
looked around and instinctively removed his tie. It was alm
eleven. The lounge was deep and long and dark with color
beer signs flashing in the painted windows.

He looked at the note again, just to be sure. "Dear M
McDeere: Please meet me at Ernie's Lounge on Winches
tonight—late. It's about Eddie Lomax. Very importa
Tammy Hemphill, his secretary."

The note had been tacked on the door to the kitchen wl
he arrived home. He remembered her from the one visit
Eddie's office, back in November. He remembered the ti
leather skirt, huge breasts, bleached hair, red sticky lips
smoke billowing from her nose. And he remembered the st
about her husband, Elvis.

The door opened without incident, and he slid inside. A r

pool tables covered the left half of the room. Through the
rkness and black smoke, he could make out a small dance
or in the rear. To the right was a long saloon-type bar
owded with cowboys and cowgirls, all drinking Bud
ngnecks. No one seemed to notice him. He walked quickly to
e end of the bar and slid onto the stool. "Bud longneck," he
d the bartender.

Tammy arrived before the beer. She was sitting and waiting
a crowded bench by the pool tables. She wore tight washed
ns, faded denim shirt and kinky red high-heels. The hair
d just received a fresh bleaching.

"Thanks for coming," she said into his face. "I've been wait-
g for four hours. I knew of no other way to find you."

Mitch nodded and smiled as if to say, "It's okay. You did the
ht thing."

"What's up?" he said.

She looked around. "We need to talk, but not here."

"Where do you suggest?"

"Could we maybe drive around?"

"Sure, but not in my car. It, uh, it may not be a good idea."

"I've got a car. It's old, but it'll do."

Mitch paid for the beer and followed her to the door. A
wpoke sitting near the door said, "Getta loada this. Guy
ows up with a suit and picks her up in thirty seconds."
tch smiled at him and hurried out the door. Dwarfed in a
w of massive mud-eating machinery was a well-worn Volks-
gen Rabbit. She unlocked it, and Mitch doubled over and
eezed into the cluttered seat. She pumped the accelerator
e times and turned the key. Mitch held his breath until it
rted.

"Where would you like to go?" she asked.

Where we can't be seen, Mitch thought. "You're driving."

"You're married, aren't you?" she asked.

"Yes. You?"

"Yes, and my husband would not understand this situation
ht here. That's why I chose that dump back there. We never
there."

She said this as if she and her husband were discriminating
tics of dark redneck dives.

"I don't think my wife would understand either. She's out [of?] town, though."

Tammy drove in the direction of the airport. "I've got [an?] idea," she said. She clutched the steering wheel tightly a[nd?] spoke nervously.

"What's on your mind?" Mitch asked.

"Well, you heard about Eddie."

"Yes."

"When did you last see him?"

"We met ten days or so before Christmas. It was sort o[f?] secret meeting."

"That's what I thought. He kept no records of the work [he?] was doing for you. Said you wanted it that way. He didn't t[ell?] me much. But me and Eddie, well, we, uh, we were . [..?] close."

Mitch could think of no response.

"I mean, we were very close. Know what I mean?"

Mitch grunted and sipped the longneck.

"And he told me things I guess he wasn't supposed to t[ell?] me. Said you had a real strange case, that some lawyers in yo[ur?] firm had died under suspicious circumstances. And that y[ou?] always thought somebody was following and listening. Tha[t's?] pretty weird for a law firm."

So much for the confidentiality, thought Mitch. "That it i[s?]"

She turned, made the exit to the airport and headed for [the?] acres of parked cars.

"And after he finished his work for you, he told me on[ce,?] just once, in bed, that he thought he was being followed. T[his?] was three days before Christmas. And I asked him who it w[as?] He said he didn't know, but mentioned your case and som[e?] thing about it was probably related to the same people w[ho?] were following you. He didn't say much."

She parked in the short-term section near the terminal.

"Who else would follow him?" Mitch asked.

"No one. He was a good investigator who left no trail[. I?] mean, he was an ex-cop and an ex-con. He was very stre[et?] smart. He got paid to follow people and collect dirt. No o[ne?] followed him. Never."

"So who killed him?"

"Whoever was following him. The paper made like he [was?]

ight snooping on some rich guy and was wasted. It's not
e."

Suddenly, from out of nowhere, she produced a filter-tip
00 and shot a flame at the end. Mitch rolled down the win-
w.

"Mind if I smoke?" she asked.

"No, just blow it that way," he said, pointing to her win-
w.

"Anyway, I'm scared. Eddie was convinced the people fol-
ving you are extremely dangerous and extremely smart.
ry sophisticated, was what he said. And if they killed him,
at about me? Maybe they think I know something. I haven't
en to the office since the day he was killed. Don't plan to go
ck."

"I wouldn't if I were you."

"I'm not stupid. I worked for him for two years and learned
ot. There's a lot of nuts out there. We saw all kinds."

"How did they shoot him?"

"He's got a friend in Homicide. Guy told me confidentially
at Eddie got hit three times in the back of the head, point
nk range, with a .22 pistol. And they don't have a clue. He
d me it was a very clean, professional job."

Mitch finished the longneck and laid the bottle on the floor-
ard with a half dozen empty beer cans. A very clean, profes-
nal job.

"It doesn't make sense," she repeated. "I mean, how could
yone sneak up behind Eddie, somehow get in the back seat
d shoot him three times in the back of the head? And he
sn't even supposed to be there."

"Maybe he fell asleep and they ambushed him."

"No. He took all kinds of speed when he worked late at
ght. Stayed wired."

"Are there any records at the office?"

"You mean about you?"

"Yeah, about me."

"I doubt it. I never saw nothing in writing. He said you
nted it that way."

"That's right," Mitch said with relief.

They watched a 727 lift off to the north. The parking lot
rated.

"I'm really scared, Mitch. Can I call you Mitch?"

"Sure. Why not?"

"I think he got killed because of the work he did for y
That's all it could be. And if they'd kill him because he kn
something, they probably assume I know it too. What do y
think?"

"I wouldn't take any chances."

"I might disappear for a while. My husband does a li
nightclub work, and we can get mobile if we have to. I have
told him all this, but I guess I have to. What do you think

"Where would you go?"

"Little Rock, St. Louis, Nashville. He's laid off, so we
move around, I guess." Her words trailed off. She lit anoth
one.

A very clean, professional job, Mitch repeated to hims
He glanced at her and noticed a small tear on her cheek. S
was not ugly, but the years in lounges and nightclubs w
taking their toll. Her features were strong, and minus
bleach and heavy makeup she would be somewhat attract
for her age. About forty, he guessed.

She took a mighty drag and sent a cloud of smoke surg
from the Rabbit. "I guess we're in the same boat, aren't we
mean, they're after both of us. They've killed all those lawy
now Eddie, and I guess we're next."

Don't hold back, baby, just blurt it out. "Look, let's do t
We need to keep in touch. You can't call me on the phone, a
we can't be seen together. My wife knows everything, and
tell her about this little meeting. Don't worry about her. O
a week, write me a note and tell me where you are. Wh
your mother's name?"

"Doris."

"Good. That's your code name. Sign the name Doris on a
thing you send me."

"Do they read your mail too?"

"Probably so, Doris, probably so."

19

AT FIVE P.M., Mitch turned off the light in his office, grabbed both briefcases and stopped at Nina's desk. Her phone was glued to one shoulder while she typed the IBM. She saw him and reached in a drawer for an ᵥelope. "This is your confirmation at the Capital Hilton," ₑ said into the receiver.

"The dictation is on my desk," he said. "See you Monday."
ₑ took the stairs to the fourth floor, to Avery's office in the ᵣner, where a small riot was in progress. One secretary ffed files into a massive briefcase. Another one spoke ᵣply to Avery, who was yelling on the phone to someone ₑ. A paralegal shot orders to the first secretary.

Avery slammed the phone down. "Are you ready!" he deᵢnded at Mitch.

"Waiting for you," Mitch replied.

"I can't find the Greenmark file," a secretary snarled at the ᵣalegal.

"It was with the Rocconi file," said the paralegal.

"I don't need the Greenmark file!" Avery shouted. "How ᵢny times do I have to tell you? Are you deaf?"

189

The secretary glared at Avery. "No, I can hear very w‍
And I distinctly heard you say, 'Pack the Greenmark file.'

"The limousine is waiting," said the other secretary.

"I don't need the damned Greenmark file!" Avery shout‍

"How about Rocconi?" asked the paralegal.

"Yes! Yes! For the tenth time. I need the Rocconi file!"

"The airplane is waiting too," said the other secretary.

One briefcase was slammed shut and locked. Avery d‍
through a pile of documents on his desk. "Where's the Fen‍
file? Where are any of my files? Why can't I ever find a fil‍

"Here's Fender," said the first secretary as she stuffed it i‍
another briefcase.

Avery stared at a piece of notepaper. "All right. Do I h‍
Fender, Rocconi, Cambridge Partners, Greene Group, Son‍
Capps to Otaki, Burton Brothers, Galveston Freight and M‍
Quade?"

"Yes, yes, yes," said the first secretary.

"That's all of them," said the paralegal.

"I don't believe it," Avery said as he grabbed his jack‍
"Let's go." He strode through the door with the secretar‍
paralegal and Mitch in pursuit. Mitch carried two briefca‍
the paralegal had two, and a secretary had one. The other s‍
retary scribbled notes as Avery barked the orders and dema‍
he wanted carried out while he was away. The entour‍
crowded onto the small elevator for the ride to the first flo‍
Outside, the chauffeur sprang into action, opening doors a‍
loading it all in the trunk.

Mitch and Avery fell into the back seat.

"Relax, Avery," Mitch said. "You're going to the Caym‍
for three days. Just relax."

"Right, right. I'm taking with me enough work for a mor‍
I've got clients screaming for my hide, threatening suits‍
legal malpractice. I'm two months behind, and now you‍
leaving for four days of boredom at a tax seminar in Washi‍
ton. You're timing is great, McDeere. Just great."

Avery opened a cabinet and mixed a drink. Mitch declin‍
The limo moved around Riverside Drive in the rush-hour tr‍
fic. After three swallows of gin, the partner breathed deep‍

"Continuing education. What a joke," Avery said.

"You did it when you were a rookie. And if I'm not m‍

ken, you spent a week not long ago at that international tax
minar in Honolulu. Or did you forget?"

'It was work. All work. Are you taking your files with
u?"

'Of course, Avery. I'm expected to attend the tax seminar
ght hours a day, learn the latest tax revisions Congress has
stowed upon us and in my spare time bill five hours a day."

'Six, if you can. We're behind, Mitch."

'We're always behind, Avery. Fix another drink. You need
unwind."

'I plan to unwind at Rumheads."

Mitch thought of the bar with its Red Stripe, dominoes,
rts and, yes, string bikinis. And the girl.

'Is this your first flight on the Lear?" Avery asked, more
axed now.

'Yes. I've been here seven months, and I'm just now seeing
e plane. If I had known this last March, I'd have gone to
rk with a Wall Street firm."

'You're not Wall Street material. You know what those guys
? They've got three hundred lawyers in a firm, right? And
h year they hire thirty new associates, maybe more. Every-
dy wants a job because it's Wall Street, right? And after
ut a month they get all thirty of them together in one big
m and inform them they're expected to work ninety hours
veek for five years, and at the end of five years, half of them
ll be gone. The turnover is incredible. They try to kill the
okies, bill them out at a hundred, hundred-fifty an hour,
ke a bundle off them, then run them off. That's Wall Street.
d the little boys never get to see the firm plane. Or the firm
no. You are truly lucky, Mitch. You should thank God every
y that we chose to accept you here at good old Bendini,
mbert & Locke."

"Ninety hours sounds like fun. I could use the rest."

"It'll pay off. Did you hear what my bonus was last year?"

"No."

"Four-eight-five. Not bad, huh? And that's just the bonus."

"I got six thousand," Mitch said.

"Stick with me and you'll be in the big leagues soon
ough."

"Yeah, but first I gotta get my continuing legal education."

Ten minutes later the limo turned into a drive that led to row of hangars. Memphis Aero, the sign said. A sleek silv Lear 55 taxied slowly toward the terminal. "That's it," Ave said.

The briefcases and luggage were loaded quickly onto t plane, and within minutes they were cleared for takeoff. Mit fastened his seat belt and admired the leather-and-brass cab It was lavish and luxurious, and he had expected nothing le Avery mixed another drink and buckled himself in.

An hour and fifteen minutes later, the Lear began its desce into Baltimore-Washington International Airport. After it ta ied to a stop, Avery and Mitch descended to the tarmac a opened the baggage door. Avery pointed to a man in a unifor standing near a gate. "That's your chauffeur. The limo is front. Just follow him. You're about forty minutes from t Capital Hilton."

"Another limo?" Mitch asked.

"Yeah. They wouldn't do this for you on Wall Street."

They shook hands, and Avery climbed back on the pla The refueling took thirty minutes, and when the Lear took and turned south, he was asleep again.

Three hours later, it landed in Georgetown, Grand Cayma It taxied past the terminal to a very small hangar where would spend the night. A security guard waited on Avery a his luggage and escorted him to the terminal and through c toms. The pilot and copilot ran through the post flight ritu They too were escorted through the terminal.

After midnight, the lights in the hangar were extinguish and the half dozen planes sat in the darkness. A side do opened, and three men, one of them Avery, entered a walked quickly to the Lear 55. Avery opened the baggage co partment, and the three hurriedly unloaded twenty-five hea cardboard boxes. In the muggy tropical heat, the hangar w like an oven. They sweated profusely but said nothing until boxes were out of the plane.

"There should be twenty-five. Count them," Avery said to muscle-bound native with a tank top and a pistol on his h The other man held a clipboard and watched intently as if

a receiving clerk in a warehouse. The native counted
kly, sweat dripping onto the boxes.

Yes. Twenty-five."

How much?" asked the man with the clipboard.

Six and a half million."

All cash?"

All cash. U.S. dollars. Hundreds and twenties. Let's get it
ed."

Where's it going?"

QuebecBank. They're waiting for us."

hey each grabbed a box and walked through the dark to
side door, where a comrade was waiting with an Uzi. The
s were loaded into a dilapidated van with CAYMAN PRODUCE
ciled badly on the side. The armed natives sat with guns
vn as the receiving clerk drove away from the hangar in
direction of downtown Georgetown.

istration began at eight outside the Century Room on the
zanine. Mitch arrived early, signed in, picked up the heavy
book of materials with his name printed neatly on the
r and went inside. He took a seat near the center of the
room. Registration was limited to two hundred, the bro-
e said. A porter served coffee, and Mitch spread the Wash-
on *Post* before him. The news was dominated by a dozen
es of the beloved Redskins, who were in the Super Bowl
n.

he room filled slowly as tax lawyers from around the coun-
gathered to hear the latest developments in tax laws that
ged daily. A few minutes before nine, a clean cut, boyish
ney sat to Mitch's left and said nothing. Mitch glanced at
and returned to the paper. When the room was packed,
moderator welcomed everyone and introduced the first
ker. Congressman something or other from Oregon, chair-
of a House Ways and Means subcommittee. As he took
odium for what was supposed to be a one hour presenta-
the attorney to Mitch's left leaned over and offered his
.

Ii, Mitch," he whispered. "I'm Grant Harbison, FBI." He
ed Mitch a card.

e congressman started with a joke that Mitch did not

hear. He studied the card, holding it near his chest. T
were five people seated within three feet of him. He di
know anyone in the room, but it would be embarrassir
anyone knew he was holding an FBI card. After five min
Mitch shot a blank stare at Harbison.

Harbison whispered, "I need to see you for a few minu
"What if I'm busy?" Mitch asked.

The agent slid a plain white envelope from his seminar r
book and handed it to Mitch. He opened it near his ches
was handwritten. Across the top, in small but imposing let
the words read simply: "Office of the Director—FBI."

The note read:

> Dear Mr. McDeere:
> I would like to speak with you for a few
> moments during lunch. Please follow the
> instructions of Agent Harbison. It won't
> take long. We appreciate your cooperation.
>   Thanks.
>   F. Denton Voyles
>   Director

Mitch folded the letter in the envelope and slowly plac
in his notebook. We appreciate your cooperation. From
Director of the FBI. He realized the importance at this
ment of maintaining his composure, of keeping a stra
calm face as if it was simply routine. But he rubbed his
ples with both hands and stared at the floor in front of him
closed his eyes and felt dizzy. The FBI. Sitting next to l
Waiting on him. The Director and hell knows who else. '
rance would be close at hand.

Suddenly, the room exploded in laughter at the cong
man's punch line. Harbison leaned quickly toward Mitch
whispered, "Meet me in the men's room around the corne
ten minutes." The agent left his notebooks on the table
exited among the laughter.

Mitch flipped to the first section of the notebook and
tended to study the materials. The congressman was detai
his courageous battle to protect tax shelters for the wea
while at the same time easing the burden on the working c
Under his fearless guidance, the subcommittee had refuse

ort legislation limiting deductions for oil and gas explora-
. He was a one-man army on the Hill.

itch waited fifteen minutes, then another five, then began
ghing. He needed water, and with hand over mouth he slid
veen the chairs to the back of the room and out the rear
r. Harbison was in the men's room washing his hands for
tenth time.

itch walked to the basin next to him and turned on the
water. "What are you boys up to?" Mitch asked.

arbison looked at Mitch in the mirror. "I'm just following
rs. Director Voyles wants to personally meet you, and I
sent to get you."

And what might he want?"

wouldn't want to steal his thunder, but I'm sure it's
er important."

itch cautiously glanced around the rest room. It was
ty. "And what if I'm too busy to meet with him?"

arbison turned off the water and shook his hands into the
n. "The meeting is inevitable, Mitch. Let's not play games.
n your little seminar breaks for lunch, you'll find a cab,
ber 8667, outside to the left of the main entrance. It will
you to the Vietnam Veterans Memorial, and we'll be
e. You must be careful. Two of them followed you here
Memphis."

wo of whom?"

he boys from Memphis. Just do as we say and they'll
r know."

moderator thanked the second speaker, a tax professor
New York University, and dismissed them for lunch.

itch said nothing to the taxi driver. He sped away like a
iac, and they were soon lost in traffic. Fifteen minutes
, they parked near the Memorial.

Don't get out yet," the driver said with authority. Mitch
not move. For ten minutes, he did not move or speak.
lly, a white Ford Escort pulled alongside the cab and
ked. It then drove away.

he driver stared ahead and said, "Okay. Go to the Wall.
y'll find you after about five minutes."

itch stepped to the sidewalk, and the cab left. He stuck his

hands deep in the pockets of his wool overcoat and wal
slowly to the Memorial. Bitter wind gusts from the north s
tered leaves in all directions. He shivered and flipped the co
of his coat around his ears.

A solitary pilgrim sat rigidly in a wheelchair and stare
the Wall. He was covered with a heavy quilt. Under his o
sized camouflage beret, a pair of aviator's sunglasses cove
his eyes. He sat near the end of the wall, near the name
those killed in 1972. Mitch followed the years down the s
walk until he stopped near the wheelchair. He searched
names, suddenly oblivious to the man.

He breathed deeply and was aware of a numbness in his
and stomach. He looked slowly downward, and then, near
bottom, there it was. Engraved neatly, matter-of-factly,
like all the others, was the name Rusty McDeere.

A basket of frozen and wilted flowers sat on its side nex
the monument, inches under his name. Mitch gently laid t
to one side and knelt before the Wall. He touched the engra
letters of Rusty's name. Rusty McDeere. Age eighteen,
ever. Seven weeks in Vietnam when he stepped on a
mine. Death was instantaneous, they said. They always
that, according to Ray. Mitch wiped a small tear and s
staring at the length of the Wall. He thought of the fifty-e
thousand families who had been told that death was insta
neous and no one suffered over there.

"Mitch, they're waiting."

He turned and looked at the man in the wheelchair, the
human in sight. The aviator's glasses stared at the Wall and
not look up. Mitch glanced around in all directions.

"Relax, Mitch. We've got the place sealed off. They're
watching."

"And who are you?" Mitch asked.

"Just one of the gang. You need to trust us, Mitch.
Director has important words, words that could save y
life."

"Where is he?"

The man in the wheelchair turned his head and loo
down the sidewalk. "Start walking that way. They'll
you."

Mitch stared for a moment longer at his brother's name

ked behind the wheelchair. He walked past the statue of
three soldiers. He walked slowly, waiting, with hands deep
nis pockets. Fifty yards past the monument, Wayne Tar-
ce stepped from behind a tree and walked beside him.
ep walking," he said.

Why am I not surprised to see you here?" Mitch said.

Just keep walking. We know of at least two goons from
mphis who were flown in ahead of you. They're at the same
el, next door to you. They did not follow you here. I think
lost them."

What the hell's going on, Tarrance?"

You're about to find out. Keep walking. But relax, no one is
ching you, except for about twenty of our agents."

Twenty?"

Yeah. We've got this place sealed off. We want to make sure
ie bastards from Memphis don't show up here. I don't ex-
t them."

Who are they?"

The Director will explain."

Why is the Director involved?"

You ask a lot of questions, Mitch."

And you don't have enough answers."

arrance pointed to the right. They left the sidewalk and
led for a heavy concrete bench near a footbridge leading to
iall forest. The water on the pond below was frozen white.
Have a seat," Tarrance instructed. They sat down. Two
walked across the footbridge. Mitch immediately recog-
d the shorter one as Voyles. F. Denton Voyles, Director of
FBI under three Presidents. A tough-talking, heavy-
ded crime buster with a reputation for ruthlessness.
litch stood out of respect when they stopped at the bench.
les stuck out a cold hand and stared at Mitch with the
e large, round face that was famous around the world.
y shook hands and exchanged names. Voyles pointed to
bench. Tarrance and the other agent walked to the foot-
ge and studied the horizon. Mitch glanced across the pond
saw two men, undoubtedly agents with their identical
k trench coats and close haircuts, standing against a tree a
dred yards away.

oyles sat close to Mitch, their legs touching. A brown fe-

197

dora rested to one side of his large, bald head. He was at [?] seventy, but the dark green eyes danced with intensity [?] missed nothing. Both men sat still on the cold bench with t[?] hands stuck deep in their overcoats.

"I appreciate you coming," Voyles started.

"I didn't feel as though I had a choice. You folks have b[?] relentless."

"Yes. It's very important to us."

Mitch breathed deeply. "Do you have any idea how [?] fused and scared I am? I'm totally bewildered. I would lik[?] explanation, sir."

"Mr. McDeere, can I call you Mitch?"

"Sure. Why not."

"Fine. Mitch, I am a man of very few words. And what [?] about to tell you will certainly shock you. You will be h[?] fied. You may not believe me. But I assure you it's all true, [?] with your help we can save your life."

Mitch braced himself and waited.

"Mitch, no lawyer has ever left your law firm alive. T[?] have tried, and they were killed. Two were about to leave, [?] they died last summer. Once a lawyer joins Bendini, Lam[?] & Locke, he never leaves, unless he retires and keeps his m[?] shut. And by the time they retire, they are a part of the [?] spiracy and cannot talk. The firm has an extensive surveilla[?] operation on the fifth floor. Your house and car are bug[?] Your phones are tapped. Your desk and office are wired. V[?] ally every word you utter is heard and recorded on the [?] floor. They follow you, and sometimes your wife. They [?] here in Washington as we speak. You see, Mitch, the fir[?] more than a firm. It is a division of a very large business, a [?] profitable business. A very illegal business. The firm is [?] owned by the partners."

Mitch turned and watched him closely. The Director loc[?] at the frozen pond as he spoke.

"You see, Mitch, the law firm of Bendini, Lambert & L[?] is owned by the Morolto crime family in Chicago. The M[?] The Mob. They call the shots from up there. And that's [?] we're here." He touched Mitch firmly on the knee and st[?] at him from six inches away. "It's Mafia, Mitch, and illeg[?] hell."

don't believe it," he said, frozen with fear. His voice was
k and shrill.

he Director smiled. "Yes you do, Mitch. Yes you do. You've
n suspicious for some time now. That's why you talked to
nks in the Caymans. That's why you hired that sleazy in-
igator and got him killed by those boys on the fifth floor.
know the firm stinks, Mitch."

itch leaned forward and rested his elbows on his knees.
stared at the ground between his shoes. "I don't believe it,"
numbled weakly.

As far as we can tell, about twenty-five percent of their
nts, or I should say your clients, are legitimate. There are
e very good lawyers in that firm, and they do tax and secu-
:s work for rich clients. It's a very good front. Most of the
you've worked on so far have been legit. That's how they
rate. They bring in a new rookie, throw money at him, buy
BMW, the house, all that jazz, wine and dine and go to the
mans, and they work his ass off with what is really legiti-
e legal stuff. Real clients. Real lawyer stuff. That goes on
a few years, and the rookie doesn't suspect a thing, right?
a great firm, great bunch of guys. Plenty of money. Hey,
ything's wonderful. Then after five or six years, when the
ey is really good, when they own your mortgage, when
have a wife and kids and everything is so secure, they drop
bomb and tell the truth. There's no way out. It's the Mafia,
ch. Those guys don't play games. They'll kill one of your
dren or your wife, they don't care. You're making more
ey than you could possibly make anywhere else. You're
kmailed because you've got a family that doesn't mean a
ned thing to the Mob, so what do you do, Mitch? You stay.
can't leave. If you stay you make a million and retire
ng with your family intact. If you want to leave, you'll
d up with your picture on the wall in the first-floor library.
y're very persuasive."

itch rubbed his temples and began shivering.

ook, Mitch, I know you must have a thousand questions.
y. So I'll just keep talking and tell you what I know. The
dead lawyers all wanted out after they learned the truth.
never talked to the first three, because, frankly, we knew
ing about the firm until seven years ago. They've done an

199

excellent job of staying quiet and leaving no trail. The 1 three just wanted out, probably, so they got out. In cof Hodge and Kozinski were different. They approached us, over the course of a year we had several meetings. T dropped the bomb on Kozinski after he'd been there for se years. He told Hodge. They whispered between themse for a year. Kozinski was about to make partner and wanted before that happened. So he and Hodge made the fatal deci: to get out. They never suspected the first three were killed at least they never mentioned it to us. We sent Wayne 1 rance to Memphis to bring them in. Tarrance is an organi crime specialist from New York. He and the two were get real close when that thing happened in the Caymans. Th guys in Memphis are very good, Mitch. Don't ever forget t They've got the money and they hire the best. So after Ho and Kozinski were killed, I made the decision to get the fi If we can bust that firm, we can indict every significant m ber of the Morolto family. There could be over five hund indictments. Tax evasion, laundering, racketeering, just w ever you want. It could destroy the Morolto family, and would be the single most devastating blow to organized cr in the past thirty years. And, Mitch, it's all in the files at quiet little Bendini firm in Memphis."

"Why Memphis?"

"Ah, good question. Who would suspect a small firm Memphis, Tennessee? There's no mob activity down there. a quiet, lovely, peaceful city by the river. It could've been D ham or Topeka or Wichita Falls. But they chose Memphis. big enough, though, to hide a forty-man firm. Perfect choi

"You mean every partner . . ." His words trailed off.

"Yes, every partner knows and plays by the rules. We pect that most of the associates know, but it's hard to There's so much we don't know, Mitch. I can't explain l the firm operates and who's in on it. But we strongly suspe lot of criminal activity down there."

"Such as?"

"Tax fraud. They do all the tax work for the Morolto bu: They file nice, neat, proper-looking tax returns each year report a fraction of the income. They launder money

.y. They set up legitimate businesses with dirty money.
.t bank in St. Louis, big client, what is it?"

Commercial Guaranty."

Right, that's it. Mafia owned. Firm does all its legal work.
rolto takes in an estimated three hundred million a year
n gambling, dope, numbers, everything. All cash, right?
st of it goes to those banks in the Caymans. How does it
ve from Chicago to the islands? Any idea? The plane, we
bect. That gold-plated Lear you flew up here on runs about
e a week to Georgetown."

litch sat straight and watched Tarrance, who was out of
ring range and standing now on the footbridge. "So why
't you get your indictments and bust it all up?"

We can't. We will, I assure you. I've assigned five agents to
project in Memphis and three here in Washington. I'll get
n, Mitch, I promise you. But we must have someone from
inside. They are very smart. They have plenty of money.
·y're extremely careful, and they don't make mistakes. I am
vinced that we must have help from you or another mem-
of the firm. We need copies of files, copies of bank records,
ies of a million documents that can only come from within.
impossible otherwise."

And I have been chosen."

And you have been chosen. If you decline, then you can go
your way and make plenty of money and in general be a
cessful lawyer. But we will keep trying. We'll wait for the
t new associate and try to pick him off. And if that doesn't
·k, we'll move in on one of the older associates. One with
rage and morals and guts to do what's right. We'll find our
1 one day, Mitch, and when that happens we'll indict you
1g with all the rest and ship your rich and successful ass off
·rison. It will happen, son, believe me."

t that moment, at that place and time, Mitch believed him.
·. Voyles, I'm cold. Could we walk around?"

Sure, Mitch."

hey walked slowly to the sidewalk and headed in the direc-
of the Vietnam Memorial. Mitch glanced over his shoul-
Tarrance and the other agent were following at a distance.
other agent in dark brown sat suspiciously on a park bench
the sidewalk.

"Who was Anthony Bendini?" Mitch asked.

"He married a Morolto in 1930. The old man's son-in-
They had an operation in Philadelphia back then, and he
stationed there. Then, in the forties, for some reason, he
sent to Memphis to set up shop. He was a very good law
though, from what we know."

A thousand questions flooded his brain and fought to
asked. He tried to appear calm, under control, skeptical.

"What about Oliver Lambert?"

"A prince of a guy. The perfect senior partner, who
happened to know all about Hodge and Kozinski and the p
to eliminate them. The next time you see Mr. Lambert aro
the office, try to remember that he is a cold-blooded murde
Of course, he has no choice. If he didn't cooperate, they'd
him floating somewhere. They're all like that, Mitch. T
started off just like you. Young, bright, ambitious, then s
denly one day they were in over their heads with no plac
go. So they play along, work hard, do a helluva job putting
a good front and looking like a real respectable little law fi
Each year or so they recruit a bright young law student fro
poor background, no family money, with a wife who wa
babies, and they throw money at him and sign him up."

Mitch thought of the money, the excessive salary fro
small firm in Memphis, and the car and low-interest mortg
He was headed for Wall Street and had been sidetracked by
money. Only the money.

"What about Nathan Locke?"

The Director smiled. "Locke is another story. He grew u
poor kid in Chicago and was running errands for old M
Morolto by the time he was ten. He's been a hood all his
Scratched his way through law school, and the old man s
him South to work with Anthony Bendini in the white-co
crime division of the family. He was always a favorite of
old man."

"When did Morolto die?"

"Eleven years ago at the age of eighty-eight. He has
slimy sons, Mickey the Mouth and Joey the Priest. Mic
lives in Las Vegas and has a limited role in the family busin
Joey is the boss."

The sidewalk reached an intersection with another one

distance to the left, the Washington Monument reached
ward in the bitter wind. To the right, the walkway led to
Wall. A handful of people were now staring at it, searching
the names of sons and husbands and friends. Mitch headed
the Wall. They walked slowly.

Mitch spoke softly. "I don't understand how the firm can do
much illegal work and keep it quiet. That place is full of
etaries and clerks and paralegals."

Good point, and one I cannot fully answer. We think it
rates as two firms. One is legitimate, with the new associ-
, most of the secretaries and support people. Then, the
ior associates and partners do the dirty work. Hodge and
inski were about to give us plenty of information, but they
er made it. Hodge told Tarrance once that there was a
up of paralegals in the basement he knew little about. They
ked directly for Locke and Milligan and McKnight and a
other partners, and no one was really sure what they did.
retaries know everything, and we think that some of them
probably in on it. If so, I'm sure they're well paid and too
ed to talk. Think about it, Mitch. If you work there mak-
great money with great benefits, and you know that if you
too many questions or start talking you wind up in the
r, what do you do? You keep your mouth shut and take the
ey."

hey stopped at the beginning of the Wall, at a point where
black granite began at ground level and started its run of
feet until it angled into the second row of identical panels.
y feet away, an elderly couple stared at the wall and cried
ly. They huddled together, for warmth and strength. The
her bent down and laid a framed black-and-white photo at
base of the Wall. The father laid a shoebox full of high
ool memorabilia next to the photo. Football programs, class
ures, love letters, key rings and a gold chain. They cried
ler.

Mitch turned his back to the Wall and looked at the Wash-
on Monument. The Director watched his eyes.

So what am I supposed to do?" Mitch asked.

First of all, keep your mouth shut. If you start asking ques-
s, your life could be in danger. Your wife's also. Don't have
kids in the near future. They're easy targets. It's best to

play dumb, as if everything is wonderful and you still pla[n]
be the world's greatest lawyer. Second, you must make a d[eci]
sion. Not now, but soon. You must decide if you will coope[rate]
or not. If you choose to help us, we will of course mak[e it]
worth your while. If you choose not to, then we will conti[nue]
to watch the firm until we decide to approach another a[sso]
ciate. As I said, one of these days we'll find someone with g[uts]
and nail those bastards. And the Morolto crime family as [we]
know it will cease to exist. We'll protect you, Mitch, and y[ou]
never have to work again in your life."

"What life? I'll live in fear forever, if I live. I've heard sto[ries]
of witnesses the FBI has supposedly hidden. Ten years la[ter]
the car explodes as they back out the driveway to go to w[ork.]
The body is scattered over three blocks. The Mob never [for-]
gets, Director. You know that."

"They never forget, Mitch. But I promise you, you and y[our]
wife will be protected."

The Director looked at his watch. "You'd better get bac[k or]
they'll be suspicious. Tarrance will be in touch. Trust h[im,]
Mitch. He's trying to save your life. He has full authority [to]
act on my behalf. If he tells you something, it's coming fr[om]
me. He can negotiate."

"Negotiate what?"

"Terms, Mitch. What we give you in return for what [you]
give us. We want the Morolto family, and you can deliver. [You]
name your price, and this government, working through [the]
FBI, will deliver. Within reason, of course. And that's com[ing]
from me, Mitch." They walked slowly along the Wall [and]
stopped by the agent in the wheelchair. Voyles stuck out [his]
hand. "Look, there's a taxi waiting where you came in, n[um]
ber 1073. Same driver. You'd better leave now. We will [not]
meet again, but Tarrance will contact you in a couple of d[ays.]
Please think about what I said. Don't convince yourself [the]
firm is invincible and can operate forever, because I will [not]
allow it. We will make a move in the near future, I prom[ise]
that. I just hope you're on our side."

"I don't understand what I'm supposed to do."

"Tarrance has the game plan. A lot will depend upon [you]
and what you learn once you're committed."

"Committed?"

That's the word, Mitch. Once you commit, there's no turn-
back. They can be more ruthless than any organization on
h."

Why did you pick me?"

We had to pick someone. No, that's not true. We picked you
ause you have the guts to walk away from it. You have no
ily except a wife. No ties, no roots. You've been hurt by
ry person you ever cared for, except Abby. You raised your-
, and in doing so became self-reliant and independent. You
't need the firm. You can leave it. You're hardened and
used beyond your years. And you're smart enough to pull
f, Mitch. You won't get caught. That's why we picked you.
d day, Mitch. Thanks for coming. You'd better get back."

oyles turned and walked quickly away. Tarrance waited at
end of the Wall, and gave Mitch a quick salute, as if to say,
long—for now."

20

AFTER MAKING the obligatory stop in Atlanta,
Delta DC9 landed in a cold rain at Memphis Inte
tional. It parked at Gate 19, and the tightly pac
crowd of business travelers quickly disembarked. Mitch
ried only his briefcase and an *Esquire*. He saw Abby wai
near the pay phones and moved quickly through the pack.
threw the briefcase and magazine against the wall and b
hugged her. The four days in Washington seemed lil
month. They kissed again and again, and whispered softl

"How about a date?" he asked.

"I've got dinner on the table and wine in the cooler,"
said. They held hands and walked through the mob push
down the concourse in the general direction of the lug
pickup.

He spoke quietly. "Well, we need to talk, and we can't c
at home."

She gripped his hand tighter. "Oh?"

"Yes. In fact, we need to have a long talk."

"What happened?"

"It'll take a while."

"Why am I suddenly nervous?"

Just keep cool. Keep smiling. They're watching."

he smiled and glanced to her right. "Who's watching?"

"I'll explain in just a moment."

Mitch suddenly pulled her to his left. They cut through the
[...]e of human traffic and darted into a dark, crowded lounge
[...] of businessmen drinking and watching the television
[...]ve the bar and waiting for their flights. A small, round
[...]e covered with empty beer mugs had just been vacated,
[...] they sat with their backs to the wall and a view of the bar
[...] the concourse. They sat close together, within three feet of
[...]ther table. Mitch stared at the door and analyzed every face
[...] walked in. "How long are we going to be here?" she
[...]ed.

[...]Why?"

[...]he slid out of the full length fox and folded it on the chair
[...]ss the table. "What exactly are you looking for?"

[...]ust keep smiling for a moment. Pretend you really missed
[...] Here, give me a kiss." He pecked her on the lips, and they
[...]ed into each other's eyes. He kissed her cheek and re-
[...]ed to the door. A waiter rushed to the table and cleaned it
[...] They ordered wine.

[...]he smiled at him. "How was your trip?"

[...]Boring. We were in class eight hours a day, for four days.
[...]er the first day, I hardly left the hotel. They crammed six
[...]ths' worth of tax revisions into thirty-two hours."

[...]Did you get to sightsee?"

[...]e smiled and looked dreamily at her. "I missed you, Abby.
[...]re than I've ever missed anyone in my life. I love you. I
[...]k you're gorgeous, absolutely stunning. I do not enjoy
[...]eling alone and waking up in a strange hotel bed without
[...]. And I have something horrible to tell you."

[...]he stopped smiling. He slowly looked around the room.
[...]y were three deep at the bar and yelling at the Knicks-
[...]ers game. The lounge was suddenly louder.

[...]I'll tell you about it," he said, "But there's a very good
[...]nce someone is in here right now watching us. They can-
[...] hear, but they can observe. Just smile occasionally, al-
[...]ugh it will be hard."

[...]he wine arrived, and Mitch began his story. He left noth-
[...] out. She spoke only once. He told her about Anthony

207

Bendini and old man Morolto, and then Nathan Locke gr
ing up in Chicago and Oliver Lambert and the boys on
fifth floor.

Abby nervously sipped her wine and tried valiantly to
pear as the normal loving wife who missed her husband
was now enjoying immensely his recollection of the tax se
nar. She watched the people at the bar, sipped a little
occasionally grinned at Mitch as he told of the money laun
ing and the murdered lawyers. Her body ached with fear.
breath was wildly irregular. But she listened, and pretend

The waiter brought more wine as the crowd thinned.
hour after he started, Mitch finished in a low whisper.

"And Voyles said Tarrance would contact me in a few
to see if I will cooperate. He said goodbye and walked aw

"And this was Tuesday?" she asked.

"Yes. The first day."

"What did you do the rest of the week?"

"I slept little, ate little, walked around with a dull head
most of the time."

"I think I feel one coming."

"I'm sorry, Abby. I wanted to fly home immediately and
you. I've been in shock for three days."

"I'm in shock now. I'm not believing this, Mitch. This is
a bad dream, only much worse."

"And this is only the beginning. The FBI is dead seri
Why else would the Director himself meet with me, an in
nificant rookie lawyer from Memphis, in fifteen-de
weather on a concrete park bench? He's assigned five agen
Memphis and three in Washington, and he said they'll sp
whatever it takes to get the firm. So if I keep my mouth s
ignore them and go about my business of being a good
faithful member of Bendini, Lambert & Locke, one day th
show up with arrest warrants and haul everybody away.
if I choose to cooperate, you and I will leave Memphis in
dead of the night after I hand the firm to the feds, and we'
off and live in Boise, Idaho, as Mr. and Mrs. Wilbur G
We'll have plenty of money, but we'll have to work to a
suspicion. After my plastic surgery, I'll get a job drivi
forklift in a warehouse, and you can work part time at a
care. We'll have two, maybe three kids and pray every n

t people we've never met keep their mouths shut and forget
ut us. We'll live every hour of every day in morbid fear of
ng discovered."

That's perfect, Mitch, just perfect." She was trying hard
to cry.

He smiled and glanced around the room. "We have a third
ion. We can walk out that door, buy two tickets to San
go, sneak across the border and eat tortillas for the rest of
lives."

Let's go."

But they'd probably follow us. With my luck, Oliver Lam-
t will be waiting in Tijuana with a squad of goons. It won't
k. Just a thought."

What about Lamar?"

I don't know. He's been here six or seven years, so he prob-
y knows. Avery's a partner, so he's very much a part of the
spiracy."

And Kay?"

Who knows. It's very likely none of the wives know. I've
ught about it for four days, Abby, and it's a marvelous
t. The firm looks exactly like it's supposed to look. They
ld fool anyone. I mean, how would you and I or any other
spective recruit even think of such an operation? It's per-
. Except, now the feds know about it."

And now the feds expect you to do their dirty work. Why
they pick you, Mitch? There are forty lawyers in the firm."

Because I knew nothing about it. I was a sitting duck. The
is not sure when the partners spring the surprise on the
ciates, so they couldn't take a chance with anyone else. I
pened to be the new guy, so they set the trap as soon as I
sed the bar exam."

bby chewed her lip and held back tears. She looked
kly at the door across the dark room. "And they listen to
ything we say," she said.

No. Just every phone call and conversation around the
se and in the cars. We're free to meet here or in most res-
ants, and there's always the patio. But I suggest we move
her away from the sliding door. To be safe, we need to
k behind the storage shed and whisper softly."

Are you trying to be funny? I hope not. This is no time for

jokes. I'm so scared, angry, confused, mad as hell and not
where to turn. I'm afraid to speak in my own house. I w
every word I utter on the phone, even if it's a wrong num
Every time the phone rings, I jump and stare at it. And
this."

"You need another drink."

"I need ten drinks."

Mitch grabbed her wrist and squeezed firmly. "Wait a
ute. I see a familiar face. Don't look around."

She held her breath. "Where?"

"On the other side of the bar. Smile and look at me."

Sitting on a barstool and staring intently at the TV w
well-tanned blond with a loud blue-and-white alpine swe
Fresh from the slopes. But Mitch had seen the tan and
blond bangs and the blond mustache somewhere in Wash
ton. Mitch watched him carefully. The blue light from
tube illuminated his face. Mitch hid in the dark. The
lifted a bottle of beer, hesitated, then, there!, shot a glance
the corner where the McDeeres huddled closely together.

"Are you sure?" Abby asked through clenched teeth.

"Yes. He was in Washington, but I can't place him. In fa
saw him twice."

"Is he one of them?"

"How am I supposed to know?"

"Let's get out of here."

Mitch laid a twenty on the table and they left the airpo

Driving her Peugeot, he raced through the short-term par
lot, paid the attendant and sped away toward midtown. A
five minutes of silence, she leaned across and whispered in
ear, "Can we talk?"

He shook his head. "Well, how's the weather been wh
was away?"

Abby rolled her eyes and looked through the passenger
dow. "Cold," she said. "Chance of light snow tonight."

"It was below freezing the entire week in Washington."

Abby looked flabbergasted at this revelation. "Any sno
she asked with raised eyebrows and wide eyes as if enthra
with the conversation.

"No. Just raw cold."

"What a coincidence! Cold here and cold there."

Mitch chuckled to himself. They rode silently on the inter-
te loop. "So who's gonna win the Super Bowl?" he asked.
"Oilers."

"Think so, huh? I'm for the Redskins. That's all they talked
out in Washington."

"My, my. Must be a real fun city."

More silence. Abby placed the back of her hand over her
uth and concentrated on the taillights ahead. At this mo-
nt of bewilderment, she would take her chances in Tijuana.
r husband, number three in his class (at Harvard), the one
th Wall Street firms rolling out the red carpet, the one who
uld have gone anywhere, to any firm, had signed up with the
. Mafia! With five dead lawyers notched on their belts, they
st surely wouldn't hesitate with number six. Her husband!
en the many conversations with Kay Quin swirled around
r brain. The firm encourages babies. The firm permits wives
work, but not forever. The firm hires no one with family
ney. The firm demands loyalty to the firm. The firm has the
vest turnover rate in the country. Small wonder.

Mitch watched her carefully. Twenty minutes after they left
airport, the Peugeot parked in the carport next to the
1W. They held hands and walked to the end of the drive-
y.

"This is crazy, Mitch."

"Yes, but it's real. It will not go away."

"What do we do?"

"I don't know, babe. But we gotta do it quick, and we can't
ke mistakes."

"I'm scared."

"I'm terrified."

rrance did not wait long. One week after he waved goodbye
Mitch at the Wall, he spotted him walking hurriedly in the
d in the direction of the Federal Building on North Main,
ht blocks from the Bendini Building. He followed him for
o blocks, then slid into a small coffee shop with a row of
ndows facing the street, or the mall, as it was called. Cars
re prohibited on Main Street in Memphis. The asphalt had
n covered with tile when the boulevard had ceased being a

211

street and had been transformed into the Mid-America Ma
An occasional useless and desolate tree rose from the tile a
stretched its barren limbs between the buildings. Winos a
urban nomads drifted aimlessly from one side of the mall
the other, begging for money and food.

Tarrance sat at a front window and watched in the distar
as Mitch disappeared into the Federal Building. He order
coffee and a chocolate doughnut. He checked his watch. It v
10 A.M. According to the docket, McDeere had a brief heari
in Tax Court at this moment. It should be very brief, the cle
of the court had informed Tarrance. He waited.

Nothing is ever brief in court. An hour later, Tarrar
moved his face closer to the window and studied the scatte
bodies walking quickly in the distance. He drained his cof
cup for the third time, laid two dollars on the table and sto
hidden in the door. As Mitch approached on the other side
the mall, Tarrance moved swiftly toward him.

Mitch saw him and slowed for a second.

"Hello, Mitch. Mind if I walk with you?"

"Yes, I mind, Tarrance. It's dangerous, don't you think?"

They walked briskly and did not look at each other. "L
at that store over there," Tarrance said, pointing to their rig
"I need a pair of shoes." They ducked into Don Pang's Ho
of Shoes. Tarrance walked to the rear of the narrow store a
stopped between two rows of fake Reeboks at $4.99 for t
pairs. Mitch followed him and picked up a pair of size te
Don Pang or some other Korean eyed them suspiciously I
said nothing. They watched the front door through the rac

"The Director called me yesterday," Tarrance said with
moving his lips. "He asked about you. Said it was time y
made a decision."

"Tell him I'm still thinking."

"Have you told the boys at the office?"

"No. I'm still thinking."

"That's good. I don't think you should tell them."
handed Mitch a business card. "Keep this. There are two nu
bers on the back. Use either one from a pay phone. You'll g
recorder, so just leave a message and tell me exactly when a
where to meet you."

Mitch put the card in his pocket.

;uddenly, Tarrance ducked lower. "What is it!" Mitch de-
nded.

'I think we've been caught. I just saw a goon walk past the
re and look in. Listen to me, Mitch, and listen carefully.
lk with me out of the store right now, and the instant we
out the door, yell at me to get lost and shove me away. I'll
like I want to fight, and you run in the direction of your
ce."

'You're gonna get me killed, Tarrance."

'Just do as I say. As soon as you get to the office, report this
ident to the partners. Tell them I cornered you and you got
ay as soon as possible."

)utside, Mitch shoved harder than necessary and yelled,
et the hell away from me! And leave me alone!" He ran two
cks to Union Avenue, then walked to the Bendini Building.
stopped in the men's room on the first floor to catch his
ath. He stared at himself in the mirror and breathed deeply
times.

Avery was on the phone, with two lights holding and blink-
. A secretary sat on the sofa, ready with a steno pad for the
laught of commands. Mitch looked at her and said, "Would
step outside, please. I need to speak with Avery in pri-
e." She stood and Mitch escorted her to the door. He closed

Avery watched him closely and hung up. "What's going
" he asked.

Mitch stood by the sofa. "The FBI just grabbed me as I was
urning from Tax Court."

Damn! Who was it?"

Same agent. Guy by the name of Tarrance."

Avery picked up the phone and kept talking. "Where did it
pen?"

On the mall. North of Union. I was just walking alone,
ding my own business."

Is this the first contact since that other thing?"

Yes. I didn't recognize the guy at first."

Avery spoke into the receiver. "This is Avery Tolleson. I
d to speak to Oliver Lambert immediately. . . . I don't
e if he's on the phone. Interrupt him, and now."

What's going on, Avery?" Mitch asked.

"Hello, Oliver. Avery here. Sorry for the interrupti[on]. Mitch McDeere is here in my office. A few minutes ago he w[as] walking back from the Federal Building when the FBI ag[ent] approached him on the mall. . . . What? Yes, he just wall[ked] in my office and told me about it. . . . All right, we'll be th[ere] in five minutes." He hung up. "Relax, Mitch. We've b[een] through this before."

"I know, Avery, but this does not make sense. Why wo[uld] they bother with me? I'm the newest man in the firm."

"It's harassment, Mitch. Pure and simple. Nothing but [har]assment. Sit down."

Mitch walked to the window and looked at the river in [the] distance. Avery was a cool liar. It was now time for [the] "they're just picking on us" routine. Relax, Mitch. Re[lax.] With eight FBI agents assigned to the firm and the Direc[tor,] Mr. Denton Voyles himself, monitoring the case daily? Re[lax.] He'd just been caught whispering to an FBI agent insid[e a] dollar shoe store. And now he was forced to act like he was [an] ignorant pawn being preyed upon by the evil forces of [the] federal government. Harassment? Then why was the goon [fol]lowing him on a routine walk to the courthouse? Answer th[at,] Avery.

"You're scared, aren't you?" Avery asked as he put his a[rm] around him and gazed out the window.

"Not really. Locke explained it all last time. I just wish t[hey] would leave me alone."

"It's a serious matter, Mitch. Don't take it lightly. Let's w[alk] over and see Lambert."

Mitch followed Avery around the corner and down the h[all.] A stranger in a black suit opened the door for them, t[hen] closed it. Lambert, Nathan Locke and Royce McKnight st[ood] near the small conference table. Again, a tape recorder sa[t on] the table. Mitch sat across from it. Black Eyes sat at the hea[d of] the table and glared at Mitch.

He spoke with a menacing frown. There were no smile[s in] the room. "Mitch, has Tarrance or anyone else from the [FBI] contacted you since the first meeting last August?"

"No."

"Are you certain?"

Mitch slapped the table. "Dammit! I said no! Why don't you me under oath?"

Locke was startled. They were all startled. A heavy, tense nce followed for thirty seconds. Mitch glared at Black s, who retreated ever so slightly with a casual movement of head.

Lambert, ever the diplomat, the mediator, intervened. ok, Mitch, we know this is frightening."

Damn right it is. I don't like it at all. I'm minding my own iness, working my ass off ninety hours a week, trying to be hing but a good lawyer and member of this firm, and for unknown reason I keep getting these little visits from the . Now, sir, I would like some answers."

Locke pressed the red button on the recorder. "We'll talk ut that in a minute. First, you tell us everything that hap-ed."

It's very simple, Mr. Locke. I walked to the Federal Build- at ten for an appearance before Judge Kofer on the Mal- n Delaney case. I was there about an hour, and I finished business. I left the Federal Building, and I was walking in direction of our office—in a hurry, I might add. It's about nty degrees out there. A block or two north of Union, this Tarrance came out of nowhere, grabbed my arm and hed me into a small store. I started to knock the hell out of , but, after all, he is an FBI agent. And I didn't want to ke a scene. Inside, he tells me he wants to talk for a minute. illed away from him, and ran to the door. He followed me, d to grab me, and I shoved him away. Then I ran here, t straight to Avery's office, and here we are. That's all that said. Play by play, everything."

What did he want to talk about?"

I didn't give him a chance, Mr. Locke. I have no plans to to any FBI agent unless he has a subpoena."

Are you sure it's the same agent?"

. think so. I didn't recognize him at first. I haven't seen him e last August. Once inside the store, he pulled his badge gave me his name again. At that point, I ran."

ocke pressed another button and sat back in the chair. bert sat behind him and smiled ever so warmly. "Listen, ch, we explained this last time. These guys are getting

bolder and bolder. Just last month they approached Jack
drich while he was eating lunch in a little grill on Sec
Street. We're not sure what they're up to, but Tarrance is
of his mind. It's nothing but harassment."

Mitch watched his lips but heard little. As Lambert sp
he thought of Kozinski and Hodge and their pretty wid
and children at the funerals.

Black Eyes cleared his throat. "It's a serious matter, Mi
But we have nothing to hide. They could better spend th
time investigating our clients if they suspect wrongdo
We're lawyers. We may represent people who flirt with
law, but we have done nothing wrong. This is very baffling
us."

Mitch smiled and opened his hands. "What do you want
to do?" he asked sincerely.

"There's nothing you can do, Mitch," said Lambert. "]
stay away from this guy, and run if you see him. If he so m
as looks at you, report it immediately."

"That's what he did," Avery said defensively.

Mitch looked as pitiful as possible.

"You can go, Mitch," Lambert said. "And keep us poste
He left the office by himself.

DeVasher paced behind his desk and ignored the partn
"He's lying, I tell you. He's lying. The son of a bitch is lyin
know he's lying."

"What did your man see?" asked Locke.

"My man saw something different. Slightly different.
very different. He says McDeere and Tarrance walked sor
nonchalantly into the shoe store. No physical intimidation
Tarrance. None at all. Tarrance walks up, they talk, and b
sort of duck into the store. My man says they disappear
the back of the store, and they're back there for three, ma
four minutes. Then another one of our guys walks by
store, looks in and sees nothing. Evidently, they saw our n
because within seconds they come flying out of the store v
McDeere shoving and yelling. Something ain't right, I
you."

"Did Tarrance grab his arm and force him into the sto
Nathan Locke asked slowly, precisely.

"Hell no. And that's the problem. McDeere went voluntar-
, and when he said the guy grabbed his arm, he's lying. My
an says he thinks they would've stayed in there for a while if
ey hadn't seen us."

"But you're not sure of that," Nathan Locke said.

"I wasn't sure, dammit. They didn't invite me into the
re."

DeVasher kept pacing while the lawyers stared at the floor.
e unwrapped a Roi-Tan and crammed it into his fat mouth.
Finally, Oliver Lambert spoke. "Look, DeVasher, it's very
ssible McDeere is telling the truth and your man got the
ong signals. It's very possible. I think McDeere is entitled to
e benefit of the doubt."

DeVasher grunted and ignored this.

"Do you know of any contact since last August?" asked
yce McKnight.

"We don't know of any, but that doesn't mean they ain't
ked, does it now? We didn't know about those other two
til it was almost too late. It's impossible to watch every
ve they make. Impossible."

He walked back and forth by his credenza, obviously deep in
ought. "I gotta talk to him," he finally said.

"Who?"

"McDeere. It's time he and I had a little talk."

"About what?" Lambert asked nervously.

"You let me handle it, okay? Just stay out of my way."

"I think it's a bit premature," Locke said.

"And I don't give a damn what you think. If you clowns
re in charge of security, you'd all be in prison."

tch sat in his office with the door closed and stared at the
lls. A migraine was forming at the base of his skull, and he
t sick. There was a knock at the door.

"Come in," he said softly.

Avery peeked inside, then walked to the desk. "How about
ch?"

"No, thanks. I'm not hungry."

The partner slid his hands into his trouser pockets and
iled warmly. "Look, Mitch, I know you're worried. Let's
e a break. I've got to run downtown for a meeting. Why

don't you meet me at the Manhattan Club at one. We'll have
long lunch and talk things over. I've reserved the limo for yo
It'll be waiting outside at a quarter till."

Mitch managed a weak smile, as if he was touched by th
"Sure, Avery. Why not."

"Good. I'll see you at one."

At a quarter till, Mitch opened the front door and walked
the limo. The driver opened the door, and Mitch fell in. Co
pany was waiting.

A short, fat, bald headed man with a huge, bulging, hangi
neck sat smugly in the corner of the rear seat. He stuck ou
hand. "Name's DeVasher, Mitch. Nice to meet you."

"Am I in the right limo?" Mitch asked.

"Sure. Sure. Relax." The driver pulled away from the cu

"What can I do for you?" Mitch asked.

"You can listen for a while. We need to have a little tal
The driver turned on Riverside Drive and headed for the H
nando De Soto Bridge.

"Where are we going?" Mitch asked.

"For a little ride. Just relax, son."

So I'm number six, thought Mitch. This is it. No, wai
minute. They were much more creative than this with th
killing.

"Mitch, can I call you Mitch?"

"Sure."

"Fine. Mitch, I'm in charge of security for the firm, and–

"Why does the firm need security?"

"Just listen to me, son, and I'll explain. The firm has
extensive security program, thanks to old man Bendini.
was a nut about security and secrecy. My job is to protect
firm, and quite frankly, we're very concerned about this F
business."

"So am I."

"Yes. We believe the FBI is determined to infiltrate our fi
in hopes of collecting information on certain clients."

"Which clients?"

"Some high rollers with questionable tax shelters."

Mitch nodded and looked at the river below. They w
now in Arkansas, with the Memphis skyline fading behi
them. DeVasher recessed the conversation. He sat like a fr

th his hands folded across the gut. Mitch waited, until it
came apparent that lapses in conversation and awkward since did not bother DeVasher. Several miles across the river,
e driver left the interstate and found a rough county road
at circled and ran back to the east. Then he turned onto a
avel road that went for a mile through low-lying bean fields
xt to the river. Memphis was suddenly visible again, across
e water.

'Where are we going?" Mitch asked, with some alarm.
"Relax. I want to show you something."

A gravesite, thought Mitch. The limo stopped on a cliff that
l ten feet to a sandbar next to the bank. The skyline stood
pressively on the other side. The top of the Bendini Build-
g was visible.

"Let's take a walk," DeVasher said.
"Where to?" Mitch asked.
"Come on. It's okay." DeVasher opened his door and walked
the rear bumper. Slowly, Mitch followed him.
"As I was saying, Mitch, we are very troubled by this con-
t with the FBI. If you talk to them, they will get bolder, then
o knows what the fools will try. It's imperative that you not
ak to them, ever again. Understand?"
"Yes. I've understood since the first visit in August."
Suddenly, DeVasher was in his face, nose to nose. He smiled
ckedly. "I have something that will keep you honest." He
ched in his sport coat and pulled out a manila envelope.
"Take a look at these," he said with a sneer, and walked
ay.

Mitch leaned on the limo and nervously opened the enve-
e. There were four photographs, black and white, eight by
, very clear. On the beach. The girl.

Oh my god! Who took these?" Mitch yelled at him.
What difference does it make. It's you, ain't it?"
here was no doubt about who it was. He ripped the photo-
phs into small pieces and threw them in DeVasher's direc-
n.

We got plenty at the office," DeVasher said calmly. "Bunch
hem. We don't want to use them, but one more little con-
sation with Mr. Tarrance or any other Fibbie and we'll
l them to your wife. How would you like that, Mitch?

Imagine your pretty little wife going to the mailbox to get h
Redbook and catalogues and she sees this strange envelope a
dressed to her. Try to think of that, Mitch. The next time y
and Tarrance decide to shop for plastic shoes, think about
Mitch. Because we'll be watching."

"Who knows about these?" Mitch asked.

"Me and the photographer, and now you. Nobody in
firm knows, and I don't plan to tell them. But if you screw
again, I suspect they'll be passing them around at lunch. I p
hardball, Mitch."

He sat on the trunk and rubbed his temples. DeVash
walked up next to him. "Listen, son. You're a very brig
young man, and you're on your way to big bucks. Don't scr
it up. Just work hard, play the game, buy new cars, build b
ger homes, the works. Just like all the other guys. Don't try
be no hero. I don't want to use the pictures."

"Okay, okay."

21

⌐OR SEVENTEEN DAYS and seventeen nights, the
troubled lives of Mitch and Abby McDeere proceeded
quietly without interference from Wayne Tarrance or
of his confederates. The routines returned. Mitch worked
hteen hours a day, every day of the week, and never left the
ce for any reason except to drive home. Lunch was at the
k. Avery sent other associates to run errands or file motions
appear in court. Mitch seldom left his office, the fifteen-by-
een sanctuary where he was certain Tarrance could not get
1. If possible, he stayed out of the halls and men's rooms
l coffee room. They were watching, he was sure. He was
sure who they were, but there was no doubt that a bunch
olks were vitally interested in his movements. So he stayed
is desk, with the door shut most of the time, working dili-
tly, billing like crazy and trying to forget that the building
l a fifth floor and on the fifth floor was a short, fat, mean
le bastard named DeVasher who had a collection of photo-
phs that could ruin him.

With each uneventful day, Mitch withdrew even more into
asylum and became even more hopeful that perhaps the
episode in the Korean shoe store had scared Tarrance or

maybe gotten him fired. Maybe Voyles would just simply f
get the entire operation, and Mitch could continue along
happy way of getting rich and making partner and buyi
everything in sight. But he knew better.

To Abby, the house was a prison, though she could co
and go at will. She worked longer hours at school, spent m
time walking the malls and made at least one trip each day
the grocery store. She watched everyone, especially men
dark suits who looked at her. She wore black sunglasses
they could not see her eyes. She wore them when it was ra
ing. Late at night, after supper alone while she waited for hi
she stared at the walls and resisted the temptation to inve
gate. The phones could be examined with a magnifying gl
The wires and mikes could not be invisible, she told hers
More than once she thought of finding a book on such devi
so she could identify them. But Mitch said no. They were
the house, he assured her, and any attempt to find them co
be disastrous.

So she moved silently around her own house, feeling
lated and knowing it could not last much longer. They b
knew the importance of appearing normal, of sounding n
mal. They tried to engage in normal talk about how the
went, about the office and her students, about the weath
about this and that. But the conversations were flat, of
forced and strained. When Mitch was in law school the lo
making had been frequent and rowdy; now it was practic
nonexistent. Someone was listening.

Midnight walks around the block became a habit. Afte
quick sandwich each night, they would deliver the rehear
lines about needing exercise and head for the street. They h
hands and walked in the cold, talking about the firm and
FBI, and which way to turn; always the same conclusion: th
was no way out. None. Seventeen days and seventeen nig

The eighteenth day brought a new twist. Mitch was
hausted by 9 P.M. and decided to go home. He had wor
nonstop for fifteen and a half hours. At two hundred per
usual, he walked the halls of the second floor, then took
stairs to the third floor. He casually checked each office to
who was still working. No one on the third floor. He follow
the stairs to the fourth floor and walked the wide rectang

allway as if in search of something. All lights except one were f. Royce McKnight was working late. Mitch eased by his fice without being seen. Avery's door was closed, and Mitch abbed the doorknob. It was locked. He walked to the library own the hall, looking for a book he did not need. After two eeks of the casual late-night inspections, he had found no osed circuit cameras above the halls or offices. They just lisn, he decided. They do not see.

He said goodbye to Dutch Hendrix at the front gate and ove home. Abby was not expecting him at such an early ur. He quietly unlocked the door from the carport and eased to the kitchen. He flipped on a light switch. She was in the droom. Between the kitchen and the den was a small foyer ith a rolltop desk where Abby left each day's mail. He laid s briefcase softly on the desk, then saw it. A large brown velope addressed with a black felt marker to Abby McDeere. o return address. Scrawled in heavy black letters were the ords PHOTOGRAPHS—DO NOT BEND. His heart stopped first, en his breathing. He grabbed the envelope. It had been ened.

A heavy layer of sweat broke across his forehead. His mouth as dry and he could not swallow. His heart returned with the ry of a jackhammer. The breathing was heavy and painful. e was nauseous. Slowly, he backed away from the desk, holdg the envelope. She's in the bed, he thought. Hurt, sick, devtated and mad as hell. He wiped his forehead and tried to llect himself. Face it like a man, he said.

She was in the bed, reading a book with the television on. he dog was in the backyard. Mitch opened the bedroom door, d Abby bolted upright in horror. She almost screamed at the truder, until she recognized him.

"You scared me, Mitch!"

Her eyes glowed with fear, then fun. They had not been ying. They looked fine, normal. No pain. No anger. He uld not speak.

"Why are you home?" she demanded, sitting up in bed, smilg now.

Smiling? "I live here," he said weakly.

"Why didn't you call?"

"Do I have to call before I can come home?" His breathing was now almost normal. She was fine!

"It would be nice. Come here and kiss me."

He leaned across the bed and kissed her. He handed her the envelope. "What's this?" he asked nonchalantly.

"You tell me. It's addressed to me, but there was nothing inside. Not a thing." She closed her book and laid it on the night table.

Not a thing! He smiled at her and kissed her again. "Are you expecting photographs from anyone?" he asked in complete ignorance.

"Not that I know of. Must be a mistake."

He could almost hear DeVasher laughing at this very moment on the fifth floor. The fat little bastard was standing there somewhere in some dark room full of wires and machines with a headset stretched around his massive bowling ball of a head, laughing uncontrollably.

"That's strange," Mitch said. Abby pulled on a pair of jeans and pointed to the backyard. Mitch nodded. The signal was simple, just a quick point or a nod of the head in the direction of the patio.

Mitch laid the envelope on the rolltop desk and for a second touched the scrawled markings on it. Probably DeVasher's handwriting. He could almost hear him laughing. He could see his fat face and nasty smile. The photographs had probably been passed around during lunch in the partners' dining room. He could see Lambert and McKnight and even Avery gawking admiringly over coffee and dessert.

They'd better enjoy the pictures, dammit. They'd better enjoy the remaining few months of their bright and rich and happy legal careers.

Abby walked by and he grabbed her hand. "What's for dinner?" he asked for the benefit of those listening.

"Why don't we go out? We should celebrate since you're home at a decent hour."

They walked through the den. "Good idea," said Mitch. They eased through the rear door, across the patio and into the darkness.

"What is it?" Mitch asked.

"You got a letter today from Doris. She said she's in Nash-

lle, but will return to Memphis on the twenty-seventh of
ebruary. She says she needs to see you. It's important. It was
very short letter."

"The twenty-seventh! That was yesterday."

"I know. I presume she's already in town. I wonder what
e wants."

"Yeah, and I wonder where she is."

"She said her husband had an engagement here in town."

"Good. She'll find us," Mitch said.

athan Locke closed his office door and pointed DeVasher in
e direction of the small conference table near the window.
he two men hated each other and made no attempt to be
rdial. But business was business, and they took orders from
e same man.

"Lazarov wanted me to talk to you, alone," DeVasher said.
've spent the past two days with him in Vegas, and he's very
xious. They're all anxious, Locke, and he trusts you more
an anyone else around here. He likes you more than he likes
e."

"That's understandable," Locke said with no smile. The rip-
es of black around his eyes narrowed and focused intensely
DeVasher.

"Anyway, there are a few things he wants us to discuss."

"I'm listening."

"McDeere's lying. You know how Lazarov's always bragged
out having a mole inside the FBI. Well, I've never believed
m, and still don't, for the most part. But according to
zarov, his little source is telling him that there was some
nd of secret meeting involving McDeere and some FBI
avyweights when your boy was in Washington back in Janu-
y. We were there, and our men saw nothing, but it's impossi-
e to track anyone twenty-four hours a day without getting
ught. It's possible he could've slipped away for a little while
thout our knowledge."

"Do you believe it?"

"It's not important whether I believe it. Lazarov believes it,
d that's all that matters. At any rate, he told me to make
eliminary plans to, uh, take care of him."

"Damn DeVasher! We can't keep eliminating people."

"Just preliminary plans, nothing serious. I told Lazarov thought it was much too early and that it would be a mistak But they are very worried, Locke."

"This can't continue, De Vasher. I mean, damn! We have rep tations to consider. We have a higher casualty rate than rigs. People will start talking. We're gonna reach a point whe no law student in his right mind would take a job here."

"I don't think you need to worry about that. Lazarov has p a freeze on hiring. He told me to tell you that. He also wants know how many associates are still in the dark."

"Five, I think. Let's see, Lynch, Sorrell, Buntin, Myers ar McDeere."

"Forget McDeere. Lazarov is convinced he knows mu more than we think. Are you certain the other four kno nothing?"

Locke thought for a moment and mumbled under h breath. "Well, we haven't told them. You guys are listeni and watching. What do you hear?"

"Nothing, from those four. They sound ignorant and act if they suspect nothing. Can you fire them?"

"Fire them! They're lawyers, DeVasher. You don't fire la yers. They're loyal members of the firm."

"The firm is changing, Locke. Lazarov wants to fire the on who don't know and stop hiring new ones. It's obvious t Fibbies have changed their strategy, and it's time for us change as well. Lazarov wants to circle the wagons and pl the leaks. We can't sit back and wait for them to pick off o boys."

"Fire them," Locke repeated in disbelief. "This firm h never fired a lawyer."

"Very touching, Locke. We've disposed of five, but nev fired one. That's real good. You've got a month to do it, so sta thinking of a reason. I suggest you fire all four at one tim Tell them you lost a big account and you're cutting back."

"We have clients, not accounts."

"Okay, fine. Your biggest client is telling you to fire Lync Sorrell, Buntin and Myers. Now start making plans."

"How do we fire those four without firing McDeere?"

"You'll think of something, Nat. You got a month. Get rid them and don't hire any new boys. Lazarov wants a tight litt hit where everyone can be trusted. He's scared, Nat. Scared and mad. I don't have to tell you what could happen if one of our boys spilled his guts."

"No, you don't have to tell me. What does he plan to do with McDeere?"

"Right now, nothing but the same. We're listening twenty-four hours a day, and the kid has never mentioned a word to his wife or anyone else. Not a word! He's been corralled twice by Tarrance, and he reported both incidents to you. I still think the second meeting was somewhat suspicious, so we're being very careful. Lazarov, on the other hand, insists there was a meeting in Washington. He's trying to confirm. He said his sources knew little, but they were digging. If in fact McDeere met with the Fibbies up there and failed to report it, then I'm sure Lazarov will instruct me to move quickly. That's why he wants preliminary plans to take McDeere out."

"How do you plan to do it?"

"It's too early. I haven't given it much thought."

"You know he and his wife are going to the Caymans in two weeks for a vacation. They'll stay in one of our condos, the usual."

"We wouldn't do it there again. Too suspicious. Lazarov instructed me to get her pregnant."

"McDeere's wife?"

"Yep. He wants them to have a baby, a little leverage. She's on the pill, so we gotta break in, take her little box, match up the pills and replace them with placebos."

At this, the great black eyes saddened just a touch and looked through the window. "What the hell's going on, DeVasher?" he asked softly.

"This place is about to change, Nat. It appears as though the feds are extremely interested, and they keep pecking away. One day, who knows, one of your boys may take the bait, and you'll all leave town in the middle of the night."

"I don't believe that, DeVasher. A lawyer here would be a fool to risk his life and his family for a few promises from the feds. I just don't believe it will happen. These boys are too smart and they're making too much money."

"I hope you're right."

22

T HE LEASING AGENT leaned against the rear of t
elevator and admired the black leather miniskirt fro
behind. He followed it down almost to the knees, whe
it ended and the seams in the black silk stockings began a
snaked downward to black heels. Kinky heels, with little r
bows across the toes. He slowly worked his way back up t
seams, past the leather, pausing to admire the roundness of h
rear, then upward to the red cashmere sweater, which from h
vantage point revealed little but from the other side was qui
impressive, as he had noticed in the lobby. The hair land
just below the shoulder blades and contrasted nicely with t
red. He knew it was bleached, but add the bleach to the leath
mini and the seams and the kinky heels and the tight sweat
hugging those things around the front, add all that togeth
and he knew this was a woman he could have. He would li
to have her in the building. She just wanted a small office. T
rent was negotiable.

The elevator stopped. The door opened, and he followed h
into the narrow hall. "This way"—he pointed, flipping on
light switch. In the corner, he moved in front of her and stu
a key in a badly aged wooden door.

"It's just two rooms," he said, flipping on another switch. "About two hundred square feet."

She walked straight to the window. "The view is okay," Tammy said, staring into the distance.

"Yes, a nice view. The carpet is new. Painted last fall. Rest room's down the hall. It's a nice place. The entire building's been renovated within the past eight years." He stared at the back seams as he spoke.

"It's not bad," Tammy said, not in response to anything he had mentioned. She continued to stare out the window. "What's the name of this place?"

"The Cotton Exchange Building. One of the oldest in Memphis. It's really a prestigious address."

"How prestigious is the rent?"

He cleared his throat and held a file before him. He did not look at the file. He was gaping at the heels now. "Well, it's such a small office. What did you say you needed it for?"

"Secretarial work. Free-lance secretarial." She moved to the other window, ignoring him. He followed every move.

"I see. How long will you need it?"

"Six months, with an option for a year."

"Okay, for six months we can lease it for three-fifty a month."

She did not flinch or look from the window. She slid her right foot out of the shoe and rubbed the left calf with it. The seam continued, he observed, under the heel and along the bottom of the foot. The toenails were . . . red! She cocked her ear to the left and leaned on the windowsill. His file was shaking.

"I'll pay two-fifty a month," she said with authority.

He cleared his throat. There was no sense being greedy. The tiny rooms were dead space, useless to anyone else, and had not been occupied in years. The building could use a free-lance secretary. Hell, he might even need a free-lance secretary.

"Three hundred, but no less. This building is in demand. Ninety percent occupied right now. Three hundred a month, and that's too low. We're barely covering costs at that."

She turned suddenly, and there they were. Staring at him. The cashmere was stretched tightly around them. "The ad said there were furnished offices available," she said.

"We can furnish this one," he said, eager to cooperat
"What do you need?"

She looked around the office. "I would like a secretarial de
with credenza in here. Several file cabinets. A couple of chai
for clients. Nothing fancy. The other room does not have to I
furnished. I'll put a copier in there."

"No problem," he said with a smile.

"And I'll pay three hundred a month, furnished."

"Good," he said as he opened a file and withdrew a bla
lease. He laid it on a folding table and began writing.

"Your name?"

"Doris Greenwood." Her mother was Doris Greenwoo
and she had been Tammy Inez Greenwood before she ran
on Buster Hemphill, who later became (legally) Elvis Aar
Hemphill, and life had pretty much been downhill since. H
mother lived in Effingham, Illinois.

"Okay, Doris," he said with an effort at suaveness, as if th
were now on a first name basis and growing closer by t
moment. "Home address?"

"Why do you need that?" she asked with irritation.

"Well, uh, we just need that information."

"It's none of your business."

"Okay, okay. No problem." He dramatically scratched o
that portion of the lease. He hovered above it. "Let's see. We
run it from today, March 2, for six months until September
Is that okay?"

She nodded and lit a cigarette.

He read the next paragraph. "Okay, we require a three-hu
dred-dollar deposit and the first month's rent in advance."

From a pocket in the tight black leather skirt, she produce
roll of cash. She counted six one-hundred-dollar bills and la
them on the table. "Receipt, please," she demanded.

"Certainly." He continued writing.

"What floor are we on?" she asked, returning to the w
dows.

"Ninth. There's a ten percent late charge past the fifteen
of the month. We have the right to enter at any reasonal
time to inspect. Premises cannot be used for any illegal p
pose. You pay all utilities and insurance on contents. You

e parking space in the lot across the street, and here are two ys. Any questions?"

"Yeah. What if I work odd hours? I mean, real late at night."

"No big deal. You can come and go as you please. After dark e security guard at the Front Street door will let you pass."

Tammy stuck the cigarette between her sticky lips and ılked to the table. She glanced at the lease, hesitated, then ;ned the name of Doris Greenwood.

They locked up, and he followed her carefully down the hall the elevator.

By noon the next day, the odd assortment of furniture had en delivered and Doris Greenwood of Greenwood Services ranged the rented typewriter and the rented phone next to :h other on the secretarial desk. Sitting and facing the type-"iter, she could look slightly to her left out of the window d watch the traffic on Front Street. She filled the desk draw-; with typing paper, notepads, pencils, odds and ends. She ıced magazines on the filing cabinets and the small table tween the two chairs where her clients would sit.

There was a knock at the door. "Who is it?" she asked.

"It's your copier," a voice answered.

She unlocked the door and opened it. A short, hyperactive tle man named Gordy rushed in, looked around the room d said rudely, "Okay, where do you want it?"

"In there," Tammy said, pointing to the eight-by-ten empty ɔm with no door on the hinges. Two young men in blue iforms pushed and pulled the cart holding the copier.

Gordy laid the paperwork on her desk. "It's a mighty big pier for this place. We're talking ninety copies a minute with :ollator and automatic feed. It's a big machine."

'Where do I sign?" she asked, ignoring the small talk.

He pointed with the pen. "Six months, at two-forty a ɔnth. That includes service and maintenance and five hun-:d sheets of paper for the first two months. You want legal letter sized?"

'Legal."

'First payment due on the tenth, and same thereafter for e months. Operator's manual is on the rack. Call me if you 'e any questions."

The two servicemen gawked at the tight stonewashed jeans

231

and the red heels and slowly left the office. Gordy ripped the yellow copy and handed it to her. "Thanks for the bus ness," he said.

She locked the door behind them. She walked to the wind next to her desk and looked north, along Front. Two blocks on the opposite side, floors four and five of the Bendini Bui ing were visible.

He kept to himself with his nose buried deep in the books a the piles of paperwork. He was too busy for any of the except Lamar. He was very much aware that his withdrav was not going unnoticed. So he worked harder. Perhaps th would not be suspicious if he billed twenty hours a day. P haps money could insulate him.

Nina left a box of cold pizza when she checked out af lunch. He ate it while he cleared his desk. He called Ab Said he was going to see Ray and that he would return Memphis late Sunday. He eased through the side door a into the parking lot.

For three and a half hours, he raced along Interstate 40 w his eyes on the rearview mirror. Nothing. He never saw the They probably just call ahead, he thought, and wait for h somewhere up there. In Nashville, he made a sudden exit i downtown. Using a map he had scribbled, he darted in and of traffic, making U-turns wherever possible and in gene driving like a nut. To the south of town, he turned quic into a large apartment complex and cruised between the bu ings. It was nice enough. The parking lots were clean and faces were white. All of them. He parked next to the office a locked the BMW. The pay phone by the covered pool work He called a cab and gave an address two blocks away. He between the buildings, down a side street, and arrived p cisely with the cab. "Greyhound bus station," he said to driver. "And in a hurry. I've got ten minutes."

"Relax, pal. It's only six blocks away."

Mitch ducked low in the rear seat and watched the tra The driver moved with a slow confidence and seven minu later turned onto Eighth Street. He stopped in front of station. Mitch threw two fives over the seat and darted into terminal. He bought a one way ticket on the four-thirty bus lanta. It was four thirty-one, according to the clock on the ll. The clerk pointed through the swinging doors. "Bus No. 4," she said. "Leaving in a moment."

The driver slammed the baggage door, took his ticket and lowed Mitch onto the bus. The first three rows were filled th elderly blacks. A dozen more passengers were scattered ward the rear. Mitch walked slowly down the aisle, gazing at ch face and seeing no one. He took a window seat on the urth row from the rear. He slipped on a pair of sunglasses d glanced behind him. No one. Dammit! Was it the wrong s? He stared out the dark windows as the bus moved quickly o traffic. They would stop in Knoxville. Maybe his contact uld be there.

When they were on the interstate and the driver reached his aising speed, a man in blue jeans and madras shirt suddenly peared and slid into the seat next to Mitch. It was Tarrance. tch breathed easier.

"Where have you been?" he asked.

"In the rest room. Did you lose them?" Tarrance spoke in a v voice while surveying the backs of the heads of the passen- s. No one was listening. No one could hear.

"I never see them, Tarrance. So I cannot say if I lost them. t I think they would have to be supermen to keep my trail s time."

"Did you see our man in the terminal?"

"Yes. By the pay phone with the red Falcons cap. Black de."

"That's him. He would've signaled if they were following."

"He gave me the go-ahead."

Tarrance wore silver reflective sunglasses under a green chigan State baseball cap. Mitch could smell the fresh Juicy iit.

"Sort of out of uniform, aren't you?" Mitch said with no ile. "Did Voyles give you permission to dress like that?"

"I forgot to ask him. I'll mention it in the morning."

"Sunday morning?" Mitch asked.

"Of course. He'll wanna know all about our little bus ride. I efed him for an hour before I left town."

"Well, first things first. What about my car?"

"We'll pick it up in a few minutes and babysit it for you. I [ ] be in Knoxville when you need it. Don't worry."

"You don't think they'll find us?"

"No way. No one followed you out of Memphis, and [ ] detected nothing in Nashville. You're clean as a whistle."

"Pardon my concern. But after that fiasco in the shoe stor[ ] know you boys are not above stupidity."

"It was a mistake, all right. We—"

"A big mistake. One that could get me on the hit list."

"You covered it well. It won't happen again."

"Promise me, Tarrance. Promise me no one will ever ag[ ] approach me in public."

Tarrance looked down the aisle and nodded.

"No, Tarrance. I need to hear it from your mouth. Prom[ ] me."

"Okay, okay. It won't happen again. I promise."

"Thanks. Now maybe I can eat at a restaurant without f[ ] of being grabbed."

"You've made your point."

An old black man with a cane inched toward them, smi[ ] and walked past. The rest-room door slammed. The Gr[ ] hound rode the left lane and blew past the lawful drivers.

Tarrance flipped through a magazine. Mitch gazed into [ ] countryside. The man with the cane finished his business a[ ] wobbled to his seat on the front row.

"So what brings you here?" Tarrance asked, flipping pa[ ]

"I don't like airplanes. I always take the bus."

"I see. Where would you like to start?"

"Voyles said you had a game plan."

"I do. I just need a quarterback."

"Good ones are very expensive."

"We've got the money."

"It'll cost a helluva lot more than you think. The wa[ ] figure it, I'll be throwing away a forty year legal career at, s[ ] an average of half a million a year."

"That's twenty million bucks."

"I know. But we can negotiate."

"That's good to hear. You're assuming that you'll work, [ ] practice, as you say, for forty years. That's a very precari[ ] assumption. Just for fun, let's assume that within five years [ ]

st up the firm and indict you along with all of your buddies.
d that we obtain convictions, and you go off to prison for a
w years. They won't keep you long because you're a white-
lar type, and of course you've heard how nice the federal
ns are. But at any rate, you'll lose your license, your house,
ur little BMW. Probably your wife. When you get out, you
n open up a private investigation service like your old friend
max. It's easy work, unless you sniff the wrong underwear."

"Like I said. It's negotiable."

"All right. Let's negotiate. How much do you want?"

"For what?"

Tarrance closed the magazine, placed it under his seat and
ened a thick paperback. He pretended to read. Mitch spoke
m the corner of his mouth with his eyes on the median.

"That's a very good question," Tarrance said softly, just
ove the distant grind of the diesel engine. "What do we want
m you? Good question. First, you have to give up your ca-
r as a lawyer. You'll have to divulge secrets and records that
long to your clients. That, of course, is enough to get you
barred, but that won't seem important. You and I must
ee that you will hand us the firm on a silver platter. Once
agree, if we agree, the rest will fall in place. Second, and
st important, you will give us enough documentation to
ict every member of the firm and most of the top Morolto
ople. The records are in the little building there on Front
eet."

'How do you know this?"

Tarrance smiled. "Because we spend billions of dollars fight-
g organized crime. Because we've tracked the Moroltos for
enty years. Because we have sources within the family. Be-
se Hodge and Kozinski were talking when they were mur-
red. Don't sell us short, Mitch."

'And you think I can get the information out?"

'Yes, Counselor. You can build a case from the inside that
ll collapse the firm and break up one of the largest crime
nilies in the country. You gotta lay out the firm for us.
hose office is where? Names of all secretaries, clerks, parale-
s. Who works on what files? Who's got which clients? The
ain of command. Where on the fifth floor? What's up there?
here are the records kept? Is there a central storage area?

How much is computerized? How much is on microfilm? A
most important, you gotta bring the stuff out and hand it to
Once we have probable cause, we can go in with a small ar
and get everything. But that's an awfully big step. We go
have a very tight and solid case before we go crashing in w
search warrants."

"Is that all you want?"

"No. You'll have to testify against all of your buddies
their trials. Could take years."

Mitch breathed deeply and closed his eyes. The bus slov
behind a caravan of mobile homes split in two. Dusk was
proaching, and, one at a time, the cars in the westbound l
brightened with headlights. Testifying at trial! This, he l
not thought of. With millions to spend for the best crimi
lawyers, the trials could drag on forever.

Tarrance actually began reading the paperback, a L
L'Amour. He adjusted the reading light above them, as if
was indeed a real passenger on a real journey. After th
miles of no talk, no negotiation, Mitch removed his sungla
and looked at Tarrance.

"What happens to me?"

"You'll have a lot of money, for what that's worth. If
have any sense of morality, you can face yourself each day.
can live anywhere in the country, with a new identity
course. We'll find you a job, fix your nose, do anything
want, really."

Mitch tried to keep his eyes on the road, but it was impo
ble. He glared at Tarrance. "Morality? Don't ever ment
that word to me again, Tarrance. I'm an innocent victim,
you know it."

Tarrance grunted with a smart-ass grin.

They rode in silence for a few miles.

"What about my wife?"

"Yeah, you can keep her."

"Very funny."

"Sorry. She'll get everything she wants. How much does
know?"

"Everything." He thought of the girl on the beach. "V
almost everything."

"We'll get her a fat government job with the Social Secu

236

ministration anywhere you want. It won't be that bad,
tch."

"It'll be wonderful. Until an unknown point in the future
en one of your people opens his or her mouth and lets
nething slip to the wrong person, and you'll read about me
my wife in the paper. The Mob never forgets, Tarrance.
ey're worse than elephants. And they keep secrets better
n your side. You guys have lost people, so don't deny it."

"I won't deny it. And I'll admit to you that they can be
enious when they decide to kill."

"Thanks. So where do I go?"

"It's up to you. Right now we have about two thousand
nesses living all over the country under new names with
w homes and new jobs. The odds are overwhelmingly in
r favor."

"So I play the odds?"

"Yes. You either take the money and run, or you play big-
t lawyer and bet that we never infiltrate."

"That's a hell of a choice, Tarrance."

"It is. I'm glad it's yours."

The female companion of the ancient black man with the
e rose feebly from her seat and began shuffling toward
m. She grabbed each aisle seat as she progressed. Tarrance
ned toward Mitch as she passed. He would not dare speak
h this stranger in the vicinity. She was at least ninety, half
ppled, probably illiterate, and could care less if Tarrance
eived his next breath of air. But Tarrance was instantly
te.

Fifteen minutes later, the rest-room door opened and re-
sed the sounds of the toilet gurgling downward into the pit
he Greyhound. She shuffled to the front and took her seat.

"Who is Jack Aldrich?" Mitch asked. He suspected a cover-
with this one, and he carefully watched the reaction from
corner of his eye. Tarrance looked up from the book and
ed at the seat in front of him.

"Name's familiar. I can't place him."

Mitch returned his gaze to the window. Tarrance knew. He
flinched, and his eyes had narrowed too quickly before he
wered. Mitch watched the westbound traffic.

"So who is he?" Tarrance finally asked.

237

"You don't know him?"

"If I knew him, I wouldn't ask who he was."

"He's a member of our firm. You should've known that, T rance."

"The city's full of lawyers. I guess you know them all."

"I know the ones at Bendini, Lambert & Locke, the q little firm you guys have been studying for ten years. Aldr is a six-year man who allegedly was approached by the FB couple of months ago. True or false?"

"Absolutely false. Who told you this?"

"It doesn't matter. Just a rumor around the office."

"It's a lie. We've talked to no one but you since August. have my word. And we have no plans to talk to anyone e unless, of course, you decline and we must find another p ect."

"You've never talked to Aldrich?"

"That's what I said."

Mitch nodded and picked up a magazine. They rode in lence for thirty minutes. Tarrance gave up on his novel, finally said, "Look, Mitch, we'll be in Knoxville in an hou so. We need to strike a deal, if we're going to. Director Vo will have a thousand questions in the morning."

"How much money?"

"Half a million bucks."

Any lawyer worth his salt knew the first offer had to rejected. Always. He had seen Avery's mouth drop ope shock and his head shake wildly in absolute disgust and di lief with first offers, regardless of how reasonable. Th would be counteroffers, and counter-counteroffers, and ther negotiations, but always, the first offer was rejected.

So by shaking his head and smiling at the window as if was what he expected, Mitch said no to half a million.

"Did I say something funny?" Tarrance, the nonlawyer, nonnegotiator, asked.

"That's ridiculous, Tarrance. You can't expect me to v away from a gold mine for half a million bucks. After tax net three hundred thousand at best."

"And if we close the gold mine and send all you Gu footed hotshots to jail?"

"If. If. If. If you knew so much, why haven't you done so

238

ng? Voyles said you boys have been watching and waiting ten years. That's real good, Tarrance. Do you always move fast?"

"Do you wanna take that chance, McDeere? Let's say it es us another five years, okay? After five years we bust the nt and send your ass to jail. At that point it won't make any ference how long it took us, will it? The result will be the ne, Mitch."

"I'm sorry. I thought we were negotiating, not threatening."

"I've made you an offer."

"Your offer is too low. You expect me to make a case that l hand you hundreds of indictments against a group of the iziest criminals in America, a case that could easily cost me life. And you offer a pittance. Three million, at least."

Tarrance did not flinch or frown. He received the counter- r with a good, straight poker face, and Mitch, the negotia- , knew it was not out of the ballpark.

"That's a lot of money," Tarrance said, almost to himself. "I i't think we've ever paid that much."

"But you can, can't you?"

I doubt it. I'll have to talk to the Director."

The Director! I thought you had complete authority on s case. Are we gonna run back and forth to the Director til we have a deal?"

What else do you want?"

I've got a few things in mind, but we won't discuss them til the money gets right."

The old man with the cane apparently had weak kidneys. stood again and began the awkward wobble to the rear of bus. Tarrance again started his book. Mitch flipped ough an old copy of *Field & Stream*.

e Greyhound left the interstate in Knoxville two minutes ore eight. Tarrance leaned closer and whispered, "Take the nt door out of the terminal. You'll see a young man wearing orange University of Tennessee sweat suit standing beside a ite Bronco. He'll recognize you and call you Jeffrey. Shake ds like lost friends and get in the Bronco. He'll take you to r car."

Where is it?" Mitch whispered.

239

"Behind a dorm on campus."

"Have they checked it for bugs?"

"I think so. Ask the man in the Bronco. If they were tra[c]ing you when you left Memphis, they might be suspicious now. You should drive to Henderson. It's about fifty miles th[is] side of Nashville. There's a Holiday Inn there. Spend t[he] night and go see your brother tomorrow. We'll be watchi[ng] also, and if things look fishy, I'll find you Monday mornin[g.]"

"When's the next bus ride?"

"Your wife's birthday is Tuesday. Make reservations [for] eight at Grisanti's, that Italian place on Airways. At precis[e] nine, go to the cigarette machine in the bar, insert six quart[ers] and buy a pack of anything. In the tray where the cigaret[tes] are released, you will find a cassette tape. Buy yourself one [of] those small tape players that joggers wear with earphones a[nd] listen to the tape in your car, not at home, and sure as hell n[ot] at the office. Use the earphones. Let your wife listen to it. [It'll] be on the cassette, and I'll give you our top dollar. I'll [also] explain a few things. After you've listened to it a few tim[es,] dispose of it."

"This is rather elaborate, isn't it?"

"Yes, but we don't need to speak to each other for a couple [of] weeks. They're watching and listening, Mitch. And they['re] very good. Don't forget that."

"Don't worry."

"What was your football jersey number in high school?"

"Fourteen."

"And college?"

"Fourteen."

"Okay. Your code number is 1-4-1-4. Thursday night, fro[m a] touch tone pay phone, call 757-6000. You'll get a voice that w[ill] lead you through a little routine involving your code numb[er.] Once you're cleared, you will hear my recorded voice, an[d it] will ask you a series of questions. We'll go from there."

"Why can't I just practice law?"

The bus pulled into the terminal and stopped. "I'm going to Atlanta," Tarrance said. "I will not see you for a couple [of] weeks. If there's an emergency, call one of the two number[s I] gave you before."

Mitch stood in the aisle and looked down at the age[d]

ree million, Tarrance. Not a penny less. If you guys can
d billions fighting organized crime, surely you can find
e million for me. And, Tarrance, I have a third option. I
disappear in the middle of the night, vanish into the air. If
happens, you and the Moroltos can fight each other till
freezes over, and I'll be playing dominoes in the Carib-
."

ure, Mitch. You might play a game or two, but they'd find
within a week. And we wouldn't be there to protect you.
ng, buddy."

itch jumped from the bus and darted through the termi-

23

AT EIGHT-THIRTY A.M. on Tuesday, Nina for
neat piles out of the rubble and debris on his desk.
enjoyed this early-morning ritual of straightening
desk and planning his day. The appointment book lay u
structed on a corner of his desk. She read from it. "You h
very busy day today, Mr. McDeere."

Mitch flipped through a file and tried to ignore her. "E
day is busy."

"You have a meeting at ten o'clock in Mr. Mahan's offic
the Delta Shipping appeal."

"I can't wait," Mitch mumbled.

"You have a meeting at eleven-thirty in Mr. Tolleson's o
on the Greenbriar dissolution, and his secretary informe
it would last at least two hours."

"Why two hours?"

"I'm not paid to ask those questions, Mr. McDeere. If I
might get fired. At three-thirty, Victor Milligan wants to
with you."

"About what?"

"Again, Mr. McDeere, I'm not supposed to ask quest

you're due in Frank Mulholland's office downtown in
en minutes."

Yes, I know. Where is it?"

The Cotton Exchange Building. Four or five blocks up
it at Union. You've walked by it a hundred times."

Fine. What else?"

Shall I bring you something back from lunch?"

No, I'll grab a sandwich downtown."

Wonderful. Do you have everything for Mulholland?"

He pointed to the heavy black briefcase and said nothing.
left, and seconds later Mitch walked down the hall, down
stairs and out the front door. He paused for a second under
streetlight, then turned and walked quickly toward down-
n. The black briefcase was in his right hand, the burgundy
kin attaché was in his left. The signal.

In front of a green building with boarded windows, he
ped next to a fire hydrant. He waited a second, then
sed Front Street. Another signal.

On the ninth floor of the Cotton Exchange Building,
amy Greenwood of Greenwood Services backed away
a the window and put on her coat. She locked the door
nd her and pushed the elevator button. She waited. She
about to encounter a man who could easily get her killed.
itch entered the lobby and went straight to the elevators.
noticed no one in particular. A half dozen businessmen
e in the process of talking as they came and went. A
an was whispering into a pay phone. A security guard
red near the Union Avenue entrance. He pushed the ele-
r button and waited, alone. As the door opened, a young
cut Merrill Lynch type in a black suit and sparkling
g tips stepped into the elevator. Mitch had hoped for a
ary ride upward.

ulholland's office was on the seventh floor. Mitch pushed
even button and ignored the kid in the black suit. As the
tor moved, both men dutifully stared at the blinking
bers above the door. Mitch eased to the rear of the small
tor and set the heavy briefcase on the floor, next to his
foot. The door opened on the fourth floor, and Tammy
ed nervously in. The kid glanced at her. Her attire was
rkably conservative. A simple, short knit dress with no

243

plunging necklines. No kinky shoes. Her hair was tinted [
soft shade of red. He glanced again and pushed the CLOSE D
button.

Tammy brought aboard a large black briefcase, identica
Mitch's. She ignored his eyes, stood next to him, quietly
ting it next to his. On the seventh floor, Mitch grabbed
briefcase and left the elevator. On the eighth floor, the
young man in the black suit made his departure, and on
ninth floor Tammy picked up the heavy black briefcase fu
files from Bendini, Lambert & Locke and took it to her of
She locked and bolted the door, quickly removed her coat
went to the small room where the copier was waiting
running. There were seven files, each at least an inch th
She laid them neatly on the folding table next to the co
and took the one marked "Koker-Hanks to East Texas Pi
She unhooked the aluminum clasp, removed the contents f
the file and carefully placed the stack of documents and let
and notes into the automatic feed. She pushed the PRINT bu
and watched as the machine made two perfect copies of ev
thing.

Thirty minutes later, the seven files were returned to
briefcase. The new files, fourteen of them, were locked a
in a fireproof file cabinet hidden in a small closet, which
also locked. Tammy placed the briefcase near the door,
waited.

Frank Mulholland was a partner in a ten man firm that spe
ized in banking and securities. His client was an old man
had founded and built a chain of do-it-yourself hardware st
and at one point had been worth eighteen million before
son and a renegade board of directors took control and for
him into retirement. The old man sued. The comp
countersued. Everybody sued everybody, and the suits
countersuits had been hopelessly deadlocked for eight
months. Now that the lawyers were fat and happy, it was
to talk settlement. Bendini, Lambert & Locke handled the
advice for the son and the new board, and two months ea
Avery had introduced Mitch to the hostilities. The plan wa
offer the old man a five million dollar package of comp
stock, convertible warrants and a few bonds.

Mulholland was not impressed with the plan. His client was greedy, he explained repeatedly, and he knew he would ever regain control of the company. His company, remem— But five million was not enough. Any jury of any degree intelligence would be sympathetic to the old man, and a fool ld see the lawsuit was worth at least, well . . . at least nty million!

fter an hour of sliding proposals and offers and counterof— across Mulholland's desk, Mitch had increased the package ight million and the old man's lawyer said he might con— r fifteen. Mitch politely repacked his attaché case and Mul— and politely escorted him to the door. They promised to t again in a week. They shook hands like best friends.

he elevator stopped on the fifth floor, and Tammy walked ally inside. It was empty, except for Mitch. When the door ed, he said, "Any problems?"

"Nope. Two copies are locked away."

"How long did it take?"

"Thirty minutes."

stopped on the fourth floor, and she picked up the empty fcase. "Noon tomorrow?" she asked.

"Yes," he replied. The door opened and she disappeared the fourth floor. He rode alone to the lobby, which was ty except for the same security guard. Mitchell McDeere, rney-at-law, hurried from the building with a heavy brief— in each hand and walked importantly back to his office.

celebration of Abby's twenty-fifth birthday was rather lued. Through the dim candlelight in a dark corner of anti's, they whispered and tried to smile at each other. It difficult. Somewhere at that moment in the restaurant an sible FBI agent was holding a cassette tape that he would rt into a cigarette machine in the lounge at precisely nine ck, and Mitch was supposed to be there seconds later to eve it without being seen or caught by the bad guys, who— they were and whatever they looked like. And the tape ld reveal just how much cold hard cash the McDeeres ld receive in return for evidence and a subsequent life on run.

hey picked at their food, tried to smile and carry on an

extended conversation, but mainly they fidgeted and glar
at their watches. The dinner was brief. By eight forty-five
were finished with the plates. Mitch left in the direction of
rest room, and he stared into the dark lounge as he walked
The cigarette machine was in the corner, exactly when
should be.

They ordered coffee, and at exactly nine Mitch returne
the lounge, to the machine, where he nervously inserted
quarters and pulled the lever under Marlboro Lights, in m
ory of Eddie Lomax. He quickly reached into the tray, took
cigarettes and, fishing around in the darkness, found the
sette tape. The pay telephone next to the machine rang, an
jumped. He turned and surveyed the lounge. It was en
except for two men at the bar watching the television bel
and above the bartender. Drunk laughter exploded fro
dark corner far away.

Abby watched every step and move until he sat across f
her. She raised her eyebrows. "And?"

"I got it. Your basic black Sony cassette tape." Mitch si
coffee and smiled innocently while quickly surveying
crowded dining room. No one was watching. No one car

He handed the check and the American Express card to
waiter. "We're in a hurry," he said rudely. The waite
turned within seconds. Mitch scribbled his name.

The BMW was indeed wired. Heavily wired. Tarra
gang had very quietly and very thoroughly examined it
magnifying glasses while waiting for the Greyhound four
earlier. Expertly wired, with terribly expensive equipmen
pable of hearing and recording the slightest sniffle or co
But the bugs could only listen and record; they could
track. Mitch thought that was awfully nice of them, ju
listen but not follow the movements of the BMW.

It left the parking lot of Grisanti's with no conversa
between its occupants. Abby carefully opened a portable
recorder and placed the cassette inside. She handed Mitc
earphones, which he stuck onto his head. She pushed the
button. She watched him as he listened and drove aiml
toward the interstate.

The voice belonged to Tarrance: "Hello Mitch. Toda
Tuesday, February 25, sometime after nine P.M. Happy B

to your lovely wife. This tape will run about ten minutes, I instruct you to listen to it carefully, once or twice, then pose of it. I had a face-to-face meeting with Director Voyles Sunday and briefed him on everything. By the way, I ened the bus ride. Director Voyles is very pleased with the y things are going, but he thinks we've talked long enough. wants to cut a deal, and rather quickly. He explained to me no uncertain terms that we have never paid three million lars and we're not about to pay it to you. He cussed a lot, to make a long story short, Director Voyles said we could a million cash, no more. He said the money would be posited in a Swiss bank and no one, not even the IRS, would r know about it. A million dollars, tax free. That's our best l, and Voyles said you can go to hell if you said no. We're na bust that little firm, Mitch, with or without you."

Mitch smiled grimly and stared at the traffic racing past m on the I-240 loop. Abby watched for a sign, a signal, a nt or groan, anything to indicate good news or bad. She l nothing.

The voice continued: "We'll take care of you, Mitch. You'll e access to FBI protection anytime you think you need it. 'll check on you periodically, if you want. And if you want move on to another city after a few years, we'll take care of You can move every five years if you want, and we'll pick up tab and find jobs for you. Good jobs with the VA or Social urity or Postal Service. Voyles said we'd even find you a h-paying job with a private government contractor. You ne it, Mitch, and it's yours. Of course, we'll provide new ntities for you and your wife, and you can change every r if you desire. No problem. Or if you got a better idea, ll listen. You wanna live in Europe or Australia, just say so. 'll get special treatment. I know we're promising a lot, ch, but we're dead serious and we'll put it in writing. We'll a million in cash, tax free, and set you up wherever you ose. So that's the deal. And in return, you must hand us the n, and the Moroltos. We'll talk about that later. For now, r time is up. Voyles is breathing down my neck, and things st happen quickly. Call me at that number Thursday night ine from the pay phone next to the men's rest room in uston's on Poplar. So long, Mitch."

He sliced a finger across his throat, and Abby pushed stop button, then REWIND. He handed her the earphones, a she began to listen intently.

It was an innocent walk in the park, two lovebirds hold. hands and strolling casually through the cool, clear moonlig They stopped by a cannon and gazed at the majestic ri inching ever so slowly toward New Orleans. The same cann where the late Eddie Lomax once stood in a sleet storm a delivered one of his last investigative reports.

Abby held the cassette in her hand and watched the ri below. She had listened to it twice and refused to leave it the car, where who knows who might snatch it. After week practicing silence, and then speaking only outdoors, wo were becoming difficult.

"You know, Abby," Mitch finally said as he tapped wooden wheel of the cannon, "I've always wanted to w with the post office. I had an uncle once who was a rural n carrier. That would be neat."

It was a gamble, this attempt at humor. But it worked. hesitated for three seconds, then laughed slightly, and he co tell she indeed thought it was funny. "Yeah, and I could n floors in a VA hospital."

"You wouldn't have to mop floors. You could change b pans, something meaningful, something inconspicuous. W live in a neat little white frame house on Maple Street Omaha. I'd be Harvey and you'd be Thelma, and we'd nee short, unassuming last name."

"Poe," Abby added.

"That's great. Harvey and Thelma Poe. The Poe fam We'd have a million dollars in the bank but couldn't spen dime because everyone on Maple Street would know it then we'd become different, which is the last thing we wa

"I'd get a nose job."

"But your nose is perfect."

"Abby's nose is perfect, but what about Thelma's? W have to get it fixed, don't you think?"

"Yeah, I suppose." He was immediately tired of the hun and became quiet. Abby stepped in front of him, and draped his arms over her shoulders. They watched a tug

248

y push a hundred barges under the bridge. An occasional
ud dimmed the moonlight, and the cool winds from the
st rose intermittently, then dissipated.

"Do you believe Tarrance?" Abby asked.

"In what way?"

"Let's suppose you do nothing. Do you believe one day
y'll eventually infiltrate the firm?"

"I'm afraid not to believe."

"So we take the money and run?"

"It's easier for me to take the money and run, Abby. I have
:hing to leave behind. For you, it's different. You'll never see
ır family again."

"Where would we go?"

"I do not know. But I wouldn't want to stay in this country.
e feds cannot be trusted entirely. I'll feel safer in another
ıntry, but I won't tell Tarrance."

"What's the next step?"

"We cut a deal, then quickly go about the job of gathering
ough information to sink the ship. I have no idea what they
nt, but I can find it for them. When Tarrance has enough,
disappear. We take our money, get our nose jobs and disap-
ır."

"How much money?"

"More than a million. They're playing games with the
ney. It's all negotiable."

"How much will we get?"

"Two million cash, tax free. Not a dime less."

"Will they pay it?"

"Yes, but that's not the question. The question is, will we
e it and run?"

$he was cold, and he draped his coat over her shoulders. He
d her tightly. "It's a rotten deal, Mitch," she said, "but at
st we'll be together."

"The name's Harvey, not Mitch."

"Do you think we'll be safe, Harvey?"

"We're not safe here."

"I don't like it here. I'm lonely and scared."

"I'm tired of being a lawyer."

"Let's take the money and haul ass."

"You've got a deal, Thelma."

She handed the cassette tape to him. He glanced at it, th
threw it far below, beyond Riverside Drive, in the direction
the river. They held hands and strolled quickly through
park toward the BMW parked on Front Street.

24

⌐OR ONLY the second time in his career, Mitch was al-
◄ lowed to visit the palatial dining room on the fifth floor.
Avery's invitation came with the explanation that the
⸱tners were all quite impressed with the seventy-one hours
 week he averaged in billing for the month of February,
⸱ thus they wished to offer the small reward of lunch. It was
⸱ invitation no associate could turn down, regardless of
⸱edules and meetings and clients and deadlines and all the
⸱er terribly important and urgently critical aspects of ca-
⸱rs at Bendini, Lambert & Locke. Never in history had an
⸱ociate said no to an invitation to the dining room. Each
⸱ived two invitations per year. Records were kept.

⸱Mitch had two days to prepare for it. His first impulse was
⸱decline, and when Avery first mentioned it a dozen lame
⸱uses crossed his mind. Eating and smiling and chatting and
⸱ernizing with criminals, regardless of how rich and pol-
⸱d, was less attractive than sharing a bowl of soup with a
⸱neless down at the bus station. But to say no would be a
⸱vous breach of tradition. And as things were going, his
⸱vements were already suspicious enough.

⸱o he sat with his back to the window and forced smiles and

small talk in the direction of Avery and Royce McKnight a
of course, Oliver Lambert. He knew he would eat at the sa
table with those three. Knew it for two days. He knew th
would watch him carefully but nonchalantly, trying to det
any loss of enthusiasm, or cynicism, or hopelessness. A
thing, really. He knew they would hang on his every wo
regardless of what he said. He knew they would lavish pra
and promises upon his weary shoulders.

Oliver Lambert had never been more charming. Seven
one hours a week for a February for an associate was a fi
record, he said as Roosevelt served prime ribs. All the partn
were amazed, and delighted, he explained softly while gla
ing around the room. Mitch forced a smile and sliced his se
ing. The other partners, amazed or indifferent, were talk
idly and concentrating on the food. Mitch counted eighte
active partners and seven retirees, those with the khakis a
sweaters and relaxed looks about them.

"You have remarkable stamina, Mitch," Royce McKni,
said with a mouthful. He nodded politely. Yes, yes, I prac
my stamina all the time, he thought to himself. As much
possible, he kept his mind off Joe Hodge and Marty Kozin
and the other three dead lawyers memorialized on the w
downstairs. But it was impossible to keep his mind off
pictures of the girl in the sand, and he wondered if they
knew. Had they all seen the pictures? Passed them arou
during one of these little lunches when it was just the partn
and no guests? DeVasher had promised to keep them to h
self, but what's a promise from a thug? Of course they'd s
them. Voyles said every partner and most of the associa
were in on the conspiracy.

For a man with no appetite, he managed the food nicely.
even buttered and devoured an extra roll, just to appear n
mal. Nothing wrong with his appetite.

"So you and Abby are going to the Caymans next wee
Oliver Lambert said.

"Yes. It's her spring break, and we booked one of the con
two months ago. Looking forward to it."

"It's a terrible time to go," Avery said in disgust. "We'r
month behind right now."

"We're always a month behind, Avery. So what's another
ek? I guess you want me to take my files with me?"
"Not a bad idea. I always do."
"Don't do it, Mitch," Oliver Lambert said in mock protest.
his place will be standing when you return. You and Abby
erve a week to yourselves."

"You'll love it down there," Royce McKnight said, as if
tch had never been and that thing on the beach didn't hap-
1 and no one knew anything about any photographs.

"When do you leave?" Lambert asked.

"Sunday morning. Early."

"Are you taking the Lear?"

"No. Delta nonstop."

ambert and McKnight exchanged quick looks that Mitch
s not supposed to see. There were other looks from the
er tables, occasional quick glances filled with curiosity that
tch had caught since he entered the room. He was there to
noticed.

"Do you scuba-dive?" asked Lambert, still thinking about
Lear versus the Delta nonstop.

No, but we plan to do some snorkeling."

There's a guy on Rum Point, on the north end, name of
rian Bench, who's got a great dive lodge and will certify
1 in one week. It's a hard week, lot of instruction, but it's
rth it."

n other words, stay away from Abanks, Mitch thought.
"hat's the name of the lodge?" he asked.

"Rum Point Divers. Great place."

Aitch frowned intelligently as if making a mental note of
helpful advice. Suddenly, Oliver Lambert was hit with
ness. "Be careful, Mitch. It brings back memories of Marty
1 Joe."

Avery and McKnight stared at their plates in a split-second
morial to the dead boys. Mitch swallowed hard and almost
ered at Oliver Lambert. But he kept a straight face, even
naged to look sad with the rest of them. Marty and Joe and
ir young widows and fatherless children. Marty and Joe,
young wealthy lawyers expertly killed and removed be-
e they could talk. Marty and Joe, two promising sharks

253

eaten by their own. Voyles had told Mitch to think of Ma
and Joe whenever he saw Oliver Lambert.

And now, for a mere million bucks, he was expected to
what Marty and Joe were about to do, without getting caug
Perhaps a year from now the next new associate would
sitting here and watching the saddened partners talk ab
young Mitch McDeere and his remarkable stamina and wha
helluva lawyer he would have been but for the accident. H
many would they kill?

He wanted two million. Plus a couple of other items.

After an hour of important talk and good food, the lur
began breaking up as partners excused themselves, spoke
Mitch and left the room. They were proud of him, they sa
He was their brightest star of the future. The future
Bendini, Lambert & Locke. He smiled and thanked them.

About the time Roosevelt served the banana cream pie a
coffee, Tammy Greenwood Hemphill of Greenwood Servi
parked her dirty brown Rabbit behind the shiny Peugeot
the school parking lot. She left the motor running. She te
four steps, stuck a key into the trunk of the Peugeot and
moved the heavy black briefcase. She slammed the trunk a
sped away in the Rabbit.

From a small window in the teachers' lounge, Abby sip
coffee and stared through the trees, across the playground a
into the parking lot in the distance. She could barely see
car. She smiled and checked her watch. Twelve-thirty,
planned.

Tammy weaved her way carefully through the noon tra
in the direction of downtown. Driving was tedious wh
watching the rearview mirror. As usual, she saw nothing. S
parked in her designated place across the street from the C
ton Exchange Building.

There were nine files in this load. She arranged them ne
on the folding table and began making copies. Sigalas P
ners, Lettie Plunk Trust, HandyMan Hardware and two f
bound loosely with a thick rubber band and marked AVE
FILES. She ran two copies of every sheet of paper in the f
and meticulously put them back together. In a ledger book,
entered the date, time and name of each file. There were n

enty-nine entries. He said there would eventually be about
ty. She placed one copy of each file into the locked and
den cabinet in the closet, then repacked the briefcase with
original files and one copy of each.

ursuant to his instructions, a week earlier she had rented in
name an eight-by-eight storage room at the Summer Ave-
Mini Storage. It was fourteen miles from downtown, and
rty minutes later she arrived and unlocked number 38C. In
mall cardboard box she placed the other copies of the nine
s and scribbled the date on the end of the flap. She placed it
t to three other boxes on the floor.

At exactly 3 P.M., she wheeled into the parking lot, stopped
ind the Peugeot, opened its trunk and left the briefcase
ere she'd found it.

econds later, Mitch stepped from the front door of the
ndini Building and stretched his arms. He breathed deeply
gazed up and down Front Street. A lovely spring day. Five
cks to the north and nine floors up, in the window, he no-
d the blinds had been pulled all the way down. The signal.
od. Everything's fine. He smiled to himself, and returned to
office.

three o'clock in the morning, Mitch eased out of bed and
etly pulled on a pair of faded jeans, flannel law school shirt,
ite insulated socks and a pair of old work boots. He wanted
look like a truck driver. Without a word, he kissed Abby,
o was awake, and left the house. East Meadowbrook was
erted, as were all the streets between home and the inter-
te. Surely they would not follow him at this hour.

He drove Interstate 55 south for twenty-five miles to
atobia, Mississippi. A busy, all-night truck stop called the
5 shone brightly a hundred yards from the four-lane. He
ted through the trucks to the rear where a hundred semis
re parked for the night. He stopped next to the Truck Wash
and waited. A dozen eighteen-wheelers inched and weaved
und the pumps.

black guy wearing a Falcons football cap stepped from
und the corner and stared at the BMW. Mitch recognized
as the agent in the bus terminal in Knoxville. He killed
engine and stepped from the car.

"McDeere?" the agent asked.

"Of course. Who else? Where's Tarrance?"

"Inside in a booth by the window. He's waiting."

Mitch opened the door and handed the keys to the age[nt.] "Where are you taking it?"

"Down the road a little piece. We'll take care of it. You w[ill] clean coming out of Memphis. Relax."

He climbed into the car, eased between two diesel pum[ps] and headed for the interstate. Mitch watched his little BM[W] disappear as he entered the truck-stop café. It was three for[ty-] five.

The noisy room was filled with heavy middle-aged m[en] drinking coffee and eating store-bought pies. They pic[ked] their teeth with colored toothpicks and talked of bass fish[ing] and politics back at the terminal. Many spoke with l[ong] Northern twangs. Merle Haggard wailed from the jukebo[x.]

The lawyer moved awkwardly toward the rear until he s[aw] in an unlit corner a familiar face hidden beneath aviator's s[un] shades and the same Michigan State baseball cap. Then [the] face smiled. Tarrance was holding a menu and watching [the] front door. Mitch slid into the booth.

"Hello, good buddy," Tarrance said. "How's the truckin[g?]"

"Wonderful. I think I prefer the bus, though."

"Next time we'll try a train or something. Just for vari[ety.] Laney get your car?"

"Laney?"

"The black dude. He's an agent, you know."

"We haven't been properly introduced. Yes, he's got my [car.] Where is he taking it?"

"Down the interstate. He'll be back in an hour or so. W[e'll] try to have you on the road by five so you can be at the of[fice] by six. We'd hate to mess up your day."

"It's already shot to hell."

A partially crippled waitress named Dot ambled by and [de-] manded to know what they wanted. Just coffee. A surge [of] Roadway drivers swarmed in the front door and filled up [the] café. Merle could barely be heard.

"So how are the boys at the office?" Tarrance asked che[er-] fully.

'Everything's fine. The meters are ticking as we speak and
everyone's getting richer. Thanks for asking."

'No problem."

'How's my old pal Voyles doing?" Mitch asked.

'He's quite anxious, really. He called me twice today and
repeated for the tenth time his desire to have an answer from
you. Said you'd had plenty of time and all that. I told him to
relax. Told him about our little roadside rendezvous tonight
and he got real excited. I'm supposed to call him in four hours,
to be exact."

'Tell him a million bucks won't do it, Tarrance. You boys
like to brag about spending billions fighting organized crime,
so I say throw a little my way. What's a couple of million cash
to the federal government?"

'So it's a couple of million now?"

'Damned right it's a couple of million. And not a dime less.
I want a million now and a million later. I'm in the process of
copying all of my files, and I should be finished in a few days.
Legitimate files, I think. If I gave them to anyone I'd be perma-
nently disbarred. So when I give them to you, I want the first
million. Let's just call it good faith money."

'How do you want it paid?"

'Deposited in an account in a bank in Zurich. But we'll
discuss the details later."

Dot slid two saucers onto the table and dropped two mis-
matched cups on them. She poured from a height of three feet
and splashed coffee in all directions. "Free refills," she
grunted, and left.

'And the second million?" Tarrance asked, ignoring the cof-

'When you and I and Voyles decide I've supplied you with
enough documents to get the indictments, then I get half. After I testify for the last time, I get the other half. That's incredibly fair, Tarrance."

'It is. You've got a deal."

Mitch breathed deeply, and felt weak. A deal. A contract.
An agreement. One that could never be put in writing, but
one that was terribly enforceable nonetheless. He sipped the
coffee but didn't taste it. They had agreed on the money. He
was on a roll. Keep pushing.

"And there's one other thing, Tarrance."

The head lowered and turned slightly to the right. "Yeal

Mitch leaned closer, resting on his forearms. "It won't c
you a dime, and you boys can pull it off with no sweat. Oka

"I'm listening."

"My brother Ray is at Brushy Mountain. Seven years u
parole. I want him out."

"That's ridiculous, Mitch. We can do a lot of things, but
damned sure can't parole state prisoners. Federal maybe,
not state. No way."

"Listen to me, Tarrance, and listen good. If I hit the r
with the Mafia on my tail, my brother goes with me. Sort
like a package deal. And I know if Director Voyles wants
out of prison, he'll get out of prison. I know that. Now,
boys just figure out a way to make it happen."

"But we have no authority to interfere with state prisoner

Mitch smiled and returned to his coffee. "James Earl
escaped from Brushy Mountain. And he had no help from
outside."

"Oh, that's great. We attack the prison like commandos
rescue your brother. Beautiful."

"Don't play dumb with me, Tarrance. It's not negotiabl

"All right, all right. I'll see what I can do. Anything e
Any more surprises?"

"No, just questions about where we go and what we
Where do we hide initially? Where do we hide during the
als? Where do we live for the rest of our lives? Just mi
questions like that."

"We can discuss it later."

"What did Hodge and Kozinski tell you?"

"Not enough. We've got a notebook, a rather thick notebo
in which we've accumulated and indexed everything we kn
about the Moroltos and the firm. Most of it's Morolto cr
their organization, key people, illegal activities and so on.
need to read it all before we start to work."

"Which, of course, will be after I've received the first
lion."

"Of course. When can we see your files?"

"In about a week. I've managed to copy four files that bel
to someone else. I may get my hands on a few more of tho

'Who's doing the copying?"

'None of your business."

Tarrance thought for a second and let it pass. "How many
s?"

'Between forty and fifty. I have to sneak them out a few at a
ne. Some I've worked on for eight months, others only a
ek or so. As far as I can tell, they're all legitimate clients."

'How many of these clients have you personally met?"

'Two or three."

'Don't bet they're all legitimate. Hodge told us about some
mmy files, or sweat files as they are known to the partners,
t have been around for years and every new associate cuts
teeth on them; heavy files that require hundreds of hours
l make the rookies feel like real lawyers."

'Sweat files?"

'That's what Hodge said. It's any easy game, Mitch. They
e you with the money. They smother you with work that
ks legitimate and for the most part probably is legitimate.
en, after a few years, you've unwittingly become a part of
conspiracy. You're nailed, and there's no getting out. Even
, Mitch. You started work in July, eight months ago, and
've probably already touched a few of the dirty files. You
n't know it, had no reason to suspect it. But they've already
you up."

Two million, Tarrance. Two million and my brother."

arrance sipped the lukewarm coffee and ordered a piece of
onut pie as Dot came within earshot. He glanced at his
ch and surveyed the crowd of truckers, all smoking ciga-
es and drinking coffee and talking relentlessly.

le adjusted the sunglasses. "So what do I tell Mr. Voyles?"

Tell him we ain't got a deal until he agrees to get Ray out of
on. No deal, Tarrance."

We can probably work something out."

'm confident you can."

When do you leave for the Caymans?"

arly Sunday. Why?"

ust curious, that's all."

Well, I'd like to know how many different groups will be
wing me down there. Is that asking too much? I'm sure

259

we'll attract a crowd, and frankly, we had hoped for a li[tt]
privacy."

"Firm condo?"

"Of course."

"Forget privacy. It's probably got more wires than a swit[ch]
board. Maybe even some cameras."

"That's comforting. We might stay a couple of nights
Abanks Dive Lodge. If you boys are in the neighborhood, s[top]
by for a drink."

"Very funny. If we're there, it'll be for a reason. And y[ou]
won't know it."

Tarrance ate the pie in three bites. He left two bucks on [the]
table and they walked to the dark rear of the truck stop. [The]
dirty asphalt pavement vibrated under the steady hum of [an]
acre of diesel engines. They waited in the dark.

"I'll talk to Voyles in a few hours," Tarrance said. "W[hy]
don't you and your wife take a leisurely Saturday-aftern[oon]
drive tomorrow?"

"Anyplace in particular?"

"Yeah. There's a town called Holly Springs thirty miles [east]
of here. Old place, full of antebellum homes and Confeder[ate]
history. Women love to drive around and look at the old m[an-]
sions. Make your appearance around four o'clock and w[e'll]
find you. Our buddy Laney will be driving a bright red Ch[evy]
Blazer with Tennessee plates. Follow him. We'll find a pl[ace]
and talk."

"Is it safe?"

"Trust us. If we see or smell something, we'll break [it.]
Drive around town for an hour, and if you don't see Lan[ey,]
grab a sandwich and go back home. You'll know they were
close. We won't take chances."

"Thanks. A great bunch of guys."

Laney eased around the corner in the BMW and jum[ped]
out. "Everything's clear. No trace of anyone."

"Good," Tarrance said. "See you tomorrow, Mitch. Ha[ppy]
truckin'." They shook hands.

"It's not negotiable, Tarrance," Mitch said again.

"You can call me Wayne. See you tomorrow."

25

◀ HE BLACK THUNDERHEADS and driving rain had
long since cleared the tourists from Seven Mile Beach
when the McDeeres, soaked and tired, arrived at the
ry condominium duplex. Mitch backed the rented Mitsu-
i jeep over the curb, across the small lawn and up to the
t door. Unit B. His first visit had been to Unit A. They
ared to be identical, except for the paint and trim. The
fit, and they grabbed and threw luggage as the clouds
t and the rain grew thicker.

nce inside and dry, they unpacked in the master bedroom
airs with a long balcony facing the wet beach. Cautious
their words, they inspected the town house and checked
each room and closet. The refrigerator was empty, but the
was very well stocked. Mitch mixed two drinks, rum and
e, in honor of the islands. They sat on the balcony with
feet in the rain and watched the ocean churn and spill
rd the shore. Rumheads was quiet and barely visible in
distance. Two natives sat at the bar, drinking and watch-
he sea.

hat's Rumheads over there," Mitch said, pointing with
rink.

"Rumheads?"

"I told you about it. It's a hot spot where tourists drink [and?] the locals play dominoes."

"I see." Abby was unimpressed. She yawned and sank lo[w] into the plastic chair. She closed her eyes.

"Oh, this is great, Abby. Our first trip out of the coun[try,] our first real honeymoon, and you're asleep ten minutes a[fter] we hit land."

"I'm tired, Mitch. I packed all night while you were sl[eep]ing."

"You packed eight suitcases—six for you and two for [me.] You packed every garment we own. No wonder you w[ere] awake all night."

"I don't want to run out of clothes."

"Run out? How many bikinis did you pack? Ten? Twel[ve?]"

"Six."

"Great. One a day. Why don't you put one on?"

"What?"

"You heard me. Go put on that little blue one with high [legs] and a couple of strings around front, the one that weighs h[alf a] gram and cost sixty bucks and your buns hang out when [you] walk. I wanna see it."

"Mitch, it's raining. You've brought me here to this is[land] during the monsoon season. Look at those clouds. Dark [and] thick and extremely stationary. I won't need any bikinis [this] week."

Mitch smiled and began rubbing her legs. "I rather like [the] rain. In fact, I hope it rains all week. It'll keep us inside, in [the] bed, sipping rum and trying to hurt each other."

"I'm shocked. You mean you actually want sex? We'v[e al]ready done it once this month."

"Twice."

"I thought you wanted to snorkel and scuba dive all we[ek.]"

"Nope. There's probably a shark out there waiting for [me.]"

The winds blew harder and the balcony was b[eing] drenched.

"Let's go take off our clothes," Mitch said.

After an hour, the storm began to move. The rain slacke[ned,] then turned to a soft drizzle, then it was gone. The sky l[it]

262

d as the dark, low clouds left the tiny island and headed
theast, toward Cuba. Shortly before its scheduled depar-
: over the horizon, the sun suddenly emerged for a brief
ore. It emptied the beach cottages and town homes and
dos and hotel rooms as the tourists strolled through the
l toward the water. Rumheads was suddenly packed with
: throwers and thirsty beachcombers. The domino game
:ed up where it had left off. The reggae band next door at
Palms tuned up.

litch and Abby walked aimlessly along the edge of the wa-
in the general direction of Georgetown, away from the
: where the girl had been. He thought of her occasionally,
of the photographs. He had decided she was a pro and had
i paid by DeVasher to seduce and conquer him in front of
hidden cameras. He did not expect to see her this time.

s if on cue, the music stopped, the beach strollers froze and
:hed, the noise at Rumheads quietened as all eyes turned to
:h the sun meet the water. Gray and white clouds, the
ing remnants of the storm, lay low on the horizon and
: with the sun. Slowly they turned shades of orange and
w and red, pale shades at first, then, suddenly, brilliant
·s. For a few brief moments, the sky was a canvas and the
splashed its awesome array of colors with bold strokes.
n the bright orange ball touched the water and within
nds was gone. The clouds became black and dissipated. A
man sunset.

h great fear and caution, Abby slowly maneuvered the jeep
ugh the early-morning traffic in the shopping district. She
from Kentucky. She had never driven on the left side of
road for any substantial period of time. Mitch gave direc-
s and watched the rearview mirror. The narrow streets
sidewalks were already crowded with tourists window-
•ping for duty-free china, crystal, perfume, cameras and
·lry.

itch pointed to a hidden side street, and the jeep darted
·een two groups of tourists. He kissed her on the cheek.
meet you right here at five."

3e careful," she said. "I'll go to the bank, then stay on the
h near the condo."

He slammed the door and disappeared between two s▮
shops. The alley led to a wider street that led to Hogsty ▮
He ducked into a crowded T-shirt store filled with racks
rows of tourist shirts and straw hats and sunglasses. He
lected a gaudy green and orange flowered shirt and a Pan▮
hat. Two minutes later he darted from the store into the ▮
seat of a passing taxi. "Airport," he said. "And make it q▮
Watch your tail. Someone may be following."

The driver made no response, just eased past the bank b▮
ings and out of town. Ten minutes later he stopped in fro▮
the terminal.

"Anybody follow us?" Mitch asked, pulling money fron
pocket.

"No, mon. Four dollars and ten cents."

Mitch threw a five over the seat and walked quickly int▮
terminal. The Cayman Airways flight to Cayman Brac w▮
leave at nine. At a gift shop Mitch bought a cup of coffee
hid between two rows of shelves filled with souvenirs.
watched the waiting area and saw no one. Of course, he ha
idea what they looked like, but he saw no one sniffing aro
and searching for lost people. Perhaps they were following
jeep or combing the shopping district looking for him.
haps.

For seventy-five Cayman dollars he had reserved the last
on the ten-passenger, three-engine Trislander. Abby had m
the reservation by pay phone the night they arrived. At
last possible second, he jogged from the terminal onto
tarmac and climbed on board. The pilot slammed and lo▮
the doors, and they taxied down the runway. No other pl
were visible. A small hangar sat to the right.

The ten tourists admired the brilliant blue sea and said ▮
during the twenty minute flight. As they approached Cay▮
Brac, the pilot became the tour guide and made a wide c
around the small island. He paid special attention to the
bluffs that fell into the sea on the east end. Without the bl
he said, the island would be as flat as Grand Cayman.
landed the plane softly on a narrow asphalt strip.

Next to the small white frame building with the word
PORT painted on all sides, a clean cut Caucasian waited
watched the passengers quickly disembark. He was Rick ▮

, special agent, and sweat dripped from his nose and glued shirt to his back. He stepped slightly forward. "Mitch," he d almost to himself.

Mitch hesitated and then walked over.

"Car's out front," Acklin said.

"Where's Tarrance?" Mitch looked around.

"He's waiting."

"Does the car have air conditioning?"

"Afraid not. Sorry."

The car was minus air, power anything and signal lights. It s a 1974 LTD, and Acklin explained as they followed the sty road that there simply was not much of a selection of tal cars on Cayman Brac. And the U.S. government had ted the car was because he and Tarrance had been unable find a taxi. They were lucky to find a room, on such late ice.

The small neat homes were closer together, and sea ap-red. They parked in the sand parking lot of an establish-nt called Brac Divers. An aging pier jutted into the water l anchored a hundred boats of all sizes. To the west along beach a dozen thatched-roof cabins sat two feet above the d and housed divers who came from around the world. xt to the pier was an open-air bar, nameless, but complete h a domino game and a dartboard. Oak-and-brass fans hung m the ceiling through the rafters and rotated slowly and ntly, cooling the domino players and the bartender.

Vayne Tarrance sat at a table by himself drinking a Coke l watching a dive crew load a thousand identical yellow ks from the pier onto a boat. Even for a tourist, his dress s hysterical. Dark sunglasses with yellow frames, brown w sandals, obviously brand-new, with black socks, a tight waiian luau shirt with twenty loud colors and a pair of gold n shorts that were very old and very short and covered little he shiny, sickly white legs under the table. He waved his ke at the two empty chairs.

Nice shirt, Tarrance," Mitch said in undisguised amuse-nt.

Thanks. You gotta real winner yourself."

Nice tan too."

Yeah, yeah. Gotta look the part, you know."

The waiter hovered nearby and waited for them to spea Acklin ordered a Coke. Mitch said he wanted a Coke with splash of rum in it. All three became engrossed with the di boat and the divers loading their bulky gear.

"What happened in Holly Springs?" Mitch finally asked.

"Sorry, we couldn't help it. They followed you out of Me phis and had two cars waiting in Holly Springs. We could get near you."

"Did you and your wife discuss the trip before you left asked Acklin.

"I think so. We probably mentioned it around the house couple of times."

Acklin seemed satisfied. "They were certainly ready for ye A green Skylark followed you for about twenty miles, then lost. We called it off then."

Tarrance sipped his Coke and said, "Late Saturday night Lear left Memphis and flew nonstop to Grand Cayman. think two or three of the goons were on board. The plane early Sunday morning and returned to Memphis."

"So they're here and they're following us?"

"Of course. They probably had one or two people on plane with you and Abby. Might have been men, women both. Could've been a black dude or an Oriental woman. W knows? Remember, Mitch, they have plenty of money. The are two that we recognize. One was in Washington when y were there. A blond fellow, about forty, six-one, maybe s two, with real short hair, almost a crew cut, and real stro Nordic-looking features. He moves quickly. We saw him y terday driving a red Escort he got from Coconut Car Rent on the island."

"I think I've seen him," Mitch said.

"Where?" asked Acklin.

"In a bar in the Memphis airport the night I returned fr Washington. I caught him watching me, and I thought at time that I had seen him in Washington."

"That's him. He's here."

"Who's the other one?"

"Tony Verkler, or Two-Ton Tony as we call him. He's a with an impressive record of convictions, most of it in C cago. He's worked for Morolto for years. Weighs about th

dred pounds and does a great job of watching people be-
se no one would ever suspect him."

He was at Rumheads last night," Acklin added.

Last night? We were there last night."

With great ceremony, the dive boat pushed from the pier
headed for open water. Beyond the pier, fishermen in
ir small catboats pulled their nets and sailors navigated
ir brightly colored catamarans away from land. After a gen-
and dreamy start, the island was awake now. Half the boats
to the pier had left or were in the process of leaving.

So when did you boys get in town?" Mitch asked, sipping
drink, which was more rum than Coke.

Sunday night," Tarrance answered while watching the
e boat slowly disappear.

Just out of curiosity, how many men do you have on the
nds?"

Four men, two women," said Tarrance. Acklin became
te and deferred all conversation to his supervisor.

And why exactly are you here?" Mitch asked.

Oh, several reasons. Number one, we wanted to talk to you
nail down our little deal. Director Voyles is terribly anx-
s about reaching an agreement you can live with. Number
, we want to watch them to determine how many goons
here. We'll spend the week trying to identify these people.
island is small, and it's a good place to observe."

And number three, you wanted to work on your suntan?"
Acklin managed a slight giggle. Tarrance smiled and then
wned. "No, not exactly. We're here for your protection."

My protection?"

Yes. The last time I sat at this very table I was talking to Joe
dge and Marty Kozinski. About nine months ago. The day
ore they were killed, to be exact."

And you think I'm about to be killed?"

No. Not yet."

Mitch motioned at the bartender for another drink. The
ino game grew heated, and he watched the natives argue
drink beer.

Look, boys, as we speak the goons, as you call them, are
bably following my wife all over Grand Cayman. I'll be
of nervous until I get back. Now, what about the deal?"

Tarrance left the sea and the dive boat and stared at Mit "Two million's fine, and—"

"Of course it's fine, Tarrance. We agreed on it, did we no

"Relax, Mitch. We'll pay a million when you turn over all your files. At that point, there's no turning back, as they s You're in up to your neck."

"Tarrance, I understand that. It was my suggestion, reme ber."

"But that's the easy part. We really don't want your fi because they're clean files. Good files. Legitimate files. want the bad files, Mitch, the ones with indictments writ all over them. And these files will be much harder to come But when you do so, we'll pay another half million. And rest after the last trial."

"And my brother?"

"We'll try."

"Not good enough, Tarrance. I want a commitment."

"We can't promise to deliver your brother. Hell, he's go least seven more years."

"But he's my brother, Tarrance. I don't care if he's a se murderer sitting on death row waiting for his last meal. I my brother, and if you want me, you have to release him.

"I said we'll try, but we can't commit. There's no legal, mal, legitimate way to get him out, so we must try ot means. What if he gets shot during the escape?"

"Just get him out, Tarrance."

"We'll try."

"You'll throw the power and resources of the FBI in ass ing my brother in escaping from prison, right, Tarrance?"

"You have my word."

Mitch sat back in his chair and took a long sip of his dr Now the deal was final. He breathed easier and smiled in direction of the magnificent Caribbean.

"So when do we get your files?" Tarrance asked.

"Thought you didn't want them. They're too clean, rem ber?"

"We want the files, Mitch, because when we get the f then we've got you. You've proved yourself when you han your files, your license to practice law, so to speak."

"Ten to fifteen days."

How many files?"

Between forty and fifty. The small ones are an inch thick.
e big ones wouldn't fit on this table. I can't use the copiers
und the office, so we've had to make other arrangements."

Perhaps we could assist in the copying," said Acklin.

Perhaps not. Perhaps if I need your help, perhaps I'll ask
it."

How do you propose to get them to us?" Tarrance asked.
klin withdrew again.

Very simple, Wayne. When I've copied them all, and once I
the million where I want it, then I'll hand you a key to a
tain little room in the Memphis area, and you can get them
our pickup."

I told you we'd deposit the money in a Swiss bank ac-
nt," Tarrance said.

And I don't want it in a Swiss bank account, okay? I'll
ate the terms of the transfer, and it'll be done exactly as I
It's my neck on the line from now on, boys, so I call the
ts. Most of them, anyway."

arrance smiled and grunted and stared at the pier. "So you
't trust the Swiss?"

Let's just say I have another bank in mind. I work for
ey launderers, remember, Wayne, so I've become an ex-
t on hiding money in offshore accounts."

We'll see."

When do I see this notebook on the Moroltos?"

After we get your files and pay our first installment. We'll
f you as much as we can, but for the most part you're on
r own. You and I will need to meet a lot, and of course
'll be rather dangerous. May have to take a few bus rides."

Okay, but the next time I get the aisle seat."

Sure, sure. Anybody worth two million can surely pick his
on a Greyhound."

'll never live to enjoy it, Wayne. You know I won't."

ee miles out of Georgetown, on the narrow and winding
l to Bodden Town, Mitch saw him. The man was squatting
ind an old Volkswagen Beetle with the hood up as if en-
 trouble had stopped him. The man was dressed like a
ve, without tourist clothes. He could easily pass for one of

the Brits who worked for the government or the banks. was well tanned. The man held a wrench of some sort a appeared to study it and watch the Mitsubishi jeep as it roa by on the left-hand side of the road. The man was the Nore

He was supposed to have gone unnoticed.

Mitch instinctively slowed to thirty miles per hour, to w for him. Abby turned and watched the road. The narrow hi way to Bodden Town clung to the shoreline for five mi then forked, and the ocean disappeared. Within minutes Nordic's green VW came racing around a slight bend. T McDeere jeep was much closer than the Nordic anticipa Being seen, he abruptly slowed, then turned into the f white rock driveway on the ocean side.

Mitch gunned the jeep and sped to Bodden Town. Wes the small settlement he turned south and less than a mile l found the ocean.

It was 10 A.M. and the parking lot of Abanks Dive Lodge half full. The two morning dive boats had left thirty minu earlier. The McDeeres walked quickly to the bar, wh Henry was already shuffling beer and cigarettes to the dom players.

Barry Abanks leaned on a post supporting the thatched of the bar and watched as his two dive boats disappea around the corner of the island. Each would make two di at places like Bonnie's Arch, Devil's Grotto, Eden Rock Roger's Wreck Point, places he had dived and toured guided through a thousand times. Some of the places he discovered himself.

The McDeeres approached, and Mitch quietly introdu his wife to Mr. Abanks, who was not polite but not rude. T started for the small pier, where a deckhand was prepari thirty-foot fishing boat. Abanks unloaded an indecipher string of commands in the general direction of the yo deckhand, who was either deaf or unafraid of his boss.

Mitch stood next to Abanks, the captain now, and pointe the bar fifty yards away down the pier. "Do you know those people at the bar?" he asked.

Abanks frowned at Mitch.

"They tried to follow me here. Just curious," Mitch sai "The usual gang," Abanks said. "No strangers."

"Have you noticed any strangers around this morning?"

"Look, this place attracts strange people. I keep no ledger of ᵗe strange ones and the normal ones."

"Have you seen a fat American, red hair, at least three hun-
ʳed pounds?"

Abanks shook his head. The deckhand eased the boat back-
ᵃʳd, away from the pier, then toward the horizon. Abby sat
ᵑ a small padded bench and watched the dive lodge disap-
ᵉar. In a vinyl bag between her feet were two new sets of
ᵘorkeling fins and dive masks. It was ostensibly a snorkeling
ᵢp with maybe a little light fishing if they were biting. The
ᵉat man himself had agreed to accompany them, but only
ᵗer Mitch insisted and told him they needed to discuss per-
ᵘnal matters. Private matters, regarding the death of his son.

ᵒm a screened balcony on the second floor of a Cayman Kai
ᵉach house, the Nordic watched the two snorkeled heads bob
ᵈ disappear around the fishing boat. He handed the binocu-
ᵣs to Two-Ton Tony Verkler, who, quickly bored, handed
ᵉm back. A striking blonde in a black one-piece with legs cut
ᵍh, almost to the rib cage, stood behind the Nordic and took
ᵉ binoculars. Of particular interest was the deckhand.

Tony spoke. "I don't understand. If they were talking seri-
ᵘs, why the boy? Why have another set of ears around?"

"Perhaps they're talking about snorkeling and fishing," said
ᵉ Nordic.

"I don't know," said the blonde. "It's unusual for Abanks to
ᵖend time on a fishing boat. He likes the divers. There must
ᵉ a good reason for him to waste a day with two novice
ᵘorkelers. Something's up."

"Who's the boy?" asked Tony.

"Just one of the gofers," she said. "He's got a dozen."

"Can you talk to him later?" asked the Nordic.

"Yeah," said Tony. "Show him some skin, snort some candy.
ᵉ'll talk."

"I'll try," she said.

"What's his name?" asked the Nordic.

"Keith Rook."

• • • •

Keith Rook maneuvered the boat alongside the pier at Ru
Point. Mitch, Abby and Abanks climbed from the boat an
headed for the beach. Keith was not invited to lunch. H
stayed behind and lazily washed the deck.

The Shipwreck Bar sat inland a hundred yards under
heavy cover of rare shade trees. It was dark and damp wit
screened windows and squeaky ceiling fans. There was no re
gae, dominoes, or dartboard. The noon crowd was quiet wit
each table engrossed in its own private talk.

The view from their table was out to sea, to the north. The
ordered cheeseburgers and beer—island food.

"This bar is different," Mitch observed quietly.

"Very much so," said Abanks. "And with good reason. It's
hangout for drug dealers who own many of the nice hom
and condos around here. They fly in on their private jets, d
posit their money in our many fine banks and spend a few day
around here checking their real estate."

"Nice neighborhood."

"Very nice, really. They have millions and they keep
themselves."

The waitress, a husky, well-mixed mulatto, dropped thr
bottles of Jamaican Red Stripe on the table without saying
word. Abanks leaned forward on his elbows with his hea
lowered, the customary manner of speaking in the Shipwre
Bar. "So you think you can walk away?" he said.

Mitch and Abby leaned forward in unison, and all thr
heads met low in the center of the table, just over the bee
"Not walk, but run. Run like hell, but I'll get away. And I
need your help."

Abanks thought about this for a moment and raised his head. I
shrugged. "But what am I to do?" He took the first sip of h
Red Stripe.

Abby saw her first, and it would take a woman to spot a
other woman straining ever so elegantly to eavesdrop on the
little conversation. Her back was to Abanks. She was a sol
blonde partially hidden under cheap black rubber sunglass
that covered most of her face, and she had been watching t
ocean and listening a bit too hard. When the three of the
leaned over, she sat up straight and listened like hell. She w
by herself at a table for two.

Abby dug her fingernails into her husband's leg, and their ble became quiet. The blonde in black listened, then turned her table and her drink.

ayne Tarrance had improved his wardrobe by Friday of Cay-an Week. Gone were the straw sandals and tight shorts and enybop sunglasses. Gone were the sickly-pale legs. Now they ere bright pink, burned beyond recognition. After three days the tropical outback known as Cayman Brac, he and Acklin, ting on behalf of the U.S. government, had pounced on a ther cheap room on Grand Cayman, miles from Seven Mile each and not within walking distance of any remote portion the sea. Here they had established a command post to moni-r the comings and goings of the McDeeres and other inter-ted people. Here, at the Coconut Motel, they had shared a hall room with two single beds and cold showers. Wednesday orning, they had contacted the subject, McDeere, and re-uested a meeting as soon as possible. He said no. Said he was o busy. Said he and his wife were honeymooning and had no ne for such a meeting. Maybe later, was all he said.

Then late Thursday, while Mitch and Abby were enjoying illed grouper at the Lighthouse on the road to Bodden wn, Lancy, Agent Laney, dressed in appropriate island garb d looking very much like an island Negro, stopped at their ble and laid down the law. Tarrance insisted on a meeting. Chickens had to be imported into the Cayman Islands, and t the best ones. Only medium-grade chickens, to be con-med not by native islanders but by Americans away from me without this most basic staple. Colonel Sanders had the mnedest time teaching the island girls, though black or close it, how to fry chicken. It was foreign to them.

And so it was that Special Agent Wayne Tarrance, of the onx, arranged a quick secret meeting at the Kentucky Fried nicken franchise on the island of Grand Cayman. The only ch franchise. He thought the place would be deserted. He as wrong.

A hundred hungry tourists from Georgia, Alabama, Texas d Mississippi packed the place and devoured extra crispy th cole slaw and creamed potatoes. It tasted better in Tu-lo, but it would do.

Tarrance and Acklin sat in a booth in the crowded restaurant and nervously watched the front door. It was not too late to abort. There were just too many people. Finally, Mitch entered, by himself, and stood in the long line. He brought his little red box to their table and sat down. He did not say hello or anything. He began eating the three-piece dinner for which he paid $4.89, Cayman dollars. Imported chicken.

"Where have you been?" Tarrance asked.

Mitch attacked a thigh. "On the island. It's stupid to meet here, Tarrance. Too many people."

"We know what we're doing."

"Yeah, like the Korean shoe store."

"Cute. Why wouldn't you see us Wednesday?"

"I was busy Wednesday. I didn't want to see you Wednesday. Am I clean?"

"Of course you're clean. Laney would've tackled you at the front door if you weren't clean."

"This place makes me nervous, Tarrance."

"Why did you go to Abanks?"

Mitch wiped his mouth and held the partially devoured thigh. A rather small thigh. "He's got a boat. I wanted to fish and snorkel, so we cut a deal. Where were you, Tarrance? In submarine trailing us around the island?"

"What did Abanks say?"

"Oh, he knows lots of words. Hello. Give me a beer. Who's following us? Buncha words."

"They followed you, you know?"

"They! Which they? Your they or their they? I'm being followed so much I'm causing traffic jams."

"The bad guys, Mitch. Those from Memphis and Chicago and New York. The ones who'll kill you tomorrow if you get real cute."

"I'm touched. So they followed me. Where'd I take them? Snorkeling? Fishing? Come on, Tarrance. They follow me, you follow them, you follow me, they follow you. If I slam on brakes I get twenty noses up my ass. Why are we meeting here, Tarrance? This place is packed."

Tarrance glanced around in frustration.

Mitch closed his chicken box. "Look, Tarrance, I'm nervous and I've lost my appetite."

"Relax. You were clean coming from the condo."

"I'm always clean, Tarrance. I suppose Hodge and Kozinski ere clean every time they moved. Clean at Abanks'. Clean on e dive boat. Clean at the funerals. This was not a good idea, arrance. I'm leaving."

"Okay. When does your plane leave?"

"Why? You guys plan to follow? Will you follow me or em? What if they follow you? What if we all get real con-sed and I follow everybody?"

"Come on, Mitch."

"Nine-forty in the morning. I'll try to save you a seat. You n have the window next to Two-Ton Tony."

"When do we get your files?"

Mitch stood with his chicken box. "In a week or so. Give me n days, and, Tarrance, no more meetings in public. They kill wyers, remember, not stupid FBI agents."

26

AT EIGHT Monday morning, Oliver Lambert and Nathan Locke were cleared through the concrete wall of the fifth floor and walked through the maze of small rooms and offices. DeVasher was waiting. He closed the door behind them and pointed to the chairs. His walk was not quick. The night had been a long losing battle with the vodka. The eyes were red and the brain expanded with each breath.

"I talked with Lazarov yesterday in Las Vegas. I explained as best I could why you boys were so reluctant to fire your four lawyers, Lynch, Sorrell, Buntin and Myers. I gave him all your good reasons. He said he'd think about it, but in the meantime, make damned sure those four work on nothing but clean files. Take no chances and watch them closely."

"He's really a nice guy, isn't he?" Oliver Lambert said.

"Oh yes. A real charmer. He said Mr. Morolto has asked about the firm once a week for six weeks now. Said they're all anxious."

"What did you tell him?"

"Told him things are secure, for now. Leaks are plugged, for now. I don't think he believes me."

"What about McDeere?" asked Locke.

"He had a wonderful week with his wife. Have you ever en her in a string bikini? She wore one all week. Outstandg! We got some pictures, just for fun."

"I didn't come here to look at pictures," Locke snapped.

"You don't say. They spent an entire day with our little pal banks, just the three of them and a deckhand. They played in e water, did some fishing. And they did a lot of talking. bout what, we don't know. Never could get close enough. t it makes me very suspicious, guys. Very suspicious."

"I don't see why," said Oliver Lambert. "What can they talk out besides fishing and diving, and, of course, Hodge and ozinski? And so they talk about Hodge and Kozinski, what's e harm?"

"He never knew Hodge and Kozinski, Oliver," said Locke. Vhy would he be so interested in their deaths?"

"Keep in mind," said DeVasher, "that Tarrance told him at eir first meeting that the deaths were not accidental. So now 's Sherlock Holmes looking for clues."

"He won't find any, will he, DeVasher?"

"Hell no. It was a perfect job. Oh sure, there are a few answered questions, but the Caymanian police damned sure n't answer them. Neither can our boy McDeere."

"Then why are you worried?" asked Lambert.

"Because they're worried in Chicago, Ollie, and they pay me al good money to stay worried down here. And until the bbies leave us alone, everybody stays worried, okay?"

"What else did he do?"

"The usual Cayman vacation. Sex, sun, rum, a little shop ng and sightseeing. We had three people on the island, and ey lost him a couple of times, but nothing serious, I hope. ke I've always said, you can't trail a man twenty-four hours a y, seven days a week, without getting caught. So we have to y it cool sometimes."

"You think McDeere's talking?" asked Locke.

"I know he lies, Nat. He lied about the incident in the Ko an shoe store a month ago. You guys didn't want to believe but I'm convinced he went into that store voluntarily be use he wanted to talk with Tarrance. One of our guys made nistake, got too close, so the little meeting broke up. That 't McDeere's version, but that's what happened. Yeah, Nat,

I think he's talking. Maybe he meets with Tarrance and tel[l] him to go to hell. Maybe they're smoking dope together. [I] don't know."

"But you have nothing concrete, DeVasher," Ollie said.

The brain expanded and pressed mightily against the sku[ll.] It hurt too much to get mad. "No, Ollie, nothing like Hod[ge] and Kozinski, if that's what you mean. We had those boys [on] tape and knew they were about to talk. McDeere's a little di[f]ferent."

"He's also a rookie," said Nat. "An eight-month lawyer w[ho] knows nothing. He's spent a thousand hours on sweat file[s,] and the only clients he's handled have been legitimate. Avery['s] been extremely careful about the files McDeere's touche[d.] We've talked about it."

"He has nothing to say, because he knows nothing," adde[d] Ollie. "Marty and Joe knew a helluva lot, but they'd been he[re] for years. McDeere's a new recruit."

DeVasher gently massaged his temples. "So you've hired [a] real dumb-ass. Let's just suppose the FBI has a hunch who o[ur] biggest client is. Okay. Think along with me. And let's ju[st] suppose Hodge and Kozinski fed them enough to confirm t[he] identity of this particular client. See where I'm going? A[nd] let's suppose the Fibbies have told McDeere all they kno[w,] along with a certain amount of embellishment. Suddenly, yo[ur] ignorant rookie recruit is a very smart man. And a very da[n]gerous one."

"How do you prove this?"

"We step up surveillance, for starters. Put his wife und[er] twenty-four-hour watch. I've already called Lazarov and [re]quested more men. Told him we needed some fresh faces. I['m] going to Chicago tomorrow to brief Lazarov, and maybe M[r.] Morolto. Lazarov thinks Morolto has a lead on a mole with[in] the Bureau, some guy who's close to Voyles and will sell info[r]mation. But it's expensive, supposedly. They wanna asse[ss] things and decide where to go."

"And you'll tell them McDeere's talking?" asked Locke.

"I'll tell them what I know and what I suspect. I'm afra[id] that if we sit back and wait for concrete, it might be too la[te.] I'm sure Lazarov will wanna discuss plans to eliminate hi[m]

"Preliminary plans?" Ollie asked, with a touch of hope.

"We've passed the preliminary stage, Ollie."

he Hourglass Tavern in New York City faces Forty-sixth reet, near its corner with Ninth Avenue. A small, dark hole--the-wall with twenty-two seats, it grew to fame with its pensive menu and fifty-nine-minute time limit on each meal. n the walls not far above the tables, hourglasses with white nd silently collect the seconds and minutes until the tavern's mekeeper—the waitress—finally makes her calculations and lls time. Frequented by the Broadway crowd, it is usually cked, with loyal fans waiting on the sidewalk.

Lou Lazarov liked the Hourglass because it was dark and ivate conversations were possible. Short conversations, un-r fifty-nine minutes. He liked it because it was not in Little aly, and he was not Italian, and although he was owned by cilians, he did not have to eat their food. He liked it because was born and spent the first forty years of his life in the eater district. Then corporate headquarters was moved to hicago, and he was transferred. But business required his esence in New York at least twice a week, and when the usiness included meeting a member of equal stature from an-her family, Lazarov always suggested the Hourglass. Tuber-ii had equal stature, and a little extra. Reluctantly, he agreed the Hourglass.

Lazarov arrived first and did not wait for a table. He knew om experience the crowd thinned around 4 P.M., especially Thursdays. He ordered a glass of red wine. The waitress pped the hourglass above his head, and the race was on. He t at a front table, facing the street, his back to the other oles. He was a heavy man of fifty-eight, with a thick chest d ponderous belly. He leaned hard on the red checkered lecloth and watched the traffic on Forty-sixth.

Thankfully, Tubertini was prompt. Less than a fourth of the ite sand was wasted on him. They shook hands politely, iile Tubertini scornfully surveyed the tiny sliver of a restau-it. He flashed a plastic smile at Lazarov and glared at his seat the window. His back would face the street, and this was remely irritating. And dangerous. But his car was just out-

side with two of his men. He decided to be polite. He deft
maneuvered around the tiny table and sat down.

Tubertini was polished. He was thirty-seven, the son-in-la
of old man Palumbo himself. Family. Married his only daug
ter. He was beautifully thin and tanned with his short bla
hair oiled to perfection and slicked back. He ordered red win

"How's my pal Joey Morolto?" he asked with a perfect br
liant smile.

"Fine. And Mr. Palumbo?"

"Very ill, and very ill-tempered. As usual."

"Please give him my regards."

"Certainly."

The waitress approached and looked menacingly at t
timepiece. "Just wine," said Tubertini. "I won't be eating."

Lazarov looked at the menu and handed it to her. "Sauté
blackfish, with another glass of wine."

Tubertini glanced at his men in the car. They appeared to
napping. "So, what's wrong in Chicago?"

"Nothing's wrong. We just need a little information, tha
all. We've heard, unconfirmed of course, that you have a ve
reliable man somewhere deep in the Bureau, somewhere clo
to Voyles."

"And if we do?"

"We need some information from this man. We have a sm
unit in Memphis, and the Fibbies are trying like hell to in
trate. We suspect one of our employees may be working wi
them, but we can't seem to catch him."

"And if you caught him?"

"We'd slice out his liver and feed it to the rats."

"Serious, huh?"

"Extremely serious. Something tells me the feds ha
targeted our little unit down there, and we've grown qu
nervous."

"Let's say his name is Alfred, and let's say he's very close
Voyles."

"Okay. We need a very simple answer from Alfred. We ne
to know, yes or no, if our employee is working with the F
bies."

Tubertini watched Lazarov and sipped his wine. "Alfr
specializes in simple answers. He prefers the yes and no va

y. We've used him twice, only when it's critical, and both mes it was a question of 'Are the feds coming here or there?' e's extremely cautious. I don't think he would provide too any details."

"Is he accurate?"

"Deadly accurate."

"Then he should be able to help us. If the answer is yes, we ove accordingly. If no, the employee is off the hook and it's asiness as usual."

"Alfred's very expensive."

"I was afraid so. How much?"

"Well, he has sixteen years with the Bureau and is a career an. That's why he's so cautious. He has much to lose."

"How much?"

"Half a million."

"Damn!"

"Of course, we have to make a small profit on the transac- n. After all, Alfred is ours."

"A small profit?"

"Quite small, really. Most of it goes to Alfred. He talks to ɔyles daily, you know. His office is two doors down."

"All right. We'll pay."

Tubertini flashed a conquering smile and tasted his wine. "I ink you lied, Mr. Lazarov. You said it was a small unit in emphis. That's not true, is it?"

"No."

"What's the name of this unit?"

"The Bendini firm."

"Old man Morolto's daughter married a Bendini."

"That's it."

"What's the employee's name?"

"Mitchell McDeere."

"It might take two or three weeks. Meeting with Alfred is a ajor production."

"Yes. Just be quick about it."

27

I T WAS HIGHLY UNUSUAL for wives to appear at t
quiet little fortress on Front Street. They were certai
welcome, they were told, but seldom invited. So Ab
McDeere arrived through the front door, into the recepti
area uninvited and unannounced. It was imperative that s
see her husband, she insisted. The receptionist phoned N
on the second floor, and within seconds she appeared in a r
and warmly greeted her boss's wife. Mitch was in a meeti
she explained. He's always in a damned meeting, Abby
plied. Get him out! They rushed to his office, where Ab
closed the door and waited.

Mitch was observing another one of Avery's chaotic dep
tures. Secretaries bumped into each other and packed bri
cases while Avery yelled into the phone. Mitch sat on the s
with a legal pad and watched. His partner was scheduled
two days on Grand Cayman. April 15 loomed on the calen
like a date with a firing squad, and the banks down there
certain records that had become critical. It was all work, Av
insisted. He talked about the trip for five days, dreading
cursing it, but finding it completely unavoidable. He wo
take the Lear, and it was now waiting, said a secretary.

Probably waiting with a load of cash, thought Mitch.

Avery slammed the phone down and grabbed his coat. Nina walked through the door and glared at Mitch. "Mr. McDeere, your wife is here. She says it's an emergency."

The chaos became silent. He looked blankly at Avery. The secretaries froze. "What is it?" he asked, standing.

"She's in your office," Nina said.

"Mitch, I've gotta go," Avery said. "I'll call you tomorrow. I hope things are okay."

"Sure." He followed Nina down the stairs, saying nothing, his office. Abby sat on his desk. He closed and locked the door. He watched her carefully.

"Mitch, I have to go home."

"Why? What's happened?"

"My father just called at school. They found a tumor in one Mother's lungs. They're operating tomorrow."

He breathed deeply. "I'm so sorry." He did not touch her. he was not crying.

"I must go. I've taken a leave of absence at school."

"For how long?" It was a nervous question.

She looked past him, to the Ego Wall. "I don't know, Mitch. e need some time apart. I'm tired of a lot of things right now, d I need time. I think it will be good for both of us."

"Let's talk about it."

"You're too busy to talk, Mitch. I've been trying to talk for x months, but you can't hear me."

"How long will you be gone, Abby?"

"I don't know. I guess it depends on Mother. No, it depends a lot of things."

"You're scaring me, Abby."

"I'll be back, I promise. I don't know when. Maybe a week. aybe a month. I need to sort out some things."

"A month?"

"I don't know, Mitch. I just need some time. And I need to with Mother."

"I hope she's okay. I mean that."

"I know. I'm going home to pack a few things, and I'll leave an hour or so."

"All right. Be careful."

"I love you, Mitch."

He nodded and watched as she opened the door. There w
no embrace.

On the fifth floor, a technician rewound the tape and push
the emergency button direct to DeVasher's office. He appear
instantly and slapped the headphones over his extra-large c
nium. He listened for a moment. "Rewind," he demanded. I
was quiet for another moment.

"When did this happen?" he asked.

The technician looked at a panel of digital numbers. "T
minutes fourteen seconds ago. In his office, second floor."

"Damn, damn. She's leaving him, ain't she? No talk of se
ration or divorce before this?"

"No. You would've known about it. They've argued ab
his workaholic routine, and he hates her parents. But nothi
like this."

"Yeah, yeah. Check with Marcus and see if he's heard a
thing before. Check the tapes, in case we've missed somethi
Damn, damn, damn!"

Abby started for Kentucky, but did not make it. An hour w
of Nashville, she left Interstate 40, and turned north on Hi
way 13. She had noticed nothing behind her. She drove eig
at times, then fifty. Nothing. At the small town of Clarksvi
near the Kentucky line, she abruptly turned east on Highw
112. An hour later she entered Nashville through a cou
highway, and the red Peugeot was lost in city traffic.

She parked it in the long-term section at Nashville Airp
and caught a shuttle to the terminal. In a rest room on the fi
floor she changed into khaki walking shorts, Bass loafers an
navy knit pullover. It was a cool outfit, a little out of seas
but she was headed for warmer weather. She pulled her sho
der-length hair into a ponytail and forced it under her col
She changed sunglasses and stuffed the dress, heels and pa
hose into a canvas gym bag.

Almost five hours after she left Memphis, she walked to
Delta boarding gate and presented her ticket. She asked fc
window seat.

No Delta flight in the free world can bypass Atlanta,
fortunately she was not forced to change planes. She waited

:r window and watched darkness fall on the busy airport.
:e was nervous, but tried not to think about it. She drank a
:ass of wine and read a *Newsweek*.

Two hours later she landed in Miami and left the plane. She
:alked rapidly through the airport, catching stares but ignor-
:g them. They're just the usual everyday stares of admiration
:d lust, she told herself. Nothing more.

At the one and only Cayman Airways boarding gate, she
·oduced her round-trip ticket and the required birth certifi-
:te and driver's license. Wonderful people, these Caymanians,
:t they won't allow you in their country unless you've al-
·ady purchased a ticket to get out. Please come and spend
·ur money, then leave. Please.

She sat in a corner of the crowded room and tried to read. A
·ung father with a pretty wife and two babies kept staring at
·r legs, but no one else noticed her. The flight to Grand Cay-
·an would leave in thirty minutes.

·fter a rough start, Avery gained momentum and spent seven
·urs at the Royal Bank of Montreal, Georgetown, Grand
·ayman branch. When he left at 5 P.M., the complimentary
·nference room was filled with computer printouts and ac-
·unt summaries. He would finish tomorrow. He needed
·cDeere, but circumstances had worked to seriously curtail
·s travel plans. Avery was now exhausted and thirsty. And
·ings were hot on the beach.

At Rumheads, he picked up a beer at the bar and worked his
·ell-tanned body through the crowd to the patio, where he
·oked for a table. As he strode confidently past the domino
·me, Tammy Greenwood Hemphill, of Greenwood Services,
·rvously but nonchalantly entered the crowd and sat on a
·ol at the bar. She watched him. Her tan was store-bought,
·achine-inflicted, with some areas browner than others. But
· the whole, it was an enviable tan for late March. The hair
·as now colored, not bleached, to a soft sandy blond, and the
·akeup likewise had been tempered. The bikini was state of
·e art, bright fluorescent orange that demanded attention.
·e large breasts hung wonderfully and stretched the strings
·d patches to their limit. The small patch across the rear was
·efully incapable of covering anything. She was forty, but

twenty sets of hungry eyes followed her to the bar, where s
ordered a club soda and fired up a cigarette. She smoked it, a
watched him.

He was a wolf. He looked good, and he knew it. He sipp
his beer and slowly examined every female within fifty yar
He locked into one, a young blonde, and seemed ready
pounce when her man arrived and she sat in his lap. He sipp
his beer and continued to survey.

Tammy ordered another club soda, with a twist of lime, a
started for the patio. The wolf locked into the big breasts i
mediately and watched them bounce his way.

"Mind if I sit down?" she asked.

He half stood and reached for the chair. "Please do." It wa
great moment for him. Of all the hungry wolves lusti
around the bar and patio at Rumheads, she picked him. He
had younger babes, but at this moment at this place, she w
the hottest.

"I'm Avery Tolleson. From Memphis."

"Nice to meet you. I'm Libby. Libby Lox from Birmi
ham." Now she was Libby. She had a sister named Libby
mother named Doris, and her name was Tammy. And s
hoped to hell she could keep it all straight. Although she w
no rings, she had a husband whose legal name was Elvis, a
he was supposed to be in Oklahoma City impersonating t
King, and probably screwing teenage girls with LOVE
TENDER T-shirts.

"What brings you here?" Avery asked.

"Just fun. Got in this morning. Staying at the Palms. Yo

"I'm a tax lawyer; and believe it or not, I'm here on bu
ness. I'm forced to come down several times a year. Real t
ture."

"Where are you staying?"

He pointed. "My firm owns those two condos over the
It's a nice little write-off."

"Very pretty."

The wolf did not hesitate. "Would you like to see them?"
She giggled like a sophomore. "Maybe later."

He smiled at her. This would be easy. He loved the islan

"What're you drinking?" he asked.

"Gin and tonic. Twist of lime."

He left for the bar, and returned with the drinks. He moved
s chair closer to her. Now their legs were touching. The
easts were resting comfortably on the table. He looked down
tween them.

"Are you alone?" Obvious question, but he had to ask it.

"Yeah. You?"

"Yeah. Do you have plans for dinner?"

"Not really."

"Good. There's this great cookout there at the Palms begin-
ng at six. The best seafood on the island. Good music. Rum
nch. The works. No dress code."

"I'm game."

They moved closer together, and his hand was suddenly be-
een her knees. His elbow nestled next to her left breast, and
e smiled. She smiled. This was not altogether unpleasant, she
ought, but there was business at hand.

The Barefoot Boys began to tune up, and the festival began.
achcombers from all directions flocked to the Palms. Na-
es in white jackets and white shorts lined up folding tables
d laid heavy cotton cloths over them. The smell of boiled
rimp and grilled amberjack and barbecued shark filled the
ach. The lovebirds, Avery and Libby, walked hand in hand
to the courtyard of the Palms and lined up for the buffet.

For three hours they dined and danced, drank and danced,
d fell madly in heat over each other. Once he became drunk,
e returned to straight club soda. Business was at hand. By
n, he was sloppy and she led him away from the dance floor,
the condo next door. He attacked her at the front door, and
ey kissed and groped for five minutes. He managed the key,
d they were inside.

"One more drink," she said, ever the party girl. He went to
e bar and fixed her a gin and tonic. He was drinking scotch
d water. They sat on the balcony outside the master bed-
om and watched a half moon decorate the gentle sea.

She had matched him drink for drink, he thought, and if she
uld handle another, then so could he. But nature was calling
ain, and he excused himself. The scotch and water sat on the
cker table between them, and she smiled at it. Much easier
at she had prayed for. She took a small plastic packet from

the orange strap between her legs and dumped two tablets chloral hydrate into his drink. She sipped her gin and toni

"Drink it up, big boy," she said when he returned. "I' ready for bed."

He grabbed his whiskey and gulped it down. The taste bu had been numb for hours. He took another swallow, then b gan to relax. Another swallow. His head wobbled from shou der to shoulder, and finally his chin hit his chest. The breat ing became heavy.

"Sleep well, lover boy," she said to herself.

With a man of a hundred eighty pounds, two shots of chlor hydrate would induce a dead sleep for ten hours. She took h glass and gauged what was left. Not much. Eight hours, to safe. She rolled him out of the chair and dragged him to t bed, head first, then feet. Very gently, she pulled his yellow and-blue surfer shorts down his legs and laid them on the flo She stared for a long second, then tucked the sheets and bla kets around him. She kissed him good night.

On the dresser she found two key rings, eleven keys. Dow stairs in the hall between the kitchen and the great room wi a view of the beach, she found the mysterious locked do Mitch had found in November. He had paced off every roo upstairs and down, and determined this room to be at le fifteen by fifteen. It was suspicious because the door was met and because it was locked, and because a small STORAGE si was affixed to it. It was the only labeled room in the condo. week earlier in Unit B, he and Abby had found no such roo

One key ring held a key to a Mercedes, two keys to t Bendini Building, a house key, two apartment keys and a de key. The keys on the other ring were unmarked and fair generic. She tried it first, and the fourth key fit. She held h breath and opened the door. No electric shocks, no alar nothing. Mitch told her to open the door, wait five minut and, if nothing happened, then turn on the light.

She waited ten minutes. Ten long and frightful minut Mitch had speculated that Unit A was used by the partne and trusted guests, and that Unit B was used by the associat and others who required constant surveillance. Thus, hoped, Unit A would not be laden with wires and cameras a recorders and alarms. After ten minutes, she opened the do

e and turned on the light. She waited again, and heard
hing. The room was square, about fifteen by fifteen, with
te walls, no carpet, and, as she counted, twelve fireproof
l size file cabinets. Slowly, she walked over to one and
ed the top drawer. It was unlocked.

he turned off the light, closed the door and returned to the
room upstairs, where Avery was now comatose and snor-
loudly. It was ten-thirty. She would work like crazy for
t hours and quit at six in the morning.

ear a desk in a corner, three large briefcases sat neatly in a
. She grabbed them, turned off the lights and left through
front door. The small parking lot was dark and empty with
avel drive leading to the highway. A sidewalk ran next to
shrubbery in front of both units and stopped at a white
rd fence along the property line. A gate led to a slight
sy knoll, with the first building of the Palms just over it.

was a short walk from the condos to the Palms, but the
fcases had grown much heavier when she reached Room
It was on the first floor, front side, with a view of the pool
not of the beach. She was panting and sweating when she
cked on the door.

bby yanked it open. She took the briefcases and placed
n on the bed. "Any problems?"

Not yet. I think he's dead." Tammy wiped her face with a
el and opened a can of Coke.

Where is he?" Abby was all business, no smiles.

n his bed. I figure we've got eight hours. Until six."

Did you get in the room?" Abby asked as she handed her a
of shorts and a bulky cotton shirt.

Yeah. There's a dozen big file cabinets, unlocked. A few
board boxes and other junk, but not much else."

A dozen?"

Yeah, tall ones. All legal size. We'll be lucky to finish by

was a single motel room with a queen size bed. The sofa,
e table and bed were pushed to the wall, and a Canon
del 8580 copier with automatic feed and collator sat in the
er with engines running. On lease from Island Office Sup-
it came at the scalper's price of three hundred dollars for
ty-four hours, delivered. It was the newest and largest

rental copier on the island, the salesman had explained, an
was not excited about parting with it for only a day. But A
charmed him and began laying hundred-dollar bills on
counter. Two cases of copy paper, ten thousand sheets,
next to the bed.

They opened the first briefcase and removed six thin f
"Same type of files," Tammy mumbled to herself. She
hitched the two-prong clasp on the inside of the file and
moved the papers. "Mitch says they're very particular ab
their files," Tammy explained as she unstapled a ten-page
ument. "He says lawyers have a sixth sense and can alm
smell if a secretary or a clerk has been in a file. So you'll h
to be careful. Work slowly. Copy one document, and when
restaple it, try to line up with the old staple holes. It's tedi
Copy only one document at a time, regardless of the num
of pages. Then put it back together slowly and in order. T
staple your copy so everything stays in order."

With the automatic feed, the ten-page document took e
seconds.

"Pretty fast," Tammy said.

The first briefcase was finished in twenty minutes. Tam
handed the two key rings to Abby and picked up two n
empty, all-canvas Samsonite handbags. She left for the cor

Abby followed her out the door, then locked it. She wal
to the front of the Palms, to Tammy's rented Nissan Sta
Dodging at oncoming traffic from the wrong side of the r
she drove along Seven Mile Beach and into Georgetown. T
blocks behind the stately Swiss Bank Building, on a narr
street lined with neat frame houses, she found the one ow
by the only locksmith on the island of Grand Cayman.
least, he was the only one she'd been able to locate with
assistance. He owned a green house with open windows
white trim around the shutters and the doors.

She parked in the street and walked through the sand to
tiny front porch, where the locksmith and his neighbors w
drinking and listening to Radio Cayman. Solid-gold reg
They quietened when she approached, and none of t
stood. It was almost eleven. He had said that he would do
job in his shop out back, and that his fees were modest,

t he would like a fifth of Myers's Rum as a down payment
ore he started.

Mr. Dantley, I'm sorry I'm late. I've brought you a little
." She held out the fifth of rum.

Mr. Dantley emerged from the darkness and took the rum.
inspected the bottle. "Boys, a bottle of Myers's."

Abby could not understand the chatter, but it was obvious
gang on the porch was terribly excited about the bottle of
ers's. Dantley handed it to them and led Abby behind his
ise to a small outbuilding full of tools and small machines
a hundred gadgets. A single yellow light bulb hung from
ceiling and attracted mosquitoes by the hundreds. She
ded Dantley the eleven keys, and he carefully laid them on
are section of a cluttered workbench. "This will be easy,"
said without looking up.

Although he was drinking at eleven at night, Dantley ap-
red to be in control. Perhaps his system had built an immu-
y to rum. He worked through a pair of thick goggles, drill-
and carving each replica. After twenty minutes, he was
shed. He handed Abby the two original sets of keys and
ir copies.

Thank you, Mr. Dantley. How much do I owe you?"

They were quite easy," he drawled. "A dollar per key."

he paid him quickly and left.

nmy filled the two small suitcases with the contents of the
drawer of the first file cabinet. Five drawers, twelve cabi-
s, sixty trips to the copier and back. In eight hours. It could
done. There were files, notebooks, computer printouts and
e files. Mitch said to copy it all. He was not exactly sure
t he was looking for, so copy it all.

he turned off the light and ran upstairs to check on lover
. He had not moved. The snoring was in slow motion.

he Samsonites weighed thirty pounds apiece, and her arms
ed when she reached Room 188. First trip out of sixty, she
ld not make it. Abby had not returned from Georgetown,
ammy unloaded the suitcases neatly on the bed. She took
drink from her Coke and left with the empty bags. Back to
condo. Drawer two was identical. She fitted the files in
er into the suitcases and strong-armed zippers. She was

sweating and gasping for breath. Four packs a day, [ ]
thought. She vowed to cut back to two. Maybe even one p[ ]
Up the stairs to check on him. He had not breathed since [ ]
last trip.

The copier was clicking and humming when she retur[ ]
from trip two. Abby was finishing the second briefcase, ab[ ]
to start on the third.

"Did you get the keys?" Tammy asked.

"Yeah, no problem. What's your man doing?"

"If the copier wasn't running, you could hear him snori[ ]
Tammy unpacked into another neat stack on the bed. [ ]
wiped her face with a wet towel and left for the condo.

Abby finished the third briefcase and started on the st[ ]
from the file cabinets. She quickly got the hang of the a[ ]
matic feed, and after thirty minutes she moved with the [ ]
cient grace of a seasoned copy-room clerk. She fed copies
unstapled and restapled while the machine clicked rapidly
spat the reproductions through the collator.

Tammy arrived from trip three out of breath and with s[ ]
dripping from her nose. "Third drawer," she reported. "[ ]
still snoring." She unzipped the suitcases and made ano[ ]
neat pile on the bed. She caught her breath, wiped her face
loaded the now copied contents of drawer one into the b[ ]
For the rest of the night, she would be loaded coming [ ]
going.

At midnight, the Barefoot Boys sang their last song, and [ ]
Palms settled down for the night. The quiet hum of the co[ ]
could not be heard outside Room 188. The door was [ ]
locked; the shades pulled tightly, and all lights extinguis[ ]
except for a lamp near the bed. No one noticed the tired l[ ]
dripping with sweat, lugging the same two suitcases to [ ]
from the room.

After midnight they did not speak. They were tired, [ ]
busy and scared, and there was nothing to report except l[ ]
boy's movements in bed, if any. And there was none, [ ]
around 1 A.M., when he subconsciously rolled onto his s[ ]
where he stayed for about twenty minutes, then returne[ ]
his back. Tammy checked on him with each visit and as[ ]
herself each time what she would do if his eyes sudd[ ]
opened and he attacked. She had a small tube of Mace in [ ]

rts pocket, just in case a confrontation occurred and escape
:ame necessary. Mitch had been vague on the details of such
escape. Just don't lead him back to the motel room, he said.
: him with the Mace, then run like crazy and scream,
ape!"

3ut after twenty-five trips, she became convinced he was
irs away from consciousness. And it was bad enough hiking
: a pack mule to and from, but she also had to climb the
rs, fourteen of them, each trip to check on Casanova. So she
nt to check every other trip. Then one out of three.

3y 2 A.M., halfway through the project, they had copied the
tents from five of the file cabinets. They had made over
r thousand copies, and the bed was covered with neat little
:ks of materials. Their copies stood along the wall next to
sofa in seven even rows almost waist high.

"hey rested for fifteen minutes.

five-thirty the first flicker of sunrise rose in the east, and
y forgot about being tired. Abby quickened her movements
ind the copier and hoped it would not burn up. Tammy
bed the cramps in her calves and walked quickly back to
condo. It was either trip number fifty-one or fifty-two. She
lost count. It would be her last trip for a while. He was
ting.
he opened the door and went straight to the storage room,
sual. She set the packed Samsonites on the floor, as usual.
quietly walked up the stairs, into the bedroom, and froze.
ry was sitting on the edge of the bed, facing the balcony.
heard her and turned slowly to face her. His eyes were
llen and glazed. He scowled at her.
istinctively, she unbuttoned the khaki shorts and they fell
he floor. "Hey, big boy," she said, trying to breathe nor-
ly and act like a party girl. She walked to the edge of the
where where he was sitting. "You're up kinda early. Let's
some more sleep."
is gaze returned to the window. He said nothing. She sat
de him and rubbed the inside of his thigh. She slid her
l up the inside of his leg, and he did not move.
Are you awake?" she asked.
o response.

"Avery, talk to me, baby. Let's get some more sleep. It's dark out there."

He fell sideways, onto his pillow. He grunted. No attemp[t] speech. Just a grunt. Then he closed his eyes. She lifted his onto the bed and covered him again.

She sat by him for ten minutes, and when the snoring turned to its former intensity, she slid into the shorts and to the Palms.

"He woke up, Abby!" she reported in panic. "He woke then passed out again."

Abby stopped and stared. Both women looked at the which was covered with uncopied documents.

"Okay. Take a quick shower," Abby said coolly. "The[n] get in bed with him and wait. Lock the door to the sto[rage] room, and call me when he wakes up and gets in the sho[wer]. I'll keep copying what's left, and we'll try to move it l[ate] after he goes to work."

"That's awfully risky."

"It's all risky. Hurry."

Five minutes later, Tammy/Doris/Libby with the brigh[t] ange string bikini made another trip—without the suitcas[e] to the condo. She locked the front door and the storage [door] and went to the bedroom. She removed the orange top crawled under the covers.

The snoring kept her awake for fifteen minutes. The[n] dozed. She sat up in bed to prevent sleep. She was sca[red] sitting there in bed with a nude man who would kill her i[f] knew. Her tired body relaxed, and sleep became unavoida[ble]. She dozed again.

Lover boy broke from his coma at three minutes past nine[.] moaned loudly and rolled to the edge of the bed. His ey[es] were stuck together. They opened slowly, and the bright came piercing through. He moaned again. The head weigh[ed] hundred pounds and rocked awkwardly from right to shifting the brain violently each time. He breathed deeply, the fresh oxygen went screaming through his temples. right hand caught his attention. He tried to raise it, bu[t] nerve impulses would not penetrate the brain. Slowly it w[as]

294

and he squinted at it. He tried to focus with the right eye
, then the left. The clock.

e looked at the digital clock for thirty seconds before he
ld decipher the red numbers. Nine-oh-five. Damn! He was
ected at the bank at nine. He moaned. The woman!

he had felt him move and heard his sounds, and she lay still
1 her eyes shut. She prayed he would not touch her. She
him staring.

or this career rogue and bad boy, there had been many
govers. But none like this. He looked at her face and tried
emember how good she had been. He could always remem-
that, if nothing else. Regardless of the size of the hangover,
ould always remember the women. He watched her for a
nent, then gave it up.

Damn!" he said as he stood and tried to walk. His feet were
lead boots and only reluctantly complied with his wishes.
braced himself against the sliding door to the balcony.

he bathroom was twenty feet away, and he decided to go
it. The desk and dresser served as braces. One painful,
nsy step after another, and he finally made it. He hovered
/e the toilet and relieved himself.

ae rolled to face the balcony, and when he finished she felt
sit on her side of the bed. He gently touched her shoulder.
oby, wake up." He shook her, and she bolted stiff.

Wake up, dear," he said. A gentleman.

ae gave him her best sleepy smile. The morning-after smile
alfillment and commitment. The Scarlett O'Hara smile the
ning after Rhett nailed her. "You were great, big boy," she
ed with her eyes closed.

1 spite of the pain and nausea, in spite of the lead boots and
ling-ball head, he was proud of himself. The woman was
ressed. Suddenly, he remembered that he was great last
.t.

ook, Libby, we've overslept. I gotta go to work. I'm al-
y late."

Not in the mood, huh?" she giggled. She prayed he wasn't
ae mood.

Naw, not now. How about tonight?"

'll be here, big boy."

Good. I gotta take a shower."

"Wake me up when you get out."

He stood and mumbled something, then locked the b
room door. She slid across the bed to the phone and ca
Abby. After three rings, she answered.

"He's in the shower."

"Are you okay?"

"Yeah. Fine. He couldn't do it if he had to."

"What took so long?"

"He wouldn't wake up."

"Is he suspicious?"

"No. He remembers nothing. I think he's in pain."

"How long will you be there?"

"I'll kiss him goodbye when he gets out of the shower.
maybe fifteen minutes."

"Okay. Hurry." Abby hung up, and Tammy slid to her
of the bed. In the attic above the kitchen, a recorder clic
reset itself and was ready for the next call.

By ten-thirty, they were ready for the final assault on
condo. The contraband was divided into three equal pa
Three daring raids in open daylight. Tammy slid the sl
new keys into her blouse pocket and took off with the
cases. She walked quickly, her eyes darting in all direct
behind the sunglasses. The parking lot in front of the co
was still empty. Traffic was light on the highway.

The new key fit, and she was inside. The key to the sto
door also fit, and five minutes later she left the condo.
second and third trips were equally quick and uneven
When she left the storage room for the last time, she studi
carefully. Everything was in order, just as she found it.
locked the condo and took the empty, well-worn Samso
back to her room.

For an hour they lay beside each other on the bed
laughed at Avery and his hangover. It was over now, for
most part, and they had committed the perfect crime.
lover boy was a willing but ignorant participant. It had b
easy, they decided.

The small mountain of evidence filled eleven and a half
rugated storage boxes. At two-thirty, a native with a straw
and no shirt knocked on the door and announced he was t

outfit called Cayman Storage. Abby pointed at the boxes.
[wit]h no place to go and no hurry to get there, he took the first
[box] and ever so slowly carried it to his van. Like all the na-
[tive]s, he operated on Cayman time. No hurry, mon.

[T]hey followed him in the Stanza to a warehouse in George-
[tow]n. Abby inspected the proposed storage room and paid
[hi]m for three months' rental.

28

WAYNE TARRANCE sat on the back row of
11:40 P.M. Greyhound from Louisville to Indiana
lis to Chicago. Although he sat by himself, the
was crowded. It was Friday night. The bus left Kent
thirty minutes earlier, and by now he was convinced so
thing had gone wrong. Thirty minutes, and not a wor
signal from anyone. Maybe it was the wrong bus. Ma
McDeere had changed his mind. Maybe a lot of things.
rear seat was inches above the diesel engine, and Wayne
rance, of the Bronx, now knew why Greyhound Frequent
ers fought for the seats just behind the driver. His L
L'Amour vibrated until he had a headache. Thirty min
Nothing.

The toilet flushed across the aisle, and the door flew o
The odor filtered out, and Tarrance looked away, to the so
bound traffic. From nowhere, she slid into the aisle seat
cleared her throat. Tarrance jerked to his right, and there
was. He'd seen her before, somewhere.

"Are you Mr. Tarrance?" She wore jeans, white co
sneakers and a heavy green rag sweater. She hid behind
glasses.

Yeah. And you?"

he grabbed his hand and shook it firmly. "Abby McDeere."

I was expecting your husband."

I know. He decided not to come, and so here I am."

Well, uh, I sort of wanted to talk to him."

Yes, but he sent me. Just think of me as his agent."

arrance laid his paperback under the seat and watched the

way. "Where is he?"

Why is that important, Mr. Tarrance? He sent me to talk

ness, and you're here to talk business. So let's talk."

Okay. Keep your voice down, and if anybody comes down

aisle, grab my hand and stop talking. Act like we're mar-

or something. Okay? Now, Mr. Voyles—do you know

he is?"

I know everything, Mr. Tarrance."

Good. Mr. Voyles is about to stroke out because we haven't

Mitch's files yet. The good files. You understand why

're important, don't you?"

Very much so."

So we want the files."

And we want a million dollars."

Yes, that's the deal. But we get the files first."

No. That's not the deal. The deal, Mr. Tarrance, is that we

the million dollars exactly where we want it, then we hand

the files."

You don't trust us?"

That's correct. We don't trust you, Voyles or anyone else.

money is to be deposited by wire transfer to a certain

bered account in a bank in Freeport, Bahamas. We will

ediately be notified, and the money will then be wired by

another bank. Once we have it where we want it, the files

yours."

Where are the files?"

n a mini-storage in Memphis. There are fifty-one files in

ll boxed up real neat and proper like. You'll be impressed.

do good work."

We? Have you seen the files?"

Of course. Helped box them up. There are these surprises

ox number eight."

Okay. What?"

"Mitch was able to copy three of Avery Tolleson's files,
they appear to be questionable. Two deal with a comp
called Dunn Lane, Ltd., which we know to be a Mafia-
trolled corporation chartered in the Caymans. It was es
lished with ten million laundered dollars in 1986. The files
with two construction projects financed by the corporat
You'll find it fascinating reading."

"How do you know it was chartered in the Caymans?
how do you know about the ten million? Surely that's n
the files."

"No, it's not. We have other records."

Tarrance thought about the other records for six mile
was obvious he wouldn't see them until the McDeeres had
first million. He let it pass.

"I'm not sure we can wire the money as you wish wit
first getting the files." It was a rather weak bluff. She re
perfectly and smiled.

"Do we have to play games, Mr. Tarrance? Why don't
just give us the money and quit sparring."

A foreign student of some sort, probably an Arab, saunt
down the aisle and into the rest room. Tarrance froze
stared at the window. Abby patted his arm like a real
friend. The flushing sounded like a short waterfall.

"How soon can this happen?" Tarrance asked. She was
touching him anymore.

"The files are ready. How soon can you round up a mi
bucks?"

"Tomorrow."

Abby looked out the window and talked from the left co
of her mouth. "Today's Friday. Next Tuesday, at ten A.M.
ern time, Bahamas time, you transfer by wire the million
lars from your account at the Chemical Bank in Manhatta
a numbered account at the Ontario Bank in Freeport.
clean, legitimate wire transfer—take about fifteen second

Tarrance frowned and listened hard. "What if we don't
an account at the Chemical Bank in Manhattan?"

"You don't now, but you will Monday. I'm sure you've
someone in Washington who can handle a simple wire t
fer."

"I'm sure we do."

Good."

But why the Chemical Bank?"

Mitch's orders, Mr. Tarrance. Trust him, he knows what doing."

see he's done his homework."

He always does his homework. And there's something you to always remember. He's much smarter than you are."

Tarrance snorted and faked a light chuckle. They rode in ace for a mile or two, each thinking of the next question answer.

Okay," Tarrance said, almost to himself. "And when do we the files?"

hen the money's safe in Freeport, we'll be notified. nesday morning before ten-thirty, you'll receive at your mphis office a Federal Express package with a note and the to the mini-storage."

So I can tell Mr. Voyles we'll have the files by Wednesday noon?"

e shrugged and said nothing. Tarrance felt stupid for asking the question. Quickly, he thought of a good one.

We'll need the account number in Freeport."

t's written down. I'll give it to you when the bus stops."

he particulars were now complete. He reached under the and retrieved his book. He flipped pages and pretended to . "Just sit here a minute," he said.

Any questions?" she asked.

eah. Can we talk about these other records you mened?"

ure."

Vhere are they?"

Good question. The way the deal was explained to me, we ld first get the next installment, a half million, I believe, in rn for enough evidence to allow you to obtain the indictts. These other records are part of the next installment."

rrance flipped a page. "You mean you've already obtained uh, dirty files?"

Ve have most of what we need. Yes, we have a bunch of files."

Vhere are they?"

She smiled softly and patted his arm. "I assure you the not in the mini-storage with the clean files."

"But you have possession of them?"

"Sort of. Would you like to see a couple?"

He closed the book and breathed deeply. He looked at "Certainly."

"I thought so. Mitch says we'll give you ten inches of d ments on Dunn Lane, Ltd.—copies of bank records, corpo charters, minutes, bylaws, officers, stockholders, wire tran records, letters from Nathan Locke to Joey Morolto, wor papers, a hundred other juicy morsels that'll make you sleep. Wonderful stuff. Mitch says you can probably get t indictments just from the Dunn Lane records."

Tarrance hung on every word, and believed her. "When I see it?" he asked quietly but so eagerly.

"When Ray is out of prison. It's part of the deal, ren ber?"

"Aw yes. Ray."

"Aw yes. He goes over the wall, Mr. Tarrance, or you forget the Bendini firm. Mitch and I will take our paltry lion and disappear into the night."

"I'm working on it."

"Better work hard." It was more than a threat, and he k it. He opened the book again and stared at it.

Abby pulled a Bendini, Lambert & Locke business from her pocket and dropped in on the book. On the back had written the account number: 477DL-19584, Ontario B Freeport.

"I'm going back to my seat near the front, away from engine. Are we clear about next Tuesday?"

"No problems, mon. Are you getting off in Indianapol

"Yes."

"Where are you going?"

"To my parents' home in Kentucky. Mitch and I are rated."

She was gone.

Tammy stood in one of a dozen long, hot lines at Miami toms. She wore shorts, sandals, halter top, sunglasses a straw hat and looked just like the other thousand weary

302

returning from the sun-drenched beaches of the Carib-
. In front of her were two ill-tempered newlyweds carry-
bags of duty-free liquor and perfume and obviously in the
dle of a serious disagreement. Behind her were two brand-
Hartman leather suitcases filled with enough documents
records to indict forty lawyers. Her employer, also a law-
had suggested she purchase luggage with little wheels on
bottom so they could be pulled through the Miami Inter-
onal Airport. She also had a small overnight bag with a
clothes and a toothbrush, to look legitimate.

bout every ten minutes, the young couple moved forward
nches, and Tammy followed with her baggage. An hour
she entered the line, she made it to the checkpoint.

No declarations!" the agent snapped in broken English.

No!" she snapped back.

e nodded at the big leather bags. "What's in there?"

Papers."

Papers?"

Papers."

What kind of papers?"

oilet paper, she thought. I spend my vacations traveling
Caribbean collecting toilet paper. "Legal documents, crap
that. I'm a lawyer."

Yeah, yeah." He unzipped the overnight bag and glanced
Okay. Next!"

e carefully pulled the bags, just so. They were inclined to
over. A bellboy grabbed them and loaded all three pieces
a two-wheeler. "Delta Flight 282, to Nashville. Gate 44,
course B," she said as she handed him a five dollar bill.

ammy and all three bags arrived in Nashville at midnight
rday. She loaded them into her Rabbit and left the airport.
he suburb of Brentwood, she parked in her designated
ing place and, one at a time, pulled the Hartmans into a
bedroom apartment.

xcept for a rented foldaway sofa, there was no furniture.
unpacked the suitcases in the bedroom and began the te-
s process of arranging the evidence. Mitch wanted a list of
document, each bank record, each corporation. He
ted it just so. He said one day he would pass through in a
hurry, and he wanted it all organized.

For two hours she took inventory. She sat on the floor
made careful notes. After three one-day trips to Grand
man, the room was beginning to fill. Monday she would l
again.

She felt like she'd slept three hours in the past two w
But it was urgent, he said. A matter of life and death.

Tarry Ross, alias Alfred, sat in the darkest corner of the lo
of the Washington Phoenix Inn. The meeting would be t
bly brief. He drank coffee and waited on his guest.

He waited and vowed to wait only five more minutes.
cup shook when he tried to sip it. Coffee splashed on the t
He looked at the table and tried desperately not to
around. He waited.

His guest arrived from nowhere and sat with his back t
wall. His name was Vinnie Cozzo, a thug from New Y
From the Palumbo family.

Vinnie noticed the shaking cup and the spilled coffee.
lax, Alfred. This place is dark enough."

"What do you want?" Alfred hissed.

"I wanna drink."

"No time for drinks. I'm leaving."

"Settle down, Alfred. Relax, pal. There ain't three peop
here."

"What do you want?" he hissed again.

"Just a little information."

"It'll cost you."

"It always does." A waiter ventured by, and Vinnie ord
Chivas and water.

"How's my pal Denton Voyles?" Vinnie asked.

"Kiss my ass, Cozzo. I'm leaving. I'm walking outta he

"Okay, pal. Relax. I just need some info."

"Make it quick." Alfred scanned the lounge. His cup
empty, most of it on the table.

The Chivas arrived, and Vinnie took a good drink. "C
little situation down in Memphis. Some of the boys're
worried about it. Ever hear of the Bendini firm?"

Instinctively, Alfred shook his head in the negative. Al
say no, at first. Then, after careful digging, return with a
little report and say yes. Yes, he'd heard of the Bendini

their prized client. Operation Laundromat. Voyles him-
had named it and was so proud of his creativity.

innie took another good drink. "Well, there's a guy down
e named McDeere, Mitchell McDeere, who works for this
dini firm, and we suspect he's also playing grab-ass with
r people. Know what I mean? We think he's selling info on
dini to the feds. Just need to know if it's true. That's all."

lfred listened with a straight face, although it was not easy.
knew McDeere's blood type and his favorite restaurant in
nphis. He knew that McDeere had talked to Tarrance half
ozen times now and that tomorrow, Tuesday, McDeere
ıld become a millionaire. Piece of cake.

'll see what I can do. Let's talk money."

innie lit a Salem Light. "Well, Alfred, it's a serious matter.
ı't gonna lie. Two hundred thousand cash."

lfred dropped the cup. He pulled a handkerchief from his
pocket and furiously rubbed his glasses. "Two hundred?
ı?"

That's what I said. What'd we pay you last time?"

Seventy-five."

See what I mean. It's pretty damned serious, Alfred. Can
do it?"

Yes."

When?"

Give me two weeks."

29

A WEEK BEFORE APRIL 15, the workaholic
Bendini, Lambert & Locke reached maximum st
and ran at full throttle on nothing but adrenaline.
fear. Fear of missing a deduction or a write-off or some e
depreciation that would cost a rich client an extra millio
so. Fear of picking up the phone and calling the client
informing him that the return was now finished and, sor
say, an extra eight hundred thousand was due. Fear of
finishing by the fifteenth, and being forced to file extens
and incurring penalties and interest. The parking lot was
by 6 A.M. The secretaries worked twelve hours a day. Tem
were short. Talk was scarce and hurried.

With no wife to go home to, Mitch worked around the c
Sonny Capps had cursed and berated Avery because he c
$450,000. On earned income of twelve million. Avery
cursed Mitch, and together they plowed through the C
files again, digging and cursing. Mitch created two very e
tionable write-offs that lowered it to $320,000. Capps sa
was considering a new tax firm. One in Washington.

With six days to go, Capps demanded a meeting with A
in Houston. The Lear was available, and Avery left at

ght. Mitch drove him to the airport, receiving instructions
ong the way.

Shortly after 1:30 A.M., he returned to the office. Three Mer-
des, a BMW and a Jaguar were scattered through the park-
g lot. The security guard opened the rear door, and Mitch
de the elevator to the fourth floor. As usual, Avery locked his
fice door. The partners' doors were always locked. At the
d of the hall, a voice could be heard. Victor Milligan, head of
x, sat at his desk and said ugly things to his computer. The
her offices were dark and locked.

Mitch held his breath and stuck a key into Avery's door. The
ob turned, and he was inside. He switched on all the lights
d went to the small conference table where he and his part-
r had spent the day and most of the night. Files were stacked
e bricks around the chairs. Papers thrown here and there.
S reg. books were piled on top of each other.

Mitch sat at the table and continued his research for Capps.
cording to the FBI notebook, Capps was a legitimate busi-
ssman who had used the firm for at least eight years. The
bbies weren't interested in Sonny Capps.

After an hour, the talking stopped and Milligan closed and
ked the door. He took the stairs without saying good night.
itch quickly checked each office on the fourth floor, then the
rd. All empty. It was almost 3 A.M.

Next to the bookshelves on one wall of Avery's office, four
lid oak file cabinets sat undisturbed. Mitch had noticed them
r months but had never seen them used. The active files
re kept in three metal cabinets next to the window. Secre-
ies dug through these, usually while Avery yelled at them.
e locked the door behind him and walked to the oak cabinets.
cked, of course. He had narrowed it down to two small
ys, each less than an inch long. The first one fit the first
binet, and he opened it.

From Tammy's inventory of the contraband in Nashville, he
d memorized many of the names of the Cayman companies
erating with dirty money that was now clean. He thumbed
ough the files in the top drawer, and the names jumped at
n. Dunn Lane, Ltd., Eastpointe, Ltd., Virgin Bay Ltd., In-
d Contractors, Ltd., Gulf-South, Ltd. He found more famil-
names in the second and third drawers. The files were filled

with loan documents from Cayman banks, wire-trans
records, warranty deeds, leases, mortgage deeds and a th
sand other papers. He was particularly interested in Du
Lane and Gulf-South. Tammy had recorded a significant nu
ber of documents for these two companies.

He picked out a Gulf-South file full of wire-transfer recor
and loan documents from the Royal Bank of Montreal. I
walked to a copier in the center of the fourth floor and turn
it on. While it warmed, he casually glanced around. The pl
was dead. He looked along the ceilings. No cameras. He h
checked it many times before. The ACCESS NUMBER li
flashed, and he punched in the file number for Mrs. Let
Plunk. Her tax return was sitting on his desk on the seco
floor, and it could spare a few copies. He laid the contents
the automatic feed, and three minutes later the file was copi
One hundred twenty-eight copies, charged to Lettie Plu
Back to the file cabinet. Back to the copier with another st
of Gulf-South evidence. He punched in the access number
the file of Greenmark Partners, a real estate development co
pany in Bartlett, Tennessee. Legitimate folks. The tax retu
was sitting on his desk and could spare a few copies. Nine
one, to be exact.

Mitch had eighteen tax returns sitting in his office waiti
to be signed and filed. With six days to go, he had finished
deadline work. All eighteen received automatic billings
copies of Gulf-South and Dunn Lane evidence. He had scr
bled their access numbers on a sheet of notepaper, and it sat
the table next to the copier. After using the eighteen numbe
he accessed with three numbers borrowed from Lamar's f
and three numbers borrowed from the Capps files.

A wire ran from the copier through a hole in the wall a
down the inside of a closet, where it connected with wi
from three other copiers on the fourth floor. The wire, lar
now, ran down through the ceiling and along a baseboard
the billing room on the third floor, where a computer recor
and billed every copy made within the firm. An innocuo
looking little gray wire ran from the computer up a wall a
through the ceiling to the fourth floor, and then up to the fi
where another computer recorded the access code, the num
of copies and the location of the machine making each cop

• • • •

5 P.M., April 15, Bendini, Lambert & Locke shut down. By
, the parking lot was empty, and the expensive automobiles
ssembled two miles away behind a venerable seafood estab-
ment called Anderton's. A small banquet room was re-
ved for the annual April 15 blowout. Every associate and
ive partner was present, along with eleven retired partners.
e retirees were tanned and well rested, the actives were
gard and frayed. But they were all in a festive spirit, ready
get plastered. The stringent rules of clean living and mod-
tion would be forgotten this night. Another firm rule pro-
ited any lawyer or secretary from working on April 16.

latters of cold boiled shrimp and raw oysters sat on tables
ng the walls. A huge wooden barrel filled with ice and cold
osehead greeted them. Ten cases stood behind the barrel.
osevelt popped tops as quickly as possible. Late in the night,
would get drunk with the rest of them, and Oliver Lambert
uld call a taxi to haul him home to Jessie Frances. It was a
al.

Roosevelt's cousin, Little Bobby Blue Baker, sat at a baby
nd and sang sadly as the lawyers filed in. For now, he was
entertainment. Later, he would not be needed.

Mitch ignored the food and took an icy green bottle to a
le near the piano. Lamar followed with two pounds of
imp. They watched their colleagues shake off coats and ties
attack the Moosehead.

Get 'em all finished?" Lamar asked, devouring the shrimp.

Yeah. I finished mine yesterday. Avery and I worked on
ny Capps's until five P.M. It's finished."

How much?"

Quarter of a mill."

Ouch." Lamar turned up the bottle and drained half of it.
e's never paid that much, has he?"

No, and he's furious. I don't understand the guy. He
red twelve million from all sorts of ventures, and he's mad
ell because he had to pay two percent in taxes."

How's Avery?"

Somewhat worried. Capps made him fly to Houston last
k, and it did not go well. He left on the Lear at midnight.
d me later Capps was waiting at his office at four in the

morning, furious over his tax mess. Blamed it all on Ave
Said he might change firms."

"I think he says that all the time. You need a beer?"

Lamar left and returned with four Mooseheads. "How's ?
by's mom?"

Mitch borrowed a shrimp and peeled it. "She's okay,
now. They removed a lung."

"And how's Abby?" Lamar was watching his friend, and •
eating.

Mitch started another beer. "She's fine."

"Look, Mitch, our kids go to St. Andrew's. It's no sec
Abby took a leave of absence. She's been gone for two wee
We know it, and we're concerned."

"Things will work out. She wants to spend a little ti
away. It's no big deal, really."

"Come on, Mitch. It's a big deal when your wife lea
home without saying when she'll return. At least that's w
she told the headmaster at school."

"That's true. She doesn't know when she'll come b
Probably a month or so. She's had a hard time coping with
hours at the office."

The lawyers were all present and accounted for, so Ro
velt shut the door. The room became noisier. Bobby Blue •
requests.

"Have you thought about slowing down?" Lamar asked

"No, not really. Why should I?"

"Look, Mitch, I'm your friend, right? I'm worried ak
you. You can't make a million bucks the first year."

Oh yeah, he thought. I made a million bucks last week
ten seconds the little account in Freeport jumped from
thousand to a million ten thousand. And fifteen minutes la
the account was closed and the money was resting safely
bank in Switzerland. Aw, the wonder of wire transfer. ,
because of the million bucks, this would be the first and o
April 15 party of his short, but distinguished legal career. ,
his good friend who is so concerned about his marriage
most likely be in jail before long. Along with everyone els
the room, except for Roosevelt. Hell, Tarrance might ge
excited he'll indict Roosevelt and Jessie Frances just for
fun of it.

Then the trials. "I, Mitchell Y. McDeere, do solemnly swear tell the truth, the whole truth and nothing but the truth. So p me God." And he'd sit in the witness chair and point the ger at his good friend Lamar Quin. And Kay and the kids uld be sitting in the front row for jury appeal. Crying tly.

He finished the second beer and started the third. "I know, nar, but I have no plans to slow down. Abby will adjust. ings'll be fine."

If you say so. Kay wants you over tomorrow for a big steak. 'll cook on the grill and eat on the patio. How about it?"

Yes, on one condition. No discussion about Abby. She went ne to see her mother, and she'll be back. Okay?"

Fine. Sure."

Avery sat across the table with a plate of shrimp. He began ling them.

We were just discussing Capps," Lamar said.

That's not a pleasant subject," Avery replied. Mitch ched the shrimp intently until there was a little pile of ut six freshly peeled. He grabbed them across the table and ved the handful into his mouth.

very glared at him with tired, sad eyes. Red eyes. He strug- for something appropriate, then began eating the un- ed shrimp. "I wish the heads were still on them," he said ween bites. "Much better with the heads."

itch raked across two handfuls and began crunching. "I the tails myself. Always been a tail man."

amar stopped eating and gawked at them. "You must be ing."

Nope," said Avery. "When I was a kid in El Paso, we used o out with our nets and scoop up a bunch of fresh shrimp. d eat 'em on the spot, while they were still wiggling." mp, chomp. "The heads are the best part because of all the n juices."

Shrimp, in El Paso?"

Yeah, Rio Grande's full of them."

amar left for another round of beer. The wear, tear, stress fatigue mixed quickly with the alcohol and the room be- e rowdier. Bobby Blue was playing Steppenwolf. Even

311

Nathan Locke was smiling and talking loudly. Just one of
boys. Roosevelt added five cases to the barrel of ice.

At ten, the singing started. Wally Hudson, minus the b
tie, stood on a chair by the piano and led the howling cho
through a riotous medley of Australian drinking songs. 7
restaurant was closed now, so who cared. Kendall Mahan
next. He had played rugby at Cornell and had an amaz
repertoire of raunchy beer songs. Fifty untalented and dr
voices sang happily along with him.

Mitch excused himself and went to the rest room. A bus
unlocked the rear door, and he was in the parking lot. 7
singing was pleasant at this distance. He started for his
but instead walked to a window. He stood in the dark, nex
the corner of the building, and watched and listened. Ken
was now on the piano, leading his choir through an obs
refrain.

Joyous voices, of rich and happy people. He studied t
one at a time, around the tables. Their faces were red. T
eyes were glowing. They were his friends—family men
wives and children—all caught up in this terrible conspir

Last year Joe Hodge and Marty Kozinski were singing
the rest of them.

Last year he was a hotshot Harvard man with job offer
every pocket.

Now he was a millionaire, and would soon have a pric
his head.

Funny what a year can do.

Sing on, brothers.

Mitch turned and walked away.

Around midnight, the taxis lined up on Madison, and the r
est lawyers in town were carried and dragged into the b
seats. Of course, Oliver Lambert was the soberest of the
and he directed the evacuation. Fifteen taxis in all, with dr
lawyers lying everywhere.

At the same time, across town on Front Street, two iden
navy blue-and-yellow Ford vans with DUSTBUSTER pai
brightly on the sides pulled up to the gate. Dutch Hen
opened it and waved them through. They backed up to
rear door, and eight women with matching shirts began

ading vacuum cleaners and buckets filled with spray bottles. hey unloaded brooms and mops and rolls of paper towels. hey chattered quietly among themselves as they went rough the building. As directed from above, the technicians aned one floor at a time, beginning with the fourth. The ards walked the floors and watched them carefully.

The women ignored them and buzzed about their business emptying garbage cans, polishing furniture, vacuuming and rubbing bathrooms. The new girl was slower than the oth-s. She noticed things. She pulled on desk drawers and file binets when the guards weren't looking. She paid attention. It was her third night on the job, and she was learning her y around. She'd found the Tolleson office on the fourth or the first night, and smiled to herself.

She wore dirty jeans and ragged tennis shoes. The blue STBUSTERS shirt was extra large, to hide the figure and make r appear plump, like the other technicians. The patch above pocket read DORIS. Doris, the cleaning technician.

When the crew was half finished with the second floor, a ard told Doris and two others, Susie and Charlotte, to fol-v him. He inserted a key in the elevator panel, and it pped in the basement. He unlocked a heavy metal door, and y walked into a large room divided into a dozen cubicles. ch small desk was cluttered, and dominated by a large com-ter. There were terminals everywhere. Black file cabinets ed the walls. No windows.

"The supplies are in there," the guard said, pointing to a set. They pulled out a vacuum cleaner and spray bottles and nt to work.

"Don't touch the desks," he said.

30

MITCH TIED THE LACES of his Nike Air Cush
jogging shoes and sat on the sofa waiting by
phone. Hearsay, depressed after two weeks with
the woman around, sat next to him and tried to doze. At
actly ten-thirty, it rang. It was Abby.

There was no mushy "sweethearts" and "babes" a
"honeys." The dialogue was cool and forced.

"How's your mother?" he asked.

"Doing much better. She's up and around, but very se
Her spirits are good."

"That's good to hear. And your dad?"

"The same. Always busy. How's my dog?"

"Lonesome and depressed. I think he's cracking up."

"I miss him. How's work?"

"We survived April 15 without disaster. Everyone's in a l
ter mood. Half the partners left for vacation on the sixteer
so the place is a lot quieter."

"I guess you've cut back to sixteen hours a day?"

He hesitated, and let it sink in. No sense starting a fig
"When are you coming home?"

"I don't know. Mom will need me for a couple more we

314

afraid Dad's not much help. They've got a maid and all,
Mom needs me now." She paused, as if something heavy
s coming. "I called St. Andrew's today and told them I
uldn't be back this semester."

He took it in stride. "There are two months left in this se-
ster. You're not coming back for two months?"

"At least two months, Mitch. I just need some time, that's
"

"Time for what?"

"Let's not start it again, okay? I'm not in the mood to ar-
."

"Fine. Fine. Fine. What are you in the mood for?"

She ignored this, and there was a long pause. "How many
les are you jogging?"

"A couple. I've been walking to the track, then running
ut eight laps."

"Be careful at the track. It's awfully dark."

"Thanks."

Another long pause. "I need to go," she said. "Mom's ready
bed."

"Will you call tomorrow night?"

"Yes. Same time."

She hung up without a "goodbye" or "I love you" or any-
g. Just hung up.

Mitch pulled on his white athletic socks and tucked in his
ite long-sleeved T-shirt. He locked the kitchen door and
ted down the dark street. West Junior High School was six
cks to the east of East Meadowbrook. Behind the red brick
srooms and gymnasium was the baseball field, and farther
y at the end of a dark driveway was the football field. A
er track circled the field, and was a favorite of local jog-
.

ut not at 11 P.M., especially with no moon. The track was
rted, and that was fine with Mitch. The spring air was
t and cool, and he finished the first mile in eight minutes.
began walking a lap. As he passed the aluminum bleachers
he home side, he saw someone from the corner of his eye.
kept walking.

"Psssssssst."

Mitch stopped. "Yeah. Who is it?"

315

A hoarse, scratchy voice replied, "Joey Morolto."

Mitch started for the bleachers. "Very funny, Tarrance. A[m] I clean?"

"Sure, you're clean. Laney's sitting up there in a school b[us] with a flashlight. He flashed green when you passed, and if y[ou] see something red flash, get back to the track and make li[ke] Carl Lewis."

They walked to the top of the bleachers and into the [un]locked press box. They sat on stools in the dark and watch[ed] the school. The buses were parked in perfect order along [the] driveway.

"Is this private enough for you?" Mitch asked.

"It'll do. Who's the girl?"

"I know you prefer to meet in daylight, preferably when [a] crowd has gathered, say like a fast-food joint or a Korean sh[oe] store. But I like these places better."

"Great. Who's the girl?"

"Pretty clever, huh?"

"Good idea. Who is she?"

"An employee of mine."

"Where'd you find her?"

"What difference does it make? Why are you always ask[ing] questions that are irrelevant?"

"Irrelevant? I get a call today from some woman I've ne[ver] met, tells me she needs to talk to me about a little matter at [the] Bendini Building, says we gotta change phones, instructs [me] to go to a certain pay phone outside a certain grocery store [and] be there at a certain time, and she'll call exactly at one-thi[rty.] And I go there, and she calls at exactly one-thirty. Keep [in] mind, I've got three men within a hundred feet of the ph[one] watching everybody that moves. And she tells me to be her[e] exactly ten forty-five tonight, to have the place sealed off, [and] that you'll come trotting by."

"Worked, didn't it?"

"Yeah, so far. But who is she? I mean, now you got some[one] else involved, and that really worries me, McDeere. Who is [she] and how much does she know?"

"Trust me, Tarrance. She's my employee and she kn[ows] everything. In fact, if you knew what she knows you'd be s[cared]

indictments right now instead of sitting here bitching
out her."

Tarrance breathed deeply and thought about it. "Okay, so
me what she knows."

"She knows that in the last three years the Morolto gang and
accomplices have taken over eight hundred million bucks in
h out of this country and deposited it in various banks in
 Caribbean. She knows which banks, which accounts, the
es, a bunch of stuff. She knows that the Moroltos control at
st three hundred and fifty companies chartered in the Cay-
ns, and that these companies regularly send clean money
k into the country. She knows the dates and amounts of the
e transfers. She knows of at least forty U.S. corporations
ned by Cayman corporations owned by the Moroltos. She
ws a helluva lot, Tarrance. She's a very knowledgeable
man, don't you think?"

Tarrance could not speak. He stared fiercely into the dark-
s up the driveway.

Mitch found it enjoyable. "She knows how they take their
ty cash, trade it up to one-hundred-dollar-bills and sneak it
 of the country."

How?"

The firm Lear, of course. But they also mule it. They've got
nall army of mules, usually their minimum wage thugs and
ir girlfriends, but also students and other free-lancers, and
y'll give them ninety-eight hundred in cash and buy them a
ket to the Caymans or the Bahamas. No declarations are
uired for amounts under ten thousand, you understand.
d the mules will fly down like regular tourists with pockets
 of cash and take the money to their banks. Doesn't sound
 much money, but you get three hundred people making
nty trips a year, and that's some serious cash walking out
he country. It's also called smurfing, you know."

Tarrance nodded slightly, as if he knew.

A lot of folks wanna be smurfers when they can get free
ations and spending money. Then they've got their super
les. These are the trusted Morolto people who take a mil-
 bucks in cash, wrap it up real neat in newspaper so the
ort machines won't see it, put it in big briefcases and walk
nto the planes like everybody else. They wear coats and ties

317

and look like Wall Streeters. Or they wear sandals and str
hats and mule it in carry-on bags. You guys catch them oc
sionally, about one percent of the time, I believe, and wh
that happens the super mules go to jail. But they never talk,
they, Tarrance? And every now and then a smurfer will st
thinking about all this money in his briefcase and how eas
would be just to keep flying and enjoy all the money hims
And he'll disappear. But the Mob never forgets, and it m
take a year or two, but they'll find him somewhere. T
money'll be gone, of course, but then so will he. The M
never forgets, does it, Tarrance? Just like they won't for
about me."

Tarrance listened until it was obvious he needed to
something. "You got your million bucks."

"Appreciate it. I'm almost ready for the next installme
"Almost?"

"Yeah, me and the girl have a couple more jobs to pull. W
trying to get a few more records out of Front Street."

"How many documents do you have?"

"Over ten thousand."

The lower jaw collapsed and the mouth fell open. He sta
at Mitch. "Damn! Where'd they come from?"

"Another one of your questions."

"Ten thousand documents," said Tarrance.

"At least ten thousand. Bank records, wire transfer reco
corporate charters, corporate loan documents, internal mer
correspondence between all sorts of people. A lot of good s
Tarrance."

"Your wife mentioned a company called Dunn Lane, I
We've reviewed the files you've already given us. Pretty g
material. What else do you know about it?"

"A lot. Chartered in 1986 with ten million, which was tr
ferred into the corporation from a numbered account in Ba
de México, the same ten million that arrived in Grand Cay:
in cash on a certain Lear jet registered to a quiet little law
in Memphis, except that it was originally fourteen million
after payoffs to Cayman customs and Cayman bankers it
reduced to ten million. When the company was chartered,
registered agent was a guy named Diego Sánchez, who
pens to be a VP with Banco de México. The president w

lightful soul named Nathan Locke, the secretary was our old
l Royce McKnight and the treasurer of this cozy little corpo-
tion was a guy named Al Rubinstein. I'm sure you know
m. I don't."

"He's a Morolto operative."

"Surprise, surprise. Want more?"

"Keep talking."

"After the seed money of ten million was invested into this
nture, another ninety million in cash was deposited over the
xt three years. Very profitable enterprise. The company be-
n buying all sorts of things in the U.S.—cotton farms in
xas, apartment complexes in Dayton, jewelry stores in Bev-
y Hills, hotels in St. Petersburg and Tampa. Most of the
nsactions were by wire transfer from four or five different
nks in the Caymans. It's a basic money laundering opera-
n."

"And you've got all this documented?"

"Stupid question, Wayne. If I didn't have the documents,
w would I know about it? I only work on clean files, remem-
-?"

"How much longer will it take you?"

"Couple of weeks. Me and my employee are still snooping
und Front Street. And it doesn't look good. It'll be very
ficult to get files out of there."

"Where'd the ten thousand documents come from?"

Mitch ignored the question. He jumped to his feet and
rted for the door. "Abby and I want to live in Albuquerque.
. a big town, sort of out of the way. Start working on it."

"Don't jump the gun. There's a lot of work to do."

I said two weeks, Tarrance. I'll be ready to deliver in two
eks, and that means I'll have to disappear."

Not so fast. I need to see a few of these documents."

You have a short memory, Tarrance. My lovely wife prom-
l a big stack of Dunn Lane documents just as soon as Ray
s over the wall."

arrance looked across the dark field. "I'll see what I can
"

Mitch walked to him and pointed a finger in his face. "Lis-
to me, Tarrance, and listen closely. I don't think we're
ting through. Today is April 17. Two weeks from today is

May 1, and on May the 1 I will deliver to you, as promis‹
over ten thousand very incriminating and highly admissi‹
documents that will seriously cripple one of the largest or‹
nized crime families in the world. And, eventually, it will c‹
me my life. But I promised to do it. And you've promised
get my brother out of prison. You have a week, until April
If not, I'll disappear. And so will your case, and career."

"What's he gonna do when he gets out?"

"You and your stupid questions. He'll run like hell, tha‹
what he'll do. He's got a brother with a million dollars wh‹
an expert in money laundering and electronic banking. H‹
be out of the country within twelve hours, and he'll go find ‹
million bucks."

"The Bahamas."

"Bahamas. You're an idiot, Tarrance. That money spent ‹
than ten minutes in the Bahamas. You can't trust those corr‹
fools down there."

"Mr. Voyles doesn't like deadlines. He gets real upset."

"Tell Mr. Voyles to kiss my ass. Tell him to get the next ‹
million, because I'm almost ready. Tell him to get my brot‹
out or the deal's off. Tell him whatever you want, Tarran‹
but Ray goes over the wall in a week or I'm gone."

Mitch slammed the door and started down the bleach‹
Tarrance followed. "When do we talk again?" he yelled.

Mitch jumped the fence and was on the track. "My ‹
ployee will call you. Just do as she says."

31

NATHAN LOCKE'S ANNUAL three-day post-April
15 vacation in Vail had been canceled. By DeVasher,
on order from Lazarov. Locke and Oliver Lambert sat
the office on the fifth floor and listened. DeVasher was re-
ting the bits and pieces and trying unsuccessfully to put
puzzle together.

His wife leaves. Says she's gotta go home to her mother,
o's got lung cancer. And that she's tired of a bunch of his
p. We've detected a little trouble here and there over the
nths. She bitched a little about his hours and all, but noth-
this serious. So she goes home to Mommy. Says she don't
w when she's coming back. Mommy's sick, right? Removed
ng, right? But we can't find a hospital that's heard of Max-
Sutherland. We've checked every hospital in Kentucky, In-
na and Tennessee. Seems odd, doesn't it, fellas?"

Come on, DeVasher," Lambert said. "My wife had surgery
r years ago, and we flew to the Mayo Clinic. I know of no
requiring one to have surgery within a hundred miles of
ne. That's absurd. And these are society people. Maybe she
cked in under another name to keep it quiet. Happens all
time."

Locke nodded and agreed. "How much has he talked
her?"

"She calls about once a day. They've had some good ta
about this and that. The dog. Her mom. The office. She t
him last night she ain't coming back for at least two month

"Has she ever indicated which hospital?" asked Locke.

"Never. She's been real careful. Doesn't talk much about
surgery. Mommy is supposedly home now. If she ever left

"What're you getting at, DeVasher?" asked Lambert.

"Shut up and I'll finish. Just suppose it's all a ruse to get
outta town. To get her away from us. From what's com
down. Follow?"

"You're assuming he's working with them?" asked Lock

"I get paid for making those assumptions, Nat. I'm assum
he knows the phones are bugged, and that's why they're
careful on the phone. I'm assuming he got her outta town
protect her."

"Pretty shaky," said Lambert. "Pretty shaky."

DeVasher paced behind his desk. He glared at Ollie and
it pass. "About ten days ago, somebody makes a bunch of
usual copies on the fourth floor. Strange because it was th
in the morning. According to our records, when the co
were made only two lawyers were here. McDeere and S
Kimble. Neither of whom had any business on the fou
floor. Twenty-four access numbers were used. Three belong
Lamar Quin's files. Three belong to Sonny Capps. The ot
eighteen belong to McDeere's files. None belong to Kim
Victor Milligan left his office around two-thirty, and McDe
was working in Avery's office. He had taken him to the
port. Avery says he locked his office, but he could have for
ten. Either he forgot or McDeere's got a key. I pressed Av
on this, and he feels almost certain he locked it. But it
midnight and he was dead tired and in a hurry. Could've
gotten, right? But he did not authorize McDeere to go bac
his office and work. No big deal, really, because they had sp
the entire day in there working on the Capps return. The c
ier was number eleven, which happens to be the closest on
Avery's office. I think it's safe to assume McDeere made
copies."

"How many?"

"Two thousand and twelve."

"Which files?"

"The eighteen were all tax clients. Now, I'm sure he'd explain it all by saying he had finished the returns and was
merely copying everything. Sounds pretty legitimate, right?
Except the secretaries always make the copies, and what the
hell was he doing on the fourth floor at three A.M. running two
thousand copies? And this was the morning of April 7. How
many of your boys finish their April 15 work and run all the
copies a week early?"

He stopped pacing and watched them. They were thinking.
He had them. "And here's the kicker. Five days later his secretary entered the same eighteen access numbers on her copier
on the second floor. She ran about three hundred copies,
which, I ain't no lawyer, but I figure to be more in line. Don't
you think?"

They both nodded, but said nothing. They were lawyers,
trained to argue five sides of every issue. But they said nothing. DeVasher smiled wickedly and returned to his pacing.
"Now, we caught him making two thousand copies that cannot be explained. So the big question is: What was he copying?
If he was using wrong access numbers to run the machine,
what the hell was he copying? I don't know. All of the offices
were locked, except, of course, Avery's. So I asked Avery. He's
got a row of metal cabinets where he keeps the real files. He
keeps 'em locked, but he and McDeere and the secretaries have
been rummaging through those files all day. Could've forgot to
lock 'em when he ran to meet the plane. Big deal. Why would
McDeere copy legitimate files? He wouldn't. Like everybody
else on the fourth floor, Avery's got those four wooden cabinets with the secret stuff. No one touches them, right? Firm
rules. Not even other partners. Locked up tighter than my
ass. So McDeere can't get in without a key. Avery showed me
his keys. Told me he hadn't touched those cabinets in two
days, before the seventh. Avery has gone through those files,
and everything seems in order. He can't tell if they've been
tampered with. But can you look at one of your files and tell if
it's been copied? No, you can't. Neither can I. So I pulled the
files this morning, and I'm sending them to Chicago. They're
gonna check 'em for fingerprints. Take about a week."

"He couldn't copy those files," Lambert said.

"What else would he copy, Ollie? I mean, everythin[g] locked on the fourth floor and the third floor. Everything, [ex]cept Avery's office. And assuming he and Tarrance are wh[is]pering in each other's ears, what would he want from Aver[y's] office? Nothing but the secret files."

"Now you're assuming he's got keys," Locke said.

"Yes. I'm assuming he's made a set of Avery's keys."

Ollie snorted and gave an exasperated laugh. "This is [in]credible. I don't believe it."

Black Eyes glared at DeVasher with a nasty smile. "H[ow] would he get a copy of the keys?"

"Good question, and one that I can't answer. Avery show[ed] me his keys. Two rings, eleven keys. He keeps 'em with hi[m] all times. Firm rule, right? Like a good little lawyer's suppo[sed] to do. When he's awake, the keys are in his pocket. When h[e's] asleep away from home, the keys are under the mattress."

"Where's he traveled in the last month?" Black Eyes ask[ed.]

"Forget the trip to see Capps in Houston last week. [Too] recent. Before that, he went to Grand Cayman for two days [in] April 1."

"I remember," said Ollie, listening intently.

"Good for you, Ollie. I asked him what he did both nigh[ts] and he said nothing but work. Sat at a bar one night, but th[at's] it. Swears he slept by himself both nights." DeVasher pushe[d a] button on a portable tape recorder. "But he's lying. This [one] was made at nine fifteen, April 2, from the phone in the ma[ster] bedroom of Unit A." The tape began:

"He's in the shower." First female voice.

"Are you okay?" Second female voice.

"Yeah. Fine. He couldn't do it if he had to."

"What took so long?"

"He wouldn't wake up."

"Is he suspicious?"

"No. He remembers nothing. I think he's in pain."

"How long will you be there?"

"I'll kiss him goodbye when he gets out of the shower. [Ten,] maybe fifteen minutes."

"Okay. Hurry."

DeVasher punched another button and continued pacing[.]

e no idea who they are, and I haven't confronted Avery.
. He worries me. His wife has filed for divorce, and he's lost
trol. Chases women all the time. This is a pretty serious
ach of security, and I suspect Lazarov will go through the
f."

She talked like it was a bad hangover," Locke said.
Evidently."

You think she copied the keys?" Ollie asked.

DeVasher shrugged and sat in his worn leather chair. The
kiness vanished. "It's possible, but I doubt it. I've thought
ut it for hours. Assuming it was some woman he picked up
a bar, and they got drunk, then it was probably late when
y went to bed. How would she make copies of the keys in
middle of the night on that tiny island? I just don't think

But she had an accomplice," Locke insisted.

Yeah, and I can't figure that out. Maybe they were trying to
l his wallet and something went wrong. He carries a cou-
of thousand in cash, and if he got drunk, who knows what
old them. Maybe she planned to lift the money at the last
nd and haul ass. She didn't do it. I don't know."

No more assumptions?" Ollie asked.

Not now. I love to make them, but it goes too far to assume
e women took the keys, somehow managed to copy them
he middle of the night on the island, without his knowl-
e, and then the first one crawled back in the bed with him.
l that somehow all of this is related to McDeere and his use
he copier on the fourth floor. It's just too much."

I agree," said Ollie.

What about the storage room?" asked Black Eyes.

've thought about that, Nat. In fact, I've lost sleep think-
about it. If she was interested in the records in the storage
n, there must be some connection with McDeere, or some-
else poking around. And I can't make that connection.
s say she found the room and the records, what could she
with them in the middle of the night with Avery asleep
airs?"

She could read them."

Yeah, there's only a million. Keep in mind, now, she must
been drinking along with Avery, or he would've been

suspicious. So she's spent the night drinking and screwi
She waits until he goes to sleep, then suddenly she has t
urge to go downstairs and read bank records. It don't wo
boys."

"She could work for the FBI," Ollie said proudly.

"No, she couldn't."

"Why?"

"It's simple, Ollie. The FBI wouldn't do it because
search would be illegal and the records would be inadmissi
And there's a much better reason."

"What?"

"If she was a Fibbie, she wouldn't have used the phone.
professional would've made that call. I think she was a p
pocket."

The pickpocket theory was explained to Lazarov, who poke
hundred holes but could devise nothing better. He orde
changes in all the locks on the third and fourth floors, and
basement, and both condos on Grand Cayman. He ordere
search for all the locksmiths on the island—there couldn'
many, he said—to determine if any had reproduced keys
night of April 1 or the early morning of April 2. Bribe th
he told DeVasher. They'll talk for a little money. He order
fingerprint examination of the files from Avery's office. De
sher proudly explained he had already started this. McDee
prints were on file with the state bar association.

He also ordered a sixty-day suspension of Avery Tolle
DeVasher suggested this might alert McDeere to someth
unusual. Fine, said DeVasher, tell Tolleson to check into
hospital with chest pains. Two months off—doctor's ord
Tell Tolleson to clean up his act. Lock up his office. As
McDeere to Victor Milligan.

"You said you had a good plan to eliminate McDeere,"
Vasher said.

Lazarov grinned and picked his nose. "Yeah. I think
use the plane. We'll send him down to the islands on a l
business trip, and there will be this mysterious explosion.

"Waste two pilots?" asked DeVasher.

"Yeah. It needs to look good."

"Don't do it anywhere around the Caymans. That'll be too
ncidental."

"Okay, but it needs to happen over water. Less debris. We'll
 a big device, so they won't find much."

"That plane's expensive."

"Yeah. I'll run it by Joey first."

"You're the boss. Let me know if we can help down there."

"Sure. Start thinking about it."

"What about your man in Washington?" DeVasher asked.

"I'm waiting. I called New York this morning, and they're
 cking into it. We should know in a week."

"That would make it easy."

"Yeah. If the answer is yes, we need to eliminate him within
 nty-four hours."

"I'll start planning."

 e office was quiet for a Saturday morning. A handful of
 tners and a dozen associates loitered about in khakis and
 os. There were no secretaries. Mitch checked his mail and
 tated correspondence. After two hours he left. It was time
 visit Ray.

 or five hours, he drove east on Interstate 40. Drove like an
 t. He drove forty-five, then eighty-five. He darted into ev-
 rest stop and weigh station. He made sudden exits from
 left lane. He stopped at an underpass and waited and
 ched. He never saw them. Not once did he notice a suspi-
 is car or truck or van. He even watched a few eighteen-
 eelers. Nothing. They simply were not back there. He
 ld have caught them.

 is care package of books and cigarettes was cleared
 ugh the guard station, and he was pointed to stall number
 e. Minutes later, Ray sat through the thick screen.

"Where have you been?" he said with a hint of irritation.
 u're the only person in the entire world who visits me, and
 is is only the second time in four months."

 know. It's tax season, and I've been swamped. I'll do bet-
 I've written, though."

 Yeah, once a week I get two paragraphs. 'Hi, Ray. How's
 bunk? How's the food? How are the walls? How's the
 ek or Italian? I'm fine. Abby's great. Dog's sick. Gotta run.

I'll come visit soon. Love, Mitch.' You write some rich lett[
little brother. I really treasure them."

"Yours aren't much better."

"What have I got to say? The guards are selling dope
friend got stabbed thirty-one times. I saw a kid get ra[
Come on, Mitch, who wants to hear it?"

"I'll do better."

"How's Mom?"

"I don't know. I haven't been back since Christmas."

"I asked you to check on her, Mitch. I'm worried about [
If that goon is beating her, I want it stopped. If I could get
of here, I'd stop it myself."

"You will." It was a statement, not a question. Mitch pla[
a finger over his lips and nodded slowly. Ray leaned forw[
on his elbows and stared intently.

Mitch spoke softly. *"Español. Hable despacio."* Spanish. S[
slowly.

Ray smiled slightly. *"¿Cuándo?"* When?

"La semana próxima." Next week.

"¿Qué día?" What day?

Mitch thought for a second. *"Martes o miércoles."* Tuesda[
Wednesday.

"¿Qué tiempo?" What time?

Mitch smiled and shrugged, and looked around.

"How's Abby?" Ray asked.

"She's been in Kentucky for a couple of weeks. Her m[
er's sick." He stared at Ray and softly mouthed the w[
"Trust me."

"What's wrong with her?"

"They removed a lung. Cancer. She's smoked heavy all [
life. You should quit."

"I will if I ever get out of here."

Mitch smiled and nodded slowly. "You've got at least s[
more years."

"Yeah, and escape is impossible. They try it occasion[
but they're either shot or captured."

"James Earl Ray went over the wall, didn't he?" Mitch
ded slowly as he asked the question. Ray smiled and wat[
his brother's eyes.

"But they caught him. They bring in a bunch of mou[

328

ys with bloodhounds, and it gets pretty nasty. I don't think
yone's ever survived the mountains after they got over the
ll."

"Let's talk about something else," Mitch said.

"Good idea."

Two guards stood by a window behind the row of visitors'
oths. They were enjoying a stack of dirty pictures someone
k with a Polaroid and tried to sneak through the guard
tion. They giggled among themselves and ignored the visi-
s. On the prisoners' side, a single guard with a stick walked
signly back and forth, half asleep.

"When can I expect little nieces and nephews?" Ray asked.

"Maybe in a few years. Abby wants one of each, and she
uld start now if I would. I'm not ready."

The guard walked behind Ray, but did not look. They stared
each other, trying to read each other's eyes.

"¿Adónde voy?" Ray asked quickly. Where am I going?

"Perdido Beach Hilton. We went to the Cayman Islands last
nth, Abby and I. Had a beautiful vacation."

"Never heard of the place. Where is it?"

"In the Caribbean, below Cuba."

"¿Que es mi nombre?" What is my name?

"Lee Stevens. Did some snorkeling. The water is warm and
geous. The firm owns two condos right on Seven Mile
ch. All I paid for was the airfare. It was great."

"Get me a book. I'd like to read about it. ¿Pasaporte?"

Mitch nodded with a smile. The guard walked behind Ray
stopped. They talked of old times in Kentucky.

dusk he parked the BMW on the dark side of a suburban
l in Nashville. He left the keys in the ignition and locked
door. He had a spare in his pocket. A busy crowd of Easter
ppers moved en masse through the Sears doors. He joined
n. Inside he ducked into the men's clothing department
studied socks and underwear while watching the door.
ody suspicious. He left Sears and walked quickly through
crowd down the mall. A black cotton sweater in the win-
· of a men's store caught his attention. He found one in-
, tried it on and decided to wear it out of there, he liked it
nuch. As the clerk laid his change on the counter, he

scanned the yellow pages for the number of a cab. Back
the mall, he rode the escalator to the first floor, where he fo
a pay phone. The cab would be there in ten minutes.

It was dark now, the cool early dark of spring in the So
He watched the mall entrance from inside a singles bar.
was certain he had not been followed through the mall.
walked casually to the cab. "Brentwood," he said to the dri
and disappeared into the back seat.

Brentwood was twenty minutes away. "Savannah C
Apartments," he said. The cab searched through the spraw
complex and found number 480E. He threw a twenty over
seat and slammed the door. Behind an outside stairwel
found the door to 480E. It was locked.

"Who is it?" a nervous female voice asked from within
heard the voice and felt weak.

"Barry Abanks," he said.

Abby pulled the door open and attacked. They kissed
lently as he lifted her, walked inside and slammed the
with his foot. His hands were wild. In less than two seco
he pulled her sweater over her head, unsnapped her bra
slid the rather loose fitting skirt to her knees. They conti
kissing. With one eye, he glanced apprehensively at the ch
flimsy rented fold-a-bed that was waiting. Either that or
floor. He laid her gently on it and took off his clothes.

The bed was too short, and it squeaked. The mattress
two inches of foam rubber wrapped in a sheet. The n
braces underneath jutted upward and were dangerous.

But the McDeeres did not notice.

When it was good and dark, and the crowd of shoppers a
mall thinned for a moment, a shiny black Chevrolet Silve
pickup pulled behind the BMW and stopped. A small
with a neat haircut and sideburns jumped out, looked ar
and stuck a pointed screwdriver into the door lock o
BMW. Months later when he was sentenced, he would te
judge that he had stolen over three hundred cars and pic
in eight states, and that he could break into a car and star
engine faster than the judge could with the keys. Said his
age time was twenty-eight seconds. The judge was no
pressed.

Occasionally, on a very lucky day, an idiot would leave the
keys in the car, and the average time was reduced dramatically.
Scout had found this car with the keys. He smiled and
opened them. The Silverado raced away, followed by the
BMW.

The Nordic jumped from the van and watched. It was too
late. He was too late. The pickup just pulled up, blocked his
vision for an instant, then wham!, the BMW was gone. Stolen!
Before his very eyes. He kicked the van. Now, how would he
explain this?

He crawled back into the van and waited for McDeere.

After an hour on the couch, the pain of loneliness had been
forgotten. They walked through the small apartment holding
hands and kissing. In the bedroom, Mitch had his first viewing
of what had become known among the three as the Bendini
Papers. He had seen Tammy's notes and summaries, but not
the actual documents. The room was like a chessboard with
rows of neat stacks of papers. On two of the walls, Tammy had
tacked sheets of white poster board, then covered them with
notes and lists and flowcharts.

One day soon he would spend hours in the room, studying
the papers and preparing his case. But not tonight. In a few
minutes, he would leave her and return to the mall.

She led him back to the couch.

32

THE HALL on the tenth floor, Madison Wing, of Baptist Hospital was empty except for an orderly a male nurse writing on his clipboard. Visiting hours ended at nine, and it was ten-thirty. He eased down the spoke to the orderly, was ignored by the nurse and knocke the door.

"Come in," a strong voice said.

He pushed the heavy door open and stood by the bed.

"Hello, Mitch," Avery said. "Can you believe this?"

"What happened?"

"I woke up at six this morning with stomach cram thought. I took a shower and felt a sharp pain right her my shoulder. My breathing got heavy, and I started swea I thought no, not me. Hell, I'm forty-four, in great sl work out all the time, eat pretty good, drink a little too n maybe, but not me. I called my doctor, and he said to mee here at the hospital. He thinks it was a slight heart at Nothing serious, he hopes, but they're running tests fo next few days."

"A heart attack."

"That's what he said."

I'm not surprised, Avery. It's a wonder any lawyer in that n lives past fifty."

Capps did it to me, Mitch. Sonny Capps. This is his heart ck. He called Friday and said he'd found a new tax firm in shington. Wants all his records. That's my biggest client. I ed him almost four hundred thousand last year, about what paid in taxes. He's not mad about the attorney's fees, but furious about the taxes. It doesn't make sense, Mitch."

He's not worth dying for." Mitch looked for an IV, but did see one. There were no tubes or wires. He sat in the only ir and laid his feet on the bed.

Jean filed for divorce, you know."

I heard. That's no surprise, is it?"

Surprised she didn't do it last year. I've offered her a small une as a settlement. I hope she takes it. I don't need a nasty rce."

Vho does? thought Mitch. "What did Lambert say?"

It was kind of fun, really. In nineteen years I've never seen lose his cool, but he lost it. He told me I was drinking too h, chasing women and who knows what else. Said I had parrassed the firm. Suggested I see a psychiatrist."

very spoke slowly, deliberately, and at times with a raspy, k voice. It seemed phony. A sentence later he would forget ut it and return to his normal voice. He lay perfectly still a corpse, with the sheets tucked neatly around him. His r was good.

I think you need a psychiatrist. Maybe two."

Thanks. I need a month in the sun. Doc said he would harge me in three or four days, and that I couldn't work two months. Sixty days, Mitch. Said I cannot, under any umstances, go near the office for sixty days."

What a blessing. I think I'll have a slight heart attack."

At your pace, it's guaranteed."

What are you, a doctor now?"

No. Just scared. You get a scare like this, and you start king about things. Today is the first time in my life I've thought about dying. And if you don't think about death, don't appreciate life."

This is getting pretty heavy."

Yeah, I know. How's Abby?"

"Okay. I guess. I haven't seen her in a while."

"You'd better go see her and bring her home. And get happy. Sixty hours a week is plenty, Mitch. You'll ruin y[our] marriage and kill yourself if you work more. She wants bab[ies], then get them. I wish I had done things differently."

"Damn, Avery. When's the funeral? You're forty-four, you had a slight heart attack. You're not exactly a vegetab[le.]"

The male nurse glided in and glared at Mitch. "Visi[ting] hours are over, sir. You need to leave."

Mitch jumped to his feet. "Yeah, sure." He slapped Ave[ry's] feet and walked out. "See you in a couple of days."

"Thanks for coming. Tell Abby I said hello."

The elevator was empty. Mitch pushed the button to [the] sixteenth floor and seconds later got off. He ran two fligh[ts of] stairs to the eighteenth, caught his breath and opened the d[oor.] Down the hall, away from the elevators, Rick Acklin wat[ched] and whispered into a dead telephone receiver. He nodde[d at] Mitch, who walked toward him. Acklin pointed, and M[itch] stepped into a small area used as a waiting room by wor[ried] relatives. It was dark and empty, with two rows of fol[ding] chairs and a television that did not work. A Coke mac[hine] provided the only light. Tarrance sat next to it and fli[pped] through an old magazine. He wore a sweat suit, headb[and,] navy socks and white canvas sneakers. Tarrance the jogg[er.]

Mitch sat next to him, facing the hall.

"You're clean. They followed you from the office to [the] parking lot, then left. Acklin's in the hall. Laney's aro[und] somewhere. Relax."

"I like the headband."

"Thanks."

"I see you got the message."

"Obviously. Real clever, McDeere. I'm sitting at my [desk] this afternoon, minding my own business, trying to wor[k on] something other than the Bendini case. I've got others, [you] know. And my secretary comes in and says there's a woma[n on] the phone who wants to talk about a man named Marty K[oz-]ski. I jump from my chair, grab the phone, and of cours[e it's] your girl. She says it's urgent, as always. So I say okay, [let's] talk. No, she don't play it. She makes me drop everything [I'm] doing, run over to the Peabody, go to the lounge—what'[s]

334

ne of it? Mallards—and have a seat. So I'm sitting there,
nking about how stupid this is because our phones are
an. Dammit, Mitch, I know our phones are clean. We can
 on our phones! I'm drinking coffee and the bartender
ks over and asks if my name is Kozinski. Kozinski who? I
 Just for fun. Since we're having a ball, right? Marty
zinski, he says with a puzzled look on his face. I say yeah,
's me. I felt stupid, Mitch. And he says I have a call. I walk
 to the bar, and it's your girl. Tolleson's had a heart attack
omething. And you'll be here around eleven. Real clever."

"Worked, didn't it?"

"Yeah, and it would work just as easily if she would talk to
 on my phone in my office."

"I like it better my way. It's safer. Besides, it gets you out of
 office."

"Damned right, it does. Me and three others."

"Look, Tarrance, we'll do it my way, okay? It's my neck on
 line, not yours."

"Yeah, yeah. What the hell are you driving?"

"A rented Celebrity. Nice, huh?"

"What happened to the little black lawyer's car?"

"It had an insect problem. Full of bugs. I parked it at a mall
 urday night in Nashville and left the keys in it. Someone
rowed it. I love to sing, but I have a terrible voice. Ever
e I could drive I've done my singing in the car, alone. But
 the bugs and all, I was too embarrassed to sing. I just got
d of it."

Tarrance could not resist a smile. "That's pretty good,
Deere. Pretty good."

"You should've seen Oliver Lambert this morning when I
ked in and laid the police report on his desk. He stuttered
 stammered and told me how sorry he was. I acted like I
 real sad. Insurance will cover it, so old Oliver says they'll
 me another one. Then he says they'll go get me a rental car
 he meantime. I told him I already had one. Got it in Nash-
 Saturday night. He didn't like this, because he knew it
 insect free. He calls the BMW dealer himself, while I'm
ding there, to check on a new one for me. He asked me
 t color I wanted. I said I was tired of black and wanted a
 undy one with tan interior. I drove to the BMW place

yesterday and looked around. I didn't see a burgundy of [a] model. He told the guy on the phone what I wanted, and t[he] he tells him they don't have it. How about black, or navy[,] gray, or red, or white? No, no, no, I want a burgundy [c] They'll have to order it, he reports. Fine, I said. He hung the phone and asked me if I was sure I couldn't use anot[her] color. Burgundy, I said. He wanted to argue, but realize[d] would seem foolish. So, for the first time in ten months, I sing in my car."

"But a Celebrity. For a hotshot tax lawyer. That's go[t to] hurt."

"I can deal with it."

Tarrance was still smiling, obviously impressed. "I won[der] what the boys in the chop shop will do when they stri[p it] down and find all those bugs."

"Probably sell it to a pawnshop as stereo equipment. H[ow] much was it worth?"

"Our boys said it was the best. Ten, fifteen thousand. I d[on't] know. That's funny."

Two nurses walked by talking loudly. They turned a cor[ner] and the hall was quiet. Acklin pretended to place ano[ther] phone call.

"How's Tolleson?" Tarrance asked.

"Superb. I hope my heart attack is as easy as his. He'[ll] here for a few days, then off for two months. Nothing s[eri-] ous."

"Can you get in his office?"

"Why should I? I've already copied everything in it."

Tarrance leaned closer and waited for more.

"No, I cannot get in his office. They've changed the lock[s on] the third and fourth floors. And the basement."

"How do you know this?"

"The girl, Tarrance. In the last week, she's been in ev[ery] office in the building, including the basement. She's che[cked] every door, pulled on every drawer, looked in every cl[oset.] She's read mail, looked at files and rummaged through the [gar-] bage. There's not much garbage, really. The building has [big] paper shredders in it. Four in the basement. Did you k[now] that?"

336

rrance listened intently and did not move a muscle.
w did she—"

Don't ask, Tarrance, because I won't tell you."

he works there! She's a secretary or something. She's
ing you from the inside."

tch shook his head in frustration. "Brilliant, Tarrance.
called you twice today. Once at about two-fifteen and then
t an hour later. Now, how would a secretary make two
to the FBI an hour apart?"

Maybe she didn't work today. Maybe she called from
."

ou're wrong, Tarrance, and quit guessing. Don't waste
worrying about her. She works for me, and together we'll
er the goods to you."

What's in the basement?"

ne big room with twelve cubicles, twelve busy desks and
usand file cabinets. Electronically wired file cabinets. I
it's the operations center for their money-laundering ac-
es. On the walls of the cubicles, she noticed names and
numbers of dozens of banks in the Caribbean. There's
nuch information lying around down there. They're very
ul. There's a smaller room off to the side, heavily locked,
ull of computers larger than refrigerators."

ounds like the place."

is, but forget it. There's no way to get the stuff out with-
lerting them. Impossible. I know of only one way to bring
oods out."

kay."

search warrant."

orget it. No probable cause."

isten to me, Tarrance. This is how it's gonna be, okay. I
give you all the documents you want. But I can give you
u need. I have in my possession over ten thousand docu-
s, and although I have not reviewed all of them, I've seen
gh to know that if you had them, you could show them to
ge and get a search warrant for Front Street. You can take
cords I have now and obtain indictments for maybe half
rm. But the same documents will get your search warrant
consequently, a truckload of indictments. There's no
way to do it."

Tarrance walked to the hall and looked around. Empty. He stretched his legs and walked to the Coke machine. He le[aned] on it and looked through the small window to the east. "[...] only half the firm?"

"Initially, only half. Plus a number of retired partners. [Scat]tered through my documents are various names of part[ners] who've set up the bogus Cayman companies with Mo[rolto] money. Those indictments will be easy. Once you have a[ll the] records, your conspiracy theory will fall in place and yo[u'll] indict everyone."

"Where did you get the documents?"

"I got lucky. Very lucky. I sort of figured the firm had [more] sense than to keep the Cayman bank records in this coun[try. I] had a hunch the records might be in the Caymans. F[ortu]nately, I was right. We copied the documents in the Caym[ans.]"

"We?"

"The girl. And a friend."

"Where are the records now?"

"You and your questions, Tarrance. They're in my po[sses]sion. That's all you need to know."

"I want those documents from the basement."

"Listen to me, Tarrance. Pay attention. The documen[ts in] the basement are not coming out until you go in with a se[arch] warrant. It is impossible, do you hear?"

"Who are the guys in the basement?"

"Don't know. I've been there ten months and never [seen] them. I don't know where they park or how they get in [and] out. They're invisible. I figure the partners and the boys i[n the] basement do the dirty work."

"What kind of equipment is down there?"

"Two copiers, four shredders, high-speed printers an[d all] those computers. State of the art."

Tarrance walked to the window, obviously deep in tho[ught]. "That makes sense. Makes a lot of sense. I've always wond[ered] how the firm, with all those secretaries and clerks and pa[rale]gals, could maintain such secrecy about Morolto."

"It's easy. The secretaries and clerks and paralegals k[now] nothing about it. They're kept busy with the real clients. [The] partners and senior associates sit in their big offices and d[o]

xotic ways to launder money, and the basement crew does
grunt work. It's a great setup."

o there are plenty of legitimate clients?"

Hundreds. They're talented lawyers with an amazing cli-
le. It's a great cover."

And you're telling me, McDeere, that you've got the docu-
ts now to support indictments and search warrants?
ve got them—they're in your possession?"

That's what I said."

n this country?"

es, Tarrance, the documents are in this country. Very
to here, actually."

rrance was fidgety now. He rocked from one foot to the
r and cracked his knuckles. He was breathing quickly.
at else can you get out of Front Street?"

Nothing. It's too dangerous. They've changed the locks,
that sort of worries me. I mean, why would they change
ocks on the third and fourth floors and not on the first and
d? I made some copies on the fourth floor two weeks ago,
don't think it was a good idea. I'm getting bad vibes. No
records from Front Street."

hat about the girl?"

he no longer has access."

rrance chewed his fingernails, rocking back and forth.
staring at the window. "I want the records, McDeere, and
t them real soon. Like tomorrow."

hen does Ray get his walking papers?"

oday's Monday. I think it's set up for tomorrow night.
wouldn't believe the cussing I've taken from Voyles. He's
o pull every string in the book. You think I'm kidding?
alled in both senators from Tennessee, and they person-
lew to Nashville to visit the governor. Oh, I've been
d, McDeere. All because of your brother."

e appreciates it."

hat's he gonna do when he gets out?"

l take care of that. You just get him out."

o guarantees. If he gets hurt, it ain't our fault."

ch stood and looked at his watch. "Gotta run. I'm sure
ne's out there waiting for me."

hen do we meet again?"

"She'll call. Just do as she says."

"Oh, come on, Mitch! Not that routine again. She can ta[ll]
me on my phone. I swear! We keep our lines clean. Please
that again."

"What's your mother's name, Tarrance?"

"What? Doris."

"Doris?"

"Yeah, Doris."

"Small world. We can't use Doris. Whom did you ta[ke to]
your senior prom?"

"Uh, I don't think I went."

"I'm not surprised. Who was your first date, if you [had]
one?"

"Mary Alice Brenner. She was hot too. She wanted m[e."]

"I'm sure. My girl's name is Mary Alice. The next [time]
Mary Alice calls, you do exactly as she says, okay?"

"I can't wait."

"Do me a favor, Tarrance. I think Tolleson's faking, an[d I]
got a weird feeling his fake heart attack is somehow rela[ted to]
me. Get your boys to snoop around here and check ou[t his]
alleged heart attack."

"Sure. We have little else to do."

33

◀ UESDAY MORNING the office buzzed with concern
for Avery Tolleson. He was doing fine. Running tests.
No permanent damage. Overworked. Stressed out.
s did it. Divorce did it. Leave of absence.

na brought a stack of letters to be signed. "Mr. Lambert
d like to see you, if you're not too busy. He just called."
ine. I'm supposed to meet Frank Mulholland at ten. Do
now that?"

f course I know that. I'm the secretary. I know every-
. Your office or his?"

tch looked at his appointment book and pretended to
h. Mulholland's office. In the Cotton Exchange Building.
is," he said with a frown.

ou met there last time, didn't you? Didn't they teach you
turf in law school? Never, I repeat, never meet two
in a row on the adversary's turf. It's unprofessional. It's
ol. Shows weakness."

ow can you ever forgive me?"

ait till I tell the other girls. They all think you're so cute
macho. When I tell them you're a wimp, they'll be
ed."

341

"They need to be shocked, with a cattle prod."

"How's Abby's mother?"

"Much better. I'm going up this weekend."

She picked up two files. "Lambert's waiting."

Oliver Lambert pointed at the stiff sofa and offered c[...]
He sat perfectly erect in a wing chair and held his cup [...]
British aristocrat. "I'm worried about Avery," he said.

"I saw him last night," Mitch said. "Doctor's forcing a [...]
month retirement."

"Yes, that's why you're here. I want you to work [...]
Victor Milligan for the next two months. He'll get mo[...]
Avery's files, so it's familiar territory."

"That's fine. Victor and I are good friends."

"You'll learn a lot from him. A genius at taxation. Read[...]
books a day."

Great, thought Mitch. He should average ten a da[...]
prison. "Yes, he's a very smart man. He's helped me ou[...]
jam or two."

"Good. I think you'll get along fine. Try and see him s[...]
time this morning. Now, Avery had some unfinished bus[...]
in the Caymans. He goes there a lot, as you know, to meet [...]
certain bankers. In fact, he was scheduled to leave tomo[...]
for a couple of days. He told me this morning you're fan[...]
with the clients and the accounts, so we need you to go.[...]

The Lear, the loot, the condo, the storage room, th[...]
counts. A thousand thoughts flashed in his mind. It di[...]
add up. "The Caymans? Tomorrow?"

"Yes, it's quite urgent. Three of his clients are in dire [...]
of summaries of their accounts and other legal work. I w[...]
Milligan to go, but he's due in Denver in the morning. [...]
said you could handle it."

"Sure I can handle it."

"Fine. The Lear will take you. You'll leave around noo[...]
return by commercial flight late Friday. Any problems?[...]

Yes, many problems. Ray was leaving prison. Tarranc[...]
demanding the contraband. A half million bucks had [...]
collected. And he was scheduled to disappear anytime.

"No problems."

He walked to his office and locked the door. He kick[...]
his shoes, lay on the floor and closed his eyes.

342

elevator stopped on the seventh floor, and Mitch bolted
the stairs to the ninth. Tammy opened the door and locked
behind him. He walked to the window.

"Were you watching?" he asked.

"Of course. The guard by your parking lot stood on the
walk and watched you walk here."

"Wonderful. Even Dutch follows me."

He turned and inspected her. "You look tired."

"Tired? I'm dead. In the past three weeks I've been a janitor,
secretary, a lawyer, a banker, a whore, a courier and a private
investigator. I've flown to Grand Cayman nine times, bought
five sets of new luggage and hauled back a ton of stolen documents. I've driven to Nashville four times and flown ten. I've
read so many bank records and legal crap I'm half blind. And
when it's bedtime, I put on my little Dustbusters shirt and
play maid for six hours. I've got so many names, I've written
them on my hand so I won't get confused."

"I've got another for you."

"This doesn't surprise me. What?"

"Mary Alice. From now on, when you talk to Tarrance,
you're Mary Alice."

"Let me write that down. I don't like him. He's very rude on
the phone."

"I've got great news for you."

"I can't wait."

"You can quit Dustbusters."

"I think I'll lie down and cry. Why?"

"It's hopeless."

"I told you that a week ago. Houdini couldn't get files out of
there, copy them and sneak them back in without getting
caught."

"Did you talk to Abanks?" Mitch asked.

"Yes."

"Did he get the money?"

"Yes. It was wired Friday."

"Is he ready?"

"He said he was."

"Good. What about the forger?"

"I'm meeting with him this afternoon."

"Who is he?"

"An ex-con. He and Lomax were old pals. Eddie said he the best documents man in the country."

"He'd better be. How much?"

"Five thousand. Cash, of course. New IDs, passports, d er's licenses and visas."

"How long will it take him?"

"I don't know. When do you need it?"

Mitch sat on the edge of the rented desk. He breathed dee and tried to think. To calculate. "As soon as possible. I thou I had a week, but now I don't know. Just get it as soor possible. Can you drive to Nashville tonight?"

"Oh yes. I'd love to. I haven't been there in two days."

"I want a Sony camcorder with a tripod set up in the room. Buy a case of tapes. And I want you to stay there, by phone, for the next few days. Review the Bendini Pa again. Work on your summaries."

"You mean I have to stay there?"

"Yeah. Why?"

"I've ruptured two disks sleeping on that couch."

"You rented it."

"What about the passports?"

"What's the guy's name?"

"Doc somebody. I've got his number."

"Give it to me. Tell him I'll call in a day or so. How m money do you have?"

"I'm glad you asked. I started with fifty thousand, right? spent ten thousand on airfare, hotels, luggage and rental And I'm still spending. Now you want a video camera. fake IDs. I'd hate to lose money on this deal."

Mitch started for the door. "How about another fifty t sand?"

"I'll take it."

He winked at her and closed the door, wondering i would ever see her again.

The cell was eight by eight, with a toilet in a corner and of bunk beds. The top bunk was uninhabited and had bee a year. Ray lay on the bottom bunk with wires running his ears. He spoke to himself in a very foreign language. T

At that moment on that floor, it was safe to bet he was the
y soul listening to Berlitz jabber in Turkish. There was
et talk up and down the hall, but most lights were out.
ven o'clock, Tuesday night.

he guard walked silently to his cell. "McDeere," he said
ly, secretly, through the bars. Ray sat on the edge of the
, under the bunk above, and stared at him. He removed the
es.

Warden wants to see you."

ure, he thought, the warden's sitting at his desk at 11 P.M.
ting on me. "Where are we going?" It was an anxious ques-
.

Put your shoes on and come on."

ay glanced around the cell and took a quick inventory of
worldly possessions. In eight years he had accumulated a
k-and-white television, a large cassette player, two card-
rd boxes full of tapes and several dozen books. He made
e dollars a day working in the prison laundry, but after
rettes there had been little to spend on tangibles. These
e his only assets. Eight years.

he guard fitted a heavy key in the door and slid it open a
inches. He turned off the light. "Just follow me, and no
stuff. I don't know who you are, mister, but you got some
vy-duty friends."

ther keys fit other doors, and they were outside under the
ketball hoop. "Stay behind me," the guard said.

ay's eyes darted around the dark compound. The wall
ned like a mountain in the distance, beyond the courtyard
walking area where he had paced a thousand miles and
ked a ton of cigarettes. It was sixteen feet tall in the day-
t, but looked much larger at night. The guard towers were
yards apart and well lit. And heavily armed.

he guard was casual and unconcerned. Of course, he had a
form and a gun. He moved confidently between two cinder
k buildings, telling Ray to follow and be cool. Ray tried to
cool. They stopped at the corner of a building, and the
rd gazed at the wall, eighty feet away. Floodlights made a
tine sweep of the courtyard, and they backed into the dark-
.

Thy are we hiding? Ray asked himself. Are those guys up

there with the guns on our side? He would like to know bef
he made any dramatic moves.

The guard pointed to the exact spot on the wall where Ja
Earl Ray and his gang went over. A rather famous spot, st
ied and admired by most of the inmates at Brushy Mount
Most of the white ones anyway. "In about fifteen minu
they'll throw a ladder up there. The wire has already been
on top. You'll find a heavy rope on the other side."

"Mind if I ask a few questions?"

"Make it quick."

"What about all these lights?"

"They'll be diverted. You'll have total darkness."

"And those guns up there?"

"Don't worry. They'll look the other way."

"Dammit! Are you sure?"

"Look, man, I've seen some inside jobs before, but this t
the cake. Warden Lattemer himself planned this one. I
right up there." The guard pointed to the nearest tower.

"The warden?"

"Yep. Just so nothing'll go wrong."

"Who's throwing up the ladder?"

"Coupla guards."

Ray wiped his forehead with his sleeve and breathed dee
His mouth was dry and his knees were weak.

The guard whispered, "There'll be a dude waiting for
His name is Bud. White dude. He'll find you on the other s
and just do what he says."

The floodlights swept through again, then died. "
ready," the guard said. Darkness settled in, followed b
dreadful silence. The wall was now black. From the nea
tower, a whistle blew two short signals. Ray knelt
watched.

From behind the next building, he could see the silhou
running to the wall. They grabbed at something in the g
then hoisted it.

"Run, dude," the guard said. "Run!"

Ray sprinted with his head low. The homemade ladder
in place. The guards grabbed his arms and threw him to
first step. The ladder bounced as he scurried up the two
fours. The top of the wall was two feet wide. A generous o

had been cut in the coiled barbed wire. He slid through
hout touching it. The rope was right where it was sup-
ed to be, and he eased down the outside of the wall. Eight
t from pay dirt, he turned loose and jumped. He squatted
l looked around. Still dark. The floodlights were on hold.
'he clearing stopped a hundred feet away, and the dense
ods began. "Over here," the voice said calmly. Ray started
it. Bud was waiting in the first cluster of black bushes.
Hurry. Follow me."

Ray followed him until the wall was out of sight. They
oped in a small clearing next to a dirt trail. He stuck out a
d. "I'm Bud Riley. Kinda fun, ain't it?"

Unbelievable. Ray McDeere."

ud was a stocky man with a black beard and a black beret.
wore combat boots, jeans and a camouflage jacket. No gun
s in sight. He offered Ray a cigarette.

Who are you with?" Ray asked.

Nobody. I just do a little free-lance work for the warden.
y usually call me when somebody goes over the wall.
irse, this is a little different. Usually I bring my dogs. I
ught we'd wait here for a minute until the sirens go off, so
can hear. Wouldn't be right if you didn't get to hear 'em. I
in, they're sorta in your honor."

That's okay. I've heard them before."

Yeah, but it's different out here when they go off. It's a
utiful sound."

Look, Bud, I—"

Just listen, Ray. We got plenty of time. They won't chase
, much."

Much?"

Yeah, they gotta make a big scene, wake ever'body up, just
a real escape. But they ain't coming after you. I don't
w what kinda pull you got, but it's something."

he sirens began screaming, and Ray jumped. Lights flashed
ss the black sky, and the faint voices of the tower guards
e audible.

See what I mean?"

Let's go," Ray said, and began walking.

My truck's just up the road a piece. I brought you some
hes. Warden gave me your sizes. Hope you like them."

Bud was out of breath when they reached the truck. [He] quickly changed into the olive Duckheads and navy co[tton] work shirt. "Very nice, Bud," he said.

"Just throw them prison clothes in the bushes."

They drove the winding mountain trail for two miles, t[hen] turned onto blacktop. Bud listened to Conway Twitty and [said] nothing.

"Where are we going, Bud?" Ray finally asked.

"Well, the warden said he didn't care and really didn't w[ant] to know. Said it was up to you. I'd suggest we get to a big t[own] where there's a bus station. After that, you're on your ow[n]."

"How far will you drive me?"

"I got all night, Ray. You name the town."

"I'd like to get some miles behind us before I start hang[ing] around a bus station. How about Knoxville?"

"Knoxville it is. Where are you going from there?"

"I don't know. I need to get out of the country."

"With your friends, that should be no problem. Be care[ful] though. By tomorrow, your picture will be hanging in e[very] sheriff's office in ten states."

Three cars with blue lights came blazing over the hil[l in] front of them. Ray ducked onto the floorboard.

"Relax, Ray. They can't see you."

He watched them disappear through the rear wind[ow.] "What about roadblocks?"

"Look, Ray. Ain't gonna be no roadblocks, okay? Trust [me."] Bud stuck a hand in a pocket and threw a wad of cash on [the] seat. "Five hundred bucks. Hand-delivered by the warden. [You] got some stout friends, buddy."

34

WEDNESDAY MORNING. Tarry Ross climbed the stairs to the fourth floor of the Phoenix Inn. He paused on the landing outside the hall door and ~~ht~~ his breath. Sweat beaded across his eyebrows. He re~~moved~~ the dark sunglasses and wiped his face with the sleeve ~~of h~~is overcoat. Nausea hit below the belt, and he leaned on ~~the~~ stair rail. He dropped his empty briefcase on the concrete ~~and~~ sat on the bottom step. His hands shook like severe palsy, ~~and~~ he wanted to cry. He clutched his stomach and tried not to ~~do~~ it.

~~T~~he nausea passed, and he breathed again. Be brave, man, be ~~brav~~e. There's two hundred thousand waiting down the hall. ~~If y~~ou got guts, you can go in there and get it. You can walk ~~out~~ with it, but you must have courage. He breathed deeper, ~~and~~ his hands settled down. Guts, man, guts.

~~T~~he weak knees wobbled, but he made it to the door. Down ~~the h~~all, past the rooms. Eighth door on the right. He held his ~~brea~~th, and knocked.

~~Se~~conds passed. He watched the dark hall through the dark ~~glass~~es and could see nothing. "Yeah," a voice inside said, ~~mil~~es away.

"It's Alfred." Ridiculous name, he thought. Where'd it c
from?

The door cracked, and a face appeared behind the l
chain. The door closed, then opened wide. Alfred walked

"Good morning, Alfred," Vinnie Cozzo said war
"Would you like coffee?"

"I didn't come here for coffee," Alfred snapped. He pl
the briefcase on the bed and stared at Cozzo.

"You're always so nervous, Alfred. Why don't you re
There's no way you can get caught."

"Shut up, Cozzo. Where's the money?"

Vinnie pointed to a leather handbag. He stopped smil
"Talk to me, Alfred."

The nausea hit again, but he kept his feet. He stared at tl
His heart beat like pistons. "Okay, your man, McDeere,
been paid a million bucks already. Another million is on
way. He's delivered one load of Bendini documents and cl
to have ten thousand more." A sharp pain hit his groin, an
sat on the edge of the bed. He removed his glasses.

"Keep talking," Cozzo demanded.

"McDeere's talked to our people many times in the las
months. He'll testify at the trials, then hit the road as a
tected witness. He and his wife."

"Where are the other documents?"

"Dammit, I don't know. He won't tell. But they're read
be delivered. I want my money, Cozzo."

Vinnie threw the handbag on the bed. Alfred opened it
the briefcase. He attacked the stacks of bills, his hands sha
violently.

"Two hundred thousand?" he asked desperately.

Vinnie smiled. "That was the deal, Alfred. I got anothe
for you in a couple of weeks."

"No way, Cozzo. I can't take any more of this." He slam
the briefcase shut and ran to the door. He stopped and trie
calm himself. "What will you do with McDeere?" he as
staring at the door.

"What do you think, Alfred?"

He bit his lip, clenched the briefcase and walked from
room. Vinnie smiled and locked the door. He pulled a

m his pocket and placed a call to the Chicago home of Mr.
u Lazarov.

Tarry Ross walked in panic down the hall. He could see
le from behind the glasses. Seven doors down, almost to the
vator, a huge hand reached from the darkness and pulled
a into a room. The hand slapped him hard, and another fist
ded in his stomach. Another fist to the nose. He was on the
•r, dazed and bleeding. The briefcase was emptied on the
l.

Ie was thrown into a chair, and the lights came on. Three
l agents, his comrades, glared at him. Director Voyles
lked up to him, shaking his head in disbelief. The agent
h the huge, efficient hands stood nearby, within striking
:ance. Another agent was counting money.

Voyles leaned into his face. "You're a traitor, Ross. The low-
form of scum. I can't believe it."

Ross bit his lip and began sobbing.

Who is it?" Voyles asked intently.

The crying was louder. No answer.

Voyles swung wildly and slapped Ross's left temple. He
•eked in pain. "Who is it, Ross? Talk to me."

Vinnie Cozzo," he blurted between sobs.

I know it's Cozzo! Dammit! I know that! But what did you
him?"

•ears ran from his eyes and blood poured from his nose. His
y shook and gyrated pitifully. No answer.

Voyles slapped him again, and again. "Tell me, you little son
bitch. Tell me what Cozzo wants." He slapped him again.

•oss doubled over and dropped his head on his knees. The
ng softened.

Two hundred thousand dollars," an agent said.

•oyles dropped to one knee and almost whispered to Ross.
it McDeere, Ross? Please, oh please, tell me it's not
Deere. Tell me, Tarry, tell me it's not McDeere."

•arry stuck his elbows on his knees and stared at the floor.
blood dripped neatly into one little puddle on the carpet.

check, Tarry. You don't get to keep your money. You're
the way to jail. You're a disgrace, Tarry. You're a slimy
•e scuzzball of a chicken, and it's over. What could possibly
•ained by keeping secrets? Gut check, Tarry."

Voyles was pleading softly. Sinners, won't you co
"Please say it ain't McDeere, Tarry, please tell me it ain't

Tarry sat straight and wiped his eyes with his fingers.
breathed deeply. Cleared his throat. He bit his lip, loo
squarely at Voyles and nodded.

DeVasher had no time for the elevator. He ran down the st
to the fourth floor, to the corner, a power one, and barged i
Locke's office. Half the partners were there. Locke, Lamb
Milligan, McKnight, Dunbar, Denton, Lawson, Banal
Kruger, Welch and Shottz. The other half had been s
moned.

A quiet panic filled the room. DeVasher sat at the hea
the conference table, and they gathered around.

"Okay, boys. It's not time to haul ass and head for Br;
Not yet, anyway. We confirmed this morning that he
talked extensively to the Fibbies, that they have paid hi
million cash, that they have promised another million, tha
has certain documents that are believed to be fatal. This c
straight from the FBI. Lazarov and a small army are flying
Memphis as we speak. It appears as though the damage has
been done. Yet. According to our source—a very high ran]
Fibbie—McDeere has over ten thousand documents in his
session, and he is ready to deliver. But he has only deliver
few so far. We think. Evidently, we have caught this thin
time. If we can prevent further damage, we should be ok;
say this, even though they have some documents. Obviou
they don't have much or they would've been here with se;
warrants."

DeVasher was onstage. He enjoyed this immensely.
spoke with a patronizing smile and looked at each of the v
ried faces. "Now, where is McDeere?"

Milligan spoke. "In his office. I just talked to him. He
pects nothing."

"Wonderful. He's scheduled to leave in three hours
Grand Cayman. Correct, Lambert?"

"That's correct. Around noon."

"Boys, the plane will never make it. The pilot will lan
New Orleans for an errand, then he'll take off for the isl
About thirty minutes over the Gulf, the little blip will di

r from radar, forever. Debris will scatter over a thirty-
are-mile area, and no bodies will ever be found. It's sad, but
essary."

The Lear?" asked Denton.

Yes, son, the Lear. We'll buy you another toy."

We're assuming a lot, DeVasher," Locke said. "We're as-
ning the documents already in their possession are harm-
s. Four days ago you thought McDeere had copied some of
ry's secret files. What gives?"

They studied the files in Chicago. Yeah, they're full of in-
ninating evidence, but not enough to move with. They
ldn't get the first conviction. You guys know the damning
terials are on the island. And, of course, in the basement.
one can penetrate the basement. We checked the files in the
do. Everything looked in order."

ocke was not satisfied. "Then where did the ten thousand
e from?"

You're assuming he has ten thousand. I rather doubt it.
p in mind, he's trying to collect another one million bucks
ore he takes off. He's probably lying to them and snooping
und for more documents. If he had ten thousand, why
ldn't the Fibbies have them by now?"

Then what's to fear?" asked Lambert.

The fear is the unknown, Ollie. We don't know what he's
except that he's got a million bucks. He's no dummy, and
ust might stumble across something if left alone. We can-
allow that to happen. Lazarov, you see, said to blow his ass
a the air. Quote unquote."

There's no way a rookie associate could find and copy that
y incriminating records," Kruger said boldly, and looked
und the group for approval. Several nodded at him with
nse frowns.

Why is Lazarov coming?" asked Dunbar, the real estate
. He said "Lazarov" as if Charles Manson was coming to
er.

That's a stupid question," DeVasher snapped, and looked
und for the idiot. "First, we've got to take care of McDeere
hope the damage is minimal. Then we'll take a long look at
unit and make whatever changes are necessary."

Locke stood and glared at Oliver Lambert. "Make s[ure] McDeere's on that plane."

Tarrance, Acklin and Laney sat in stunned silence and [lis]tened to the speaker phone on the desk. It was Voyles in W[ash]ington, explaining exactly what had happened. He wo[uld] leave for Memphis within the hour. He was almost desper[ate].

"You gotta bring him in, Tarrance. And quick. Co[mpany] doesn't know that we know about Tarry Ross, but Ross [told] him McDeere was on the verge of delivering the records. T[hey] could take him out at any time. You've got to get him. N[ow.] Do you know where he is?"

"He's at the office," Tarrance said.

"Okay. Fine. Bring him in. I'll be there in two hour[s. I] wanna talk to him. Goodbye."

Tarrance punched the phone, then dialed the number.

"Who are you calling?" Acklin asked.

"Bendini, Lambert & Locke. Attorneys-at-law."

"Are you crazy, Wayne?" Laney asked.

"Just listen."

The receptionist answered the phone. "Mitch McDe[ere,] please," Tarrance said.

"One moment, please," she said. Then the secretary: "[Mr.] McDeere's office."

"I need to speak to Mitchell McDeere."

"I'm sorry, sir. He's in a meeting."

"Listen, young lady, this is Judge Henry Hugo, and he['s] supposed to be in my courtroom fifteen minutes ago. W[e're] waiting for him. It's an emergency."

"Well, I see nothing on his calendar for this morning."

"Do you schedule his appointments?"

"Well, yes, sir."

"Then it's your fault. Now get him on the phone."

Nina ran across the hall and into his office. "Mitch, there['s a] Judge Hugo on the phone. Says you're supposed to be in c[ourt] right now. You'd better talk to him."

Mitch jumped to his feet and grabbed the phone. He [was] pale. "Yes," he said.

"Mr. McDeere," Tarrance said. "Judge Hugo. You're [late] for my court. Get over here."

Yes, Judge." He grabbed his coat and briefcase and
wned at Nina.

I'm sorry," she said. "It's not on your calendar."

Mitch raced down the hall, down the stairs, past the recep-
ist and out the front door. He ran north on Front Street to
ion and darted through the lobby of the Cotton Exchange
lding. On Union, he turned east and ran toward the Mid-
merica Mall.

he sight of a well-dressed young man with a briefcase run-
g like a scared dog may be a common sight in some cities,
not in Memphis. People noticed.

He hid behind a fruit stand and caught his breath. He saw
one running behind him. He ate an apple. If it came to a
race, he hoped Two-Ton Tony was chasing him.

He had never been particularly impressed with Wayne Tar-
ce. The Korean shoe store was a fiasco. The chicken place
Grand Cayman was equally dumb. His notebook on the
roltos would bore a Cub Scout. But his idea about a May-
code, a "don't ask questions just run for your life" alert, was
rilliant idea. For a month, Mitch knew if Judge Hugo
ed, he had to hit the door on a dead run. Something bad
gone wrong, and the boys on the fifth floor were moving
Where was Abby? he thought.

few pedestrians walked in pairs along Union. He wanted
owded sidewalk, but there was none. He stared at the cor-
of Front and Union and saw nothing suspicious. Two
ks east, he casually entered the lobby of the Peabody and
ed for a phone. On the mezzanine overlooking the lobby,
ound a neglected one in a short hallway near the men's
n. He dialed the Memphis office of the Federal Bureau of
stigation.

Wayne Tarrance, please. It's an emergency. This is Mitch
Deere."

arrance was on the phone in seconds. "Mitch, where are
"

Okay, Tarrance, what's going on?"

Where are you?"

'm out of the building, Judge Hugo. I'm safe for now.
t's happened?"

Mitch, you've gotta come in."

"I don't have to do a damned thing, Tarrance. And I wo until you talk to me."

"Well, we've, uh, we've had a slight problem. There's be small leak. You need—"

"Leak, Tarrance? Did you say leak? There's no such thin a small leak. Talk to me, Tarrance, before I hang up this ph and disappear. You're tracing this call, aren't you, Tarra I'm hanging up."

"No! Listen, Mitch. They know. They know we've b talking, and they know about the money and the files."

There was a long pause. "A small leak, Tarrance. Sou like the dam burst. Tell me about this leak, and quick."

"God this hurts. Mitch, I want you to know how much hurts. Voyles is devastated. One of our senior men sold information. We caught him this morning at a hotel in W ington. They paid him two hundred thousand for the stor you. We're in shock, Mitch."

"Oh, I'm touched. I'm truly concerned over your shock pain, Tarrance. I guess now you want me to run down ther your office so we can all sit around and console each othe

"Voyles will be there by noon, Mitch. He's flying in his top people. He wants to meet with you. We'll get you o town."

"Right. You want me to rush into your arms for protect You're an idiot, Tarrance. Voyles is an idiot. You're all id And I'm a fool for trusting you. Are you tracing this Tarrance?"

"No!"

"You're lying. I'm hanging up, Tarrance. Sit tight and call you in thirty minutes from another phone."

"No! Mitch, listen. You're dead if you don't come in."

"Goodbye, Wayne. Sit by the phone."

Mitch dropped the receiver and looked around. He wa to a marble column and peeked at the lobby below. The d were swimming around the fountain. The bar was deserte table was surrounded with rich old ladies sipping their tea gossiping. A solitary guest was registering.

Suddenly, the Nordic stepped from behind a potted tree stared at him. "Up there!" he yelled across the lobby t accomplice. They watched him intently and glanced at rway under him. The bartender looked up at Mitch, then he Nordic and his friend. The old ladies stared in silence. Call the police!" Mitch yelled as he backed away from the ng. Both men sprang across the lobby and hit the stairs. ch waited five seconds, and returned to the railing. The ender had not moved. The ladies were frozen.

here were heavy noises on the stairs. Mitch sat on the rail- dropped his briefcase, swung his legs over, paused, then ped twenty feet onto the carpet of the lobby. He fell like a , but landed squarely on both feet. Pain shot through his es and hips. The football knee buckled, but did not col- e.

ehind him, next to the elevators, was a small haberdashery windows full of ties and Ralph Lauren's latest. He ped into it. A kid of no more than nineteen waited eagerly nd the counter. There were no customers. An outside r opened onto Union.

s that door locked?" Mitch asked calmly.

es, sir."

You wanna make a thousand dollars cash? Nothing illegal." ch quickly peeled off ten hundred-dollar bills and threw n on the counter.

Jh, sure. I guess."

Nothing illegal, okay? I swear. I wouldn't get you in trou- Unlock that door, and when two men come running in in about twenty seconds, tell them I ran through that and jumped in a cab."

he kid smiled even brighter and raked up the money. e. No problem."

Where's the dressing room?"

es, sir, over there next to the closet."

Jnlock the door," Mitch said as he slid into the dressing a and sat down. He rubbed his knees and ankles.

e clerk was straightening ties when the Nordic and his ner ran through the door from the lobby. "Good morn- " he said cheerfully.

Did you see a man running through here, medium build, gray suit, red tie?"

es, sir. He just ran through there, through that door, and ped in a cab."

"A cab! Damn!" The door opened and closed, and the s[t]
was silent. The kid walked to a shoe rack near the clo[se]
"They're gone, sir."

Mitch was rubbing his knees. "Good. Go to the door
watch for two minutes. Let me know if you see them."

Two minutes later, he was back. "They're gone."

Mitch kept his seat and smiled at the door. "Great. I w[ant]
one of those kelly green sport coats, forty-four long, and a [pair]
of white buckskins, ten D. Bring them here, would you? [And]
keep watching."

"Yes, sir." He whistled around the store as he collected [the]
coat and shoes, then slid them under the door. Mitch ya[nked]
off his tie and changed quickly. He sat down.

"How much do I owe you?" Mitch asked from the roo[m.]

"Well, let's see. How about five hundred?"

"Fine. Call me a cab, and let me know when it's outsi[de.]"

Tarrance walked three miles around his desk. The call [was]
traced to the Peabody, but Laney arrived too late. He was [here]
now, sitting nervously with Acklin. Forty minutes afte[r the]
first call, the secretary's voice blasted through the inter[com.]
"Mr. Tarrance. It's McDeere."

Tarrance lunged at the phone. "Where are you?"

"In town. But not for long."

"Look, Mitch, you won't last two days on your own. Th[ey'll]
fly in enough thugs to start another war. You've got to l[et us]
help you."

"I don't know, Tarrance. For some strange reason I [just]
don't trust you boys right now. I can't imagine why. Just [a]
feeling."

"Please, Mitch. Don't make this mistake."

"I guess you want me to believe you boys can protect m[e for]
the rest of my life. Sorta funny, isn't it, Tarrance? I cut a [deal]
with the FBI, and I almost get gunned in my own o[ffice.]
That's real protection."

Tarrance breathed deeply into the phone. There was a [long]
pause. "What about the documents? We've paid you a m[illion]
for them."

"You're cracking up, Tarrance. You paid me a millio[n]

358

clean files. You got them, and I got the million. Of course,
was just part of the deal. Protection was also a part of it."

Give us the damned files, Mitch. They're hidden some-
re close to us, you told me that. Take off if you want to,
leave the files."

Won't work, Tarrance. Right now I can disappear, and the
oltos may or may not come after me. If you don't get the
you don't get the indictments. If the Moroltos don't get
cted, maybe, if I'm lucky, one day they'll just forget about
I gave them a real scare, but no permanent damage. Hell,
may even hire me back one of these days."

ou don't really believe that. They'll chase you until they
you. If we don't get the records, we'll be chasing too. It's
simple, Mitch."

hen I'll put my money on the Moroltos. If you guys find
irst, there'll be a leak. Just a small one."

ou're outta your mind, Mitch. If you think you can take
million and ride into the sunset, you're a fool. They'll
goons on camels riding the deserts looking for you. Don't
, Mitch."

oodbye, Wayne. Ray sends his regards."

he line was dead. Tarrance grabbed the phone and threw
ainst the wall.

itch glanced at the clock on the airport wall. He punched
other call. Tammy answered.

Hello, sweetheart. Hate to wake you."

on't worry, the couch kept me awake. What's up?"

Major trouble. Get a pencil and listen very carefully. I
have a second to waste. I'm running, and they're right
d me."

ire away."

irst, call Abby at her parents'. Tell her to drop everything
get out of town. She doesn't have time to kiss her mother
bye or to pack any clothes. Tell her to drop the phone, get
r car and drive away. And don't look back. She takes
state 55 to Huntington, West Virginia, and goes to the
rt. She flies from Huntington to Mobile. In Mobile, she
a car and drives east on Interstate 10 to Gulf Shores, then
on Highway 182 to Perdido Beach. She checks in at the

Perdido Beach Hilton under the name of Rachel James. she waits. Got that?"

"Yeah."

"Second. I need you to get on a plane and fly to Memphi called Doc, and the passports, etc., are not ready. I cussed but to no avail. He promised to work all night and have t ready in the morning. I will not be here in the morning you will. Get the documents."

"Yes, sir."

"Third. Get on a plane and get back to the apartmen Nashville. Sit by the phone. Do not, under any circumsta leave the phone."

"Got it."

"Fourth. Call Abanks."

"Okay. What are your travel plans?"

"I'm coming to Nashville, but I'm not sure when I' there. I gotta go. Listen, Tammy, tell Abby she could be within the hour if she doesn't run. So run, dammit, run!

"Okay, boss."

He walked quickly to Gate 22 and boarded the 10:04 flight to Cincinnati. He clutched a magazine full of one tickets, all bought with MasterCard. One to Tulsa on A can Flight 233, leaving at 10:14, and purchased in the na Mitch McDeere; one to Chicago on Northwest Flight leaving at 10:15, and purchased in the name of Mit McDeere; one to Dallas on United Flight 562, leaving at and purchased in the name of Mitchell McDeere; and o Atlanta on Delta Flight 790, leaving at 11:10, and purchas the name of Mitchell McDeere.

The ticket to Cincinnati had been bought with cash, i name of Sam Fortune.

Lazarov entered the power office on the fourth floor and head bowed. DeVasher faced him like a scared, whipped The partners studied their shoelaces and held their bow

"We can't find him," DeVasher said.

Lazarov was not one to scream and cuss. He took great in being cool under pressure. "You mean he just got up walked out of here?" he asked coolly.

There was no answer. None was needed.

'All right, DeVasher, this is the plan. Send every man
ı've got to the airport. Check with every airline. Where's his
?"

'In the parking lot."

'That's great. He left here on foot. He walked out of your
le fortress on foot. Joey'll love this. Check with every rental
company. Now, how many honorable partners do we have
e."

'Sixteen present."

'Divide them up in pairs and send them to the airports in
ami, New Orleans, Houston, Atlanta, Chicago, L.A., San
ncisco and New York. Roam the concourses of these air-
ts. Live in these airports. Eat in these airports. Watch the
ernational flights in these airports. We'll send reinforce-
nts tomorrow. You honorable esquires know him well, so
find him. It's a long shot, but what have we got to lose? It'll
p you counselors busy. And I hate to tell you boys, but
se hours are not billable. Now, where's his wife?"
Danesboro, Kentucky. At her parents'."
Go get her. Don't hurt her, just bring her in."
Do we start shredding?" DeVasher asked.
We'll wait twenty-four hours. Send someone to Grand Cay-
1 and destroy those records. Now hurry, DeVasher."
he power office emptied.

les stomped around Tarrance's desk and barked com-
ds. A dozen lieutenants scribbled as he yelled. "Cover the
ort. Check every airline. Notify every office in every major
. Contact customs. Do we have a picture of him?"
We can't find one, sir."
Find one, and find it quick. It needs to be in every FBI and
oms office by tonight. He's on the run. Son of a bitch!"

35

THE BUS left Birmingham shortly before 2
Wednesday. Ray sat in the rear and studied every
son who climbed in and found a seat. He looked sp
He had taken a cab to a mall in Birmingham and in th
minutes had purchased a new pair of faded Levi's, a p
short-sleeved golf shirt and a pair of red-and-white Reeb
He had also eaten a pizza and received a severe Marine-s
haircut. He wore aviator sunshades and an Auburn cap.

A short, fat, dark-skinned lady sat next to him.

He smiled at her. "*¿De dónde es usted?*" he asked. Where
you from?

Her face broke into unrestrained delight. A wide smil
vealed few teeth. "*México,*" she said proudly. "*¿Habla espai*
she asked eagerly.

"*Sí.*"

For two hours, they jabbered in Spanish as the bus r
along to Montgomery. She had to repeat occasionally, bu
surprised himself. He was eight years out of practice a
little rusty.

Behind the bus, Special Agents Jenkins and Jones follo
in a Dodge Aries. Jenkins drove while Jones slept. The

become boring ten minutes out of Knoxville. Just routine
veillance, they were told. If you lose him, no big deal. But
not to lose him.

e flight from Huntington to Atlanta was two hours away,
Abby sat in a secluded corner of a dark lounge watching.
watching. In the chair next to her was a carry-on bag.
ntrary to her urgent instructions, she had packed a tooth-
sh, makeup and a few clothes. She had also written a note
er parents, giving a brief story about how she had to run to
mphis, needed to see Mitch, everything's fine, don't worry,
s and kisses, love, Abby. She ignored the coffee and
ched the arriving and departing.

he did not know if he was dead or alive. Tammy said he
scared, but very much in control. As always. She said he
flying to Nashville, and she, Tammy, was flying to Mem-
s. Confusing, but she was certain he knew what he was
ng. Get to Perdido Beach and wait.

bby had never heard of Perdido Beach. And she was cer-
he'd never been there either.

he lounge was nerve-racking. Every ten minutes a drunk
nessman would venture over and throw something sugges-
at her. Get lost, she said a dozen times.

fter two hours, they boarded. Abby was stuck in the aisle
. She buckled her belt and relaxed. And then she saw her.
he was a striking blonde with high cheekbones and a firm
that was almost unfeminine, yet strong and attractive.
y had seen the partial face before. Partial, because the eyes
e covered, as before. She looked at Abby and glanced away
he passed and went to her seat somewhere in the rear.

he Shipwreck Bar! The blonde in the Shipwreck Bar. The
de who was eavesdropping on her and Mitch and Abanks.
y had found her. And if they had found her, where was
husband? What had they done to him? She thought of the
-hour drive from Danesboro to Huntington, through the
ding mountain roads. She had driven like a maniac. They
d not have followed her.

hey taxied from the terminal and minutes later lifted off
Atlanta.

r a second time in three weeks, Abby watched dusk from

the inside of a 727 at the airport in Atlanta. She and
blonde. They were on the ground for thirty minutes and t
left for Mobile.

From Cincinnati, Mitch flew to Nashville. He arrived at 6 p
Wednesday, long after the banks had closed. He foun
U-Haul truck rental place in the phone book and flagged a
He rented one of the smaller models, a sixteen-footer.
paid cash, but was forced to use his driver's license and a cr
card for a deposit. If DeVasher could track him to a U-H
place in Nashville, so be it. He bought twenty cardboard p
ing boxes and left for the apartment.

He had not eaten since Tuesday night, but he was in l
Tammy had left a bag of microwave popcorn and two be
He ate like a pig. At eight, he made his first call to the Per
Beach Hilton. He asked for Lee Stevens. He had not arri
she said. He stretched out on the den floor and thought
hundred things that could happen to Abby. She could be
in Kentucky and he wouldn't know. He couldn't call.

The couch had not been folded, and the cheap sheets h
off the end and fell to the floor. Tammy was not much
housework. He looked at the small, temporary bed
thought of Abby. Only five nights ago, they had tried to
each other on the bed. Hopefully, she was on the plane. Al

In the bedroom, he sat on the unopened Sony box and
veled at the roomful of documents. Across the carpet she
built perfect columns of paper, all painstakingly divided
Cayman banks and Cayman companies. On top of each s
was a yellow legal pad, with the company name followe
pages of dates and entries. And names!

Even Tarrance could follow the paper trail. A grand
would eat it up. The U.S. Attorney would call press co
ences. And the trial juries would convict, and convict and
vict.

Special Agent Jenkins yawned into the telephone receiver
punched the numbers to the Memphis office. He had not
in twenty-four hours. Jones was snoring in the car.

"FBI," a male voice said.

"Yeah, who's there?" Jenkins asked. Just a routine chec

Acklin."

Hey, Rick. This is Jenkins. We've—"

Jenkins! Where have you been? Hold on!"

nkins quit yawning and looked around the bus terminal.
angry voice yelled into the earpiece.

Jenkins! Where are you?" It was Wayne Tarrance.

We're at the bus station in Mobile. We've lost him."

You what? How could you lose him?"

nkins was suddenly alert and leaning into the phone.
it a minute, Wayne. Our instructions were to follow him
eight hours to see where he went. Routine, you said."

I can't believe you lost him."

Wayne, we weren't told to follow him for the rest of his
Eight hours, Wayne. We've followed for twenty hours, and
disappeared. What's the big deal?"

Why haven't you called in before now?"

Ve called in twice. In Birmingham and Montgomery. Line
busy both times. What's going on, Wayne?"

ust a minute."

nkins grabbed the phone tighter and waited. Another
e: "Hello, Jenkins?"

es."

Director Voyles here. What the hell happened?"

nkins held his breath and looked wildly around the termi-
"Sir, we lost him. We followed him for twenty hours, and
n he got off the bus here in Mobile, we lost him in the
rd."

hat's great, son. How long ago?"

wenty minutes."

ll right, listen. We desperately need to find him. His
her has taken our money and disappeared. Call the locals
in Mobile. Tell them who you are, and that an escaped
derer is on the loose in town. They've probably got Ray
eere's name and picture stuck to the walls. His mother
in Panama City Beach, so alert every local between there
Mobile. I'm sending in our troops."

kay. I'm sorry, sir. We weren't told to trail him forever."

Ve'll discuss it later."

· · · · ·

At ten, Mitch called the Perdido Beach Hilton for the seco[nd]
time. He asked for Rachel James. No arrival. He asked for
Stevens. One moment, she said. Mitch sat on the floor [and]
waited intently. The line to the room was ringing. Aft[er a]
dozen rings, someone picked up.

"Yeah." It was quick.

"Lee?" Mitch asked.

A pause. "Yeah."

"This is Mitch. Congratulations."

Ray fell on the bed and closed his eyes. "It was so e[asy,]
Mitch. How'd you do it?"

"I'll tell you when we have time. Right now, there a[re a]
bunch of folks trying to kill me. And Abby. We're on the r[un.]"

"Who, Mitch?"

"It would take ten hours to tell the first chapter. We'll [talk]
later. Write this number down. 615-889-4380."

"That's not Memphis."

"No, it's Nashville. I'm in an apartment that's servin[g as]
mission control. Memorize that number. If I'm not here, [the]
phone will be answered by a girl named Tammy."

"Tammy?"

"It's a long story. Just do as I say. Sometime tonight, A[bby]
will check in there under the name of Rachel James. She'[s]
in a rented car."

"She's coming here!"

"Just listen, Ray. The cannibals are chasing us, but we['re a]
step ahead of them."

"Ahead of who?"

"The Mafia. And the FBI."

"Is that all?"

"Probably. Now listen to me. There is a slight chance [she]
is being followed. You've got to find her, watch her and m[ake]
damned sure no one is behind her."

"And if they are?"

"Call me, and we'll talk about it."

"No problem."

"Don't use the phone except to call this number. An[d I]
can't talk much."

"I've got a bunch of questions, little brother."

"And I've got the answers, but not now. Take care of my wife and call me when she gets there."

"Will do. And, Mitch, thanks."

"*Adios.*"

An hour later she turned off Highway 182 onto the winding driveway to the Hilton. She parked the four door Cutlass with Alabama tags and walked nervously under the sprawling veranda to the front doors. She stopped for a second, looked behind her at the driveway and went inside.

Two minutes later, a yellow cab from Mobile stopped under the veranda, behind the shuttle vans. Ray watched the cab. A woman was in the back seat leaning forward and talking to the driver. They waited a minute. She pulled money from her purse and paid him. She got out and waited until the cab drove away. The woman was a blonde, and that was the first thing he noticed. Very shapely, with tight black corduroy pants. And black sunglasses, which seemed odd to him because it was pushing midnight. She walked suspiciously to the front doors, waited a minute, then went in. He watched her carefully. He moved toward the lobby.

The blonde approached the only clerk behind the registration desk. "A single room, please," he heard her say.

The clerk slid a registration form across the counter. The blonde wrote her name and asked, "That lady who just checked in before me, what's her name? I think she's an old friend."

The clerk flipped through the registration cards. "Rachel Jones."

"Yeah, that's her. Where's she from?"

"It's a Memphis address," the clerk said.

"What's her room number? I'd like to say hello."

"I can't give room numbers," the clerk said.

The blonde quickly pulled two twenties from her purse and slid them across the counter. "I just want to say hello."

The clerk took the money. "Room 622."

The woman paid in cash. "Where are the phones?"

"Around the corner," the clerk said. Ray slid around the corner and found four pay phones. He grabbed a middle one and began talking to himself.

The blonde took a phone on the end and turned her back him. She spoke softly. He could hear only pieces.

". . . checked in . . . Room 622 . . . Mobile . . . sor help . . . I can't . . . an hour? . . . yes . . . hurry . . ."

She hung up, and he talked louder into his dead phone.

Ten minutes later, there was a knock at the door. T blonde jumped from the bed, grabbed her .45 and stuck it the corduroys under the shirt. She ignored the safety cha and cracked the door.

It burst open and knocked her against the wall. Ray lung at her, grabbed the gun, and pinned her to the floor. With h face in the carpet, he stuck the barrel of the .45 in her ear. ' you make a sound, I'll kill you!"

She stopped struggling and closed her eyes. No response

"Who are you?" Ray demanded. He pushed the bar deeper into her ear. Again, no response.

"Not a move, not a sound. Okay? I'd love to blow your he off."

He relaxed, still sitting on her back, and ripped open h flight bag. He dumped its contents on the floor and found pair of clean tennis socks. "Open your mouth," he demand

She did not move. The barrel returned to her ear, and s slowly opened her mouth. Ray crammed the socks in betwe her teeth, then tightly blindfolded her with the silk nightshi He bound her feet and hands with panty hose, then ripped t bedsheets into long strips. The woman did not move. When finished the binding and gagging, she resembled a mumm He slid her under the bed.

The purse contained six hundred dollars in cash and a wal with an Illinois driver's license. Karen Adair from Chica; Date of birth: March 4, 1962. He took the wallet and gun.

The phone rang at 1 A.M., and Mitch was not asleep. He was bank records up to his waist. Fascinating bank records. High incriminating.

"Hello," he answered cautiously.

"Is this mission control?" The voice was in the vicinity o loud jukebox.

"Where are you, Ray?"

"A joint called the FloraBama lounge. Right on the state ne."

"Where's Abby?"

"She's in the car. She's fine."

Mitch breathed easier and grinned into the phone. He lis-ned.

"We had to leave the hotel. A woman followed Abby in— me woman you saw in some bar in the Caymans. Abby is ying to explain everything. The woman followed her all day d showed up at the hotel. I took care of her, and we disap-ared."

"You took care of her?"

"Yeah, she wouldn't talk, but she's out of the way for a short me."

"Abby's fine?"

"Yeah. We're both dead tired. Exactly what do you have in ind?"

"You're about three hours away from Panama City Beach. I ow you're dead tired, but you need to get away from there. et to Panama City Beach, ditch the car and get two rooms at e Holiday Inn. Call me when you check in."

"I hope you know what you're doing."

"Trust me, Ray."

"I do, but I'm beginning to wish I was back in prison."

"You can't go back, Ray. We either disappear or we're dead."

36

THE CAB STOPPED at a red light in downtown Nashville, and Mitch hopped out on stiff and aching legs. He limped through the busy intersection dodging the morning traffic.

The Southeastern Bank Building was a thirty-story glass cylinder, designed along the same lines as a tennis-ball can. The tint was dark, almost black. It stood prominently away from the street corner amidst a maze of sidewalks and fountains and manicured greenery.

Mitch entered the revolving doors with a swarm of employees rushing to work. In the marble-laden atrium he found the directory and rode the escalators to the third floor. He opened a heavy glass door and walked into a large circular office. A striking woman of forty or so watched him from behind the glass desk. She offered no smile.

"Mr. Mason Laycook, please," he said.

She pointed. "Have a seat."

Mr. Laycook wasted no time. He appeared from around the corner and was as sour as his secretary. "May I help you?" he asked through his nose.

Mitch stood. "Yes, I need to wire a little money."

"Yes. Do you have an account at Southeastern?"

"Yes."

"And your name?"

"It's a numbered account." In other words, you don't get a name, Mr. Laycook. You don't need a name.

"Very well. Follow me." His office had no windows, no view. A row of keyboards and monitors sat on the credenza behind his glass desk. Mitch sat down.

"The account number, please."

It came from memory. "214-31-35."

Laycook pecked at his keyboard and watched a monitor. That's a Code Three account, opened by a T. Hemphill, with access only by her and a certain male meeting the following physical requirements: approximately six feet tall, one seventy-five to one eighty-five, blue eyes, brown hair, about twenty-five or twenty-six years old. You fit that description, sir." Laycook studied the screen. "And the last four digits of your Social Security number are?"

"8585."

"Very well. You are accessed. Now what can I do for you?"

"I want to wire in some funds from a bank in Grand Cayman."

Laycook frowned and took a pencil from his pocket. "Which bank in Grand Cayman?"

"Royal Bank of Montreal."

"What type of account?"

"It's a numbered account."

"I presume you have the number?"

"499DFH2122."

Laycook wrote the number and stood. "I'll be just a moment." He left the room.

Ten minutes passed. Mitch tapped his bruised feet and looked at the monitors across the desk.

Laycook returned with his supervisor, Mr. Nokes, a vice president or something. Nokes introduced himself from behind the desk. Both men appeared nervous. They stared downward at Mitch.

Nokes did the talking. He held a small sheet of computer paper. "Sir, that is a restricted account. You must have certain information before we can start the wire."

Mitch nodded confidently.

"The dates and amounts of the last three deposits, sir
They watched him intensely, knowing he would fail.

Again, it came from memory. No notes. "February third
this year, six and a half million. December fourteenth, la
year, nine point two million. And October eighth, last yea
eleven million."

Laycook and Nokes gaped at the small printout. Nokes ma
aged a tiny professional smile. "Very well. You are cleared
the Pen number."

Laycook stood ready with his pencil.

"Sir, what is your Pen number?" Nokes asked.

Mitch smiled and recrossed his damaged legs. "72083."

"And the terms of the wire?"

"Ten million dollars wired immediately into this bank, a
count 214-31-35. I'll wait."

"It's not necessary to wait, sir."

"I'll wait. When the wire is complete, I've got a few mo
for you."

"We'll be a moment. Would you like some coffee?"

"No. Thanks. Do you have a newspaper?"

"Certainly," Laycook said. "On the table there."

They scurried from the office, and Mitch's pulse began
descent. He opened the Nashville *Tennessean* and scanned thr
sections before he found a brief paragraph about the escape
Brushy Mountain. No picture. Few details. They were safe
the Holiday Inn on the Miracle Strip in Panama City Bea
Florida.

Their trail was clear, so far. He thought. He hoped.

Laycook returned alone. He was friendly now. A real ba
slapper. "Wire's complete. The money is here. Now what c
we do for you?"

"I want to wire it out. Most of it, anyway."

"How many transfers?"

"Three."

"Give me the first one."

"A million dollars to the Coast National Bank in Pensac
to a numbered account, accessible to only one person, a wh
female, approximately fifty years of age. I will provide
with the Pen number."

"Is this an existing account?"

"No. I want you to open it with the wire."

"Very well. The second transfer?"

"One million dollars to the Dane County Bank in Danesro, Kentucky, to any account in the name of Harold or Maxe Sutherland, or both. It's a small bank, but it has a correondent relationship with United Kentucky in Louisville."

"Very well. The third transfer?"

"Seven million to the Deutschbank in Zurich. Account mber 772-03BL-600. The remainder of the money stays re."

"This will take about an hour," Laycook said as he wrote.

"I'll call you in an hour to confirm."

"Very well."

"Thank you, Mr. Laycook."

Each step was painful, but the pain was not felt. He moved a controlled jog down the escalators and out of the building.

the top floor of the Royal Bank of Montreal, Grand Cayn branch, a secretary from Wire Transfers slid a computer ntout under the very pointed and proper nose of Randolph good. She had circled an unusual transfer of ten million. usual because the money in this account did not normally urn to the United States and unusual because it went to a k they had never dealt with. Osgood studied the printout l called Memphis. Mr. Tolleson was on leave of absence, the retary informed him. Then Nathan Locke? he asked. Mr. cke is out of town. Victor Milligan? Mr. Milligan is away).

Osgood placed the printout in the pile of things to do tomor-.

ng the Emerald Coast of Florida and Alabama, from the skirts of Mobile east through Pensacola, Fort Walton Beach, stin and Panama City, the warm spring night had been ceful. Only one violent crime along the coast. A young man was robbed, beaten and raped in her room at the dido Beach Hilton. Her boyfriend, a tall blond headed man h strong Nordic features, had found her bound and gagged

in her room. His name was Rimmer, Aaron Rimmer, and
was from Memphis.

The real excitement of the night was a massive manhunt
the Mobile area for the escaped murderer, Ray McDeere. H
had been seen arriving at the bus station after dark. His m
shot was on the front page of the morning paper, and befo
ten, three witnesses had come forth and reported sightin
His movements were traced across Mobile Bay to Foley, A
bama, then to Gulf Shores.

Since the Hilton is only ten miles from Gulf Shores alo
Highway 182, and since the only known escaped murder
was in the vicinity when the only violent crime occurred, t
conclusion was quick and inescapable. The hotel's night cle
made a probable ID of Ray McDeere, and the records reflect
that he checked in around nine-thirty as a Mr. Lee Steve
And he paid cash. Later, the victim checked in and was
tacked. The victim also identified Mr. Ray McDeere.

The night clerk remembered that the victim asked abou
Rachel James, who checked in five minutes before the vict
and paid cash. Rachel James vanished sometime during t
night without bothering to check out. Likewise for R
McDeere, alias Lee Stevens. A parking-lot attendant mad
probable ID of McDeere and said he got in a white four-dc
Cutlass with a woman between midnight and one. Said s
was driving and appeared to be in a hurry. Said they went e
on 182.

Calling from his room on the sixth floor of the Hilton, Aar
Rimmer anonymously told a Baldwin County sheriff's dep
to check the car rental companies in Mobile. Check them
an Abby McDeere. That's your white Cutlass, he told him

From Mobile to Miami, the search began for the Cutl
rented from Avis by Abby McDeere. The sheriff's investiga
promised to keep the victim's boyfriend, Aaron Rimm
posted on all developments.

Mr. Rimmer would wait at the Hilton. He shared a ro
with Tony Verkler. Next door was his boss, DeVasher. Fo
teen of his friends sat in their rooms on the seventh floor a
waited.

•   •   •   •

took seventeen trips from the apartment to the U-Haul, but
noon the Bendini Papers were ready for shipment. Mitch
sted his swollen legs. He sat on the couch and wrote instruc-
ns to Tammy. He detailed the transactions at the bank and
d her to wait a week before contacting his mother. She
uld soon be a millionaire.

He set the telephone in his lap and prepared himself for an
pleasant task. He called the Dane County Bank and asked
r Hugh Sutherland. It was an emergency, he said.

"Hello," his father-in-law answered angrily.

"Mr. Sutherland, this is Mitch. Have you—"

"Where's my daughter. Is she okay?"

"Yes. She's fine. She's with me. We'll be leaving the country
r a few days. Maybe weeks. Maybe months."

"I see," he replied slowly. "And where might you being
ing?"

"Not sure. We'll just knock around for a while."

"Is something wrong, Mitch?"

"Yes, sir. Something is very wrong, but I can't explain now.
aybe one of these days. Watch the newspapers closely. You'll
a major story out of Memphis within two weeks."

"Are you in danger?"

"Sort of. Have you received any unusual wire transfers this
rning?"

"As a matter of fact we have. Somebody parked a million
cks here about an hour ago."

"That somebody was me, and the money is yours."

There was a very long pause. "Mitch, I think I deserve an
planation."

"Yes, sir, you do. But I can't give you one. If we make it
ely out of the country, you'll be notified in a week or so.
joy the money. Gotta run."

Mitch waited a minute and called Room 1028 at the Holiday
, Panama City Beach.

"Hello." It was Abby.

"Hi, babe. How are you?"

"Terrible, Mitch. Ray's picture is on the cover of every
wspaper down here. At first it was the escape and the fact
t someone saw him in Mobile. Now the TV news is claim-
he is the prime suspect in a rape last night."

"What! Where!"

"At the Perdido Beach Hilton. Ray caught that blonde f. lowing me into the hotel. He jumped her in her room and ti her up. Nothing serious. He took her gun and her money, a now she's claiming she was beaten and raped by R McDeere. Every cop in Florida is looking for the car I rent last night in Mobile."

"Where's the car?"

"We left it about a mile west of here at a big condo devele ment. I'm so scared, Mitch."

"Where's Ray?"

"He's lying on the beach trying to sunburn his face. T picture in the paper is an old one. He's got long hair and lo real pale. It's not a good picture. Now he's got a crew cut a he's trying to turn pink. I think it will help."

"Are both rooms in your name?"

"Rachael James."

"Listen, Abby. Forget Rachel and Lee and Ray and Ab Wait until almost dark, then leave the rooms. Just walk aw About a half a mile east is a small motel called the Blue Ti You and Ray enjoy a little walk on the beach until you find You go to the desk and get two rooms next to each other. I in cash. Tell them your name is Jackie Nagel. Got that? Jac Nagel. Use that name, because when I get there I'll ask for

"What if they don't have two rooms next to each other?"

"Okay, if anything goes wrong, two doors down is anot dump called the Seaside. Check in there. Same name. I'm le ing here now, say one o'clock, and I should be there in hours."

"What if they find the car?"

"They'll find it, and they'll throw a blanket over Pana City Beach. You've got to be careful. After dark, try to sn into a drugstore and buy some hair dye. Cut your hair tremely short and dye it blond.

"Blond!"

"Or red. I don't give a damn. But change it. Tell Ray no leave his room. Do not take any chances."

"He's got a gun, Mitch."

"Tell him I said not to use it. There will be a thousand c around there, probably tonight. He can't win a gunfight."

"I love you, Mitch. I'm so scared."

"It's okay to be scared, babe. Just keep thinking. They don't
ow where you are, and they can't catch you if you move. I'll
there by midnight."

mar Quinn, Wally Hudson and Kendall Mahan sat in the
nference room on the third floor and contemplated their
xt move. As senior associates, they knew about the fifth floor
d the basement, about Mr. Lazarov and Mr. Morolto, about
odge and Kozinski. They knew that when one joined the
m, one did not leave.

They told their stories about the Day. They compared it to
: day they learned the sad truth about Santa Claus. A sad
d frightening day, when Nathan Locke talked to them in his
ice and told them about their biggest client. And then he
roduced them to DeVasher. They were employees of the
orolto family, and they were expected to work hard, spend
:ir handsome paychecks and remain very quiet about it. All
ee did. There had been thoughts of leaving, but never seri-
s plans. They were family men. In time, it sort of went
ay. There were so many clean clients to work for. So much
rd, legitimate work.

The partners handled most of the dirty work, but growing
iority had brought increasing involvement in the conspira-
 They would never be caught, the partners assured them.
ey were too smart. They had too much money. It was a
rfect cover. Of particular concern at the conference table
s the fact that the partners had skipped town. There was
: a single partner in Memphis. Even Avery Tolleson had
appeared. He had walked out of the hospital.

They talked about Mitch. He was out there somewhere,
red and running for his life. If DeVasher caught him, he
s dead and they would bury him like Hodge and Kozinski.
t if the feds caught him, they got the records, and they got
 firm, which, of course, included the three of them.

What if, they speculated, no one caught him? What if he
de it, just vanished? Along with his documents, of course.
at if he and Abby were now somewhere on a beach, drink-
 rum and counting their money? They liked this thought
 talked about it for a while.

Finally, they decided to wait until tomorrow. If Mitch w
gunned down somewhere, they would stay in Memphis. If
was never found, they would stay in Memphis. If the fe
caught him, they would hit the road, Jack.

Run, Mitch, run!

The rooms at the Blue Tide Motel were narrow and tacl
The carpet was twenty years old and badly worn. The b
spreads had cigarette burns. But luxury was unimportant.

After dark Thursday, Ray stood behind Abby with a pair
scissors and snipped delicately around her ears. Two tow
under the chair were covered with her dark hair. She watch
him carefully in the mirror next to the antique color televis
and was free with her instructions. It was a boyish cut, w
above the ears, with bangs. He stepped back and admired
work.

"Not bad," he said.

She smiled and brushed hair from her arms. "I guess I n
to color it now," she said sadly. She walked to the tiny ba
room and closed the door.

She emerged an hour later as a blonde. A yellowish blon
Ray was asleep on the bedspread. She knelt on the dirty car
and scooped up the hair.

She picked it from the floor and filled a plastic garbage k
The empty dye bottle and the applicator were thrown in w
the hair, and she tied the bag. There was a knock at the do

Abby froze, and listened. The curtains were pulled tigh
She slapped Ray's feet. Another knock. Ray jumped from
bed and grabbed the gun.

"Who is it?" she whispered loudly at the window.

"Sam Fortune," he whispered back.

Ray unlocked the door, and Mitch stepped in. He grab
Abby and bear-hugged Ray. The door was locked, the li
turned off, and they sat on the bed in the darkness. He I
Abby tightly. With so much to say, the three said nothing

A tiny, weak ray of light from the outside filtered under
curtains and, as minutes passed, gradually lit the dresser
television. No one spoke. There were no sounds from the I
Tide. The parking lot was virtually empty.

[can almost explain why I'm here," Ray finally said, "but
 not sure why you're here."

We've got to forget why we're here," Mitch said, "and con-
:rate on leaving here. All together. All safe."

Abby's told me everything," Ray said.

[don't know everything," she said. "I don't know who's
;ing us."

['m assuming they're all out there," Mitch said. "DeVasher
 his gang are nearby. Pensacola, I would guess. It's the
'est airport of any size. Tarrance is somewhere along the
:t directing his boys in their all-out search for Ray
)eere, the rapist. And his accomplice, Abby McDeere."

What happens next?" Abby asked.

They'll find the car, if they haven't already done so. That
 pinpoint Panama City Beach. The paper said the search
nded from Mobile to Miami, so now they're spread out.
:n they find the car, they zero in here. Now, there's a thou-
[cheap motels just like this one along the Strip. For twelve
s, nothing but motels, condos and T-shirt shops. That's a
)f people, a lot of tourists with shorts and sandals, and
orrow we'll be tourists too, shorts, sandals, the whole bit. I
:e even if they have a hundred men after us, we've got two
uree days."

)nce they decide we're here, what happens?" she asked.

You and Ray could have simply abandoned the car and
n off in another one. They can't be certain we're on the
), but they'll start looking here. But they're not the Ge-
>. They can't crash a door and search without probable
e."

)eVasher can," Ray said.

'eah, but there's a million doors around here. They'll set
oadblocks and watch every store and restaurant. They'll
to every hotel clerk, show them Ray's mug shot. They'll
m like ants for a few days, and with luck, they'll miss us."

What are you driving, Mitch?" Ray asked.

. U-Haul."

don't understand why we don't get in the U-Haul, right
, and haul ass. I mean, the car is sitting a mile down the
, just waiting to be found, and we know they're coming. I
ve haul it."

"Listen, Ray. They might be setting roadblocks right n
Trust me. Did I get you out of prison? Come on."

A siren went screaming past on the strip. They froze,
listened to it fade away.

"Okay, gang," Mitch said, "we're moving out. I don't
this place. The parking lot is empty and too close to the h
way. I've parked the U-Haul three doors down at the ele
Sea Gull's Rest Motel. I've got two lovely rooms there.
roaches are much smaller. We're taking a quiet stroll on
beach. Then we get to unpack the truck. Sound exciting?

37

OEY MOROLTO and his squad of storm troopers landed
at the Pensacola airport in a chartered DC-9 before sunrise
Friday. Lazarov waited with two limos and eight rented
s. He briefed Joey on the past twenty-four hours as the
voy left Pensacola and traveled east on Highway 98. After
our of briefing, they arrived at a twelve-floor condo called
Sandpiper, in the middle of the Strip at Destin. An hour
n Panama City Beach. The penthouse on the top floor had
n procured by Lazarov for only four thousand dollars a
k. Off-season rates. The remainder of the twelfth floor and
f the eleventh had been leased, for the goons.

r. Morolto snapped orders like an agitated drill sergeant.
ommand post was set up in the great room of the pent-
se, overlooking the calm emerald water. Nothing suited
. He wanted breakfast, and Lazarov sent two vans to a
champs supermarket nearby. He wanted McDeere, and
rov asked him to be patient.

y daybreak, the troops had settled into their condos. They
ed.

hree miles away along the beach, and within view of the
lpiper, F. Denton Voyles and Wayne Tarrance sat on the

balcony of an eighth-floor room at the Sandestin Hilton. Th
drank coffee, watched the sun rise gently on the horizon a
talked strategy. The night had not gone well. The car had
been found. No sign of Mitch. With sixty FBI agents and h
dreds of locals scouring the coast, they should have at le
found the car. With each passing hour, the McDeeres w
farther away.

In a file by a coffee table inside were the warrants. For l
McDeere, the warrant read: escape, unlawful flight, robb
and rape. Abby's sin was merely being an accomplice. T
charges for Mitch required more creativity. Obstruction of
tice and a nebulous racketeering charge. And of course the
standby, mail fraud. Tarrance was not sure where the m
fraud fit, but he worked for the FBI and had never seen a c
that did not include mail fraud.

The warrants were issued and ready and had been fully
cussed with dozens of reporters from newspapers and tel
sion stations throughout the Southeast. Trained to mainta
stone face and loathe the press, Tarrance was having a deli
ful time with the reporters.

Publicity was needed. Publicity was critical. The author
must find the McDeeres before the Mob did.

Rick Acklin ran through the room to the balcony. "They
found the car!"

Tarrance and Voyles jumped to their feet. "Where?"

"Panama City Beach. In the parking lot of a high rise."

"Call our men in, every one of them!" Voyles yelled. "S
searching everywhere. I want every agent in Panama C
Beach. We'll turn the place inside out. Get all the locals
can. Tell them to set up roadblocks on every highway
gravel road in and out of there. Dust the car for prints. Wh
the town look like?"

"Similar to Destin. A twelve mile strip along the beach w
hotels, motels, condos, the works," Acklin answered.

"Start our men door to door at the hotels. Is her compo
ready?"

"Should be," Acklin said.

"Get her composite, Mitch's composite, Ray's composite
Ray's mug shot in the hands of every agent and cop. I w

ople walking up and down the Strip waving those damn nposites."

"Yes, sir."

"How far away is Panama City Beach?"

"About fifty minutes due east."

"Get my car."

e phone woke Aaron Rimmer in his room at the Perdido ach Hilton. It was the investigator with the Baldwin unty Sheriff's Department. They found the car, Mr. Rim- r, he said, in Panama City Beach. Just a few minutes ago. out a mile from the Holiday Inn. On Highway 98. Sorry in about the girl, he said. Hope she's doing better, he said.

Mr. Rimmer said thanks, and immediately called Lazarov at Sandpiper. Ten minutes later, he and his roommate, Tony, DeVasher and fourteen others were speeding east. Panama y Beach was three hours away.

n Destin, Lazarov mobilized the storm troopers. They ved out quickly, piled into the vans and headed east. The zkrieg had begun.

ook only a matter of minutes for the U-Haul to become a item. The assistant manager of the rental company in hville was a guy named Billy Weaver. He opened the office y Friday morning, fixed his coffee and scanned the paper. the bottom half of the front page, Billy read with interest story about Ray McDeere and the search along the coast. d then Abby was mentioned. Then the escapee's brother, ch McDeere, was mentioned. The name rang a bell.

illy opened a drawer and flipped through the records of tanding rentals. Sure enough, a man named McDeere had ted a sixteen-footer late Wednesday night. M. Y. McDeere, the signature, but the driver's license read Mitchell Y. m Memphis.

eing a patriot and honest taxpayer, Billy called his cousin Metro Police. The cousin called the Nashville FBI office, fifteen minutes later, the U-Haul was a hot item.

arrance took the call on the radio while Acklin drove. les was in the back seat. A U-Haul? Why would he need a aul? He left Memphis without his car, clothes, shoes or

toothbrush. He left the dog unfed. He took nothing with hi
so why the U-Haul?

The Bendini records, of course. Either he left Nashvi
with the records in the truck or he was in the truck en route
get them. But why Nashville?

Mitch was up with the sun. He took one long, lustful look
his wife with the cute blond hair and forgot about sex. It co
wait. He let her sleep. He walked around the stacks of boxe:
the small room and went to the bathroom. He showe:
quickly and slipped on a gray sweat suit he'd bought at a V
Mart in Montgomery. He eased along the beach for a half n
until he found a convenience store. He bought a sackful
Cokes, pastries and chips, sunglasses, caps and three news
pers.

Ray was waiting by the U-Haul when he returned. T
spread the papers on Ray's bed. It was worse than they
pected. Mobile, Pensacola and Montgomery had front p
stories with composites of Ray and Mitch, along with the n
shot again. Abby's composite had not been released, accord
to the Pensacola paper.

As composites go, they were close here and there and ba
off in other areas. But it was hard to be objective. Hell, Mi
was staring at his own composite and trying to give an ur
ased opinion about how close it was. The stories were ful
all sorts of wild statements from one Wayne Tarrance, spe
agent, FBI. Tarrance said Mitchell McDeere had been spot
in the Gulf Shores–Pensacola area; that he and Ray both w
known to be heavily armed and extremely dangerous; **t**
they had vowed not to be taken alive; that reward money
being gathered; that if anyone saw a man who faintly res
bled either of the McDeere brothers, please call the local
lice.

They ate pastries and decided the composites were not cl
The mug shot was even comical. They eased next door
woke Abby. They began unpacking the Bendini Papers
assembling the video camera.

At nine, Mitch called Tammy, collect. She had the new
and passports. He instructed her to Federal Express then
Sam Fortune, front desk, Sea Gull's Rest Motel, 16694 H

)8, West Panama City Beach, Florida. She read to him the
-page story about himself and his small gang. No com-
:s.

told her to ship the passports, then leave Nashville.
: four hours to Knoxville, check into a big motel and call
it Room 39, Sea Gull's Rest. He gave her the number.

FBI agents knocked on the door of the old ragged trailer
> San Luis. Mr. Ainsworth came to the door in his under-
They flashed their badges.

› whatta you want with me?" he growled.

agent handed him the morning paper. "Do you know
two men?"

studied the paper. "I guess they're my wife's boys.
ır met them."

ıd your wife's name is?"

a Ainsworth."

here is she?"

. Ainsworth was scanning the paper. "At work. At the
: Hut. Say they're around here, huh?"

s, sir. You haven't seen them?"

:ll no. But I'll get my gun."

ıs your wife seen them?"

ɔt to my knowledge."

ıanks, Mr. Ainsworth. We've got orders to set up watch
ın the street, but we won't bother you."

›od. These boys are crazy. I've always said that."

ıile away, another pair of agents parked discreetly next
Vaffle Hut and set up watch.

ɔn, all highways and county roads into the coast around
ıa City Beach were blocked. Along the Strip, cops
:d traffic every four miles. They walked from one T-shirt
›o the next, handing out composites. They posted them
bulletin boards in Shoney's, Pizza Hut, Taco Bell and a
more fast-food places. They told the cashiers and wait-
to keep their eyes open for the McDeeres. Very danger-
ople.

ırov and his men camped at the Best Western, two miles
f the Sea Gull's Rest. He rented a large conference room

and set up command. Four of his troops were dispatch
raid a T-shirt shop, and they returned with all sorts of to
clothes and straw hats and caps. He rented two Ford Es
and equipped them with police scanners. They patrolle
Strip and listened to the endless squawking. They immedi
caught the search for the U-Haul and joined in. DeVasher
tegically spread the rented vans along the Strip. They sat i
cently in large parking lots and waited with their radios

Around two, Lazarov received an emergency call fro
employee on the fifth floor of the Bendini Building.
things. First, an employee snooping around the Cayman
found an old locksmith who, after being paid, recalled ma
eleven keys around midnight of April 1. Eleven keys, on
rings. Said the woman, a very attractive American, a bru
with nice legs, had paid cash and was in a hurry. Said the
had been easy, except for the Mercedes key. He wasn't
about that one. Second, a banker from Grand Cayman c
Thursday at 9:33 A.M., ten million dollars had been wired
the Royal Bank of Montreal to the Southeastern Bank in N
ville.

Between four and four-thirty, the police scanners went
The squawking was nonstop. A clerk at the Holiday Inn
a probable ID of Abby, as the woman who paid cash fo
rooms at 4:17 A.M., Thursday. She paid for three nights
had not been seen since the rooms were cleaned around o
Thursday. Evidently, neither room had been slept in T
day night. She had not checked out, and the rooms were
for through noon Saturday. The clerk saw no sign of a
accomplice. The Holiday Inn was swamped with cops and
agents and Morolto thugs for an hour. Tarrance himself i
rogated the clerk.

They were there! Somewhere in Panama City Beach.
and Abby were confirmed. It was suspected Mitch was
them, but it was unconfirmed. Until 4:58, Friday afterno

The bombshell. A county deputy pulled into a cheap
and noticed the gray-and-white hood of a truck. He w
between two buildings and smiled at the small U-Haul
hidden neatly between a row of two-story rooms and a

age Dumpster. He wrote down all the numbers on the
k and called it in.

hit! In five minutes the motel was surrounded. The owner
ged from the front office and demanded an explanation.
looked at the composites and shook his head. Five FBI
es flapped in his face, and he became cooperative.
ccompanied by a dozen agents, he took the keys and went
to door. Forty-eight doors.

ily seven were occupied. The owner explained as he un-
d doors that it was a slow time of the year at the Beach-
er Inn. All of the smaller motels struggle until Memorial
he explained.

en the Sea Gull's Rest, four miles to the west, was strug-

y Patrick received his first felony conviction at the age of
een and served four months for bad checks. Branded as a
, he found honest work impossible, and for the next
ty years worked unsuccessfully as a small-time criminal.
rifted across the country shoplifting, writing bad checks
reaking into houses here and there. A small, frail nonvio-
man, he was severely beaten by a fat, arrogant county
ty in Texas when he was twenty-seven. He lost an eye
ost all respect for the law.

months earlier, he landed in Panama City Beach and
l an honest job paying four bucks an hour working the
shift at the front and only desk of the Sea Gull's Rest
l. Around nine, Friday night, he was watching TV when
arrogant county deputy swaggered through the door.

ot a manhunt going on," he announced, and laid copies of
omposites and mug shot on the dirty counter. "Looking
e folks. We think they're around here."

dy studied the composites. The one of Mitchell Y.
ere looked pretty familiar. The wheels in his small-time
ous brain began to churn.

h his one good eye, he looked at the fat, arrogant county
y and said, "Ain't seen them. But I'll keep an eye out."
ney're dangerous," the deputy said.

're the dangerous one, Andy thought.

st these up on the wall there," the deputy instructed.

Do you own this damned place? Andy thought. "I'm s
but I'm not authorized to post anything on the walls."

The deputy froze, cocked his head sideways and glare
Andy through thick sunglasses. "Listen, Peewee, I author
it."

"I'm sorry, sir, but I can't post anything on the walls u
my boss tells me to."

"And where is your boss?"

"I don't know. Probably in a bar somewhere."

The deputy carefully picked up the composites, walke
hind the counter and tacked them on the bulletin board. V
he finished, he glared down at Andy and said, "I'll come
in a coupla hours. If you remove these, I'll arrest you fo
struction of justice."

Andy did not flinch. "Won't stick. They got me for tha
time in Kansas, so I know all about it."

The deputy's fat cheeks turned red and he gritted his t
"You're a little smart-ass, aren't you?"

"Yes, sir."

"You take these down and I promise you you'll go to ja
something."

"I've been there before, and it ain't no big deal."

Red lights and sirens screamed by on the Strip a few
away, and the deputy turned and watched the excitemen
mumbled something and swaggered out the door. Andy t
the composites in the garbage. He watched the squad
dodge each other on the Strip for a few minutes, then w
through the parking lot to the rear building. He knocke
the door of Room 38.

He waited and knocked again.

"Who is it?" a woman asked.

"The manager," Andy replied, proud of his title. The
opened, and the man who favored the composite of Mitch
McDeere slid out.

"Yes, sir," he said. "What's going on?"

He was nervous, Andy could tell. "Cops just came by, I
what I mean?"

"What do they want?" he asked innocently.

Your ass, Andy thought. "Just asking questions and sho
pictures. I looked at the pictures, you know."

388

Uh-huh," he said.

Pretty good pictures," Andy said.

Mr. McDeere stared at Andy real hard.

Andy said, "Cop said one of them escaped from prison.
ow what I mean. I been in prison, and I think everybody
ht to escape. You know?"

Mr. McDeere smiled, a rather nervous smile. "What's your
e?" he asked.

Andy."

've got a deal for you, Andy. I'll give you a thousand bucks
, and tomorrow, if you're still unable to recognize any-
, I'll give you another thousand bucks. Same for the next
"

wonderful deal, thought Andy, but if he could afford a
sand bucks a day, certainly he could afford five thousand a
It was the opportunity of his career.

Nope," Andy said firmly. "Five thousand a day."

r. McDeere never hesitated. "It's a deal. Let me get the
ey." He went in the room and returned with a stack of

ive thousand a day, Andy, that's our deal?"

ndy took the money and glanced around. He would count
er. "I guess you want me to keep the maids away?" Andy
d.

reat idea. That would be nice."

nother five thousand," Andy said.

r. McDeere sort of hesitated. "Okay, I've got another deal.
orrow morning, a Fed Ex package will arrive at the desk
am Fortune. You bring it to me, and keep the maids away,
'll give you another five thousand."

on't work. I do the night shift."

kay, Andy. What if you worked all weekend, around the
, kept the maids away and delivered my package? Can you
at?"

ure. My boss is a drunk. He'd love for me to work all
end."

ow much money, Andy?"

for it, Andy thought. "Another twenty thousand."

. McDeere smiled. "You got it."

Andy grinned and stuck the money in his pocket. He wa
away without saying a word, and Mitch retreated to Room

"Who was it?" Ray snapped.

Mitch smiled as he glanced between the blinds and the
dows.

"I knew we would have to have a lucky break to pull this
And I think we just found it."

38

R. MOROLTO wore a black suit and a red tie and sat at the head of the plastic-coated executive conference table in the Dunes Room of the Best Western on the ... The twenty chairs around the table were packed with ...est and brightest men. Around the four walls stood more ...s trusted troops. Though they were thick-necked killers ...did their deeds efficiently and without remorse, they ...ed like clowns in their colorful shirts and wild shorts and ...ing potpourri of straw hats. He would have smiled at ... silliness, but the urgency of the moment prevented smil- ...He was listening.

... his immediate right was Lou Lazarov, and on his imme- ...left was DeVasher, and every ear in the small room lis- ...d as the two played tag team back and forth across the

...hey're here. I know they're here," DeVasher said dramati- ...slapping both palms on the table with each syllable. The ...had rhythm.

...zarov's turn: "I agree. They're here. Two came in a car, ...came in a truck. We've found both vehicles abandoned, ...ed with fingerprints. Yes, they're here."

DeVasher: "But why Panama City Beach? It makes
sense."

Lazarov: "For one, he's been here before. Came here Ch
mas, remember? He's familiar with this place, so he fig
with all these cheap motels on the beach it's a great plac
hide for a while. Not a bad idea, really. But he's had some
luck. For a man on the run, he's carrying too much bagg
like a brother who everybody wants. And a wife. And a tr
load of documents, we presume. Typical schoolboy menta
If I gotta run, I'm taking everybody who loves me. Ther
brother rapes a girl, they think, and suddenly every co
Alabama and Florida is looking for them. Some pretty
luck, really."

"What about his mother?" Mr. Morolto asked.

Lazarov and DeVasher nodded at the great man and
knowledged this very intelligent question.

Lazarov: "No, purely coincidental. She's a very si
woman who serves waffles and knows nothing. We've wat
her since we got here."

DeVasher: "I agree. There's been no contact."

Morolto nodded intelligently and lit a cigarette.

Lazarov: "So if they're here, and we know they're here,
the feds and the cops also know they're here. We've got
people here, and they got hundreds. Odds are on them."

"You're sure they're all three together?" Mr. Morolto a

DeVasher: "Absolutely. We know the woman and the
vict checked in the same night at Perdido, that they left
three hours later she checked in here at the Holiday Inn
paid cash for two rooms and that she rented the car and
fingerprints were on it. No doubt. We know Mitch rent
U-Haul Wednesday in Nashville, that he wired ten mi
bucks of our money into a bank in Nashville Thursday m
ing and then evidently hauled ass. The U-Haul was found
four hours ago. Yes, sir, they are together."

Lazarov: "If he left Nashville immediately after the m
was wired, he would have arrived here around dark.
U-Haul was found empty, so they had to unload it somew
around here, then hide it. That was probably sometime
last night, Thursday. Now, you gotta figure they need to
sometime. I figure they stayed here last night with pla

392

ving on today. But they woke up this morning and their
s were in the paper, cops running around bumping into
a other, and suddenly the roads were blocked. So they're
ped here."

eVasher: "To get out, they've got to borrow, rent or steal a
No rental records anywhere around here. She rented a car
Mobile in her name. Mitch rented a U-Haul in Nashville in
name. Real proper ID. So you gotta figure they ain't that
ned smart after all."

azarov: "Evidently they don't have fake IDs. If they rented
r around here for the escape, the rental records would be
ie real name. No such records exist."

r. Morolto waved his hand in frustration. "All right, all
t. So they're here. You guys are geniuses. I'm so proud of
Now what?"

eVasher's turn: "The Fibbies are in the way. They're in
rol of the search, and we can't do nothing but sit and
h."

azarov: "I've called Memphis. Every senior associate in the
is on the way down here. They know McDeere and his
real well, so we'll put them on the beach and in restau-
s and hotels. Maybe they'll see something."

eVasher: "I figure they're in one of the little motels. They
give fake names, pay in cash and nobody'll be suspicious.
er people too. Less likelihood of being seen. They checked
the Holiday Inn but didn't stay long. I bet they moved on
n the Strip."

azarov: "First, we'll get rid of the feds and the cops. They
t know it yet, but they're about to move their show on
n the road. Then, early in the morning, we start door to
at the small motels. Most of these dumps have less than
rooms. I figure two of our men can search one in thirty
ites. I know it'll be slow, but we can't just sit here. Maybe
a the cops pull out, the McDeeres will breathe a little and
a mistake."

ou mean you want our men to start searching hotel
s?" Mr. Morolto asked.

Vasher: "There's no way we can hit every door, but we
try."

r. Morolto stood and glanced around the room. "So what

about the water?" he asked in the direction of Lazarov
DeVasher.

They stared at each other, thoroughly confused by the q[ues]tion.

"The water!" Mr. Morolto screamed. "What about the [wa]ter?"

All eyes shot desperately around the table and qui[ckly]
landed upon Lazarov. "I'm sorry, sir, I'm confused."

Mr. Morolto leaned into Lazarov's face. "What about [the]
water, Lou? We're on a beach, right? There's land and h[igh]ways and railroads and airports on one side, and there's w[ater]
and boats on the other. Now, if the roads are blocked and [the]
airports and railroads are out of the question, where do [you]
think they might go? It seems obvious to me they would tr[y to]
find a boat and ease out in the dark. Makes sense, don'[t]
boys?"

Every head in the room nodded quickly. DeVasher s[poke]
first. "Makes a hell of a lot of sense to me."

"Wonderful," said Mr. Morolto. "Then where are [the]
boats?"

Lazarov jumped from his seat, turned to the wall and be[gan]
barking orders at his lieutenants. "Go down to the docks! [Buy]
every fishing boat you can find for tonight and all day to[mor]row. Pay them whatever they want. Don't answer any q[ues]tions, just pay 'em the money. Get our men on those boats [and]
start patrolling as soon as possible. Stay within a mil[e of]
shore."

Shortly before eleven, Friday night, Aaron Rimmer stoo[d at]
the checkout counter at an all-night Texaco in Tallahassee [and]
paid for a root beer and twelve gallons of gas. He ne[eded]
change for the call. Outside, next to the car wash, he fli[pped]
through the blue pages and called the Tallahassee Police [De]partment. It was an emergency. He explained himself, an[d the]
dispatcher connected him with a shift captain.

"Listen!" Rimmer yelled urgently, "I'm here at this Te[xaco]
and five minutes ago I saw these convicts everybody is loo[king]
for! I know it was them!"

"Which convicts?" asked the captain.

"The McDeeres. Two men and a woman. I left Panama [City]

394

ch not two hours ago, and I saw their pictures in the paper. en I stopped here and filled up, and I saw them."

immer gave his location and waited thirty seconds for the t patrol car to arrive with blue lights flashing. It was ckly followed by a second, third and fourth. They loaded nmer in a front seat and raced him to the South Precinct. e captain and a small crowd waited anxiously. Rimmer was orted like a celebrity into the captain's office, where the e composites and mug shot were waiting on the desk.

That's them!" he shouted. "I just saw them, not ten min- s ago. They were in a green Ford pickup with Tennessee es, and it was pulling a long double-axle U-Haul trailer."

Exactly where were you?" asked the captain. The cops g on every word.

I was pumping gas, pump number four, regular unleaded, they eased into the parking lot, real suspicious like. They ced away from the pumps, and the woman got out and it inside." He picked up Abby's composite and studied it. o. That's her. No doubt. Her hair's a lot shorter, but it's . She came right back out, didn't buy a thing. She seemed ous and in a hurry to get back to the truck. I was finished iping, so I walked inside. Right when I opened the door, drove within two feet of me. I saw all three of them."

Who was driving?" asked the captain. Rimmer stared at 's mug shot. "Not him. The other one." He pointed at :h's composite.

Could I see your driver's license," a sergeant said.

immer carried three sets of identification. He handed the eant an Illinois driver's license with his picture and the e Frank Temple.

Vhich direction were they headed?" the captain asked.

ast."

t the same moment, about four miles away, Tony Verkler g up the pay phone, smiled to himself and returned to the ;er King.

ne captain was on the phone. The sergeant was copying rmation from Rimmer/Temple's driver's license and a n cops chatted excitedly when a patrolman rushed into office "Just got a call! Another sighting, at a Burger King of town. Same info! All three of them in a green Ford

pickup pulling a U-Haul. Guy wouldn't leave a name, but s
he saw their pictures in the paper. Said they pulled throu
the carry-out window, bought three sacks of food and t
off."

"It's gotta be them!" the captain said with a huge smile.

The Bay County sheriff sipped thick black coffee from a Sty
foam cup and rested his black boots on the executive con
ence table in the Caribbean Room at the Holiday Inn. I
agents were in and out, fixing coffee, whispering and updat
each other on the latest. His hero, the big man himself, Di
tor F. Denton Voyles, sat across the table and studied a st
map with three of his underlings. Imagine, Denton Voyle
Bay County. The room was a beehive of police activity. F
da state troopers filtered in and out. Radios and teleph
rang and squawked on a makeshift command post in a cor
Sheriff's deputies and city policemen from three counties
tered about, thrilled with the chase and suspense and prese
of all those FBI agents. And Voyles.

A deputy burst through the door with a wild eyed glo
sheer excitement. "Just got a call from Tallahassee! The
got two positive IDs in the last fifteen minutes! All thre
them in a green Ford pickup with Tennessee tags!"

Voyles dropped his street map and walked over to the d
ty. "Where were the sightings?" The room was silent, ex
for the radios.

"First one was at a Texaco Quick Shop. Second one was
miles away at a Burger King. They drove through the driv
window. Both witnesses were positive and gave identical I

Voyles turned to the sheriff. "Sheriff, call Tallahassee
confirm. How far away is it?"

The black boots hit the floor. "Hour and a half. Stra
down Interstate 10."

Voyles pointed at Tarrance, and they stepped into a s
room used as the bar. The quiet roar returned to mission
trol.

"If the sightings are real," Voyles said quietly in Tarran
face, "we're wasting our time here."

"Yes, sir. They sound legitimate. A single sighting coul

ake or a prank, but two that close together sound awfully
timate."

How the hell did they get out of here?"

It's gotta be that woman, Chief. She's been helping him for
onth. I don't know who she is, or where he found her, but
s on the outside watching us and feeding him whatever he
ds."

Do you think she's with them?"

Doubt it. She's probably just following closely, away from
action, and taking directions from him."

He's brilliant, Wayne. He's been planning this for
aths."

`vidently."

You mentioned the Bahamas once."

Yes, sir. The million bucks we paid him was wired to a
k in Freeport. He later told me it didn't stay there long."

You think, maybe, he's headed there?"

Who knows. Obviously he has to get out of the country. I
ed to the warden today. He told me Ray McDeere can
k five or six languages fluently. They could be going any-
re."

think we should pull out," Voyles said.

Let's get the roadblocks set up around Tallahassee. They
't last long if we've got a good description of the vehicle.
should have them by morning."

want every cop in central Florida on the highways in an
r. Roadblocks everywhere. Every Ford pickup is automati-
searched, okay? Our men will wait here until daybreak,
we'll pull up stakes."

Yes, sir," Tarrance answered with a weary grin.

d of the Tallahassee sightings spread instantly along the
rald Coast. Panama City Beach relaxed. The McDeeres
gone. For reasons unknown only to them, their flight had
ed inland. Sighted and positively identified, not once but
e, they were now somewhere else speeding desperately
rd the inevitable confrontation on the side of a dark high-

ne cops along the coast went home. A few roadblocks re-
ed through the night in Bay County and Gulf County,

the predawn hours of Saturday were almost normal. Both e
of the Strip remained blocked, with cops making cur
exams of driver's licenses. The roads north of town were
and clear. The search had moved east.

On the outskirts of Ocala, Florida, near Silver Springs
Highway 40, Tony Verkler lumbered from a 7-Eleven
stuck a quarter in a pay phone. He called the Ocala Po
Department with the urgent report that he had just seen t
three convicts everybody was looking for up around Pan
City Beach. The McDeeres! Said he saw their pictures in
paper the day before when he was driving through Pensa
and now he had just seen them. The dispatcher informed
all patrolmen were on the scene of a bad accident and ask
he would mind driving over to the police station so they c
file a report. Tony said he was in a hurry, but since it
somewhat important, he would be there in a minute.

When he arrived, the chief of police was waiting in a T-s
and blue jeans. His eyes were swollen and red, and his
was not in place. He led Tony into his office and thanked
for coming by. He took notes as Tony explained how he
pumping gas in front of the 7-Eleven, and a green Ford pic
with a U-Haul trailer behind it pulled up next to the store
a woman got out and used the phone. Tony was in the pro
he explained, of driving from Mobile to Miami and had dr
through the manhunt up around Panama City. He had
the newspapers and had been listening to his radio and k
all about the three McDeeres. Anyway, he went in and
for the gas and thought that he had seen the woman s
where before. Then he remembered the papers. He wa
over to a magazine rack in the front window and got a
look at the men. No doubt in his mind. She hung up, got
in the truck between the men, and they left. Green Ford
Tennessee plates.

The chief thanked him and called the Marion County S
iff's Department. Tony said goodbye and returned to his
where Aaron Rimmer was asleep in the back seat.

They headed north, in the direction of Panama City Be

39

ATURDAY, 7 A.M. Andy Patrick looked east and west
along the Strip, then walked quickly across the parking
lot to Room 39. He knocked gently.

fter a delay, she asked, "Who is it?"

The manager," he answered. The door opened, and the
who resembled the composite of Mitchell Y. McDeere
out. His hair was now very short and gold-colored. Andy
ed at his hair.

Good morning, Andy," he said politely while glancing
nd the parking lot.

Good morning. I was kinda wondering if you folks were
here."

r. McDeere nodded and continued to look around the
ing lot.

mean, according to the television this morning, you folks
led halfway across Florida last night."

eah, we're watching it. They're playing games, aren't
, Andy?"

ndy kicked at a rock on the sidewalk. "Television said
were three positive identifications last night. At three
rent places. Kinda strange, I thought. I was here all night,

399

working and being on the lookout and all, and I didn't see
leave. Before sunrise I sneaked across the highway to a co
shop, just over there, and as usual, there were cops in ther
sat close to them. According to them, the search has b
called off around here. They said the FBI moved out r
after the last sighting came in, around four this morning. M
of the other cops left too. They're gonna keep the S
blocked until noon and call it off. Rumor has it you've got
from the outside, and you're trying to get to the Bahama

Mr. McDeere listened closely as he watched the parking
"What else did they say?"

"They kept talking about a U-Haul truck full of st
goods, and how they found the truck, and it was empty,
how nobody can figure out how you loaded the stolen go
into a trailer and sneaked outta town right under their no
They're very impressed, all right. Of course, I didn't say n
ing, but I figured it was the same U-Haul you drove in
Thursday night."

Mr. McDeere was deep in thought and did not say anyth
He didn't appear to be nervous. Andy studied his face c
fully.

"You don't seem too pleased," Andy said. "I mean, the
are leaving and calling off the search. That's good, ain't i

"Andy, can I tell you something?"

"Sure."

"It's more dangerous now than before."

Andy thought about this for a long minute, then
"How's that?"

"The cops just wanted to arrest me, Andy. But there
some people who want to kill me. Professional killers, A
Many of them. And they're still here."

Andy narrowed his good eye and stared at Mr. McD
Professional killers! Around here? On the Strip? Andy to
step backward. He wanted to ask exactly who they were
why they were chasing him, but he knew he wouldn't
much of an answer. He saw an opportunity. "Why don't
escape?"

"Escape? How could we escape?"

Andy kicked another rock and nodded in the direction
1971 Pontiac Bonneville parked behind the office. "Well,

ld use my car. You could get in the trunk, all three of you,
I could drive you outta town. You don't appear to be
ke, so you could catch a plane and be gone. Just like that."

And how much would that cost?"

Andy studied his feet and scratched his ear. The guy was
bably a doper, he thought, and the boxes were probably
of cocaine and cash. And the Colombians were probably
r him. "That'd be pretty expensive, you know. I mean,
t now, at five thousand a day, I'm just an innocent motel
k who's not very observant. Not part of nothing, you un-
stand. But if I drive you outta here, then I become an ac-
plice, subject to indictment and jail and all that other crap
been through, you know. So it'd be pretty expensive."

How much, Andy?"

A hundred thousand."

Mr. McDeere did not flinch or react; he just kept a straight
and glanced across the beach to the ocean. Andy knew
ediately it was not out of the question.

Let me think about it, Andy. For right now, you keep your
open. Now that the cops are gone, the killers will move
This could be a very dangerous day, Andy, and I need your
. If you see anyone suspicious around here, call us quick.
re not leaving these rooms, okay?"

ndy returned to the front desk. Any fool would jump in
trunk and haul ass. It was the boxes, the stolen goods.
t's why they wouldn't leave.

he McDeeres enjoyed a light breakfast of stale pastries and
m soft drinks. Ray was dying for a cold beer, but another
to the convenience store was too risky. They ate quickly
watched the early-morning news. Occasionally a station
g the coast would flash their composites on the screen. It
ed them at first, but they got used to it.

few minutes after 9 A.M., Saturday, Mitch turned off the
vision and resumed his spot on the floor among the boxes.
picked up a stack of documents and nodded at Abby, the
era operator. The deposition continued.

rov waited until the maids were on duty, then scattered
roops along the Strip. They worked in pairs, knocking on
s, peeking in windows and sliding through dark hallways.

Most of the small places had two or three maids who kn every room and every guest. The procedure was simple, most of the time it worked. A goon would find a maid, h her a hundred-dollar bill, and show her the composites. If resisted, he would continue giving money until she bec cooperative. If she was unable to make the ID, he would as she had noticed a U-Haul truck, or a room full of boxes, or men and a woman acting suspicious or scared, or anyth unusual. If the maid was of no help, he would ask which ro were occupied, then go knock on the doors.

Start with the maids, Lazarov had instructed them. E from the beach side. Stay away from the front desks. Pret to be cops. And, if you hit pay dirt, kill them instantly and to a phone.

DeVasher placed four of the rented vans along the S near the highway. Lamar Quin, Kendall Mahan, Wally H son and Jack Aldrich posed as drivers and watched every v cle that passed. They had arrived in the middle of the nigh a private plane with ten other senior associates of Bene Lambert & Locke. In the souvenir shops and cafés, the for friends and colleagues of Mitch McDeere milled about v the tourists and secretly hoped they would not see him. partners had been called home from airports around the c try, and by midmorning they were walking the beach anc specting pools and hotel lobbies. Nathan Locke stayed bel with Mr. Morolto, but the rest of the partners disguised th selves with golf caps and sunglasses and took orders from C eral DeVasher. Only Avery Tolleson was missing. Since w ing out of the hospital, he had not been heard from. Inclu the thirty-three lawyers, Mr. Morolto had almost a hunc men participating in his private little manhunt.

At the Blue Tide Motel, a janitor took a hundred dollar looked at the composites and said he thought he might l seen the woman and one of the men check into two ro early Thursday evening. He stared at Abby's sketch and came convinced it was her. He took some more money went to the office to check the registration records. He turned with the information that the woman had checked i Jackie Nagel and paid cash for two rooms for Thursday,

and Saturday. He took some more money, and the two
men followed him to the rooms. He knocked on both
rs. No answer. He unlocked them and allowed his new
nds to inspect them. The rooms had not been used Friday
ht. One of the troops called Lazarov, and five minutes later
Vasher was poking around the rooms looking for clues. He
nd none, but the search was immediately constricted to a
-mile stretch of beach between the Blue Tide and the
chcomber, where the U-Haul was found.

he vans moved the troops closer. The partners and senior
ciates scoured the beach and restaurants. And the gunmen
cked on doors.

ly signed the Federal Express ticket at 10:35 and inspected
package for Sam Fortune. It had been shipped by Doris
enwood, whose address was listed as 4040 Poplar Avenue,
nphis, Tennessee. No phone number. He was certain it
valuable and for a moment contemplated another quick
it. But its delivery had already been contracted for. He
d along both ends of the Strip and left the office with the
kage.

fter years of dodging and hiding, Andy had subconsciously
ed himself to walk quickly in the shadows, near the cor-
, never in the open. As he turned the corner to cross the
king lot, he saw two men knocking on the door to Room 21.
room happened to be vacant, and he was immediately
icious of the two. They wore odd-fitting matching white
ts that fell almost to their knees, although it was difficult
ll exactly where the shorts stopped and the snow-white
began. One wore dark socks with battered loafers. The
r wore cheap sandals and walked in obvious pain. White
ma hats adorned their beefy heads.

ter six months on the Strip, Andy could spot a fake tour-
he one beating on the door hit it again, and when he did
y saw the bulge of a large handgun stuck in the back of his
s.

quickly retraced his quiet footsteps and returned to the
. He called Room 39 and asked for Sam Fortune.
his is Sam."
am, this is Andy at the desk. Don't look out, but there are

403

two very suspicious men knocking on doors across the park[ ]
lot."

"Are they cops?"

"I don't think so. They didn't check in here."

"Where are the maids?" Sam asked.

"They don't come in till eleven on Saturday."

"Good. We're turning off the lights. Watch them and [ ]
when they leave."

From a dark window in a closet, Andy watched the men[ ]
from door to door, knocking and waiting, occasionally get[ ]
one to open. Eleven of the forty-two rooms were occupied. [ ]
response at 38 and 39. They returned to the beach and di[s]
peared. Professional killers! At his motel.

Across the Strip, in the parking lot of a miniature [ ]
course, Andy saw two identical fake tourists talking to a [ ]
in a white van. They pointed here and there and seemed t[o]
arguing.

He called Sam. "Listen, Sam, they're gone. But this plac[e]
crawling with these people."

"How many?"

"I can see two more across the Strip. You folks better run[ ]
it."

"Relax, Andy. They won't see us if we stay in here."

"But you can't stay forever. My boss'll catch on before m[uch]
longer."

"We're leaving soon, Andy. What about the package?"

"It's here."

"Good. I need to see it. Say, Andy, what about food? C[an]
you ease across the street and get something hot?"

Andy was a manager, not a porter. But for five thousa[n]
day the Sea Gull's Rest could provide a little room ser[v]
"Sure. Be there in a minute."

Wayne Tarrance grabbed the phone and fell across the s[i]
bed in his Ramada Inn room in Orlando. He was exhaus[ ]
furious, baffled and sick of F. Denton Voyles. It was 1:30 [ ]
Saturday. He called Memphis. The secretary had nothin[g]
report, except that Mary Alice called and wanted to tal[k]
him. They had traced the call to a pay phone in Atlanta. M[ary]
Alice said she would call again at 2 P.M. to see if Wayne—

ed him Wayne—had checked in. Tarrance gave his room
nber and hung up. Mary Alice. In Atlanta. McDeere in
lahassee, then Ocala. Then no McDeere. No green Ford
kup with Tennessee plates and trailer. He had vanished
in.

he phone rang once. Tarrance slowly lifted the receiver.
ary Alice," he said softly.

Wayne baby! How'd you guess?"

Where is he?"

Who?" Tammy giggled.

McDeere. Where is he?"

Well, Wayne, you boys were close for a while, but then you
sed a wild rabbit. Now you're not even close, baby. Sorry
ell you."

We've got three positive IDs in the past fourteen hours."

Better check them out, Wayne. Mitch told me a few min-
ago he's never been to Tallahassee. Never heard of Ocala.
er driven a green Ford pickup. Never pulled a U-Haul
er. You boys bit hard, Wayne. Hook, line and sinker."

arrance pinched the bridge of his nose and breathed into
phone.

So how's Orlando?" she asked. "Gonna see Disney World
le you're in town?"

Where the hell is he!"

Wayne, Wayne, relax, baby. You'll get the documents."

arrance sat up. "Okay, when?"

Well, we could be greedy and insist on the rest of our
ey. I'm at a pay phone, Wayne, so don't bother to trace it,
? But we're not greedy. You'll get your records within
ty-four hours. If all goes well."

Where are the records?"

'll have to call you back, baby. If you stay at this number,
all you every four hours until Mitch tells me where the
ments are. But, Wayne, if you leave this number, I might
you, baby. So stay put."

'll be here. Is he still in the country?"

think not. I'm sure he's in Mexico by now. His brother
ks the language, you know?"

know." Tarrance stretched out on the bed and said to hell
it. Mexico could have them, as long as he got the records.

"Stay where you are, baby. Take a nap. You gotta be ti
I'll call around five or six."

Tarrance laid the phone on the nightstand, and took a

The dragnet lost its steam Saturday afternoon when the F
ma City Beach police received the fourth complaint f
motel owners. The cops were dispatched to the Brea
Motel, where an irate owner told of armed men harassing
guests. More cops were sent to the Strip, and before long
were searching the motels for gunmen who were searching
the McDeeres. The Emerald Coast was on the brink of w

Weary and hot, DeVasher's men were forced to work al
They spread themselves even thinner along the beach
stopped the door-to-door work. They lounged in plastic cl
around the pools, watching the tourists come and go. They
on the beach, dodging the sun, hiding behind dark sh
watching the tourists come and go.

As dusk approached, the army of goons and thugs
gunmen, and lawyers, slipped into the darkness and waite
the McDeeres were going to move, they would do it at n
A silent army waited for them.

DeVasher's thick forearms rested uncomfortably on a
cony railing outside his Best Western room. He watched
empty beach below as the sun slowly disappeared on the
zon. Aaron Rimmer walked through the sliding glass door
stopped behind DeVasher. "We found Tolleson," Rimmer

DeVasher did not move. "Where?"

"Hiding in his girlfriend's apartment in Memphis."

"Was he alone?"

"Yeah. They iced him. Made it look like a robbery."

In Room 39, Ray inspected for the hundredth time the
passports, visas, driver's licenses and birth certificates.
passport photos for Mitch and Abby were current, with p
of dark hair. After the escape, time would take care o
blondness. Ray's photo was a slightly altered Harvard
School mug shot of Mitch, with the long hair, stubbl
rough academic looks. The eyes, noses and cheekbones
similar, after careful analysis, but nothing else. The docur
were in the names of Lee Stevens, Rachel James and Sam

e, all with addresses in Murfreesboro, Tennessee. Doc did
d work, and Ray smiled as he studied each one.

bby packed the Sony video camera into its box. The tripod
folded and leaned against the wall. Fourteen videocassette
s with stick-on labels were stacked neatly on the television.
fter sixteen hours, the video deposition was over. Starting
a the first tape, Mitch had faced the camera, raised his right
d and sworn to tell the truth. He stood next to the dresser
a documents covering the floor around him. Using Tam-
s notes, summaries and flowcharts, he methodically walked
ugh the bank records first. He identified over two hundred
fifty secret accounts in eleven Cayman banks. Some had
es, but most were just numbered. Using copies of com-
r printouts, he constructed the histories of the accounts.
a deposits, wire transfers and withdrawals. At the bottom
ach document used in his deposition, he wrote with a black
ker the initials MM and then the exhibit number: MM1,
2, MM3 and so on. After Exhibit MM1485, he had identi-
nine hundred million dollars hiding in Cayman banks.
fter the bank records, he painstakingly pieced together the
cture of the empire. In twenty years, more than four hun-
Cayman corporations had been chartered by the
oltos and their incredibly rich and incredibly corrupt at-
eys. Many of the corporations owned all or pieces of each
r and used the banks as registered agents and permanent
esses. Mitch learned quickly that he had only a fraction of
records and speculated, on camera, that most documents
e hidden in the basement in Memphis. He also explained,
he benefit of the jury, that it would take a small army of
investigators a year or so to piece together the Morolto
orate puzzle. He slowly explained each exhibit, marked it
fully and filed it away. Abby operated the camera. Ray
hed the parking lot and studied the fake passports.
tch testified for six hours on various methods used by the
oltos and their attorneys to turn dirty money into clean.
y the most favored method was to fly in a load of dirty
on a Bendini plane, usually with two or three lawyers on
d to legitimate the trip. With dope pouring in by land, air
sea, U.S. customs cares little about what's leaving the
try. It was a perfect setup. The planes left dirty and came

back clean. Once the money landed on Grand Cayman, a[ ]
yer on board handled the required payoffs to Cayman cust[ ]
and to the appropriate banker. On some loads, up to twe[ ]
five percent went for bribes.

Once deposited, usually in unnamed, numbered accou[ ]
the money became almost impossible to trace. But many of[ ]
bank transactions coincided nicely with significant corpo[ ]
events. The money was usually deposited into one of a de[ ]
numbered holding accounts. Or "super accounts," as M[ ]
called them. He gave the jury these account numbers, and[ ]
names of the banks. Then, as the new corporations were e[ ]
tered, the money was transferred from the super accoun[ ]
the corporate accounts, often in the same bank. Once the e[ ]
money was owned by a legitimate Cayman corporation[ ]
laundering began. The simplest and most common me[ ]
was for the company to purchase real estate and other e[ ]
assets in the United States. The transactions were handle[ ]
the creative attorneys at Bendini, Lambert & Locke, an[ ]
money moved by wire transfer. Often, the Cayman corp[ ]
tion would purchase another Cayman corporation that[ ]
pened to own a Panama corporation that owned a hol[ ]
company in Denmark. The Danes would purchase a ball-[ ]
ing factory in Toledo and wire in the purchase money fr[ ]
subsidiary bank in Munich. And the dirty money was[ ]
clean.

After marking Exhibit MM4292, Mitch quit the deposi[ ]
Sixteen hours of testimony was enough. Tarrance and his[ ]
dies could show the tapes to a grand jury and indict at[ ]
thirty lawyers from the Bendini firm. He could show the[ ]
to a federal magistrate and get his search warrants.

Mitch had held to his end of the bargain. Although he w[ ]
not be around to testify in person, he had been paid o[ ]
million dollars and was about to deliver more than wa[ ]
pected. He was physically and emotionally drained, and s[ ]
the edge of the bed with the lights off. Abby sat in a chair[ ]
her eyes closed.

Ray peeked through the blinds. "We need a cold beer[ ]
said.

"Forget it," Mitch snapped.

Ray turned and stared at him. "Relax, little brother[ ]

k, and the store is just a short walk down the beach. I can
e care of myself."

Forget it, Ray. There is no need to take chances. We're
ving in a few hours, and if all goes well, you'll have the rest
your life to drink beer."

ay was not listening. He pulled a baseball cap firmly over
forehead, stuck some cash in his pockets and reached for
gun.

Ray, please, at least forget the gun," Mitch pleaded.

ay stuck the gun under his shirt and eased out the door. He
ked quickly in the sand behind the small motels and shops,
ing in the shadows and craving a cold beer. He stopped
ind the convenience store, looked quickly around and was
ain no one was watching, then walked to the front door.
beer cooler was in the rear.

n the parking lot next to the Strip, Lamar Quin hid under a
e straw hat and made small talk with some teenagers from
iana. He saw Ray enter the store and thought he might
ognize something. There was a casualness about the man's
le that looked vaguely familiar. Lamar moved to the front
dow and glanced in the direction of the beer cooler. The
's eyes were covered with sunglasses, but the nose and
ekbones were certainly familiar. Lamar eased inside the
ll store and picked up a sack of potato chips. He waited at
checkout counter and came face to face with the man, who
not Mitchell McDeere but greatly resembled him.

was Ray. It had to be. The face was sunburned, and the
was too short to be stylish. The eyes were covered. Same
ght. Same weight. Same walk.

How's it going?" Lamar said to the man.

Fine. You?" the voice was similar.

amar paid for his chips and returned to the parking lot. He
ly dropped the bag in a garbage can next to a phone booth
quickly walked next door to a souvenir shop to continue
search for the McDeeres.

40

DARKNESS brought a cool breeze to the beach a the Strip. The sun disappeared quickly, and there no moon to replace it. A distant ceiling of harm dark clouds covered the sky, and the water was black.

Darkness brought fishermen to the Dan Russell Pier in center of the Strip. They gathered in groups of three and along the concrete structure and stared silently as their ran into the black water twenty feet below. They leaned tionless on the railing, occasionally spitting or talking friend. They enjoyed the breeze and the quietness and the water much more than they enjoyed the occasional fish ventured by and hit a hook. They were vacationers from North who spent the same week each year at the same n and came to the pier each night in the darkness to fish marvel at the sea. Between them sat buckets full of bait small coolers full of beer.

From time to time throughout the night, a nonfisherma a pair of lovebirds would venture onto the pier and wa hundred yards to the end of it. They would gaze at the b gentle water for a few minutes, then turn and admire the of a million flickering lights along the Strip. They w

tch the inert, huddled fishermen leaning on their elbows.
e fishermen did not notice them.

The fishermen did not notice Aaron Rimmer as he casually
lked behind them around eleven. He smoked a cigarette at
end of the pier and tossed the butt into the ocean. He gazed
ng the beach and thought of the thousands of motel rooms
condos.

e Dan Russell Pier was the westernmost of the three at
ama City Beach. It was the newest, the longest and the
y one built with nothing but concrete. The other two were
r and wooden. In the center there was a small brick build-
containing a tackle shop, a snack bar and rest rooms. Only
rest rooms were open at night.

was probably a half mile east of the Sea Gull's Rest. At
en-thirty, Abby left Room 39, eased by the dirty pool and
an walking east along the beach. She wore shorts, a white
w hat and a windbreaker with the collar turned up around
ears. She walked slowly, with her hands thrust deep in the
kets like an experienced, contemplative beachcomber. Five
utes later, Mitch left the room, eased by the dirty pool and
wed her footsteps. He gazed at the ocean as he walked.
joggers approached, splashing in the water and talking
ween breaths. On a string around his neck and tucked un-
his black cotton shirt was a whistle, just in case. In all four
ets he had crammed sixty thousand in cash. He looked at
cean and nervously watched Abby ahead of him. When he
two hundred yards down the beach, Ray left Room 39 for
ast time. He locked it and kept a key. Wrapped around his
t was a forty-foot piece of black nylon rope. The gun was
k under it. A bulky windbreaker covered it all nicely.
y had charged another two thousand for the clothing and
s.

y eased by the pool and onto the beach. He watched
h and could barely see Abby. The beach was deserted.
was almost midnight, Saturday, and most of the fishermen
left the pier for another night. Abby saw three in a small
er near the rest rooms. She eased past them and noncha-
y strolled to the end of the pier, where she leaned on the
rete railing and stared at the vast blackness of the Gulf.

Red buoy lights were scattered as far as she could see. Blue a white channel lights formed a neat line to the east. A blink yellow light on some vessel inched away on the horizon. S was alone at the end of the pier.

Mitch hid in a beach chair under a folded umbrella near entrance to the pier. He could not see her, but had a good vi of the ocean. Fifty feet away, Ray sat in the darkness on a br ledge. His feet dangled in the sand. They waited. T checked their watches.

At precisely midnight, Abby nervously unzipped her wi breaker and untied a heavy flashlight. She glanced at the wa below and gripped it fiercely. She shoved it into her stom: shielded it with the windbreaker, aimed at the sea and pus the switch three times. On and off. On and off. On and off. ' green bulb flashed three times. She held it tightly and stare the ocean.

No response. She waited an eternity and two minutes la flashed again. Three times. No response. She breathed dee and spoke to herself. "Be calm, Abby, be calm. He's out th somewhere." She flashed three more times. Then waited. response.

Mitch sat on the edge of the beach chair and anxiously veyed the sea. From the corner of an eye, he saw a figure w ing, almost running from the west. It jumped onto the step the pier. It was the Nordic. Mitch bolted across the beach a him.

Aaron Rimmer walked behind the fishermen, around small building, and watched the woman in the white hat at end of the pier. She was bent over clutching something flashed again, three times. He walked silently up to her.

"Abby."

She jerked around and tried to scream. Rimmer lunge her and shoved her into the railing. From the darkness, M dived head first into the Nordic's legs, and all three went d hard onto the slick concrete. Mitch felt the gun at the Nor back. He swung wildly with a forearm and missed. Rim whirled and landed a wicked smash to Mitch's left eye. A kicked and crawled away. Mitch was blind and dazed. Rim stood quickly and reached for the gun, but never found it. charged like a battering ram and sent the Nordic crashing

412

railing. He landed four bulletlike jabs to the eyes and nose, each one drawing blood. Skills learned in prison. The Nordic to all fours, and Ray snapped his head with four powerful jabs. He groaned pitifully and fell, face first.

Ray removed the gun and handed it to Mitch, who was standing now and trying to focus with his good eye. Abby watched the pier. No one.

"Start flashing," Ray said as he unwound the rope from his waist. Abby faced the water, shielded the flashlight, found the switch and began flashing like crazy.

"What're you gonna do?" Mitch whispered, watching Ray and the rope.

"Two choices. We can either blow his brains out or drown him."

"Oh my god!" Abby said as she flashed.

"Don't fire the gun," Mitch whispered.

"Thank you," Ray said. He grabbed a short section of rope, twisted it tightly around the Nordic's neck and pulled. Mitch turned his back and stepped between the body and Abby. She did not try to watch. "I'm sorry. We have no choice," Ray mumbled almost to himself.

There was no resistance, no movement from the unconscious man. After three minutes, Ray exhaled loudly and announced, "He's dead." He tied the other end of the rope to a post, slid the body under the railing and lowered it quietly into the water.

"I'm going down first," Ray said as he crawled through the railing and eased down the rope. Eight feet under the deck of the pier, an iron cross brace was attached to two of the thick concrete columns that disappeared into the water. It made a perfect hideout. Abby was next. Ray grabbed her legs as she clutched the rope and eased downward. Mitch, with his one eye, lost his equilibrium and almost went for a swim.

But they made it. They sat on the cross brace, ten feet above the cold, dark water. Ten feet above the fish and the barnacles and the body of the Nordic. Ray cut the rope so the corpse would fall to the bottom properly before it made its ascent in a day or two.

They sat like three owls on a limb, watching the buoy lights and channel lights and waiting for the messiah to come walk-

413

ing across the water. The only sounds were the soft splash
of the waves below and the steady clicking of the flashligh

And then voices from the deck above. Nervous, anxio
panicked voices, searching for someone. Then they were ge

"Well, little brother, what do we do now?" Ray whisper

"Plan B," Mitch said.

"And what's that?"

"Start swimming."

"Very funny," Abby said, clicking away.

An hour passed. The iron brace, though perfectly loca
was not comfortable.

"Have you noticed those two boats out there?" Ray as
quietly.

The boats were small, about a mile offshore, and for the
hour had been cruising slowly and suspiciously back and fo
in sight of the beach. "I think they're fishing boats," M
said.

"Who fishes at one o'clock in the morning?" Ray asked.

The three of them thought about this. There was no ex
nation.

Abby saw it first, and hoped and prayed it was not the b
now floating toward them. "Over there," she said, poin
fifty yards out to sea. It was a black object, resting on the w
and moving slowly in their direction. They watched inte
Then the sound, like that of a sewing machine.

"Keep flashing," Mitch said. It grew closer.

It was a man in a small boat.

"Abanks!" Mitch whispered loudly. The humming n
died.

"Abanks!" he said again.

"Where the hell are you?" came the reply.

"Over here. Under the pier. Hurry, dammit!"

The hum grew louder, and Abanks parked an eight-foot
ber raft under the pier. They swung from the brace
landed in one joyous pile. They quietly hugged each o
then hugged Abanks. He revved up the five-horsepower
tric trolling motor and headed for open water.

"Where's the boat?" Mitch asked.

"About a mile out," answered Abanks.

"What happened to your green light?"

Abanks pointed to a flashlight next to the motor. "Battery
nt dead."

he boat was a forty-foot schooner that Abanks had found in
maica for only two hundred thousand. A friend waited by
e ladder and helped them aboard. His name was George, just
orge, and he spoke English with a quick accent. Abanks said
could be trusted.

"There's whiskey if you like. In the cabinet," Abanks said.
y found the whiskey. Abby found a blanket and lay down
a small couch. Mitch stood on the deck and admired his
w boat. When Abanks and George had the raft aboard,
tch said, "Let's get out of here. Can we leave now?"

'As you wish," George snapped properly.

Mitch gazed at the lights along the beach and said farewell.
went below and poured a cup of scotch.

yne Tarrance slept across the bed in his clothes. He had not
ved since the last call, six hours earlier. The phone rang
ide him. After four rings, he found it.

"Hello." His voice was slow and scratchy.

'Wayne baby. Did I wake you?"

'Of course."

'You can have the documents now. Room 39, Sea Gull's Rest
tel, Highway 98, Panama City Beach. The desk clerk is a
y named Andy, and he'll let you in the room. Be careful
h them. Our friend has them all marked real nice and pre-
:, and he's got sixteen hours of videotape. So be gentle."

I have a question," Tarrance said.

Sure, big boy. Anything."

Where did he find you? This would've been impossible
hout you."

Gee, thanks, Wayne. He found me in Memphis. We got to
friends, and he offered me a bunch of money."

How much?"

Why is that important, Wayne? I'll never have to work
n. Gotta run, baby. It's been real fun."

Where is he?"

"As we speak, he's on a plane to South America. But plea
don't waste your time trying to catch him. Wayne, baby, I lo
you, but you couldn't even catch him in Memphis. Bye now
She was gone.

41

DAWN. SUNDAY. The forty-foot schooner sped south with full sails under a clear sky. Abby was in a deep sleep in the master suite. Ray was in a scotch-induced coma on a couch. Abanks was somewhere below catching a nap.

Mitch sat on the deck sipping cold coffee and listening to George expound on the basics of sailing. He was in his late fifties, with long, gray, bleached hair and dark, sun cured skin. He was small and wiry, much like Abanks. He was Australian by birth, but twenty-eight years earlier had fled his country after the largest bank heist in its history. He and his partner split eleven million in cash and silver and went their separate ways. His partner was now dead, he had heard.

George was not his real name, but he'd used it for twenty-eight years and forgotten the real one. He discovered the Caribbean in the late sixties, and after seeing its thousands of small, primitive English-speaking islands, decided he'd found home. He put his money in banks in the Bahamas, Belize, Panama, and, of course, Grand Cayman. He built a small compound on a deserted stretch of beach on Little Cayman and spent the past twenty-one years touring the Caribbean in

417

his thirty-foot schooner. During the summer and early fall, stayed close to home. But from October to June, he lived on boat and hopped from island to island. He'd been to thr hundred of them in the Caribbean. He once spent two yea just in the Bahamas.

"There are thousands of islands," he explained. "And they never find you if you move a lot."

"Are they still looking for you?" Mitch asked.

"I don't know. I can't call and ask, you know. But I dou it."

"Where's the safest place to hide?"

"On this boat. It's a nice little yacht, and once you learn sail it, it'll be your home. Find you a little island somewhe perhaps Little Cayman or Brac—they're both still primitive and build a house. Do as I've done. And spend most of yo time on this boat."

"When do you stop worrying about being chased?"

"Oh, I still think about it, you know. But I don't wor about it. How much did you get away with?"

"Eight million, give or take," Mitch said.

"That's nice. You've got the money to do as you please, forget about them. Just tour the islands for the rest of your li There are worse things, you know."

For days they sailed toward Cuba, then around it in the dir tion of Jamaica. They watched George and listened to his tures. After twenty years of sailing through the Caribbean, was a man of great knowledge and patience. Ray, the lingu listened to and memorized words like spinnaker, mast, bo stern, aft, tiller, halyard winches, masthead fittings, shrou lifelines, stanchions, sheet winch, bow pulpit, coamings, tr som, clew outhaul, genoa sheets, mainsail, jib, jibstays, sheets, cam cleats and boom vangs. George lectured on he ing, luffing, running, blanketing, backwinding, heading trimming and pointing. Ray absorbed the language of saili Mitch studied the technique.

Abby stayed in the cabin, saying little and smiling o when necessary. Life on a boat was not something dreamed about. She missed her house and wondered w would happen to it. Maybe Mr. Rice would cut the grass

ll the weeds. She missed the shady streets and neat lawns
d the small gangs of children riding bicycles. She thought of
r dog, and prayed that Mr. Rice would adopt it. She worried
out her parents—their safety and their fear. When would
e see them again? It would be years, she decided, and she
uld live with that if she knew they were safe.

Her thoughts could not escape the present. The future was
conceivable.

During the second day of the rest of her life, she began
riting letters; letters to her parents, Kay Quin, Mr. Rice and
few friends. The letters would never be mailed, she knew,
t it helped to put the words on paper.

Mitch watched her carefully, but left her alone. He had
thing to say, really. Maybe in a few days they could talk.

By the end of the fourth day, Wednesday, Grand Cayman
s in sight. They circled it slowly once and anchored a mile
m shore. After dark, Barry Abanks said goodbye. The
cDeeres simply thanked him, and he eased away in the rub-
r raft. He would land three miles from Bodden Town at
other dive lodge, then call one of his dive captains to come
t him. He would know if anyone suspicious had been
ound. Abanks expected no trouble.

orge's compound on Little Cayman consisted of a small
in house of white-painted wood and two smaller outbuild-
gs. It was inland a quarter of a mile, on a tiny bay. The
arest house could not be seen. A native woman lived in the
allest building and maintained the place. Her name was
y.

The McDeeres settled in the main house and tried to begin
process of starting over. Ray, the escapee, roamed the
ches for hours and kept to himself. He was euphoric, but
uld not show it. He and George took the boat out for several
urs each day and drank scotch while exploring the islands.
ey usually returned drunk.

Abby spent the first days in a small room upstairs overlook-
the bay. She wrote more letters and began a diary. She
pt alone.

· · · · ·

Twice a week, Fay drove the Volkswagen bus into town f[or] supplies and mail. She returned one day with a package fro[m] Barry Abanks. George delivered it to Mitch. Inside the pac[k] age was a parcel sent to Abanks from Doris Greenwood i[n] Miami. Mitch ripped open the thick legal-sized envelope an[d] found three newspapers, two from Atlanta and one fro[m] Miami.

The headlines told of the mass indicting of the Bendini la[w] firm in Memphis. Fifty-one present and former members [of] the firm were indicted, along with thirty-one alleged membe[rs] of the Morolto crime family in Chicago. More indictmen[ts] were coming, promised the U.S. Attorney. Just the tip of t[he] iceberg. Director F. Denton Voyles allowed himself to [be] quoted as saying it was a major blow to organized crime [in] America. It should be a dire warning, he said, to legitima[te] professionals and businessmen who are tempted to hand[le] dirty money.

Mitch folded the newspapers and went for a long walk [on] the beach. Under a cluster of palms, he found some shade a[nd] sat down. The Atlanta paper listed the names of every Bendi[ni] lawyer indicted. He read them slowly. There was no joy [in] seeing the names. He almost felt sorry for Nathan Locke. [Al]most. Wally Hudson, Kendall Mahan, Jack Aldrich and, [fi]nally, Lamar Quin. He could see their faces. He knew the[ir] wives and their children. Mitch gazed across the brillia[nt] ocean and thought about Lamar and Kay Quin. He lov[ed] them, and he hated them. They had helped seduce him into t[he] firm, and they were not without blame. But they were [his] friends. What a waste! Maybe Lamar would only serve a co[u]ple of years and then be paroled. Maybe Kay and the ki[ds] could survive. Maybe.

"I love you, Mitch." Abby was standing behind him. S[he] held a plastic pitcher and two cups.

He smiled at her and waved to the sand next to him. "Wha[t's] in the pitcher?"

"Rum punch. Fay mixed it for us."

"Is it strong?"

She sat next to him on the sand. "It's mostly rum. I told F[ay] we needed to get drunk, and she agreed."

He held her tightly and sipped the rum punch. They
tched a small fishing boat inch through the sparkling water.

"Are you scared, Mitch?"

"Terrified."

"Me too. This is crazy."

"But we made it, Abby, We're alive. We're safe. We're to-
her."

"But what about tomorrow? And the next day?"

"I don't know, Abby. Things could be worse, you know. My
me could be in the paper there with the other freshly in-
ted defendants. Or we could be dead. There are worse
ngs than sailing around the Caribbean with eight million
ks in the bank."

"Do you think my parents are safe?"

"I think so. What would Morolto have to gain by harming
ur parents? They're safe, Abby."

She refilled the cups with rum punch and kissed him on the
ek. "I'll be okay Mitch. As long as we're together, I can
dle anything."

"Abby," Mitch said slowly, staring at the water, "I have a
fession to make."

"I'm listening."

"The truth is I never wanted to be a lawyer anyway."

"Oh, really."

"Naw. Secretly I've always wanted to be a sailor."

"Is that so. Have you ever made love on the beach?"

Mitch hesitated for a slight second. "Uh, no."

"Then drink up, sailor. Let's get drunk and make a baby."

THE PELICAN BRIEF

John Grisham

If you have enjoyed *The Firm*, you will certainly want to read John Grisham's compelling new thriller *The Pelican Brief*, published in hardback in July by Century.

Featuring Grisham's unique mix of legal intrigue and page-turning suspense, *The Pelican Brief* centres on the simultaneous assassination of two Supreme Court Justices, one a liberal legend, the other America's youngest and most conservative justice. The FBI is baffled: what could link their deaths?

Brilliant law student, Darby Shaw thinks she has the answer. Days of painstaking research have led her to an obscure connection between the two justices and in a meticulous but wildly speculative brief she names an unlikely suspect. A suspect who has friends at the very top. Only when she narrowly escapes the bomb which kills her lover in a New Orleans side street does she realise that her brief has fallen into the wrong hands. Someone very powerful has read it. Someone who wants her dead.

Darby sinks into the shadows of the French Quarter. Alone and terrified she moves from one anonymous hotel to another, trusting no-one. Until Gray Grantham investigative reporter at the *Washington Post* uncovers some startling evidence. He too is convinced that behind the assassinations lies the greatest cover-up since Watergate. Together they go underground, with the key to a secret that will rock the nation. Their only aim to stay alive long enough to expose the real truth behind *The Pelican Brief*.

The extract that follows is taken from the first chapter.

HE SEEMED INCAPABLE of creating such chaos, but much of what he saw below could be blamed on him. And that was fine. He was ninety-one, paralyzed, [tra]pped in a wheelchair and hooked to oxygen. His second [stro]ke seven years ago had almost finished him off, but [G]raham Rosenberg was still alive and even with tubes in his [no]se his legal stick was bigger than the other eight. He was the [onl]y legend remaining on the Court, and the fact that he was [stil]l breathing irritated most of the mob below.

[H]e sat in a small wheelchair in an office on the main floor of [the] Supreme Court Building. His feet touched the edge of the [win]dow, and he strained forward as the noise increased. He [hat]ed cops, but the sight of them standing in thick, neat lines [wa]s somewhat comforting. They stood straight and held [gro]und as the mob of at least fifty thousand screamed for [blo]od.

["]Biggest crowd ever!" Rosenberg yelled at the window. He [wa]s almost deaf. Jason Kline, his senior law clerk, stood [beh]ind him. It was the first Monday in October, the opening [day] of the new term, and this had become a traditional [cele]bration of the First Amendment. A glorious celebration. [Ro]senberg was thrilled. To him, freedom of speech meant [free]dom to riot.

["]Are the Indians out there?" he asked loudly.

[J]ason Kline leaned closer to his right ear. "Yes!"

["]With war paint?"

["]Yes! In full battle dress."

["]Are they dancing?"

["]Yes!"

[T]he Indians, the blacks, whites, browns, women, gays, tree [love]rs, Christians, abortion activists, Aryans, Nazis, atheists, [hun]ters, animal lovers, white supremacists, black suprema[cist]s, tax protestors, loggers, farmers—it was a massive sea of [pro]test. And the riot police gripped their black sticks.

["]The Indians should love me!"

["]I'm sure they do." Kline nodded and smiled at the frail [littl]e man with clenched fists. His ideology was simple; [gov]ernment over business, the individual over government, [the] environment over everything. And the Indians, give them whatever they want.

The heckling, praying, singing, chanting, and scream
grew louder, and the riot police inched closer together.
crowd was larger and rowdier than in recent years. Thi
were more tense. Violence had become common. Abort
clinics had been bombed. Doctors had been attacked
beaten. One was killed in Pensacola, gagged and bound i
the fetal position and burned with acid. Street fights w
weekly events. Churches and priests had been abused
militant gays. White supremacists operated from a do
known, shadowy, paramilitary organizations, and had beco
bolder in their attacks on blacks, Hispanics, and Asia
Hatred was now America's favorite pastime.

And the Court, of course, was an easy target. Thre
serious ones, against the justices had increased tenfold si
1990. The Supreme Court police had tripled in size. At l
two FBI agents were assigned to guard each justice,
another fifty were kept busy investigating threats.

"They hate me, don't they?" he said loudly, staring out
window.

"Yes, some of them do," Kline answered with amuseme

Rosenberg liked to hear that. He smiled and inhaled dee
Eighty percent of the death threats were aimed at him.

"See any of those signs?" he asked. He was nearly blind

"Quite a few."

"What do they say?"

"The usual. Death to Rosenberg. Retire Rosenberg.
Off the Oxygen."

"They've been waving those same damned signs for ye
Why don't they get some new ones?"

The clerk did not answer. Abe should've retired years
but they would carry him out one day on a stretcher. His t
law clerks did most of the research, but Rosenberg insiste
writing his own opinions. He did so with a heavy felt
marker and his words were scrawled across a white legal
much like a first-grader learning to write. Slow work, but
a lifetime appointment, who cared about time? The cl
proofed his opinions, and rarely found mistakes.

Rosenberg chuckled. "We oughta feed Runyan to

dians." The Chief Justice was John Runyan, a tough conservative appointed by a Republican and hated by the Indians and most other minorities. Seven of the nine had been appointed by Republican Presidents. For fifteen years Rosenberg had been waiting for a Democrat in the White House. He wanted to quit, needed to quit, but he could not stomach the idea of a right-wing Runyan type taking his beloved seat.

He could wait. He could sit here in his wheelchair and breathe oxygen and protect the Indians, the blacks, the women, the poor, the handicapped, and the environment until he was a hundred and five. And not a single person in the world could do a damned thing about it, unless they killed him. And that wouldn't be such a bad idea either.